Stories
ELIZABETH STODDARD

Stories
ELIZABETH STODDARD

Edited with an Introduction by
SUSANNE OPFERMANN *and* YVONNE ROTH

Northeastern University Press

BOSTON

Advisor to Northeastern University Press
American Literature and Culture
Marjorie Pryse

NORTHEASTERN UNIVERSITY PRESS

Copyright 2003 by Susanne Opfermann and Yvonne Roth

All rights reserved. Except for the quotation of short passages for the purposes of criticism and review, no part of this book may be reproduced in any form or by any means, electronic or mechanical, including photocopying, recording, or any information storage and retrieval system now known or to be invented, without written permission of the publisher.

Library of Congress Cataloging-in-Publication Data

Stoddard, Elizabeth, 1823–1902.
[Short stories. Selections]
Elizabeth Stoddard : stories / edited with an introduction and notes
by Susanne Opfermann and Yvonne Roth.
p. cm.
Includes bibliographical references.
ISBN 1-55553-563-1 (acid-free paper)—ISBN 1-55553-562-3 (pbk. : acid-free paper)
1. United States—Social life and customs—19th century—Fiction.
I. Opfermann, Susanne. II. Roth, Yvonne, 1969– III. Title.
PS2934.S3 A6 2003
813'.4—dc21   2002015415

Frontispiece features Mrs. R. H. Stoddard.

Designed by Steve Kress

Composed in Bembo by Coghill Composition Company in Richmond, Virginia.
Printed and bound by Maple Press in York, Pennsylvania.
The paper is Sebago Antique, an acid-free sheet.

MANUFACTURED IN THE UNITED STATES OF AMERICA

07 06 05 04 03   5 4 3 2 1

Contents

Acknowledgments vii
Introduction ix
A Note on Authorship xxxi
A Note on the Texts xxxi

One

Geography and Character: New England Stories 1

Our Christmas Party 3
Uncle Zeb 10
The Chimneys 21
Lucy Tavish's Journey 35
A Study for a Heroine 51
Mrs. Jed and the Evolution of Our Shanghais 65

Two

"A Wonderful Promise of Misery":
Stories of Love and Other Disappointments 77

A Summer Story 79
Eros and Anteros 89
Lemorne versus Huell 105
"Boots" 121
A Dead-Lock, and its Key 131
Out of the Deeps 139

Three

The De/Construction of Happy Endings 149

A Partie Carrée 151
Tuberoses 184
"Me and My Son" 200
Waiting at the Station 218

Notes 229

Acknowledgments

We would like to thank all the people who have helped to make this book possible. Our greatest debt is to James Matlack whose publication check-list in his Stoddard biography provided the starting point for our research. Moreover, he generously answered questions and shared information with us. For further assistance we are grateful to the librarians at the Library of Congress, Washington D.C., at Widener Library of Harvard University, and at Lilly Library of Indiana University, Bloomington.

While it was a joy to find and read Stoddard's stories, the process of selection for this edition was a difficult one. We greatly profited by the discussions with our students in the seminar on "Elizabeth Stoddards Erzählungen" at Frankfurt University. Many thanks to Marjorie Pryse whose support was essential at a key intermediate stage of this project. In addition, we want to express our gratitude to the following persons who helped in various ways: Tanja Milewsky and Brigitte Rathert endangered their eyesight in transcribing texts from the first publications. Klaus Lösch provided technical support. Dörte Löffert, Katja Sarkowsky, Änne Söll, Angelique Wheelock, and Astrid Wilkens helped with proofreading. Susanne Scharf and Birgit Spengler tracked down hard-to-locate information; our thanks to Birgit for her sharp-eyed rereading of the entire manuscript. Sandra Bachmann was a most enthusiastic research assistant. Janice Perry gave invaluable stylistic advice and, what is more, she was there when we needed her.

Yvonne Roth would like to thank Chris Wiser for his loving support and unshatterable optimism, which were a wonderful supply of energy. Susanne Opfermann is indebted in many ways to Helmbrecht Breinig, a Stoddard enthusiast himself. His collection of British authors would make Stoddard feel wonderfully at home—it holds almost everyone whom she quoted. To Chris, Cosmo, and Helm this book is dedicated.

Introduction

Elizabeth Stoddard tended to disagree. She vehemently rejected most labels that contemporaries applied to her and her fiction. And yet, her stories were distinctive enough that readers knew them to be hers even without an author's name. An early admirer remembered the time when *Harper's Monthly Magazine* did not yet name its contributors except in a semi-annual index. She played the game of grouping together "certain stories as the work of one author, to wait for them month by month, and verify her conclusions with much exaltation when the index became due. The writer of the stories was Mrs. E. D. B. Stoddard, . . . the creator of a new and fascinating world."[1] Among her fellow writers it was William Dean Howells who acknowledged Stoddard's unique literary voice when he said of her, "in whatever she did she left the stamp of a talent like no other, and of a personality disdainful of literary environment. In a time when most of us had to write like Tennyson, or Longfellow, or Browning, she never would write like any one but herself."[2] Stoddard struck most of her contemporaries as an unusual woman. Lilian Woodman Aldrich describes an encounter in the mid-1860s, when Stoddard was at the height of her literary productivity: "I know no prototype of Mrs. Stoddard—this singular woman, who possessed so strongly the ability to sway all men who came within her influence. Brilliant and fascinating, she needed neither beauty nor youth, her power was so much beyond such aids."[3] According to Mrs. Aldrich, Stoddard had "[n]o aura of charm whatever," and she elicited no lukewarm responses. Nor was she ever afraid of alienating her friends. She once told her poet husband and his colleagues to their faces that they were all "dreary failures as poets"—incidentally a judgment with which modern critics tend to agree.[4]

Clearly, tact was not one of Stoddard's strong points, but her radical openness was a result of the high standards she set for herself and others rather than of intentional cruelty. She was a dedicated artist who was willing to subject her own work to strict criticism. Her husband Richard was her severest reader and she respected his opinion, wryly acknowledging "the tears of rage he has cost me, the more, because he was right."[5] Stoddard's insistence on her self-realization as an artist and as a woman runs counter to the pleas for women's selflessness that were so common in Victorian America. Her attitudes are much closer to the notions of our own day. Today she is primarily known as the author of *The Morgesons*. This first novel (originally published in 1862) prompted Nathaniel Hawthorne to write her a very warm, congratulatory letter.[6] Very little else of her substantial oeuvre is in print.[7] The present collection will make available, for the first time, an important segment of her literary production of short fiction that has previously been all but neglected.[8]

The stories selected here represent the range of Stoddard's work in this genre from her beginnings in 1859 to the 1890s and demonstrate the versatility of a fascinating writer who was one of the most original and unique voices in nineteenth-century American literature. Her writing is remarkable for its almost total lack of sentimentality, her pervasive use of irony, the psychological depth of her character portraits, the intense atmospheric descriptions of New England, concise language, and the innovative use of narrative voice and structure. Gender is an important focus of Stoddard's fiction. She investigates male/female relations by analyzing emotions ranging from love and desire to disdain, aggression, and depression. She deserves recognition as a pioneer regional realist and as the predecessor of Mary Wilkins Freeman, Sarah Orne Jewett, and Kate Chopin. A realist before realism became the dominant fictional mode, Stoddard merges a wide range of literary traditions stemming from the romance of the American Renaissance, woman's fiction, and regionalism. Her experiments in narrative method, her highly original, elliptical style, and use of imagery occasionally make her a precursor of American modernism. In her own time, however, Stoddard did not achieve lasting popular success. As Richard Foster put it, "at her best she seemed to be writing for audiences not yet born."[9] We believe that at last we have a generation of readers who will fully appreciate and enjoy Stoddard's complex artistry.

Life and Career

Born Elizabeth Drew Barstow on May 6, 1823, Stoddard grew up in the small seaport town of Mattapoisett in Massachusetts.[10] She was the second of nine children of an established and fairly well-to-do family, although her father, a merchant and shipbuilder, suffered several business failures. By antebellum standards Stoddard received a good education, supplemented by her voracious reading which she was permitted to indulge in the well-stocked library of Thomas Robbins, the local Congregationalist minister. Stoddard and her father occasionally visited relatives in New York City where she greatly enjoyed the theater. During a later stay in New York she attended one of the literary soirees of Anne Lynch and there met the poet Richard Henry Stoddard, two years her junior.[11] On December 6, 1852, they were married and in 1853 the couple settled in New York City. Richard was helped in procuring a job in the New York customhouse by Nathaniel Hawthorne, who interceded with his friend, President Pierce, on Richard's behalf. For many years this position provided basic financial security, although money always remained scarce. Richard's real ambition was poetry, although he knew all too well that it took a poet like Longfellow to be able to live solely by writing verse. A man of letters up to his death, Richard tirelessly took on any literary work available. In his own words, he "contributed to all the magazines in the country, and to more newspapers than I can remember, and on all subjects, except theology and politics."[12] He also was a drama critic, editor, essayist, and book reviewer. For all of their lives the Stoddards were part of the New York literary scene, where they mingled with different generations of writers such as Alice and Phoebe Cary, Caroline Kirkland, William Cullen Bryant, George Ripley, Horace Greeley, Rufus Griswold, Nathaniel Parker Willis, Louise Chandler Moulton, and others.

Richard Stoddard's closest friends were George Boker and Bayard Taylor, and, somewhat later, Thomas Bailey Aldrich and Edmund Clarence Stedman. Stedman was to become a devoted lifelong friend to Elizabeth. The Stoddard home was the gathering place for these aspiring poets and, for a time in the late 1850s and early 1860s, the Stoddards and the Taylors hosted weekly Saturday evening receptions attended by authors, musicians, and painters. The Stoddards' close proximity to the well-known Studio Building on 10th Street, home to many of the painters of the Hudson River School, allowed them to live in a world filled with the arts. They became friends with the sculptor Launt Thompson—who made a medallion head of the Stoddards' son Willy—and the painters Jervis McEntee and Sanford Gifford. Gifford presented Elizabeth with one of his paintings and in 1867 she dedicated her third novel, *Temple House*, to him. The Stoddards were also ardent theatergoers. Edwin Booth, the most famous Hamlet of his day, was an intimate friend, and together with his wife, Mary, spent much time at the Stoddards.

In an atmosphere so charged with literature and the arts, it is perhaps not surprising that Elizabeth Stoddard should herself have taken to writing. Mentored by her husband she began writing poetry in the early 1850s. She sent her first literary efforts to Lewis Gaylord Clark, editor of the *Knickerbocker Magazine*, and to the poet Paul Hamilton Hayne, editor of *Russell's Magazine*, the southern literary journal, both of whom she had met. Her work was accepted and her career was launched. Stoddard continued to write poetry all her life and produced some excellent blank verse poems although most scholars agree that her best work is in prose, which she began writing in earnest in 1854.[13] She was engaged to write a biweekly column for the San Francisco *Daily Alta California*, the same paper in which Mark Twain began his career a few years later. As the *Alta*'s "Lady Correspondent" Elizabeth wrote letters from New York, commentaries on current developments ranging from literary events such as the publication of Thoreau's *Walden* to the Maine Liquor Law and Women's Rights. Like Fanny Fern, the famous columnist, Stoddard skillfully fashioned a provocative, unconventional, and opinionated persona for the *Alta*. Her criticism was directed at all kinds of sentimentalities, vanities, and prescribed morals. As Stoddard herself put it, this work "proved useful in two ways: teaching me to write prose and the earning of money."[14] Her engagement with the *Alta* ended four years later in 1858, by which time Stoddard had completed her literary apprenticeship. From then on she wrote mainly fiction.

Her first published story, a regional sketch, appeared in *Harper's Monthly* in January of 1859, and is included here.[15] "Our Christmas Party" is told by a child narrator who recounts a Christmas day in rural New England around 1830. Stoddard clearly makes use of autobiographical material, as she did in later stories and in her novels, but we should be careful not to overemphasize the autobiographical element in her fiction. She drew from personal experience, especially her deep knowledge of New England and its characters, but she also very consciously controlled her material and adapted it to her purposes. Her next story provides a case in point. "My Own Story" was published in May of 1860 by the most prestigious literary journal of the day, the *Atlantic Monthly*. Readers who expect it to be "Stoddard's own story" will be disappointed. The title had been suggested by the magazine's editor, James Russell Lowell.[16] The narrator tells of her emotional and romantic relationships—with her friend Laura, and with several young men. While "Our Christmas Party" is remarkable for its dense New England atmosphere, "My Own Story" is an exploration of the dynamics of gender relations. The central interest of the story lies not in its regional features but rather in its examination of the nature of passion and love. In the following years, regionalism and gender relations constituted two major themes that Stoddard continued to work out in her fiction. These stories launched Stoddard's period of greatest productivity, which lasted for the next fifteen years. Thirty-five of her nearly fifty short stories were published by 1875, as were almost all of her stories for children.

Early in her career, Stoddard occasionally belittled her stories as mere moneymaking ventures, but by the mid-1860s she had firmly established a reputation for herself as a prose writer.[17] All three of her novels appeared during the 1860s: *The Morgesons* in 1862, *Two Men* in 1865, and *Temple House* in 1867. None was the success their author had hoped for, although on the whole reviews were positive (many of them were written by friends) and appreciative of Stoddard's original voice. It seems probable that frustration stemming from lack of popular recognition prompted her, like Herman Melville before her, to give up novel writing. Stoddard was aware that her novels were considered "difficult" and she may have despaired of her readers, but she did not give up writing.[18] For the rest of her life, albeit at a much slower rate, she continued to publish stories, essays, travel pieces, poems, and late in her life, a series of personal reminiscences. She also undertook some projects together with her husband. In 1869 she and Richard co-edited *Remember. A Keepsake*, an attempt at reviving the American tradition of the gift book.[19] To this eclectic selection of poetry and prose Stoddard contributed a poem and her previously published story "The Chimneys" (included here). In 1874 she brought out a collection of her stories for children, *Lolly Dinks's Doings*, some of which had previously appeared in the *Aldine*.[20] After this book her literary productivity declined considerably, perhaps an indication of a loss of energy and hope on her part.

Moreover, financial prospects for the Stoddards, never bright, were becoming increasingly bleak. As far as Richard was concerned, it was now clear that he would not realize his ambition of achieving lasting literary fame in poetry. Friends like Bayard Taylor had far surpassed him, gaining public renown as a writer and diplomat. Illness further complicated the family's circumstances. But somehow the Stoddards kept on. Elizabeth's lagging career took an upward turn when, through the agency of Edmund Clarence Stedman, her three novels were published in slightly revised editions in 1888 and 1889. By that time the literary climate had changed in favor of regional and social realism, and theorists of realism such as William Dean Howells recognized Stoddard's novels as forerunners of the realist mode in fiction. Not only did this cause a flurry of interest in Stoddard's work but it also seems to have provided her with much needed encouragement. Her output increased noticeably over the next few years.

In 1893 Stoddard's novels were included in the exhibit celebrating women's work in literature at the Woman's building at the World's Columbian Exposition in Chicago.[21] Two years later Stoddard put together a selection of her poetry, *Poems*. She and Richard were finally reaping the fruits of their long literary labors. On March 25, 1897, the Author's Club of New York hosted a gala dinner at the Hotel Savoy in honor of Richard Henry Stoddard's long career as a man of letters. One hundred and forty guests paid their respects to Richard and to his wife. As *The Critic* reported, "[t]hroughout the evening, the speakers alluded more than once to Mrs. Stoddard's work . . . and the dinner may be said to have been in her honor as well as in that of her illustrious husband."[22] There is evidence that Stoddard considered publishing a collection of her stories in the 1890s although the project never got beyond an experimental stage. Dean Keller describes a volume "in dark red half calf" with "Stories" stamped in gold on the spine and "E. D. B. Stoddard" on the front cover, which contained seventeen stories that were carefully clipped from the magazines in which they originally appeared and bound as a book.[23] It is not known why this selection never went into production. In any case, Stoddard had the satisfaction of seeing all of her three novels reprinted once again in 1901.

Both Stoddards were deeply committed to literature. Their marriage, although not without troubles, had a secure foundation in their dedication to their literary work and their mutual support. Their loyalty to each other also helped them to weather the hardest blows that fate could deal them. Their first son, born 1855, died after a brief illness in 1861 and a second son died within days after he was born in 1859. Even their last son Lorimer, who was born in 1863, and who carried on the family's literary tradition by becoming a successful playwright and actor, preceded his parents in death in September of 1901. Less than a year later, on August 1, 1902, aged seventy-nine years, Elizabeth Stoddard died of double pneumonia. The inscription on her grave in Sag Harbor, Long Island, reads: "Elizabeth / wife of / Richard B. Henry / and mother of / Lorimer Stoddard / 1823–1902 // Novelist, Poet, / strong original thinker and / steadfast loving friend / will long be remembered."[24]

The Century of the Magazine

The nineteenth century might well be called the century of the magazine.[25] An enormous and diverse number of periodicals had already flourished in America before the Civil War and continued to increase in the post-bellum era. Almost one hundred women's magazines were dedicated to addressing their primarily female readership on issues such as domestic economy, fashion, social questions, education, and literature. There were specialized magazines for children, family newspapers, journals devoted to politics, and periodicals that focused on immigrant groups. Throughout the century most editors favored a blend of genres that combined fiction, poetry, historical pieces, cultural articles, book reviews, and articles about famous people. For writers, the periodical market proved much more lucrative than the book market. Women eagerly entered into the world of magazine publishing and they filled all roles available. They contributed fiction and poetry, and worked as journalists and reviewers. Women acted as editors, as evidenced by Margaret Fuller, editor of the transcendentalist paper *The Dial,* Caroline Kirkland who edited the *Union Magazine of Literature and Art,* and Sarah Josepha Hale, long-time editor of the most famous woman's magazine of the nineteenth century, *Godey's Lady's Book.* Some magazines were even typeset by women.

By 1860, New York City was the country's largest and most competitive literary marketplace. Stoddard's work appeared in a variety of media, extending from the elite monthlies *Atlantic* and *Harper's* to less renowned weekly papers like the *New York Leader.* All of these periodicals catered to a predominantly white middle-class audience and, with the exceptions of the *Atlantic Monthly* and *Lippincott's Magazine,* all of her publication venues were based in New York City. Through personal contacts, her husband, and her friends, Stoddard knew many of the city's editors and she usually sent her work to a New York paper or magazine. Among the close network of literary people to whom the Stoddards belonged, it was quite common to solicit friends for contributions. When in the summer of 1871 Richard Stoddard became editor of the *Aldine,* a journal that specialized in beautiful graphic art, he commissioned many of his literary friends as well as his wife. Elizabeth Stoddard contributed essays, short stories, and children's stories to the *Aldine,* twelve pieces in all during 1872 and 1873, when Richard resigned the editorship of the journal.[26] After 1885 Stoddard published mostly in the *Independent,* a New York weekly that advocated reforms such as women's suffrage and contained a wide range of literary contributions.[27]

Before 1875 the great majority of Stoddard's short stories appeared in the three periodicals published by the house of Harper. The Harpers paid well and their magazines had a high circulation; by 1860 *Harper's Monthly* sold 200,000 copies per month. Stoddard was a valued contributor to *Harper's Monthly* and in their pages she reached a wide readership. She also wrote for *Harper's Bazar* (later spelled *Bazaar*), a weekly begun in 1867 and designed as a family paper for women which extensively covered the fashions of the day. She contributed prose and poetry to *Harper's Weekly*, first issued a decade before the *Bazar* and subtitled "A Journal of Civilization." It addressed political questions, which *Harper's Monthly*, founded in 1850, eschewed. The *Monthly's* wide southern readership necessitated a careful skirting of the slavery issue in order not to alienate its southern audience. Stoddard complied with the Harpers' restrictive editorial policy but to some extent she also worked against it. The political impetus found in her novel *Two Men* (arguably Stoddard's most openly political narrative) in which she took a stand against slavery and racism, is more subdued in her short fiction. None of the stories openly criticize racist attitudes, but the attentive reader will still find references to the political ambiguities of the time. A case in point is provided by "Lemorne *versus* Huell" (*Harper's Monthly*, 1863). Stoddard inserts a brief and seemingly unmotivated exchange on the Fugitive Slave Law. The character who endorses it later turns out to be a "scoundrel." This story also employs slavery as a metaphor to illustrate the situation of the protagonist, which possibly may have led readers to ask political questions as well. Although Stoddard rarely confronts issues of race and class directly, they are of great importance as a backdrop of her tales and give them a dynamic undercurrent.

All of the Harper periodicals contained fiction as well as poetry and usually featured serialized novels. George Eliot's *Middlemarch* ran in *Harper's Weekly* from December 1871 to February 1873. Early on *Harper's Monthly* chiefly reprinted English fiction by favorite authors such as Charles Dickens and Mrs. Craik, but soon the *Monthly* also came to include American stories. As Henry Harper remembered, "[t]he general acceptance of Harper's as pre-eminently a home magazine for family reading made short stories of domestic interest, and especially well-written love-stories, a characteristic feature."[28] Stoddard provided quite a few of these. It is a remarkable commentary on her ability that she was able to retain a distinct voice while fulfilling the publishers' and audience's expectations for happy endings. She used this framework to explore the preconditions for a successful marriage. Although Stoddard did not identify herself with the women's rights movement she always endorsed the ideal of a partnership of equals. As is evident in the third section of this book, all of her stories of romance make the point that happiness is possible only when couples strive for an egalitarian relationship built on mutual consideration and respect.

From Romanticism to Realism

One might be tempted to propose that Stoddard "had it all": a literary career as well as family, a husband supportive of her work, close friends, possibly lovers. Unlike many women writers of her time who self-consciously and publicly belittled their own literary aspirations and were affected by what Sandra Gilbert and Susan Gubar have termed "anxiety of authorship," Stoddard seems to have had few difficulties in bridging the gap between the private and the public spheres.[29] Although her lack of success embittered her, as is evident from her letters, she never doubted her creative gift or her right to use it. "I *know* that I have written the truth regarding human emotion—the turbulence, the repression, the expression of Passion [sic]. Now, why don't my co-fellows acknowledge me—in spite of my faults, and manner of arrogance. . . . [I]t has been a pain to me, that I have not gained the respect of the intellects, whose intellects *I* respect."[30] Such self-assurance is quite remarkable for a nineteenth-century woman writer. Much of her unusual self-confidence may be based in her personality, in the fact that she never was afraid to adopt unpopular opinions, but credit is also due to Richard Stoddard, who recognized her original talent and always stood by her. With a twinge of irony he acknowledged that she had had "more of the quality called genius than I, who certainly had more talent than she."[31]

Stoddard's fiction defies easy classification. In the 1860s she had prided herself on the unvarnished prose portraits that she called "a plain transcript of human life."[32] But by 1888 she vehemently denied being a precursor of the literary realists and insisted: "I am *not* realistic—I am *romantic*, the very bareness and simplicity of my work is a trap for its romance."[33] Today scholars are still debating which literary school Stoddard belongs to and what her place in literary history should be. Regarded in relation to the male and female authors of her era it becomes apparent that Stoddard has affiliations to both major literary movements that critics have traditionally presented as opposites: Romanticism and Realism.

Her year of birth, 1823, places her among the younger writers of the American Renaissance—as the late flowering of romanticism in America has come to be known. Herman Melville (born 1819) was four years older, Emily Dickinson was seven years younger than Stoddard. The dark and brooding characters of her novels, indulging in their "God-forsaken independence" (as it is called in *Temple House*), are reminiscent of Hawthorne's. Stoddard's self-willed, passionate and isolated protagonists seem to be close to the world of Emily and Charlotte Brontë, whose novels she greatly admired.[34] Her interest in individual self-expression, her emphasis on states of emotional intensity, on love and rage, are quite in keeping with romantic preferences. But her dark heroes have lost their aura of mystery. They follow bourgeois occupations, they grow roses and breed fast horses, they may struggle with alcoholism but there is no hidden secret in their past, they don't have mad women locked away in the attic, their wives are right there with them. Storm-beaten old castles have been exchanged for well-ordered New England parlors, which, appearances notwithstanding, does not diminish the violence and the power struggles that take place therein. The gothic element in Stoddard's novels, never strongly pronounced, is transformed into the ordinary, the everyday. Literary history has traditionally divided American literature into two distinct periods: antebellum fiction, regarded as basically romantic; and post-Civil War fiction, regarded as predominantly realistic. This emphasis on difference has obscured the continuities between romantic and realist fiction which mark Stoddard's writing. Both literary modes fed into and were fed by the dominant system of cultural values in America that remained essentially Victorian throughout the century. As Winfried Fluck puts it: "American realism might be most fruitfully described . . . as a cultural strategy to extend and modernize basic tenets of American Victorianism in order to gain influence on the definition of American society and culture after the Civil War."[35]

The most prominent genre developed by women writers in that era, the domestic or woman's novel, characteristically combines romantic and realistic elements. Stoddard is slightly younger than the domestic novelists Harriet Beecher Stowe (born 1811) and Susan Warner (born 1819). Stoddard's plots might well be classified as "domestic fiction" but her work presents a fundamentally different outlook—she did not base her fictional world on Christian ethics. The deeply religious worldview that inspires the novels of Stowe and Warner, as well as later ones such as Louisa May Alcott's *Work* (1873), is completely absent from Stoddard's writing.[36] She did not exercise the didacticism so prevalent at the time nor did she support the Victorian view of women as pious, selfless, gentle, and forbearing creatures. She did not subscribe to the ethics of sentimentalism that extolled sympathy and other-directedness as cardinal virtues for women. Her female characters do not practice the "politics of cheerfulness," although they too struggle for power.[37] Critic Sandra Zagarell comments on Stoddard's difference to other women writers: "In a period when the voices of respectable American women writers were generally raised publicly on behalf of personal forbearance, the representation of communities and local cultures, and public reform, her most compelling project was to articulate the nature and dynamics of a woman's subjectivity."[38]

In accordance with the later realists Mark Twain (born 1835), William Dean Howells (born 1837), and Henry James (born 1843), Stoddard presents her characters as shaped by heritage, training, milieu, and above all, primal drives and desires. Not Fate but the characters themselves are responsible for their actions. She also expressed this belief in her letters: "Did you ever think that our *results* may be owing to ourselves[,] our idiosyncrasies, faults, that our misfortunes are not wholly due to idiosyncrasies outside us?" she wrote to a friend, "[t]he longer I live, the more I perceive that we are makers and marrers of our destiny."[39] In her short fiction Stoddard shows a more familiar and everyday world than in her novels. Although the stories testify to her sharp gift for observation they are less focused on the broad social history of the time. The central interest in Stoddard's writing was always a psychological one.

Like Kate Chopin (born 1851) more than thirty years later, Stoddard advocates and investigates women's subjectivity. At the same time, her concept of creative individualism links her to the male writers of American romanticism. For Stoddard, the goal of a woman's development is to know herself. Such knowledge about self and world (which also includes an awareness of her sexual nature, her erotic desire) can only be gained by experience; it is not enough to comply with social expectations and society's moral law. In Stoddard's fictional world naïveté and trust in traditional wisdom and authority are usually fraught with negative consequences. Individual responsibility and a "selfish" devotion to one's needs and wants, including sexual ones, are considered not only acceptable but essential—a feature that points forward to Chopin's Edna Pontellier in *The Awakening*. Unlike Chopin's male characters, Stoddard's men learn to accept and welcome a woman's individuality. A balance of power between the sexes needs to be achieved to ensure a reasonable happiness for both. In Rebecca Harding Davis's "The Wife's Story," a woman's attempt at self-realization ends disastrously and is denounced by the female protagonist herself.[40] In Stoddard's work, self-realization is a necessary development for a woman in order to become a fully grown person. Stoddard does not minimize the limitations by which her female characters find themselves bound. She acknowledges and explores the network of powerful social and familial conventions, dependencies, and restraints to which women are subject. And yet, to speak up about and name women's struggles is a first step to women's empowerment.

Stoddard's plots often employ conventional conflicts and formulaic elements. But if she relies on conventional material she puts it to radical use. More than anything else it is her distinct narrative voice—terse, quaint, elliptical—that gives an edge even to standard situations. Stoddard is an excellent observer and she handles dialogue with a minimum of narrative intrusion, rarely using qualifiers such as "she said" or "he growled," leaving readers to supply the degree of emphasis with which characters speak. This results in a strikingly modern ambiguity and openness of meaning, almost Hemingwayesque in its suggestiveness. Stoddard's narrators are non-judgmental. She does not subject her characters to moral censure, no matter what they do, but presents them in all their gloriously abrupt and contradictory behavior, so that readers are aware of the layered inherent tensions and multiple psychological and social forces at work. When a narrator's voice does take on a mildly ironic or semi-satirical tone (another aspect that links Stoddard's stories to those of the later regional realists), it serves to create distance between characters and readers but is never used to make readers lose respect for the characters. When she presents her audience with surprisingly sudden happy endings she manages to undermine our faith in such good fortune while at the same time making us aware how strongly we wish for such happiness. What distinguishes Stoddard from her contemporaries is this ability to write it both ways—combining the romantic and the realist elements without trivializing either, fulfilling and subverting readers' expectations at the same time, being simultaneously conventional and original.

The Stories: Eros and Irony

The sixteen stories in the present collection, chosen from nearly fifty tales that Stoddard published, represent the scope of her work in terms of tone, topic, and mode.[41] Except for "The Chimneys" and "Lemorne *versus* Huell," none of these stories were reprinted in the twentieth century. We are pleased to be able to include one story not previously listed among Stoddard's works ("A Summer Story"). The texts are grouped into three sections, to furnish readers with some thematic orientation. The first section collects stories with a strong regional focus, the second section is made up of stories that explore gender issues and challenge conventional conceptions of love relations, and the third section brings together a number of stories that combine explorations of balanced love relations with interesting narrative experiments. The latter are the kind of stories that Stoddard wrote most often. Within each grouping, the stories are presented in the order of their publication. The notes provide source and background information not readily available to modern readers.

GEOGRAPHY AND CHARACTER: NEW ENGLAND STORIES

Stoddard began her career as an author of short stories with "Our Christmas Party," an early example of regionalist writing. Late in her life, in "Mrs. Jed and the Evolution of Our Shanghais," she again devoted herself to regional fiction, which by that time had become popular with the general public. The stories in this section present rich portraits of New England and its people, their idiosyncrasies and heroism in the face of the region's slow economic decline. Stoddard sketches the New England landscape and illuminates distinct character types. Occasionally the stories make use of the vernacular. What Judith Fetterley and Marjorie Pryse have identified as the narrative strategy of women's regionalist fiction, as employed by Alice Cary, Sarah Orne Jewett, or Mary Wilkins Freeman, applies to Stoddard as well: she shares "their desire not to hold up regional characters to potential ridicule by eastern urban readers but rather to present regional experience from within, so as to engage the reader's sympathy and identification."[42] Humor, an important element in Stoddard's stories, may result from the evocation of vivid images—such as "Gran'ther" mumbling "behind a chicken leg" in "Our Christmas Party"—that work as vividly as film takes. Links between Stoddard's regionalist tales and her novels are obvious. Thus, the character of Mrs. Saunders in "Our Christmas Party" reappears in *The Morgesons*. In one of the novel's most impressive moments, Cassandra, the protagonist, finds her mother dead in the kitchen. This scene is prefigured in "Our Christmas Party" where the narrator discovers that one of the guests has died. The skill with which Stoddard portrays the sudden shock of recognition and the confusion it produces underscores her superior psychological realism.

Unlike other female regionalists Stoddard does not create a "narrative of community" as Sandra Zagarell calls it, nor does she promote a separate female value system.[43] Her characters are rarely close to each other, friendships between women are never intimate. But Stoddard's narrators admire female individuality, as is obvious in "A Study for a Heroine." It is the story of a poor clam-digger's daughter who grows to be an independent woman in spite of poverty, isolation, and class discrimination. In terms of genre it is best described as a character sketch, a literary form that emphasizes the revelation of personality rather than plot development. "Uncle Zeb" is a sketch with a male protagonist. The title recalls eighteenth-century figures of literary uncles (such as Laurence Sterne's Uncle Toby), but it also refers to Harriet Beecher Stowe's "Uncle Lot" (1834) and, because it is a study of the abuse of male power, Alice Cary's "Uncle Christopher's" (1853). Stoddard reworks the tradition of the character sketch to illustrate the interconnectedness of the psychological and the regional. Zeb's demolished house at the end of the story exemplifies the protagonist's self-destructiveness while at the same time it recalls the numerous abandoned New England houses that stood as monuments to the region's decline. Thus Stoddard once again merges character and geography.

Stoddard's regionalist fiction pays close attention to the finer distinctions of class and power at work within village communities. In "The Chimneys," the story of an unlikely courtship, Stoddard extends the popular romance formula. Here are characters who are marginalized in various ways but whose fierce sense of pride will not allow them to admit it. In this setting, the question of marriage does not remain a matter between two people, but also involves the young couple's antagonistic mothers. The mothers are part and parcel of the marriage proposal and clearly will be major influences on the couple's married life. The light tone adopted by Stoddard in many of these tales just barely veils the more serious issues that lie beneath. "Lucy Tavish's Journey" satirizes middle-class Victorian education and its culmination, the obligatory tour of Europe, by instead sending the protagonist on a train journey to the West for the finishing touches to her education. But rather than taking in the sights, Lucy finds herself beleaguered by overeager admirers and ends up being engaged before the train even reaches its destination. The story also makes the point that women, try as they may, never really escape the confines of the family—Lucy's future husband turns out to be her cousin. A woman's development remains under the control of and limited by the network of relatives.

In "Mrs. Jed and the Evolution of Our Shanghais" (1891), Stoddard presents the familiar conflict between poor but contented village folks and an ambitious outsider. In this case the newcomer is a female know-it-all whose missionary activism upsets the rural peace, a situation that Mary Wilkins Freeman later explored in *The Jamesons* (1898). In Stoddard's tale the local spinster sisters, affected by the new spirit of enterprise, successfully master the challenge of modernization and manage to develop a breed of pure white chicken. What is so remarkable about this tale of progress and progressivism, however, is Stoddard's handling of the discourse on racial improvement, survival of the fittest, and Social Darwinism in general. Published at a time when the nation debated the extension of the Chinese Exclusion Act (which was passed in 1892), the racial symbolism of the story—manifested in the focus on and establishment of white as a superior color—subtly exposes the xenophobia and racism of late nineteenth-century America.

"A WONDERFUL PROMISE OF MISERY": STORIES OF LOVE AND OTHER DISAPPOINTMENTS

A caricature in a nineteenth-century magazine shows William Dean Howells dissecting a woman's head. Years before Howells and Henry James began to earn high reputations for their masterful scrutiny of human nature, Elizabeth Stoddard had already excelled in her portrayal of motivations and desires. The stories in this section address the "dark sides" of both male and female psyches—disdain and (illegitimate) desire, aggression and fear—the struggle for power set against a middle class, often urban background. Most of these tales use a romantic surface plot as a means to explore gender roles and gendered relationships. Marriage turns out to be more of a trap than a happy ending. Thus, "A Summer Story" introduces Agnes, a middle-aged woman who is severely depressed by an unfulfilling marriage. She falls in love with a much younger man and although the affair is not consummated, the adulteress-to-be is cruelly punished. Like Edith Wharton's Ethan Frome, Agnes will be reminded of her emotional and imaginative transgression for the rest of her life. The ending's exaggerated poetic justice illustrates the double standard of the conventional moral order—Agnes is punished, but her husband suffers no such consequence for the years spent with his "soubrettes." Stoddard's style is remarkable as well. The story opens with several paragraphs of direct exposition in the form of choppy, staccato sentences that sharply contrast the characters: "Agnes Fleming was thirty, Hugh Pennock was twenty." With very few strokes Stoddard manages to sketch a devastating portrait of the state of the Flemings' marriage that culminates in a startling non sequitur: "Though claret is the coolest wine in the world, Fleming's hair was thinning." As the story develops, its melodramatic elements underscore this brilliantly atmospheric beginning.

"Eros and Anteros" can be seen as a companion piece to "Lemorne *versus* Huell," which has long been recognized as one of Stoddard's best stories. In both cases a female first-person narrator describes her romantic involvement with a man who turns out to be cruel, domineering, and of dubious morals. Margaret of "Lemorne" presents herself as a victim while she simultaneously unveils her own participation in her victimization. In language dominated by negatives that emphasize her apathy, she never dares to speak or act on her own behalf. Sue in "Eros" is aware that she is physically attracted to King but is convinced that she must not express her desire. She accepts her passive gender role in an arrangement in which men watch women and women watch themselves being watched. King's image of women is conventionally Victorian. He divides them into two categories—morally superior, sexless angels or sexualized (and therefore depraved) beings. King finds himself attracted to both types. He enjoys his affair with the sensuous Cuban washerwoman Garcia, but would never consider marrying her, and he proposes to Sue, whom he desires as the ideal wife. It is one of the story's many ironies that King cannot imagine and will never find out that Sue fulfills both of his desires. Nor does Sue dare to reach for what she wants. In this respect the story ends in a kind of stalemate. The story aligns Sue and Garcia not only as objects of male desire, but also as studies in female dependency. There is a marked class difference between the two women, but their situation differs more in degree than in kind. Sue acts as housekeeper for her brother John, an arrangement that is as advantageous and convenient for him as it is for Garcia's husband to profit by his wife's wages as a washerwoman and as a prostitute. Furthermore, the fact that Sue herself is attracted to Garcia works against conventional racist and class attitudes.

The first three stories of this section are all from the early 1860s, and the final three date from the late 1860s and early 1870s. At that time Stoddard experimented with symbolist narratives that not only echo Poe and Hawthorne but also break ground for such Freeman tales as "The Parrot." In these stories Stoddard explores further the degrees of complexity of emotional drives and desires, while challenging readers to think beyond the ending. "'Boots'" employs the conventions of the ghost story to create an ambiguous uneasiness that lingers even after the resolution of the mystery and extends to heterosexual gender relations in general. "A Dead-Lock, and Its Key" is a story of female entrapment but also of female empowerment. It is highly symbolic in Freudian terms, pitching a male and female principle against each other. The reader bears witness to a power struggle in which women actively enter into destruction of the patriarchal father's most prized possession while men become incapacitated or helplessly faint when confronted with this female force.

"Out of the Deeps" is exceptional among the stories because it focuses on male relationships, a theme Stoddard addressed mostly in her novels *Two Men* and *Temple House*. Hawthornesque in its parabolic quality, the story portrays love in the rivalry between three men, with a woman serving as a merely functional object. Throughout the tale Charlotte remains in the background; she is equally friendly towards all three male characters. The unresolved ending leaves the protagonists in a triangle similar to the one at the story's opening. This open ending frustrates our desire for a solution to the conflict and asks us to reflect on our understanding of love as an emotionally exclusive relationship. Significantly, the most emotionally intense relationships in the story exist between the men, who seem to share a closer companionship than most marriages can provide. Implicitly, Stoddard suggests that love is not restricted to heterosexual unions.

THE DE/CONSTRUCTION OF HAPPY ENDINGS

This section gathers the kind of stories that the Harper brothers preferred for their periodicals—love stories that end happily in marriage. With the exception of "Waiting at the Station" (published in *Harper's Bazar*), all of them appeared in *Harper's Monthly*. Stoddard consistently fulfilled the formulaic requirements of the typical romance, but she also expanded its range with variations of her own in terms of both plot and narrative strategy. One such variant may be called the "delayed happy ending"—"A Partie Carrée," "'Me and My Son,'" and "Waiting at the Station" all postpone the happy marriage for many years. Stoddard employs this device to illustrate what it takes to build an egalitarian relationship. When the characters first meet they are usually lacking in self-awareness and maturity, which keeps them from making the "right" decisions. Women, in particular, need experience to gain the independence of mind that is a prerequisite for a marriage of equals. As a consequence, they may be middle-aged before they find the right partner. Over and over again, the author implies that women have to achieve self-knowledge—they need to be aware of their desires. Hiding behind cultural norms of acceptable behavior amounts to an evasion of responsibility. Stoddard adheres to the prevalent Victorian belief in and enthusiasm for moral education but the lesson that she teaches is unconventional: Women (and men as well) ought not to accept anybody's superior guardianship. Women who defer to their husbands and subordinate themselves to male authority have no chance of happiness at all.

It is interesting that Stoddard's stories, as Timothy Morris suggests, "resist their own happy endings by violating narrative conventions."[44] She often combines romantic plots with unusual narrative devices. "A Partie Carrée," for example, employs a technique that is similar to "morphing" in film when the camera evolves one character's face out of another. Within the same paragraph Stoddard subtly switches narrative perspective from one character to the other, which results in a conflation of figures, and eliminates difference. She uses this most often with characters whom she has built up as contrasts. This can be confusing for readers and may disrupt the illusionary potential of the text, but it forces us to question our acceptance of stereotypical clear-cut characterization. "Tuberoses" experiments with multiple points of view by using the conventions of a play: it opens with stage directions. Instead of an omniscient narrator there are several reflector figures. Stoddard uses this device to heighten the sense of unmediated experience. Readers gain direct access to Clara's mind in its tumultuous emotional state. We witness the jumbled and confused development of her unreasoned thinking, which is reflected in the nonlinear unfolding of events. The story features two sisters who are courted by two friends, both of whom propose to the "wrong" sister before each recognizes the right partner. The couples' misunderstandings result from their rigid and overdrawn notions about appropriate gender roles. In a variation of the lesson of Jane Austen's *Pride and Prejudice* both George and Clara have to revise their position in order to understand that a true partnership is one well-balanced. Dependency and power must be mutual. Stoddard gives a sense of immediacy to her exploration of the mental state of her protagonist by employing a narrative strategy that is, for the period, quite extraordinary.

"'Me and My Son'" features many of Stoddard's strengths as an author. The story is set in New York City but includes a long flashback to the New England girlhood of Laura, the protagonist, combining both country and city settings. In a manner reminiscent of Mark Twain, laconic, deadpan description is used for comic effect. Thus Laura's hometown is introduced as follows: "It was a very respectable town; an excellent one to be born in, and perhaps a still better one to be buried in." Parataxis and enumeration create a superb satiric effect, as is evident in the brief summing up of the Calton's honeymoon: "After buying a good deal of jewelry, and going to many places of amusement, Mr. Calton went back to his business with fresh zest." Stoddard also pioneers an early form of the stream-of-consciousness technique in the description of Cousin Martha's random and unconnected thoughts as she falls asleep. The elderly Cousin Martha is a particularly noteworthy character. This apparent country bumpkin from Ohio, whose entry is a comic epiphany, is an inversion of regionalist fiction's "experienced foreigner" or outsider who upsets a peaceful rural community. As it turns out, she is much more knowledgeable about life and art than the city-dwelling Laura. Cousin Martha's mission to reanimate the depressed Laura includes her taking over part of the courtship for her absent son Lester, to whom she refers constantly in the use of the title phrase "me and my son." The story handles the ideal of romantic love with wit and irony, but does not invalidate it; Stoddard combines the satirical and the serious in her explorations of love. Throughout the author strikes a fine and delicate balance between keeping an ironic distance from her characters and taking them seriously. In "Waiting at the Station" Stoddard treats the theme of romance in a more concise way. It is an accomplished short story that successfully uses setting (a train layover) to underline the protagonist's unsettled situation. The story points toward modernism because nothing much happens on the outside and all of the important events take place in the characters' minds. There the past is open to interpretation, indeed revision. What is most striking about the happy ending in this case is the precariousness of it—how easily it could have been missed.

Even after more than one and a half centuries, Elizabeth Stoddard's accomplished and entertaining stories have lost none of their immediacy and freshness. Her aesthetic achievement extends our appreciation of the diversity of nineteenth-century American literature. Her complexity enriches our understanding of nineteenth-century literature in general and of women writers in particular. Her writing may be simply enjoyed as a good read or subjected to exacting analysis. In any case, she speaks profoundly to contemporary readers.

Notes

1. Mary Gay Humphreys includes this personal reminiscence in an evaluation of Stoddard's novels that she wrote for the *New York Times* shortly after Stoddard's death. See "Mrs. Stoddard's Novels," *New York Times*, August 23, 1902.

2. William Dean Howells, "First Impressions of Literary New York," *Harper's Monthly* 91 (June 1895): 73. Reprinted in William Dean Howells, *Literary Friends and Acquaintance* (New York: Harper, 1900), 67–90.

3. Mrs. Thomas Bailey Aldrich, *Crowding Memories* (Boston, New York: Houghton Mifflin, 1920), 14; the next quote ibid., 13.

4. Reported by George Boker in a letter to Bayard Taylor, July 30, 1874, quoted in James Matlack, "The Literary Career of Elizabeth Barstow Stoddard" (diss., Yale University, 1968), 447.

5. Stoddard in a letter to Lillian Whiting, dated August 5th [1888]; quoted in Susanne Opfermann, *Diskurs, Geschlecht und Literatur: Amerikanische Autorinnen des 19. Jahrhunderts* (Stuttgart: Metzler, 1996), 311.

6. Quoted in Matlack, 266–67. Stoddard herself quoted Hawthorne's letter in her preface to the 1901 edition of her novels.

7. Stoddard's oeuvre comprises her work as a journalist, three novels, almost fifty short stories, stories for children, essays, travel pieces, and poems. Soon after her death she was completely forgotten. It was not until the late 1960s that interest in Stoddard slowly began to revive. The Johnson Reprint Corporation brought out Stoddard's three novels in 1971, with an introduction by Richard Foster. Still, scholarly interest remained moderate. Only when Lawrence Buell and Sandra Zagarell once again edited *The Morgesons and Other Writings, Published and Unpublished, by Elizabeth Stoddard* (Philadelphia: University of Pennsylvania Press, 1985), did Stoddard receive wider attention but even today, most criticism focuses on *The Morgesons*.

8. Stoddard's short fiction has not received much scholarly comment. Exceptions are John B. Humma, "Realism and Beyond: The Imagery of Sex and Sexual Oppression in Elizabeth Stoddard's 'Lemorne *versus* Huell,'" *South Atlantic Review* 58 (January 1993): 33–47; Timothy Morris, "Elizabeth Stoddard: An Examination of Her Work as Pivot Between Exploratory Fiction and the Modern Short Story," in *American Women Short Story Writers*, ed. Julie Brown (New York, London: Garland, 1995), 33–44; Ellen Weinauer, "Alternative Economies: Authorship and Ownership in Elizabeth Stoddard's 'Collected by a Valetudinarian,'" *Studies in American Fiction* 25:2 (Autumn 1997): 167–82. For a recent list of Stoddard criticism see Jennifer Hynes, "Elizabeth Stoddard," *Nineteenth-Century American Fiction Writers*, Dictionary of Literary Biography, vol. 202 (Detroit: Gale, 1999), 231–32.

9. Richard Foster, "The Fiction of Elizabeth Stoddard: An American Discovery," in *Geschichte und Fiktion: Amerikanische Prosa im 19. Jahrhundert*, ed. Alfred Weber and Hartmut Grendel (Göttingen: Vandenhoek & Ruprecht, 1972), 162.

10. The richest source on Stoddard's life is still James Matlack's unpublished dissertation. For a brief but excellent overview see also Sandra Zagarell, "Legacy Profile: Elizabeth Barstow Stoddard (1823–1902)," *Legacy* 8:1 (Spring 1991): 39–49. Stoddard herself wrote four autobiographical articles for the *Saturday Evening Post:* "A New England Girl in Old New York" (October 14, 1899), 274–75; "My Record of the Stage" (November 4, 1899), 354–55; "Literary Folk as They Came and Went With Ourselves" (June 2, 1900), 1126–27 and (June 30, 1900), 1222–23.

11. Anne Lynch (1815–1891), later Anne Lynch Botta, kept up a well-known literary salon in New York City for more than forty years.

12. Richard Henry Stoddard, *Recollections, Personal and Literary* (New York: Barnes, 1903), 299.

13. See for example "The Wife Speaks," with which Stoddard commemorated her crystal wedding anniversary in 1867. It was published in *Lippincott's Magazine* 1 (March 1868), along with Richard's companion piece, "The Husband Speaks," a much inferior effort. Both poems are included in Elizabeth Stoddard's *Poems* (New York: Houghton Mifflin, 1895).

14. Stoddard, "Literary Folk," *Saturday Evening Post* (June 30, 1900), 1223.

15. Matlack names a reverie entitled "Phases" (signed G. D. B.) as Stoddard's first published work. It appeared in the *Literary World* in 1852. This attribution seems doubtful. In the preface to the 1901 edition of *The Morgesons* Stoddard identifies "Our Christmas Party" as her first sketch. "My Own Story" was her first attempt at a "long story," as she remembers. See "1901 Preface to *The Morgesons*" in *The Morgesons*, ed. Buell and Zagarell, 260.

16. In her 1901 Preface to *The Morgesons* Stoddard reports that the story had been previously refused by *Harper's Monthly*. Matlack reads "My Own Story" autobiographically, see Matlack, 181. Considerations of space prevented its inclusion in the present volume. It was reprinted once during the nineteenth century in the collection *Short Stories*, ed. Constance Cary Harrison (New York: Harper, 1893), 1–73.

17. In two letters to Edmund Clarence Stedman in 1863 Stoddard refers to her short story work as "bread articles" and says that she "write[s] those things for money"; both quotations in Matlack, 313 and 317.

18. "I think that my readers at a second reading overcome the obscurity of my style, or rather get through it," Stoddard commented in a letter to Lillian Whiting in the late 1880s, quoted in Opfermann, *Diskurs*, 311.

19. Gift books were annual miscellanies lavishly printed and adorned for use as Christmas or New Year's gifts. *Remember. A Keepsake*, ed. Richard and Elizabeth Stoddard (New York: Leavitt & Allen, 1869). The volume was reprinted several times with different titles; see *Bibliography of American Literature*, vol. 8, ed. Michael Winship (New Haven: Yale University Press, 1990), 12.

20. The *Aldine* was a journal distinguished for its engravings. For a brief description of the *Aldine* see Frank Luther Mott, *A History of American Magazines, 1741–1930*, vol. 3 (Cambridge: Harvard University Press, 1938), 410–12.

21. The Woman's building housed a large library with work by American and foreign women writers to which the state of New York contributed 2,500 volumes. A volume of short stories, edited by Constance Cary Harrison, intended to represent the work of the women of the State of New York in periodical literature, included Stoddard's "My Own Story" (see note 16). See also *Art and Handicraft in the Woman's Building of the World's Columbian Exposition, Chicago, 1893*, ed. Maud Howe Elliott (Paris, New York: Goupil, 1893).

22. Quoted in Matlack, 610.

23. See Dean H. Keller, "Mrs. Stoddard's 'Stories,'" *American Notes & Queries* 7 (1969): 131–33.

24. Stoddard is buried next to her husband Richard and her son Lorimer, in the Oakland Cemetery in Sag Harbor, N.Y.

25. For the history of magazines in America see Frank Luther Mott, *A History of American Magazines, 1741–1930*, 5 volumes (Cambridge: Harvard University Press, 1938–1968); and John Tebbel and Mary Ellen Zuckerman, *The Magazine in America: 1741–1990* (New York: Oxford University Press, 1991).

26. Among his list of works by Stoddard Matlack also includes those *Aldine* contributions that were signed Elizabeth B. Leonard. He thinks that Stoddard "probably wrote" these pieces; see Matlack, 485. A comparative analysis of content and style of the stories makes this highly unlikely. A person who signed E.B. Leonard also published in other journals, which supports the claim that she was a minor writer in her own right.

27. In the early 1860s, under the editorship of Henry Ward Beecher, Harriet Beecher Stowe's brother, the *Independent* was a religious paper but under Beecher's successors it became a secular periodical devoted to political discussion as well as literature.

28. J. Henry Harper, *The House of Harper: A Century of Publishing in Franklin Square* (New York: Harper, 1912), 225.

29. See Sandra Gilbert and Susan Gubar, *The Madwoman in the Attic: The Woman Writer and the Nineteenth-Century Literary Imagination* (New Haven: Yale University Press, 1979).

30. Letter to Lillian Whiting, June 20th [1888]; quoted in Opfermann, *Diskurs*, 160.

31. Richard Henry Stoddard, *Recollections*, 298.

32. Letter to Edmund Clarence Stedman, June 22, 1862; quoted in Matlack, 217.

33. Letter to Edmund Clarence Stedman, April 21, 1888; quoted in Buell and Zagarell, "Introduction" to *The Morgesons*, xxii.

34. Louise Penner discusses parallels between Stoddard and Charlotte Brontë, see "Domesticity and Self-Possession in *The Morgesons* and *Jane Eyre*," *Studies in American Fiction* 27 (1999): 131–47.

35. Winfried Fluck, "Declarations of Dependence: Revising Our View of American Realism," in *Victorianism in the United States: Its Era and Its Legacy*, ed. Steve Ickingrill and Stephen Mills (Amsterdam: VU University Press, 1992), 20.

36. For a detailed comparison of Stoddard, Stowe, and Warner see A. Jerome Croce, "A Woman Outside Her Time: Elizabeth Barstow Stoddard (1823–1910) [sic] and Nineteenth-Century American Popular Fiction," *Women's Studies* 19 (1991): 357–69. Croce compares death scenes in the fiction of these authors. While Stowe and Warner construct these scenes to demonstrate the promise of eternal life, Stoddard insists on the materiality of death and emphasizes the loss and confusion it creates among the survivors. For another comparison of Stoddard's novels to those of Stowe and Warner see Susan K. Harris, "Stoddard's *The Morgesons*: A Contextual Evaluation," *Emerson Society Quarterly* 31:1 (1985): 11–22.

37. Nancy Schnog uses the phrase "politics of cheerfulness" to define the female strategy of social control that domestic fiction widely advertised in "Changing Emotions: Moods and the Nineteenth-Century American Woman Writer," in *Inventing the Psychological: Toward a Cultural History of Emotional Life in America*, ed. Joel Pfister and Nancy Schnog (New Haven: Yale University Press, 1997), 93.

38. Sandra Zagarell, "Legacy Profile," 39.

39. Letters to Elizabeth Akers Allen (ca. 1870s); quoted in Croce, "A Woman Outside Her Time," 366.

40. Rebecca Harding Davis, "The Wife's Story," *Atlantic Monthly* 14 (July 1864): 1–19.

41. This excludes Stoddard's stories for children. The exact number of Stoddard's short stories is unknown. Matlack's extensive list of Stoddard's writings is not comprehensive, see Matlack, 625–32.

42. Fetterley and Pryse, "Introduction," in *American Women Regionalists 1850–1910*, ed. Judith Fetterley and Marjorie Pryse (New York: Norton, 1992), xii.

43. See Sandra Zagarell, "Narrative of Community: The Identification of a Genre," *SIGNS* 13:3 (Spring 1988): 498–527.

44. Morris, "Elizabeth Stoddard," 40.

A Note on Authorship

Stoddard's name was printed at the head or bottom of the following stories in one of these variants: Elizabeth Stoddard ("Mrs. Jed," "Out of the Deeps"), Mrs. Elizabeth Stoddard ("A Study for a Heroine"), and Mrs. R. H. Stoddard ("Uncle Zeb," "A Summer Story," "Eros and Anteros"). The index to *Appleton's Journal* lists Elizabeth Stoddard as author of "'Boots.'" *Harper's Monthly* identified contributors only in the indices to its volumes, which named Elizabeth Stoddard as author of "The Chimneys," "Lucy Tavish's Journey," "Lemorne *versus* Huell," "A Partie Carrée," "Tuberoses," and "'Me and My Son'" (as Mrs. R. H. Stoddard). "Our Christmas Party" was published anonymously but was claimed by Stoddard as her first sketch in her preface to the 1901 edition of her novels. Neither "A Dead-Lock, And Its Key" nor "Waiting at the Station" are identified by name in the general indices of *Harper's Weekly* and *Harper's Bazar* respectively. However, we concur with James Matlack's attribution which is based on circumstantial evidence and is supported as well by an analysis of content and style.

A Note on the Texts

All of the stories were transcribed from their original magazine publications, which are identified in the notes. We have limited ourselves to correction of obvious typographical errors. We neither modernized punctuation and spelling nor emended to impose consistency on the texts.

One

Geography and Character

New England Stories

Our Christmas Party

Twenty-five years ago the villages that whiten the rocky and deeply indented coast of Massachusetts were not as they are now. No telegraph wires stretched above them, and no iron rails ran through them, to drop idlers in their most secret places. Each village was an isolated community, governed by its social necessities. Little visiting passed between it and its neighbors. Now and then one of its young men would stray away, and come back with a strange wife; or a young woman would induce some inhabitant of another region to settle down by her for the sake of marrying her. But the parties were considered foreigners to the day of their death, and then were generally carried back and buried in their native place.

Where I lived there were no Christmas legends. No stories came down to us of the mistle-toe bough, the Yule-log, the wassail-bowl, and boar's head.[1] "Baxter's Saint's Rest,"[2] and "Edwards on the Will,"[3] were the standard books for the old; and we young ones had primers, "The Christian Drummer," "The Penitent Robber," and "Milk for Babes, or a Catechism in Verse."[4] Little Christmas cheer we found in any of them!

On the 25th of December, 1620, English mothers might have wished each other and their children, with a smile and a tear, "Merry Christmas!" At any rate the mild sarcasm was in vogue with us children, their descendants. We rose early in the morning of that day, and clamorously wished "Merry Christmas" to every body. We received many pennies in return, but the pastime was soon over, and the day became as dull as any other day; duller to me, for I was forced to celebrate it after a fashion which my mother, who was a Lady Bountiful, had devised.

She had a list of friends who seldom sat at rich men's feasts. Their sphere was narrow—they were perhaps what Kingsley calls "minute philosophers"—but their hearts were better than the hearts of the heroes which the world has anatomized and impaled in songs and epics.[5] They were alike fervent and impartial on the annual measles and fevers, the corn crop and the religious revival. They could expatiate with equal interest on a birth or a death; whether the child was "marked," or the coffin mahogany!

Christmas, at our house, was set apart for their entertainment; and I, a child, was lugged into the day's duties. If the weather was fine the day before, my mother sent me in the chaise, with Bill, our hired man, for a driver, with the invitations. They were always accepted, for they were always expected.

From year to year the party changed. One of the old people in the interval might die, but a new member would be added, and the list was always full. As it is with the king who never dies, so with the poor. They die! They live! I remember all those festivals. But here is one in its particulars.

Invitations had been sent to Miss Polly Le Brun; to the widow Chandos and her sister, Miss Carter; to Mrs. Saunders; to Jane Buck, and her grandfather, Mr. John Buck; and George Washington Jones.

The day began well for me. Mother had given me a bead work-bag, in blue and red, as a reward for the merit she expected me to attain before night. It was hilarious weather. A white frost cobwebbed the frozen ground; the passing wheels chinked a pleasant music as they rolled through the ridged ruts; and horses and oxen were enveloped in powdery clouds of vapor. The old red barn glistened with sun and frost, and the gray walls of the house looked modestly glad. It was very cold, and log fires of oak and birch were snapping and blazing in the lower rooms. All the rocking chairs in the house were ranged round the parlor hearth, their chintz-covered cushions well shaken and their frills smoothed. Two new snuff-boxes—with beautiful pictures of the Prodigal Son,[6] in a blue dress coat and knee breeches; and Joseph and his Brethren,[7] all respectably dressed—filled, one with yellow snuff, the other with black, had been placed on the mantle-shelf. The kitchen chamber had been arranged for me and for what mother called "my company"—to wit, Jane Buck and George W. Jones, both of whom were young people. The kitchen was well cleaned, for chance visitors were expected there; and sundry bundles were piled up in the buttery waiting their arrival. Mother and I were dressed and ready for the company. She had on a dark merino dress, with sleeves very full at the shoulder, and wadded, and tight to the arm from the elbow to the wrist; a long, full, black silk apron; and a lace handkerchief tucked about her throat. Her beautiful hair was simply twisted, and held up by a huge fan-topped comb of filagreed tortoise-shell. I wore a claret-colored glazed woolen frock, trimmed with gilt buttons, and a high-necked white cambric apron. My hair was "shingled," and the white skin contrasted with the short black bristles. Mother had sent Bill with "Old Gray" and the yellow-bottomed chaise for the guests; and by half past ten they had all arrived.

Miss Polly Le Brun came first, as she lived the greatest distance from us. She was arrayed in a black satin bonnet, trimmed with great bows, and a somewhat frayed black silk cloak. Underneath it was a bright figured coarse calico dress, fashionably made. She wore high-heeled morocco shoes, and her feet were very small. She was a favorite at our house, and generally staid with us a few weeks every winter. Miss Polly was a decayed gentlewoman, and had connections which were her pride. She had traveled too, for in her younger years she had visited rich relatives in Connecticut and Maine. These visits were the romance of Miss Polly's innocent life. She had picked up bits of family history—a love affair or so, and some tragic morsels that she never was tired of repeating to me after we retired at night; for it was my privilege to sleep with Miss Polly, and I was never tired of hearing her, although I generally fell asleep in the middle of each story. She was very small in person, and very neat. How she contrived to dress herself nicely, for six weeks together, with the contents of a small blue-and-white cotton handkerchief, which comprised her baggage, was a great mystery to me. Her nose looked like the beak of a parrot, and her breath whistled through it very loudly when her mouth was shut; her finger nails were always in a moulting condition. Nobody enjoyed our dinners more than Miss Polly. She was the kindest-hearted creature in the world, but she could not help feeling superior to the rest of our visitors.

Mrs. Chandos came next, with her maiden sister, Carter. Mrs. Chandos was a large, coarse-featured woman. She wore list shoes, and made no more noise than a cat in walking. The sisters were dressed alike in mourning calico, with white streaks running over the ground like lightning. They wore stiff muslin caps, bound on with black ribbon. Miss Carter was an echo of Mrs. Chandos. When she said "Yes," Miss Carter said "Yes" too. And if one laughed, so did the other. They were always knitting mixed yarn, and I had to wear the shapeless stockings—and ugly enough they were. Mrs. Chandos seated herself in the best corner, adjusted her knitting sheath, and took snuff—not by smelling it, but by laying it up in large pinches inside her nose. She then said to mother, "This ere is the tenth Christmas, marm. Your father, that helped my old man to his pension, invited me to his house just ten Christmas-days, too; and then he died, good as he was. Lord-a-marcy! how much better the punkins were then than they are nowadays!" Miss Carter said "the punkins were dreadful poor nowadays; but the squire's garden sarse always tasted better than other folks'." Mother sent to the corn-house for a specimen of the great Cape Horn squash to show them. She told them that the kind of squash was as good as the ancient pumpkin, and that they should have some of the seed to sow in their garden patch. Said patch was nearly as large as a bed-blanket, and its space was much encroached on by the old well, whose sweep towered above their humble roof. "The marvelous man!" said Mrs. Chandos; "what won't they have next!" and "*What* won't they have next!" said Miss Carter. I left them simmering in happiness, and went in search of Mrs. Saunders. I found her in the kitchen. Good Mrs. Saunders! Thou wert a noble and patient martyr! Were I a Catholic I should call thee Saint Saunders! What a nice smell of pennyroyal and spear-mint there was about her! Even when she came in the spring to make our annual mess of soft soap, and dabbled in bones and ashes, and hung over the witch-like cauldron, the herby smell never quite left her. "It hung round her still." With what tenderness she called me her "little dear!" and smoothed, or tried to smooth, my stubbed hair with her hard hands. She felt any kindness shown her, and tried to repay it. She had brought my mother some little presents from her two or three starveling acres which she tried to take care of herself, while her lazy, ugly husband smoked his pipe and hiccoughed, the day through, on the old settle in their red-raftered kitchen. The presents were lumps of turpentine in clam-shells, which she said was good for inflammation and bruises, and for drafts for the feet when any of us had a fever, which the Lord forbid! and turkeys' wings, bound with red flannel, which she thought would save boughten brooms, and answer for sweeping the ashes in the chimney corner. A few gnarled sour apples and some sweet herbs completed the gift. Mrs. Saunders wore a blue woolen gown, spun and dyed by herself. Her gray hair was not covered by a cap. Her face shone with soap and water; and she beamed all over with goodness. She tried to conceal her cares and troubles, and met every eye with a smile. She had only two long eye-teeth to show her friends; and the contrast between her forced smile and her care-worn face was indeed pitiable. She would not sit in the parlor, but wanted to help in the kitchen, and was very much in every body's way, she was so flurried and anxious. Old Mr. Buck, the miller, was there too, and was regaling himself with cheese and gingerbread, his favorite relish. He was a captious old man, and found great fault with the "select men" of the town. "They didn't do right, according to Scriptur." George Washington Jones had not ventured from his chair by the door. In case of any great embarrassment he could rush out. He was a lad of twenty, the son of a brutal father, who had nearly cuffed his wits out. Mother presented him with a two-bladed jack-knife soon after he came, and he changed it from pocket to pocket continually; he was so delighted with it, he was almost miserable. Jane Buck I carried up stairs, and placed in a chair by the fire. She was in a chilly condition; her fingers were long and red, her face pinched and blue, and her figure drawn up as if she were in misery. Her hair was almost white, and tied so tight at the back of her head that its roots round her forehead were turned into pimples. She wore a new red-and-yellow calico frock, and a little shawl was pinned over her shoulders.

I brought out my small dishes and all my treasures, but she yawned over them. I could detect no expression of interest in her face, except when the fire blazed up a little higher, and her hands, which she held over the blaze, turned still redder with the heat. No one had ever told me that the poor girl was half demented; but I had the feeling which children always have for that class of unfortunates. She was repulsive to me; but I did my best to amuse her, although I thought it very hard on my mother's part to expect so much of me.

I was in despair, and on the point of crying, when the thought struck me of inviting George Washington up stairs. I found him in the barnyard, whittling. He accepted my invitation reluctantly. Jane blushed a little when he came in; he dropped his hat under his chair, and giggled. He eyed my playthings with contempt, and said, "Them's for little gals." He offered Jane a red apple, but she shook her head; so he took a great bite from it and put it back in his pocket. He edged up to the fire by degrees, and kicked the brands spitefully, and then grew talkative, and finally succeeded in interesting Jane in an account of what he called a "blind bile," which he had had on his arm, and which kept him from hunting rabbits for a month.

I was glad when we were called down to dinner. It was all arranged on the table at once. There was chicken stew and chicken pie, a roasted goose and spare rib. The vegetables were mashed, and the sauces very strong and sweet. We had for dessert boiled custards, apple-dumplings, dried fruit stewed in sugar, and currant and elderberry wine.

Gran'ther Buck and Jane sat together. Mrs. Saunders sat as far back from the table as she dared to without the fear of toppling from her chair, and losing her dinner between the table and her mouth. George Washington held up his knife and fork, resting the handles on the cloth. Mrs. Chandos and Miss Carter looked solemn and longing, and Miss Polly watched my mother, eager to help her, as she was the carver and waiter. It was pleasant to see the hunger of the company. Gran'ther Buck, the edge of whose appetite had been dulled by his relish of cheese and gingerbread, was very polite, and handed the dishes about unremittingly, upsetting one now and then. Mrs. Chandos and Miss Carter accepted every thing, and Mrs. Saunders refused every thing. She had no occasion for any thing, she said; but she ate all that my mother quietly put on her plate.

"Gran'ther," said Jane Buck, "the mill's going to-day; I hear it."

"She's a poor creetur," said Gran'ther, apologetically, from behind a chicken leg.

Miss Polly made a hasty motion, and laid her knife down; but she caught my mother's pitying eye, and took it up again.

"Marm," said George Washington, "gimme more cramberry sarse. I'm going to Nickerson's Swamp next week, and I'll fetch you a peck on 'em." And, "Marm, would you like a skunk? Dad says they are better'n goose when they are stuffed with sage and innions, and apple sarse goes along."

Mother said she would like the cranberries, but declined the skunk.

Mrs. Chandos asked mother if she had forgotten how to make Injun meal dumplings; they ought to have been in the chicken stew, she said, instead of flour dumplings. Still, Mrs. Chandos had eaten heartily of the light crust which composed part of the stew.

"I am sure, Marm, you have got plenty of yeller meal," said Gran'ther, "for your Bill took away ten bags yesterday from my mill. But corn ain't what it used to be; it's only fit for creeturs' feed."

The dinner was finished at last. They all rose together, and put their chairs against the wall, and then looked at mother. She told them that at five o'clock tea would be ready; in the mean time they must make themselves comfortable.

Miss Polly, who, like most mercurial people, needed little naps, went up stairs to indulge herself with one. Mrs. Chandos went into the parlor, followed by Miss Carter; they resumed their knitting.

Gran'ther and George strolled off somewhere to take a nap—probably in the hay-mow—and Mrs. Saunders went into the kitchen to help wash the dishes. I begged mother to send for one of my schoolmates to come and pass the afternoon with me. She consented; and when Emma came we went up stairs together with Jane Buck, and our play amused the poor girl. When we got tired of playing (it was after four o'clock, and the shade of evening was creeping over the house), Jane Buck was snoring in her chair, and Emma and I went down stairs. Mrs. Saunders was in the kitchen fanning herself with a turkey's wing, and mother was cutting out some garments for her to take home and make up. I went into the parlor. Miss Carter was by the window. She nodded her head toward Mrs. Chandos, not wishing me to disturb her. I looked at Mrs. Chandos, and felt impelled to get near her. Her eyes were wide open, and her hands were clenched; her yarn was broken, the ball had rolled on the floor; the snuff-box had fallen from her lap, and the spilled snuff made me sneeze violently. But Mrs. Chandos did not stir—she was dead! I looked at Miss Carter. She caught my scared eyes and came forward quickly. The sight broke her heart, but she made no noise; she only wrung her withered hands, and then she picked up the ball of yarn and tried to wind it again. I called my mother. She gently led Miss Carter from the room, and all that could be done was done for the bereaved woman. She died before the next Christmas, and the family, whose name was in the "Memorial," became extinct.

Miss Polly hurried down stairs, full of compassion, but with a look which seemed to say, "What could we expect? she was so very old!" But Miss Polly was only three years younger than Mrs. Chandos!

Gran'ther Buck wiped his forehead when my mother told him of Mrs. Chandos's death.

"John Chandos was a good Christian man, though he *was* fond of Hollands;[8] but I guess Mrs. Chandos will meet him in the 'fields beyond the swelling flood.' "[9]

Gran'ther enjoyed his tea, drinking four cups scalding hot, and eating much sweet-cake. Poor Jane trembled with fear, but she brightened up when mother gave her a new bed blanket with a red rose in each corner. Mrs. Saunders went home crying with thankfulness.

And so ended our Christmas Party. Before I went to bed that night mother asked me if I did not think it a happiness to be able to bestow pleasure on those poor friends of hers? I said I was very tired of Jane Buck, and asked her when she thought Gran'ther Buck would die? Whereat she smiled, and sent me to bed. And I heard that night the story of cousin Nancy's marriage, and her bridal present of a silver porringer from Miss Polly.

Uncle Zeb

Uncle Zeb's monument is under my window in the yard,—its top in a rosebush, and its base on a bed of pinks. The stone-cutter brought it on a truck, and with an air of irreverence launched it into the present position. Uncle Zeb ordered the monument the day after he made his will, and left the duty of paying for it to his executors, although he lived long enough afterward to pay for a dozen of the most elaborate workmanship. This monument is a deceptive affair, like most tombstones; a wreath of heart's ease is carved round an open book on the square of the pedestal, and a column runs up from it, ornamented with the long stems and flowers of the white water-lily.[1] As I hang over the window-ledge, my recollections of Uncle Zeb assume the shape of imps which grin at me through the meshes of the lily-stems, and they slide their elfish fingers over the stony leaves of the book, as if they were writing the true story of a life that I alone can read.

My first remembrance of Uncle Zeb dates from an early period of childhood. One day, while I was at my Grandfather's, I heard a bustle in the front entry, and a noise like that of the dropping of trunks. Old Lizzy Bowles, an ancient hanger-on of the establishment, told me that my Uncle Zeb had "come in from a vy'ge," and that I must go into the East room and shake hands with him. I went into the room quietly, and looked out of the window first, where I saw Uncle Zeb's ship, the *Dryad*, swinging at anchor, a mile down the harbor.[2] I then turned and looked at Uncle Zeb, who was toasting himself by a roaring fire which burned in a Franklin-stove. He was in that condition of roasted helplessness, which a wood fire always engenders in one on a wet, damp day. He strove to mitigate the smart of his shins by continually changing one leg over the other, and he held his baked hands between his crimson face and the fire. He looked at me from behind them a moment, and then reached up to the mantle, and took from it a present which he brought from Liverpool. It was a red and white cow and calf of earthenware, the like of which had never been seen by any juvenile in our primeval village. As he gave it to me, he called me a trollop, and said I looked like my mother. Grandmother, who was knitting a blue stocking in a corner remote from the fire, said, "Sho, Zeb!"

This was my first interview with my relative, and my last present. I retired to the kitchen, and to old Lizzy, who told me about the cargo of crockery which she said Uncle Zeb was going to sell in New York, and make a fortune by.

Uncle Zeb was then about thirty; he had made several voyages previous to the one I spoke of, and was already well to do. My father was some years younger, and at the beginning of Uncle Zeb's sea-life, was a stripling, lounging about home in a round jacket. It sometimes happens in a well-regulated family, that one of its members is overlooked; he is never especially noticed by the rest, and his future is not thought of.

My father happened to be the ignored one in his family, and to that fact I ascribe the difference between him and his relations. His idiosyncracy got no twist from their sympathy. But my father was in love; boy as he was, he thought of marriage, and the way to live afterward. The girl he loved was a poor tailoress; in fact, she made his homespun jackets. She was older than her lover, and had made his jackets with equanimity, while he wore them in a tempestuous state of mind. Grandmother was the Squire's wife; she felt above the poor tailoress. An impartial mind would perhaps have found it difficult to establish the lines of superiority, for Grandmother herself sold milk from her kitchen every day, and did not disdain to keep the milk-score with chalk on her yellow buttery door. The tailoress was very handsome, and very resolute. She would wear feathers in her bonnet; and every Sunday she went to church dressed in better taste than anybody beside,—the handsomest Presbyterian of them all. Most of all, Grandmother disliked her because my father loved her. And Uncle Zeb had a weakness in that direction; but it was obscured by selfishness, and died out in moral laziness.

Uncle Zeb went on his voyages, and my father, who did not know what else to do, went to sea also; not having any help from Grandfather, he was obliged, of course, to ship before the mast, and went under the command of Captain Southerd, a neighboring farmer, who planted turnips, and carted wood and hay to market, in the intervals between his voyages. Nearly all the inhabitants of our little town were amphibious. The boys took to the water like spaniels; their first toys were punts, and skiffs, and rafts. The men, when they were not sailors, were ship-carpenters. The landowners put their savings into small vessels, which coasted from Maine to Florida, and even went on six months' trips into the Atlantic for whales.

Uncle Zeb and his brother did not meet often. When one was at home the other was generally away. Uncle Zeb bought up the *Dryad*, piece by piece, and went in her to all the trading ports in the world, from St. Petersburg to Calcutta. The merchants from whom he purchased his cargoes, or to whom they were consigned, invited him to their houses, and in this way he picked up bits of eccentricity, which he grafted upon his ordinary manners, and made a very strange compound of himself. At home he travestied foreign ways, and introduced unheard of fashions in Grandfather's house. He swore beautifully in all languages; but his native damns never left him, any more than his appetite forsook him for salt junk and grog, after he had learned to like what he called foreign kickshaws.³

Father plodded along on small wages, and had a remote hope of reaching the cabin. When ashore, he lounged in his round jacket, and kept on loving my mother, who waited in patience for a turn in the long lane of their courtship. She snubbed Uncle Zeb whenever she had a chance, and always inquired about Father, of him, by the name of Esau.⁴ Grandfather, as well as Uncle Zeb, grew comfortably rich. His investments in sloops and schooners were fortunate ones, and he talked of buying a ship to fit out for a whaler. Feeling the need of a helper, for the first time in his life he turned his attention toward his youngest son, who was then at home, waiting for Captain Southerd to harvest his turnips. A proposal of partnership was made to father, which he accepted; and thus his sea life ended. He was married at once, and he and Mother took to housekeeping with one feather-bed, six small silver spoons, and a hearty affection for each other. Father applied himself to business, and the house that was thus founded became in a few years one of the richest and most influential in our part of the country. Grandfather very soon saw that it would only be necessary for him to take his share of the profits, and that he could safely give up all business matters to his partner.

In a year from the date of their marriage I was born, and at the time of Uncle Zeb's arrival from Liverpool with my cow and calf, I was five years old. That voyage was the last one that Uncle Zeb made. Finding us prosperous, he concluded to retire from business. He invested his money outside of the family-interest, but considerately took up his abode with Grandfather, and indulged Grandmother with the care of him. He occupied himself with watching the domestic and business transactions of the house of A. G. & Son, and banking his money as fast as it came in.

For a few years I cannot remember much concerning Uncle Zeb; the traits I recall belong to my present knowledge of him. When I went to school, it was one of my recreations to go to Grandfather's to dinner at mid-day, and one of my miseries to sit next to Uncle Zeb at the table. His dog, "Die," squatted on the other side of him. We had to wait till Uncle Zeb was carefully helped, by himself, to all the best bits on the table. Then he would give Die a titbit, making her snap her jaws for it, and then one to me. A snarling was kept up between him and the dog through the whole meal.

He would not have the potatoes on the table, they must be kept hot on the kitchen fire; so Grandmother sat, fork in hand, watching him; when he wanted one she fished it from the kettle, and he ate it scalding hot, with noise. Grandmother occupied a child's high chair, and wore a black satin hood over her high-crowned cap. She never dined or supped till after Uncle Zeb; and I had the best of times after he and Die had retired from the table. Grandmother took excellent care of her graceless son. He wore ruffled cambric shirts; and many an afternoon when the sun's rays slanted through the narrow kitchen windows, and made her resemble, in her shining spectacles, an owl, have I seen her laboriously plait its ruffles with a case-knife. On Sundays she combed his hair; it was fine and straight, and of the color of wet sand. It was unchanged to the day of his death. On Sunday afternoon he went to church in a great camlet cloak, and carried a cane with leather tassels. He listened to the sermon with an air of respect, and broke Grandmother's heart with deriding it after he got home.

Now and then he had a visitor, some piratical looking captain, or foreign merchant; the visitor was never introduced to any of the household, but was entertained in the parlor with tumblers of red wine and equivocal stories. As he never minded whether I came or went, I sometimes had the benefit of the latter. His laughter always arrested me; it contradicted him, it was so racy and hearty. His teeth glittered in his sardonic face, and lighted it up; they were long, white, and regular, and like his hair they never changed.

Two visits per diem were Uncle Zeb's allowance for our house. The first was made an hour or so after dinner, when he loitered in the kitchen, and tickled the servant girls, or poked them with his cane. Afterward, with his hat in his hand, he sought mother, and however long his stay, he held his cane and hat as if on a visit of ceremony. He talked well; he was sarcastic and witty, and never bored anybody. The second visit was made after supper, when father was at home. There was no confidence between the brothers, and no sympathy; but they passed cigars to each other, and enveloped themselves in clouds of smoke, and discoursed through it on commonplace subjects.

As soon as I was fledged, I was sent to boarding-school. My vacations were short, and I did not observe what went on at home; things seemed to run smoothly in the grooves of habit. I accepted appearances for realities. The business of A. G. & Son had greatly increased. All the year through, their ships were arriving in port, or were fitting for sea. Our household was a gay one, and Grandfather's house was full of comers and goers. He knew little of the private affairs of the concern, but smoked his pipe, and burned holes with its falling ashes in his fine blue pantaloons, in peace and tranquility. Uncle Zeb had given up ruffled shirts, and had taken to Marryatt's novels.[5] He neither bought nor sold; he never gave advice, or asked an opinion. He had a habit of going to funerals, but he went in a cheerful state of mind, as if the deceased had done him a favor by dying. He was respected as a moneyed man. The world admires what it dare not be a consistent, selfish skeptic; and our little world gave its admiration to my hard-headed Uncle Zeb. He was cautious, because he was cold,—prudent, because he was indifferent. As a token of the respect of his townsmen, he was elected Representative, and had a seat in the State House for several years. He brought home a great many volumes of Revised Statutes, which Grandmother stored in the garret, with the dried herbs. What he did as a member of the honorable body of Representatives nobody knew. He only spoke of the toughness of the pie-crust, and the hardness of his bed at his boarding-house.

When I was eighteen I left school and came home for good. I was the only young woman in the family connexion, and was considered worthy of much attention. Uncle Zeb, however, did not like me. He had his way of exasperating me. He always talked as if he knew that I must know that virtue was only a pretence. It was a game we were all playing. It was becoming in a woman to affect modesty; it was her capital. He gave me credit for shrewdness, and he had no doubt but that I should play my cards admirably. If I grew enraged at him, he laughed at me; but sometimes I made his cold blue eyes gleam with anger by telling him one or two unpleasant truths. His manner was usually deferential to women; but his ribaldry would break out now and then, and I have known him to be as coarse as Rabelais in a room full of ladies.[6] It was done with an air, as if he were obliging us with his candid wit.

It was not long after my return from school when I perceived that something weighed on father's mind. When I accompanied him on his many drives from one business-place to another, I saw the mask of cheerfulness drop from his face; he was absent-minded and silent. One day when we were alone, I begged him to tell me what troubled him, and then he owned to me that his business affairs were vexing him; that things had been going behindhand for a year; but I must say nothing of this, for he had hopes of being able to overcome his difficulties. Independent of his business perplexities, the keeping it secret was a trouble; he dared not retrench any expense, and he feared the effect of the truth on Grandfather, who was becoming childish. We went on this way for two years; plan after plan of salvation failed; but father's energy and good temper never left him. One day I thought of Uncle Zeb. "Why wont he," I said to myself, "put some of his thousands to the wheel?" I determined to tell him the state of affairs: I did not expect much from his generosity, but something from his pride; and thought, too, that his shrewdness might enable him to make something eventually out of any loan he might offer. So I sought him, and found him lying on the floor in the East Room asleep. I roused him, and did not wait for him to open his eyes before I began my tale. When I had finished, he eyed me for a moment, and said:

"So, you'll have to come down. Your devil's pride will be broken."

I stared mutely at him, but inwardly called myself a fool.

"I'll see," he said, "about buying up the family acres when the crash comes; but as for piling my money on the ruins of your father's speculations—that I wont do. Go home; if your father knew this he would pull your ears, though he is idiot enough not to do it."

I rose from my chair, looking, no doubt, just as I felt, for he laughed, and said, "Kick me if you like."

I went home thoroughly miserable, and did not report my interview, while Uncle Zeb on his part was silent also; but I did much mischief that day, and Uncle Zeb did a good stroke of business out of the capital which I had furnished him.

About this time Grandmother was persuaded to take an assistant—one who should unite in herself the qualities of companion and housekeeper. As there exists such a race of females, one was easily found. She was a remote cousin (this race is apt to be distantly related), and lived forty miles away, in Grandmother's native place. Her name was Nancy Goring, her age thirty-five. She was poor, intelligent, proud, and adroit. She had pretty, delicate hands, a large nose, and wore her hair parted at the side of her head. Her wardrobe was neat, but scanty; and Grandmother, who believed in making people happy as far as good clothes and food went, bought material for dresses and petticoats, and the companion's first duty was to make them up. After the dresses were made, she was allowed to knit and to sweep a little; but Grandmother's pride was still too great to allow herself to be supplanted in housekeeping.

Uncle Zeb proposed the position of hair-comber to Nancy, as Grandmother's eyesight was failing, and whenever she combed his hair now she fell asleep, and made an irregular thing of it. Nancy accepted; and from that time she began to pay him all sorts of delicate attentions, from cutting his finger-nails and tying his cravat, to mixing his grog and looking over his accounts. Uncle Zeb understood Nancy's devotion to him; but Nancy was very uncertain as to the nature of his feelings for her. She was desperately bent on turning Uncle Zeb from the errors of a bachelor, into the merits of a husband. She watched him, and followed him, and grovelled about him; but all in vain. Uncle Zeb never gave way. One day Grandmother's eyes were opened. She found Nancy, with a red silk handkerchief of Uncle Zeb's in her hand, which she had rolled into a tight ball, imprecating its owner hysterically.

The next day Nancy returned to her native place.

Our evil days drew near. A ship,—the one father depended on as his last hope,—made a broken voyage, and he was obliged to succumb. The house of A. G. & Son failed. A few days before the public announcement of the failure, he told it to his family. Then Uncle Zeb played his part. He behaved as if he had received an insult from father; he glowered with rage, and cursed him for his duplicity and foolishness. How dared he disgrace the name with failure and poverty? Had he given up all his property to his creditors? He, himself, had taken what measures he could to save some little from the wreck; and then it came out that he had obtained from Grandfather every cent of his private property: deeds had been signed by Grandfather in Uncle Zeb's favor, merely, as Uncle Zeb had told him, to make him safe if ever a rainy day came along. He had not made any nice distinctions between personal property and that which belonged to the firm, but had clawed into his possession all he could, and left the reputation of it to rest on father, if possible, if the creditors should discover it, and make allowance for it in the settlement.

The failure came out, and our house was besieged from morning till night by creditors. They were the more angry for its being unexpected. They not only wanted their money, but an explanation. Father had his office closed, and staid at home to receive them. The parlor was full of Ledgers, and councils were held over them, during which his character and conduct were discussed as if he had not been present. Not being a creditor, Uncle Zeb was denied the pleasure of being a member of the council; but he came and went a dozen times a day, without speaking to one of us. He went about the shipyards poking the timber with his cane, as if he would like to hurt it, and I saw him on the wharf studying the spars of the vessels. He was taking much more exercise than he had been accustomed to, and it evidently did not agree with him.

His ownership in certain properties was denied by the creditors; but they could not prove that the large homestead which had been Grandfather's belonged to the firm; so it passed into Uncle Zeb's keeping. But the creditors increased the percentage of what father was to pay on his debts, in consequence.

So we were ruined. Father made some arrangement by which his parents were not disturbed in their way of living; but mother, and the rest of us, gave up our purple and fine linen. Although Uncle Zeb lived in his own house now, the expenses of living were not defrayed by him, but by A. G. & Son. But if he did not complain, who should? He felt contempt for father; at the same time, I believe he had some admiration for his dignity and patience. Uncle Zeb was too clear-minded not to understand himself. He began to hate himself, and this self-hatred made him reckless; from this time he gave rein to his evil nature, and his pace was awful.

The next year Grandfather died, and was buried with his fathers, who slept under the mossy slate-stones of the Puritan times. Meanwhile father had prospered; he had paid within a twelvemonth the demands of his creditors, and had something left to begin the world again.

Another female cousin had come to reside with Grandmother, who dozed perpetually, or bemoaned Grandfather piteously. The cousin's name was Sally Packer, a middle-aged woman, who lived on patent medicine, took snuff, and believed in signs. She was wonderfully ignorant, but full of that low cunning which serves such people instead of knowledge. She had a faculty for mending broadcloth, and she was always at Uncle Zeb's clothes. Her waxed thread was whizzing through them from morning till night. She did not profess to know much, she said, but she would like to see the woman who understood tailoring better. She called Uncle Zeb a "superior being," and talked to him about property;—her respect for money was immense. Her manner toward him was full of humility, and if he came near her, she made a feint of retreating, at the same time casting her small eyes upward with an adoring expression. She meekly offered her snuffbox to him whenever she took a pinch, and after a little he fell into the habit of snuffing with her. He employed a portion of his time in experimenting with alcohol. Cloudy tumblers stood on the shelves with curious mixtures in them,—a sediment of rhubarb overlaid with brandy, or gin and senna,[7] or pounded Brandreth's pills in Jamaica rum.[8] He had a theory that if physic was taken with a dram it could have no deleterious effect. Night and day he drank his compounds. He set his bed on fire; he fell on the dining-table and crashed the dishes; he rolled off his horse with his feet in the stirrup; he laid in the street. But Sally Packer was his providence; she kept harm away from him. She dragged him to bed; she washed him; she dressed him; and she fed him;—and he cursed her.

The consequence of his theories was, that one morning he woke up with a paralysis, and father was obliged to take charge of him. Tenderly and mercifully he cared for him, for he was speechless and helpless. Sally Packer hustled him about as if he were a baby. How he wanted to rail at her! His eyes glared and burned with rage, whenever he saw Father come into his room. One night his watcher was startled from a nap, by the sight of Uncle Zeb in the middle of the floor.

"My cursed tongue is loose," he said, "and I can walk. Get out of the way!"

He wrapped the counterpane round his gaunt form, and tottered down-stairs into the street. He leaned against the fence and looked up to the sky, and chafed his feeble hands, and then crept back to bed; but from that night he was better, and soon became well.

Grandmother soon followed Grandfather, and slept near him in the same narrow bed. Sally Packer asked leave to remain long enough after the funeral to put the house in order. It was granted, and it took her years to do it—in fact, the house was never in order afterward; and so she staid. She convinced Uncle Zeb that no one could take care of him better than she could. She told him that the selfish world might say she expected to be remembered in his will; but it was not so. She had a good home of her own in Swampscot; a house, which, although it was not plastered, did not leak a drop, and there was as good a well of water close to it as ever was. She was willing to stay just to keep him from being imposed on, although she didn't know but that his relations were as honest as anybody's relations.

No one imposed upon either Uncle Zeb or Sally. The Lares and Penates of the ancient household were broken; its former friends deserted it.[9] It did not agree with Sally Packer's principles to have company; her moral constitution was averse to anything like hospitality. Uncle Zeb was indifferent whether anybody came or went. So Sally kept her ground, and had her own way. Uncle Zeb cursed and ridiculed her every day of her life. She cajoled, and wrangled, and worried, and petted him. Now she complained of being worn out with hard work, and now, that it was a place her betters would be glad to be in.

Both were to be found, usually, in the kitchen of the old mansion, a low-ceiled, dingy room, with a great brick hearth, on which Sally had ranged for convenience a row of pots and kettles. A fire burned, Summer and Winter, on the great iron dogs. Sally's chair was in one corner of the hearth, where she could poke the fire, or stir the contents of the pots and kettles; her snuff-box, and comb, and an almanac, were on the shelf above the fire. Her hair was thick and gray, and she was fond of combing it when she had a leisure moment. She wore short dresses of black bombazine, which never required washing, and went barelegged; her shoes were made of coarse carpet, on account of her corns. Uncle Zeb generally reclined on a wooden settee under the window; an old wollen cloak, rolled up, served him for a pillow. At the foot of the settee, whenever Uncle Zeb reposed on it, lay an ugly dog, which was Sally's property, by name "Spot." Picked bones, the remains of Spot's feasts, were strewed under the table and under the settee. Spot had a habit of howling in his sleep, and Uncle Zeb had a habit of kicking him for it. As he declined the trouble of taking off his hat when he laid down, it suffered in looks, and resembled a pair of windless bellows. He took snuff lying down; the result to his nails, and beard, and clothes, was deplorable. After Grandmother's death he resumed the habit of dram-drinking, minus the drugs, in the full expectation of killing himself. He began then to fling his money into wild schemes; he would amuse himself with using up as much as he could of his property, he said, before he was summoned to move off for good. He had some trouble, for he would not give it away; so he built and rebuilt inconvenient houses, and drained barren fields, and planted in the sand, and blasted rocks, and made roads that led to nowhere.

Everybody now knew Uncle Zeb's character, and he and Sally were the curiosity and aversion of the neighborhood. The old house grew darker and more dismal every day. He was continually cutting doors and passages through the walls; he seemed to have an idea that they would enable him to elude some enemy that might come upon him. Sally had all the carpets taken up and put away, and all the beds stripped. She slept on a stuffed bench outside Uncle Zeb's door. All the furniture was piled away; the looking-glasses were covered, and the shutters of every room were fastened. All she wanted for daily use was congregated in the kitchen, and there she staid as if she were waiting for some event to happen.

Once in a while I lifted the latch of the porch door. Sometimes the inmates noticed me, and sometimes not. Now and then Uncle Zeb would sit up in his crumpled hat, and revive with me his recollections of his voyages, and tell me many a piquant and picturesque anecdote. Sally would also forget herself a moment, and listen with admiring "Laws, Capen Zeb." But oftener I was the silent witness of angry disputes, when she stunned me with her foolishness, and he pained me with his profanity. His common salutation to her was, "You lying jade," whereat she whimpered, or scolded, according to the mood of the moment.

Father remonstrated with him once, but Uncle Zeb drove him away. He made his will soon afterward, and ordered the monument of which I have spoken; but his constitution was an iron one, and it bore much before he had a second stroke of paralysis. When he did, his case was at once hopeless, and father again took the post of an only friend. Sally was at her wit's end. She threw the medicine out of the window, and whispered about poison. She shook Uncle Zeb to make him speak. She talked and cried over him, till father was obliged to turn her from the room.

The night he died father staid by his bedside. About one o'clock Uncle Zeb turned over, the first time he had moved since the stroke. His fingers trembled toward father's. The first kindly look he ever gave his brother, beamed in his wild eyes then. Faint broken words struggled on his lips; but it was too late for speech—"Your wife, Mary," was all he said,—so he went out of this world, an unhappy mutilated spirit.

The homestead reverted to father; but it stands empty. The doors and passages which Uncle Zeb cut are open; and the beds that Sally stripped, still stand bare. No one has been there since the day of the funeral.

The Chimneys

Facing the western sky, Ruth Bowen caught the sight of two chimneys in the sunset glow, on the edge of the wooded horizon, which belonged to a house whose inhabitants had long been hateful to her. Ezra Clark lived there, and his mother, the "Widow Nabby." She had rejected Ezra twice, and had included his mother in the rejection. Why she should stop and ponder over those chimneys, with that basis of remembrance, seems inconsistent; but she stood as one taking a fond leave—like the soldier upon the hill. At that moment Ezra was eating his supper of bread and milk, thickly dashed with huckleberries, and avowing there was nothing equal to them in their season; but his mother, who was watching him, pretended to make moan over the necessity she was under of going into the swamp to pick more for him.

"Rheumatic fever and colic would not keep you from picking every darned one, mother," Ezra said.

"Now, Ezry, you know you lie; why, I haven't dried one yet."

"Folks are crazy in huckleberry time; they are ferocious to get into the woods and swamps, where a cat-bird would be ashamed to squall."

"What do you think of them Florida swamps, where human beings live for days on huckleberries?" asked his mother, wishing to divert his mind.

"Mother, our minister will spoil you with his politics. I wish he would attend to his gospel business, and not distress you with Florida."

"Fellow-creatures, Ezry."

"There, there; go on with the huckleberry crop," exclaimed Ezra; "there's no philanthropy in that."

"That's what I meant all along, Ezry; I am glad to convince you that I had better do something."

"The combat is over, then," said Ezra, "for the present, and I'll take a smoke."

If Ruth, when she started from home in search of field lilies, had been aware of coming in sight of Ezra's chimneys, she would have taken some other path; but here she was on a lonely road, and there they were, set in the deep border of woods in the west. The enchantment of the summer eve, with its splendid sky, its odorous thickets of dog-roses, swamp-apple blossoms, and wild grapes; its sleepy birds, who could not resist the rosy brilliancy of the atmosphere, and sang faint broken songs of delight in their leafy beds; its sweet silence and repose; aggravated her remembrances against him, it offered such a contrast to his appearance in his evening's rest and leisure. His shirt-sleeves were rolled up on his arms, of course, which, like his complexion, were ham-colored, and of a hairy muscularity. Probably wisps of hay stuck in his hair, and husks of rye were dropping from his clothes; he was bare-legged, undoubtedly, and most likely was taking his supper on the old door-step. She struck from the bushes along the path straggling bits of hay which had caught from passing loads, and twisted them, viciously wishing that she could twist the whole thing out of her mind. But that was impossible; she must live where Ezra lived, and still meet the Widow Nabby. She could never probably move away from Repton, where there was but one church, one society. She walked to and fro between the thickets till the chimneys disappeared in the gloom of the woods, the sky faded, and the dew fell. When she arrived at her mother's door she thought of the errand she had been on, and that inquiries would be made for the lilies. Though her mother, Mrs. Bowen, sympathized with her in regard to Ezra Clark, she knew a scolding would come if a confession was made of such erratic unnecessary reverie; for Mrs. Bowen was matter-of-fact, and chose neither to love nor hate from any ideal point of view. Ruth concluded to say nothing concerning the chimneys, and entered the house with shawl and bonnet in her hand.

"Your aunt's vases will not be filled this evening, I perceive," said Mrs. Bowen.

Ruth shrugged her shoulders, and shook out her dress.

"What have you been doing all this time, Ruth? Your dress is awfully bedraggled."

"Bespangled you mean, mother, with dew."

"What I mean is that I have to wash and iron your dresses. Where did you go?"

"I have been walking on the upper road; the evening is lovely."

"Any mosquitoes?"

"Suppose Aunt Eliza should ask me to come and live with her?" Ruth asked, reflectively.

"I can't suppose so; it is too foolish an idea. Eliza knows that this is our place."

"I wish to leave Repton."

"No, you do not; where should we be so much respected as here? Who would care to learn that once we were respectable, when we went about begging for work? What do people think of poor widows generally? That's what I am, when you come to the bare bones of the thing. Don't ever think that I am going to throw away the result of sixteen years of labor and management. I expect to live and die with the best here."

Ruth shuddered at the idea of being in any spot where her claims to equality with the highest might not be recognized; as for asking for work any where, it could not be done.

"What ails you?" continued her mother. "Has your evening walk unsettled your mind? It is not best to speculate on any change; if you will dwell on one, take into consideration the impossibility of our ever gathering again the comforts we have now. Once give up our house, which is in order, and our furniture—all our belongings, in short—how could we ever raise money to start afresh? It has taken me years to roll together what little we have."

Ruth was silenced and convinced.

"Hannah Brown called while you were out," Mrs. Bowen began again. "She tells me she is going up to Ezra Clark's next week to quilt for Mrs. Clark, who thinks her time may come any minute, and that she had better get together all the bed-clothes Ezra's wife will need during her lifetime."

"Ezra's wife!" exclaimed Ruth, with contempt. "Where will he find her? What kind of quilts did Hannah say old Clark was getting up?"

"Furniture chintz, very handsome, which Mrs. Clark bought five years ago."

"Ezra's wife is welcome to them!"

"He will find some suitable person, I dare say—one that the old woman can manage, and one who will feel under obligation to him for a home. It is bedtime, Ruth; take all your things up stairs—I do not want to begin the morning in a litter. Those bosoms are to be stitched first thing."

"Mother," Ruth asked, drowsily, after they had been in bed some time, "haven't we got a good many bedquilts?"

"Not one," Mrs. Bowen answered, gaping, "that hasn't come to darning."

Mrs. Bowen, as she had said, was a widow, and a genteel one. Her husband had been genteel also, but his gentility did not prevent long absences from home, in one of which he died without any effects—at least none ever reached his wife; and she was obliged, at the age of thirty, to cast about her for means to live by and to bring up Ruth, then six years old. For a few years she kept an infant-school—that is, the infants went to her house, and hung about her skirts, or slept on quilts spread over the floor for their convenience. All the nice people in Repton sent their children to her, understanding they would be taught nothing beyond the alphabet. Mrs. Bowen became a familiar name to every mother in the neighborhood, and it was a matter of pride between them to serve her. The children were made the medium of presents which, in fact, amounted to supplies; and as children have sharp wits, and are able to appreciate the cunning of older minds, they were sometimes made to perceive the comparison between Ruth's home and their own, to Ruth's advantage. She flourished with them at their bed and board, and in similar clothing, and grew more genteel even than her mother. When she was sixteen Mrs. Bowen gave up her school, and took up, with Ruth's assistance, fine-sewing. They never sought work; it was brought to them, to be done at their leisure and pleasure. Both were industrious, ingenious, and capable of executing any trust that was confided to them. The natural conscience, which persons of indifferent characters sometimes possess, is a curious starting-point for reflection, if one such had time to reflect on the inconsistencies of men and women. What Mrs. Bowen and Ruth professed to do they did as if they were actuated by a high sense of duty—but they were not.

What does it matter, so long as the Reptonians felt themselves repaid in their own coin? What if some acute person now and then said that the Bowens lived for themselves alone, and did it shrewdly too? Were they not bright, cheerful, and did they not hold up their heads high while they were about it? They made the most of what they had, and in that way they were generous, bestowing agreeable sensations by means of their neatness and good taste.

Mrs. Bowen turned her gifts and money to so good an account that it was difficult to remember their origin always; her pride assimilated what was originally foreign so thoroughly, that no soul would ever have dared to remind either Ruth or herself of the fact, or play the part of "Indian Giver" with them. They made as fine an appearance in Repton as any Reptonian. Not a fashion came there that Ruth did not adopt—not a new book was heard of that she did not contrive to get, either from the circulating library in the shire town or by borrowing from the few who read in Repton. Every magazine or paper which contained any account of the outside world, taken in the town, she devoured with a zest which was accounted for by her acquaintances who thought it a desire for information. It is not easy to account for a taste in novel-reading when the one who has it is somewhat selfish and passionless, as Ruth certainly was, and still less easy to discover what the effect of novel-reading is on such a character. It did not appear that she had imbibed therefrom any romantic ideas of solitude or society; she was invited every where, and accepted all her invitations. She was a marked feature in every party, being pleasing in style and intelligent. Sifting her influence to the bottom it was nothing; but she would have been missed from Repton, and never forgotten. People expected her presence, some one said, on the same principle that quince preserves obtained—they were always made, never liked, but eaten. Mrs. Bowen had a half-sister, who lived in a distant city and was married to a merchant of some means. She sometimes sent presents to Mrs. Bowen and Ruth—small articles of taste and luxury, which Mrs. Bowen received with a sneer or a sarcasm, and Ruth with curiosity and gratification. The last gift had been a pair of painted China vases, which Ruth intended to fill with lilies; but Ezra's chimneys had filled her mind instead.

Ezra Clark's farm was not in Repton proper, but three miles from its centre. It was not a model farm. Its buildings were without paint or white-wash; tumbling stone-walls and fences of crooked rails divided its ground into cornfields, potato patches, and pasture. On the north of it was a big swamp, in the west pine woods, and to the east ran the road which led to Repton. There was nothing picturesque about the premises. There were no prize cattle, or breed horses, or fancy poultry, and no pigeons. Ezra owned some good common cows, a yoke of oxen, a horse, and quite a number of hogs. He raised hay, corn, rye, and potatoes. Mrs. Clark made butter and sold it; also apple butter and dried apples. The old orchard, whose fangs defied nature's dentistry, also sheltered a bee-hive, and was the pleasure-ground of a few hens, whose eggs and broods were sold also, together with the honey from the hive. Ezra sold hay in the spring and the rest of his crops in the fall, pork in the winter, and sometimes beef. The farm cleared between three and four hundred dollars a year, which was nearly all saved. It had paid nothing in the time of Ezra's father; but when he died Ezra took it and brought it into a paying condition. It had been his for five years, consequently he was now worth about two thousand dollars. Sometimes he thought of taking this fund to speculate with in some other part of the world: like other Yankees he could go any where and be any thing, should he choose. He might establish a trading post in Japan, or invent something in the East Indies that would keep the natives cool and make his fortune. But he never came nearer to leaving home than this vague dream brought him. There were a hundred reasons why he should stay. His mother could not live without him. Who but himself could twist and screw a profit from the mean acres they owned? Who would keep an eye upon the old age of proud Mrs. Bowen if he failed to? Lastly, who wouldn't cut him out with Ruth if he forsook his forlorn hope?

Mrs. Clark would have lived had he left her, for she loved life and the world. She was somewhat eccentric—the "Widow Nabby," pious by rule, and skeptical by nature, artful, kind-hearted, bright, and simple, and withal a remarkably handsome woman. Her features were as regular as a Greek's. She had full black eyes, and a mop of black curly hair; her feet and hands were beautiful, her form perfect, and yet she was born on the opposite side of the swamp, where she lived till she married Ezra's father, and moved on the side where she now was. She was an awful dowdy, however, being perfectly indifferent to dress and her personal appearance. Her shoes were always down at the heel; she preferred wearing them so—there was no trouble about tying them. She hated strings, buttons, and hooks and eyes, and pins scratched her; her cap was two-thirds off her head generally, which she said was owing to the obstinate curl of her hair—it would rise up wave-like. Her gowns were made of a material that never required washing, and never came to mending, but fell all away at once. Her house was arranged correspondingly, and her way of doing housework was slip-shod of course. What was the use of making her bed every morning when it was tumbled every night—she reasoned with old Sally Lane, her ancient "help," who made it up notwithstanding. If the furniture dropped apart it remained so, unless Ezra saw it, and had it mended. Occasionally she had a fit of moving what she called "Lumber" into the unused rooms, and compelling Sally and Ezra to enjoy bare floors and walls a while. She swept and dusted, she said, when the Lord willed, which was not often. Her duty was done, however, in the line of milk-pans; their "shining morning faces," when she put them out of doors on a board, propitiated the demon of cleanliness, and was the saving clause put in by her friends when they otherwise called her a "Slut." She made a sincere effort on Sundays to look something like the Repton people whom she met at the Presbyterian church; and, with the help of Sally, succeeded, though before she returned her bonnet, shawl, and collar went astray over her shoulders; and she lost so many gloves and handkerchiefs that she gave up wearing them at last, and flourished a leaf of tansy, a rose, or a dry stalk of caraway seed instead.

It was at church that Ezra began to observe Ruth, to admire, and then fall in love with her. His pew was behind the one Mrs. Bowen hired seats in, which gave him the advantage of seeing Ruth enter it, and of looking boldly at the back of her bonnet. Sometimes her silk dress rustled against him, and he smelt the Cologne water her handkerchief was perfumed with. Mrs. Bowen and Mrs. Clark were members of the church, and the symbolic cup was handed by one to the other often; but they never exchanged more than a bow outside of the church. The "Widow Nabby" and her wardrobe was a jesting theme between Mrs. Bowen and Ruth; but her wonderful old woman's beauty was never recognized by them; perhaps they never saw it. Some people never discover genius even, when it is born in the same town with themselves. I am told that one of our noted authoresses is considered a miserable housekeeper in her town, and that Mr. Tennyson is called a cross man in his. If the world discovers a man of genius these people cry: "It can't be; he was born here; we have known him always!"

Ezra was really unnoticed by Ruth, and indeed there was little about him that was noticeable. "A common, decent farmer" Mrs. Bowen would have called him, if she had spoken of him at all. He was unlike his mother, but favored his father, as she often said with an odd sigh; he was tall and angular, fair-haired, gray-eyed, and had a Roman nose. If Ruth had ever taken pains to examine his face she would have seen there a resemblance to herself. She was tall and angular also, and had fair hair; but her features were delicate and trained, as in fact was her whole self, while Ezra, as yet, was but a man in the rough. Mrs. Clark penetrated Ezra's secret about the time he learned it himself. She thought him a green, foolish boy, but did not say so; she depicted the horrors of gentility to him in her cunning way; exposed the shifts and expedients to be resorted to where there was no real basis for it, but she only made Ezra laugh. The truth was, that it was Ruth's elegant precision that had fascinated him. He had suffered his long life, without knowing it, from the disorder and confusion at home, and his mother, without his knowing this too, would have been the last model he would have chosen from. Poor mothers! But they are ignorant also. After worshiping Ruth for several years in church he suddenly took the initiatory step toward making her acquaintance, and went up to Repton to spend his evenings. This was late in the spring, at the time the young people were beginning their excursions to the woods and fields. He was acquainted with the Repton men, but had made no visits to their houses. His point of attack was a call at the minister's, where it was lawful for all to go, with a bundle of rhubarb stalks, which he presented to the minister's wife, with the hope that they would not use up too much of her sugar; and chance, who loves parochial gifts, favored him. One of his friends, Joel Barnes, was there on a parish errand.

"There's a party of us," he said, "going up your way in a few minutes, Ezra. Join it, will you? We are going to Grape Dell."

"Who's going?" Ezra asked, confidently.

"I hardly know; I asked Ruth Bowen to go, for one."

"I am not acquainted with her."

"I'll introduce you. Come, you have kept out of company long enough. I never saw you in the minister's house before."

"It is Mr. Clark's fault," remarked the minister's wife, kindly.

"I know it," answered Ezra; "but, marm, the farm is on my hands; it takes all there is of me, soul and body, to keep it from falling back on me. But I've met with a change lately. I intend to be more among folks; and, Joel, I don't care if I do go along with you, and you may introduce me to as many young women as you like."

As it was dusk when the introduction came off Ezra acquitted himself decently, though he was sure of nothing, except that Ruth Bowen was near him, and that she had said in a high clear voice, "How do you do, Mr. Clark?" and immediately added, addressing Joel Barnes:

"Where did he come from?"

"What a splendid moon, Ezra!" Joel remarked, as if he had not heard her.

"No," answered Ezra.

"What a fool!" thought Ruth.

"The girls are getting into his head," thought Joel.

Ezra thought of a way to speak significantly to Ruth. The loud talking and laughing round him saddened his heart, he could not reason why. He wished Ruth would not feel quite as gay and self-possessed while she was so near him; but of course she could not guess what was seething in his mind. At last he asked her if she liked long walks. Very much, she replied, pleasantly; he said then, that he liked walking too. "Behind the plow or dropping corn," she thought; but said "Indeed!" and spoke to someone else. When the road which led to Grape Dell was reached he suddenly conceived the idea that he should feel easier at home, and drew aside for the party to pass. As Ruth went by he called out to her astonishment, in a friendly tone:

"Good-evening, Miss Bowen!"

"That's a capital good fellow!" said Joel Barnes to Ruth a few moments afterward.

"I have seen him with the Widow Nabby for years, but never met him. Have we the prospect of much of his society in our set?"

"Perhaps he wants a wife—where else could he look for one?"

"He!"

"He appeared to be flabbergasted by you," said Joel, mischievously.

"Me!" and Ruth tossed her head and her long neck, declaring that she was not fond of jokes.

Ezra walked home very fast, and when he saw his mother burst out with, "Mother, they are walking all over."

"Who's a-walking, Ezry? Not sperrits, I trust."

"The young folks at Repton. Why can't they walk here?"

"What for?"

"Because it is pleasant."

"Ho, ho! delightful, ain't it? either with the skeeters in the swamp, the owls in the woods, or me and Sally Lane in the kitchen."

"To—to—see me, then."

"The wind is that way, is it? Ask 'em right up, Ezry; they'll sing hymns, maybe."

"Hymns be darned."

"Do have 'em, Ezry, whether or no; young feet have not trod over these floors for many a day. I wish they would dance."

"Will you dance, mother?"

"Oh, Ezra! I belong, and can't; but I'll bet a horse to a herring that Sally Lane would like to cut a caper."

He consulted with Sally; she advised cider and cookies, and, as most of their chairs refused to bear any body's weight, suggested some new ones. He went to Repton the next day and bought twelve maple-backed and rush-seated chairs, and then carried his idea to Joel Barnes.

"If you will come up to my shanty with the same party and spend the evening," he said, "I'll drive you all home in my hay-cart."

"All right," answered Joel; "say when."

"Next week some time."

"Thursday."

"That's fair. Don't expect any thing; there's a good deal of rind about mother and me, you know."

"My country friend," said Joel, "husk is what we jaded voluptuaries need."

"Be darned."

When Sally saw the chairs she was so excited that she exclaimed: "Ain't he a one to go it?"

"No," answered Mrs. Clark; "I would have burnt the house down, and moved the lot."

Ezra exchanged a look with her.

"You are right, mother; but I won't do either, and you know why."

"The mountain's a coming to Mohammed."[1]

Mrs. Clark spoke kindly to every one on the evening of the party, but made no effort to entertain.

"She has not changed her cap even," said Ruth Bowen to one of the girls. "Isn't she curious? and did you ever see such a house? Ezra has not made a mistake, has he, and put us in a deserted cattle-pen? I would not be obliged to sleep here, or touch a particle of food, for the world. But what can we expect of that poor young man, brought up in this way?"

"True enough," her friend answered; "but Mrs. Clark is a good, clever woman for all that; and Ezra is a fine young man—forehanded, too. He is looking at us."

Ruth turned her face toward him, and tried to look civil. He had watched her all the evening, and paid her several attentions, which she mutely accepted. He liked her in his own house better than ever. How graceful and neat she looked in her spotted muslin dress and little black silk apron, and with the long curls at the back of her head! But he divined her thoughts, and felt the scornful expression in her face while she spoke to her friend. He went up to her and the friend sauntered away.

"This is a poor place," he said, sharply.

She was so surprised at his sudden accost that she blushed and looked very natural.

"It is quite old, I suppose," she remarked, gently.

"Old as it is, poor, mean, filthy, I intend to bring my wife here."

Being fully recovered, she shook out her handkerchief, raised her eyebrows, and answered, "Indeed!"

"Yes, and I am going to ask you to be my wife. I have thought of you for a long time."

He was very pale, and his Roman nose looked more like a bridge than ever.

"Mercy on me," said Ruth, terribly afraid he would be overheard; "I decline the honor."

Mrs. Clark saw it all through the half-opened kitchen door. She would have flown at Ruth's throat in behalf of her offspring if it would have helped him; as it was she shook her head till her cap fell off, and she kicked it away.

"I am," continued Ezra, between his teeth, "a suitable husband for you. We both earn our living. Our mothers have to labor. I will take care of your mother in her old age. She need never make another shirt; but you would have to work and help me."

"I—never! I could never dream of such a husband as you. Please attend to your company and let me alone."

He turned away in perfect calmness, but deeply mortified. So was Ruth, and very angry. He offered her a glass of cider when it went round, but she would not take it or look at him.

"I deserve your respect," he said, holding the glass almost under her nose. "I insist upon your taking this from my hand."

She raised her eyes to his. He looked so determined that she took it; she was afraid he would make a scene if she refused, and then it would come out that she had been subjected to his ridiculous proposal. The remainder of the evening was chaos to both; Ruth was anxious to get away, and Ezra desired an end to the thing. Mrs. Clark was not sorry to see the party depart. She sent Sally Lane to bed immediately, but sat up herself till Ezra returned from Repton with the hay-cart.

"How do you think that glass of cider tasted to Ruth Bowen, Ezry?"

"I don't think."

"I do; it was as bitter as the waters of Marah."[2]

"If it was as bitter as the tears that I could shed as easy as not, she'll be very sick before morning. I took her down from the hay-cart, however; if I hadn't she would have sprained her ankle."

"I wish her pride could be sprained."

"Never mind, mother; I am going to wait a while. Good-night to you; much obliged."

With tears of vexation Ruth related to her mother what had befallen her.

"What could have possessed the jackass?" asked Mrs. Bowen; "he could not suppose you would inherit any property."

"Oh, mother," said Ruth, with heat, "I think the donkey is in love with me."

"There's no other way of accounting for it; but what encouragement had you given him?"

"Don't drive me quite crazy. You know that I never gave any body the least encouragement."

"You need not fire up. It will pass over soon; it is not likely that he will tell of his rejection."

"He is Joel's particular friend."

"I am sorry for that; what can Joel see in him?"

"I know I shall see him whenever I see Joel; I am sure of it."

And she did, Ezra solemnly went every where with Joel, if there was a prospect of meeting her. His pertinacity came to be understood, and Ruth was laughed at for her adorer. There was but one way of escape—marriage—and there was but one she would marry—Joel Barnes—Ezra's friend, who appeared to be his advocate from the fact of his allowing Ezra to hang to his skirts on all occasions. Joel was genteel. His business, that of clerk in a dry-goods store, suited her; his hands were white, his clothes always fashionable. But Joel had no intention of rescuing her from Ezra's pursuit. The summer passed without any mitigation of her troubles; Ezra was quietly friendly toward her, whether she turned her back to him, or whether she set her face in scornful rigidity opposite his. It is certain that under this *régime* he developed wonderfully, acquiring experience with his hopelessness that went far toward turning him into one of "Nature's noblemen;" that is, his farming instincts and his love of labor sat with ease and dignity upon him. But farming and labor blinded Ruth's eyes still. Nature's nobleman was poor; he had rough hands; he still said "darn" now and then. Can she be blamed? When winter came, she made it an excuse for not going out in the evening as much as formerly. Ezra could not carry the war into her dwelling; he would not quite dare to face Mrs. Bowen. It was not pleasant for Ruth to hear that Ezra was more and more tolerated; that he had been invited to the sociables for the season. She refused to join them. When he heard of it he wrote her a long letter, and proposed withdrawing from them, should she desire to go. He also wrote her some disagreeable truths concerning herself, but he repeated his offer of marriage. Ruth took no notice of the letter, and still staid away from the sociables.

"It will never do to give it up so," said her friends. "You will have to marry him to get rid of him."

"Be sure to come and take tea with me when I do," she answered.

It came to pass that Mrs. Bowen and Mrs. Clark had a slight falling out without ever having had a falling in. One snowy Sunday Mrs. Clark passed the interval between the morning and the afternoon service in the church. As Ruth was to remain at home, Mrs. Bowen started early, and they met at the stove in the entry. Bows were exchanged, but with the sudden opportunity wrath gathered in Mrs. Bowen's heart.

"I wonder your son is not at his post watching," she said. "I miss him."

"I am sorry to disappoint you marm," Mrs. Clark answered; "but he ain't coming. Where's your Ruth?"

"*She* has been obliged to make herself a prisoner."

"'Tain't on bread and water, I hope."

"If it was it would be preferable to what she is forced to have when she goes out."

"What's that, marm?"

"The attentions of your son. Can't you teach him how to keep in the place where he belongs?"

"If your Ruth's disposition and behavior won't drive him away nothing will; we must let him go to the end of his rope. I am really sorry for you, because I see you have not got over it, as *I* have; I gave Ezry up some time ago. Now, marm, let us go right in and hear the gospel preached."

Ezra from this time deserted Repton. Ruth emerged from her seclusion and went about as in former times; but she missed something—her persecution. A sting, an expectation, a flavor was gone; dullness took their place, especially after Joel Barnes became engaged to a girl entirely out of their set.

"The good times are over," was the cry. "We are going to break up; what are we to do for young men?"

But Ruth had little time either for amusement or reflection. Mrs. Bowen was taken ill; their work got behindhand, and Ruth obtained an insight into the pains and penalties of living. When her mother recovered they were obliged to make up by extra industry for the lost time, and so the weeks rolled on even up to the night on which Ruth walked out in sight of Ezra's chimneys. She did not on that occasion define all the cause of her exasperation. The roots of human nature are everlastingly the same; and yet every body is surprised at the foliage and fruit they bear. No one would have been more surprised than Ruth if she had been told that she wanted Ezra to come back. Bedquilts ran in her mind the whole of the following day; dreams of their disposal by Ezra's wife confused and afflicted her; fancies of a well-regulated house for him flitted through her mind. How much might she accomplish with her ability, industry, and neatness toward making him a prosperous man she could not help reckoning. And what would he not do for her—how indulgent, generous, and faithful she was sure she should find him! She and her mother could turn him round their little fingers if they chose. The day ended with her hating the supposititious wife and her bedquilts, and going out to walk on the same road she had walked over the night before. She sauntered nearer and nearer the chimneys, which seemed to ride down the horizon as she approached. It was the barley harvest, and it chanced that Ezra and his man were out late in a field on the border of his farm. He descried Ruth's tall figure in the "gloaming," and concluded not to drive home his loaded wagon, but sent his man on with it in advance. Ruth still walked forward without seeing him. He leaned his elbows on the wall which bordered the road, and wondered if she knew where she was going, and if she would come much nearer. She stopped a moment as if she were reflecting, which made him feel sorry and apprehensive, and started on again; her eyes fell on his head above the wall, she made up her mind instinctively to go by as if she did not see him; but when she came opposite him she said, in a trembling voice,

"Good-evening, Ezra!"

He was over the wall in an instant and beside her; for a moment both were agitated.

"Do you feel any different?" he asked at length.

She meant to say "No," and that she "never should;" but all at once she felt how lonely the road was; how lonely the world might be, and how deep the "gloaming" which would surround her.

She gave a little gasp and looked up at him. His arm was round her waist like lightning. His shirt-sleeves were rolled up, and barley straws were sticking in his hat, but she returned his kiss.

They were married, but it was a very unequal match, and nobody knew it so well as Mrs. Clark and Mrs. Bowen, though they had entirely different reasons for thinking so.

Lucy Tavish's Journey

At last the family united on the question of Lucy's taking a journey. Even her Aunt Debby Davis, who opposed her in every thing on orthodox principles, admitted that perhaps she would never see a better time to do a useless thing, and she might as well go and be done with it. No one knew how the suggestion had been started in Lucy's behalf; like an invention, probably the necessity for it gave its birth, and it rose in several minds, to be perfected among those who could carry out the plan. Valid reasons were assigned for this journey—she was eighteen years old, and with the expectation of devoting the future to the happy profession of a village school-teacher had finished the necessary education—she had never been out of her native place, nor seen a railroad, steamboat, or canal. It would be an advantage certainly to add the experiences of travel to her education, and elevate her plane above that of her associates and scholars.

"But where can she go?" Mrs. Tavish, her mother, inquired, describing the circle of the globe with pudgy hands acquainted with the making of butter-balls.

"Our relations have all died out," added Aunt Debby, "old Moses Davis, second cousin to you and me, Sarah, went off suddenly a year ago, and his farm was sold. There's no mistake about my missing the quinces I used to get every fall from his place. He was the last of the Davises, you know, except myself and yourself, Sarah."

Mr. Tavish cogitated; his rough white eyebrows went up and down as if in search of some friend to quarter his Lucy upon. She must have an object, and a hospitable destination. As he could neither leave his farm nor afford the money it would cost to accompany her, it would not be proper otherwise for her to rush blindly over some railroad, and put up at some tavern or gimcrack hotel, and order what she pleased, paying her bill like a man. She was smart enough to do it, he argued, but was too pretty, and her "sarsy" way might come upon her at the wrong moment, and fetch her trouble.

Lucy sat demure in the family conclave, but felt secretly proud of the importance her eighteen years had so unexpectedly assumed, and pleased with the prospect of a variation upon her dull life. She turned over in her mind the pages of the Geography, whose wood-cuts represented remarkable objects in nature: Niagara, the Natural Bridge in Virginia not capable of reconstruction—the Rocky Mountains, and Bunker Hill. A journey according to her ideas meant a pursuit of these famous objects, for the purpose of conveying information afterward to those of one's friends athirst for knowledge, and only able to receive it at second-hand, and of holding them in one's memory as the precious treasures of a past not to be repeated. Somehow this idea of a journey did not attract her, it lacked human interest—a Mountain could only be a large hill, and Falls mere water running swifter than a brook. Passing over these she saw with her mind's eye the pictures of cities, New York, Chicago, St. Louis; the latter stirred some vague association, striving to follow its clew she lost the thread of the conversation, but was recalled to it by the loud tones of her father, who was replying to some remark of his wife's.

"Yes," he said, "you know what I think of relations, and what I have done for yours and mine. Blood is a great deal thicker than water; it is as thick as mud. We flounder about, our eyes and mouth so full of it that none of us can tell what's right and what's wrong with us till we are parted or dead."

"Father, where's my Uncle John?" inquired Lucy.

"He moved to St. Louis in 1848," he answered. Debby looked out of the window at the mention of Uncle John's name, and Mrs. Tavish gave a loud sigh.

"Mrs. Tavish," said Mr. Tavish, angrily, "what is the matter with you?"

"Why not let me go there?" asked Lucy.

"Because I think he is dead," her father replied, hanging his head.

"He is just as much alive as I am," said Debby.

"Why shouldn't he be?" cried Mrs. Tavish.

"He is just your age."

"Lemuel Green, who went out West three years ago, told me he saw a sign over a store in St. Louis with 'JOHN TAVISH AND CO., *Leather Dealers*,' on it, and asked me if it was that brother of Seth's who disappeared so strangely some years since. I said I guessed not; that Tavish was a common name in that part of the country; but I am sure it was our John, it is just like him to be well off and happy somewhere else."

Seth Tavish gave a grim smile. "I reckon the '*Co.*' has the worth of it," he said. "Lucy, you do not remember your uncle I am sure."

"She does," interrupted Debby; "She was four years old when he went away with that wife of his."

"Sho, Debby, you forget yourself!" cried Mrs. Tavish.

"Wish I could," muttered Debby.

"I recollect," said Lucy, obtaining an opportunity for speaking, "a tall man who used to dangle his legs from the window-seat, where Aunt Debby kept her work-basket, and her saying: 'Run away, Lucy, Uncle John does not want you here.' I suppose he was my uncle."

Mr. Tavish roared, and slapped his knee. "Good for you, Debby! Well, we'll send her to Uncle John, and find out by her great ears whether he wants her now. Lucy, Puss, remember the old saying about the pitcher's going to the well one time too many."

"No one knows better than Aunt Debby," replied Lucy, "the size of my ears, she has pulled them often enough."

This discussion ended, a new one opened, from which Mr. Tavish, after affirming that he would only allow the price of a ton of hay for Lucy's outfit, withdrew. The discussion on Lucy's side regarded what outfit she *must have*, on that of Mrs. Tavish and Aunt Debby what she *could do without* in the outfit.

"I should go respectably," said Lucy.

"You will come home in rags, whatever you may start with," said Aunt Debby.

"That is to be expected," added Mrs. Tavish.

"It's all the same," retorted Lucy, "provided the glass slipper comes round to me again—when I am sitting in my old ashes."

"Glass slipper!" cried Aunt Debby; "that comes from your novel-reading. You are not fit to be trusted to go alone from here to the barn."

"Mother, I must have a stone-colored traveling dress."

"And a bag," suggested Mrs. Tavish.

"Fiddle-stick! what kind of a bag?" asked Aunt Debby.

"A morocco traveling-bag, with a steel chain."

"Don't you mean to take a trunk, Lucy?"

"Certainly; but the bag, I mean, or satchel, or portmanteau, or valise is an article to be carried in the hand, containing sandwiches, a towel, cake, a dressing-comb, my journal, a bottle of salts, pamphlet novels, a sponge, and what-nots."

Aunt Debby was silenced on that point: the sponge was thrown up.

"Borrow Lucinda Brown's bag," said Mrs. Tavish. "She's sure to have one, if it is only to go from house to house to carry her duds in."

"I never borrow, mother. I also should have a silk dress, in case I should find Uncle John fashionable; I am told that any thing except silk is inadmissible at dinner and evening parties."

"Heaven and earth! Your uncle John may be dead and buried, and the worms giving parties in his skeleton!" cried Aunt Debby, forgetting her late opinion as to his existence.

"You shall have my fawn-colored silk," said Mrs. Tavish; "Miss Lewis can make it over for you. I am quite willing for you to appear like other folks. Do, Debby, hush; recollect Lucy is a young girl."

Lucy held up three fingers, and enumerated distinctly—the traveling-dress, the traveling-bag, and the silk dress, which must be black. She would turn down her thumb, she said, for a few extras.

"The whole hay on the brook meadow wouldn't pay for what you want," said Aunt Debby.

"Well, then," said Mrs. Tavish, resolutely, "I'll sell my cheese the first of the week, up at the store; that will do it; she isn't going to take but one journey, Debby, and she shall go as Seth Tavish's daughter ought to go."

"Good soul!" exclaimed Lucy, dramatically, "Heaven has given thee a heart in the right place, though it hath bestowed upon thee a robust form. Let me kiss thee!"

As she embraced her mother, she made a wry face at Aunt Debby, who now appeared to be lost in thought.

"Now, I hope it is all settled," said Mrs. Tavish. "I'll go into the kitchen; it won't do to let your father's dinner get behindhand, journey or no journey."

"Stop!" called Aunt Debby, in a solemn voice—"it shall not be said that I did not do my part. Lucy, I will give you my watch and chain."

Lucy stared amazed, for this watch and chain she had looked upon as Aunt Debby's Baal, from childhood; and Mrs. Tavish exchanged an intelligent sympathetic glance with her sister.[1]

"I never wear it," she continued, "and never shall. You are welcome to the gift. You will need the watch on your journey, and afterward, when you keep school."

Lucy felt so severe a pang of shame at this generosity that she did not know how to give thanks. She contrived to mutter a few words, at which Aunt Debby rather grandly waved her hand and left the room.

"I am astonished, Lucy," said Mrs. Tavish, "that she should part with the watch. Your Uncle John, I may as well tell you, gave it to her. They were once engaged."

"What broke it off?"

"He behaved badly. He was wild and extravagant. Your father had a bitter quarrel with him, partly on Debby's account. At last the farm was divided; John took all the ready money, and left for parts unknown, with his wife."

"Aunt Debby ever in love! Gracious!"

"Lucy, you are a foolish child. Love is not confined to the imagination of girls and boys. It is a sober, lasting fact. The poetry books omit a great deal in their descriptions because they are meant for the like of you—young, pretty, ignorant. Debby was, and is, cruelly disappointed; in fact, she had a brain-fever which turned her hair. She is barely forty, you goose, now, and you think her an old woman. Lucy, you never saw me out of patience with her. Will you let what I have said prevail with you, and make you more gracious and affectionate with her?"

"Never was so ashamed in my life. How much *did* she love him? Now I am curious about my uncle. I declare I'll take out the watch before his face and tell him the time of day."

"There, Lucy, you need not get into any tantrum on the subject. I guess your father has concluded he was not over-reasonable with John. I surmise that Seth wants to make up, for he is a tender-hearted man."

Mr. Tavish's reason told him that the better way would be to write to "John Tavish and Co." before sending Lucy on what might prove a wild-goose chase; but pride, and possibly—clod-turner that he was—a sentiment, prevented his doing so. He chose the experiment of sending a mutual tie as embassador between himself and his brother. Several days afterward, dressed in his best, Mr. Tavish rode away from his door without giving his family any reason, and returned after an absence of a few hours. He produced what he called an "associated ticket" for Lucy, which he had purchased at Dropville—a railroad station twelve miles distant, where he had been for the purpose of conferring with the station-master.

"Now, Lucy," he said, "this combination thing will put you right through. You won't have to put your hand in your purse for a cent, unless to buy something to eat with. In three days and three nights you will be there. I've ciphered it all out. The Railroad Company is bound to take care of you, or it lies like thunder. Are you about ready?"

"No, father; the dresses I am to have are not yet bought, and my mind is not quite prepared."

"What has your mind to do with it?"

"Would you have her leave her wits at home, father?" said Mrs. Tavish. "I'll tell you what she means. She is waiting for me to sell my cheese."

"Oh, ho!"

"To piece out your generous providings."

"Oh, ho! ho!"

"Yes, she is going on the strength of my cheese."

"Well, Sally, your cheese is apt to be strong enough to take any body along. Plague take you! How much more do you want for furbelows?"

It is needless to say that Lucy's wishes were finally carried out. The morning arrived when she turned the key in her trunk, and stood before her mother dressed in a stone-colored suit, a stone-colored hat, trimmed with ivy-leaves, and holding a pretty leather bag, stuffed full of small stores.

"Good-by, mother! Eyes, look your last; arms, take your last embrace!"

Mrs. Tavish made no effort to wipe away the tears which slid off her round, shining cheeks. She hugged Lucy, begged her not to wet her feet, and told her that she must be sure to read a chapter every night in the little Testament which had been clapped into her trunk at the last moment. Lucy heroically suppressed every symptom of exultation and anticipation, kissed her mother, and patted her shoulders, and turned to Aunt Debby, who was tearless, and wore a critical expression.

"Good-by, Aunt Debby; I shall write."

"Be sure to tell us all the fashions; and if you come across any curiosities bring them home."

"Come now, Lucy," called her father from outside; "Bill's beginning to thrash."

She sprang forward, and into the wagon beside him; and as they left the village, striking the highway which led up a long hill, and from its summit showed the round of the purple autumn sky hovering over a hundred corn-fields, filled with sere stalks, dotted with elms and maples, whose leaves were amber, crimson, and green, and russet woods running like promontories into the valleys, and hills veiled in blue velvety mist, she felt as if she was riding up to Paradise; that vagary on the road before us which turns out to be nothing at all she felt to perfection. Her feelings were sustained by Bill's unvarying jog and her father's silence, which at last he broke.

"If there should be any difficulty, Lucy, after you get there, in finding your Uncle John, you must go to a private boarding-house. I made inquiries of a man who has been there, and he gave me this direction; put it in your pocket-book. I trust, however, you will have no difficulty; our information about John is to be relied on."

"How long shall I stay in case I do?"

"Till you have got an idea of the Western Country. I wish you would notice the soil, what sort of trees flourish best, and what effect the water has on your system. Who knows but that I may sell out here, and move Sally and Debby there!"

"What shall I say to Uncle John?"

"Tell him you've come to make him a short visit."

Nothing more was said till they came to the Dropville Station. Mr. Tavish then grew anxious and doubtful, but Lucy's spirits rose to a grand level with the sight of the railroad paraphernalia.

"I am not sure," he said, "that I haven't done the wrong thing to let you go. Be mighty careful of the folks you meet along your way. I hope I haven't made a mistake. What possessed me to let you go when you are all the treasure I have? Darn that John Tavish! he never was any thing but a pest to me."

"It is all right, father. I can take care of myself from here to Jericho. I shouldn't be worth naming as a New England girl if I couldn't. You have arranged every thing just as I like it."

"Expect I did calculate on your grit. There's the whistle. Now you are going. Here, give me a kiss. Don't do any thing to be ashamed of to high nor low."

And Lucy was off! A tear bedimmed her eye as she caught sight of her father and Bill at a turn of the road, the former holding down his head thoughtfully, and the latter thrashing his long tail viciously; but, as they disappeared, the novelty and excitement of her position filled her mind afresh.

In the first isolation, and dread of the approach of strangers, she kept her stone-colored veil over her face, and assumed a haughty mien if any of the passengers made a movement in her direction; but the feeling soon wore off. On the second day the veil streamed from the back of her hat, her gloves were off, her hair had become a little regardless of the eyes of strangers, and her dress was crumpled: her whole air partook of that peculiar demoralization which travel effects with those who give themselves up to it. She had even accepted a piece of sponge-cake and a *Harper's Weekly* from a dapper middle-aged gentleman, who was subservient to a brown linen surtout, and who remarked that the cake might be free from specks, but that he didn't think so, and who pointed to the fact of the remarkable similarity between the portraits of malefactors and those of the good and great men.² The absence of that old lady who governs society, Mrs. Grundy, who is never able to leave her narrow locality, the sudden, inevitable, and unlooked-for relations, caused by the abnormal conditions of traveling, established a community of interests—lasting between town and town, or for the whole journey. It had been magnetically discovered who were the "through passengers"—and they felt themselves a bettered, jolly crew—the soot, cinders, and dust, the terrifying behavior of the brakemen, watching from between the cars, and frantically pulling at cranks and cords or dancing lanterns about, together with the concise, impressive manners of the conductors, incapable of volunteering any information, answered to the perils and uncertainties of shipboard, and drew confiding souls together, whose bonds would fly asunder at the first glimpse of the destined station. The few short intervals in which the passengers were permitted to leave the train and skirmish for a meal, consisting mostly of lard and grit, apples and deleterious liquids, awoke Lucy to a bewildering sense of an outside world whose extremities were the home she had left, and St. Louis, each vague and remote, and alien to her present purpose. All she saw outside the railroad appeared automatic—the towns, with strings of puppets, whose motions would cease with the passing of the locomotive; the hill-ranges that rose and sank; the winding rivers, wide and silent, narrow and noisy, skimmed by birds, or dotted with boats; the belts of primeval woods, shady as the world of ghosts; and but for the embrace of the iron rails, as impenetrable, and the lakes, the blue eyes of the landscape, opening sleepily at the noise and fume of the perturbations of men. It all counted afterward as a wild vision in her memory.

At Chicago there was more confusion, hurry, and change than at any time before; and on starting from thence Lucy perceived that the aspect of her particular car had changed entirely—she was alone in her corner. Two veiled statues in crinoline occupied seats at the opposite end, who were evidently prepared to remain immovable through all vicissitudes, and not admit their propinquity to any fellow-beings; the other occupants were men—sharp-jawed tobacco-chewers, with wrinkled foreheads, and eyes filled with speculation. Miles rolled away, the brakemen were napping or smoking, and the conductors' appetites for tickets for the present were appeased. Lucy gazed at the flying country till her eyes ached, and then thought she would empty her traveling-bag and sort its contents for amusement. She shook, folded, and replaced them. Opening her little journal for the first time, she began to write in it with the gold pencil attached to Aunt Debby's chain, and was arrested by a voice close to her ear from the seat behind hers, which she had thought empty.

"You have traveled so far, Miss, that I reckon you have to keep that book posted up to keep run of yourself."

She turned and brought her face unpleasantly near to that of a young man who rested his elbows on the back of her seat. There was a detestable expression of admiration in his good-natured countenance which made her angry; she grew very red and her eyes sparkled. He, not intimidated, moved his elbows to get a better view, and made another attempt.

"I have been observing you some time, Miss—thought you seemed dull, and that I'd better come over and introduce myself—might as well be neighborly! I am going to Alton. My name is Torch. I was all through the war—Lieutenant of Company A, Fourth Indiana—Silver Tails. We were the boys, I assure you. We didn't run away but once."

"I wish, Sir, you would repeat the performance of this occasion," said Lucy, fiercely.

He laughed.

"I didn't run. I never do under any circumstances. I couldn't *that* day. Look here!"

In spite of herself she looked, as he rolled up his loose coat-sleeve and exposed an ugly scar running down his arm to his right hand, from which two fingers were gone.

"I spent a lively evening after the fight, when my bunch of fives was sliced into *without* chloroform; the surgeon excused himself for mislaying the last bottle. I kicked him and I cursed him; and then a New England woman came along with a lemon—the New England women carried lemons always—and *she* was almighty good to me. She said, 'Don't swear;' and I haven't cursed since. I knew your stripe as soon as I set eyes on you. Should be happy, Miss, to show you any attention in my power."

Ending with this bit of politeness he drew aside with an expression which denoted he had done all that could become a man and traveler. A broad smile passed over Lucy's face, which he perceived, and which encouraged him. He replaced his elbows and resumed:

"The war, Miss, has had the effect of making us feel free and easy every where. I am quite ready to go with our artillery to Mexico; the Mexicans need h—(beg your pardon!), and your cannon can give it to them. What is your opinion of the Mexicans? When you say *vermin, vomito,* and a want of *veracity,* they are described, in my estimation."

Lucy looked down the row on her right, and up the row on her left, to see if any body was observing this persistent, shabby young man, who was using the most offensive language she ever heard. No one appeared at all regardful of him; but she omitted to glance into the little mirror inserted in the panel at the end of the car on her side.

"Where is Mexico?" she asked, with an indifferent air.

"It is the country where hasty plates of soup are made, and military officers use the politest of talk, when it is necessary for Captain Bragg to give 'em a little more grape."

She raised her eyes to his, and met a sharp, intelligent, cool glance, which made her feel slightly afraid of him. With oozing courage, she said, abruptly:

"Mr. Torch, were you ever extinguished?"

"Old!" he answered; "old as the Alleghanies that joke is! The Torch Family came in with that range. Before that party of self-sufficient gentlemen set sail for America in 1620."

In spite of his pert reply his sand-colored complexion took on a lively red, and matched his long hair, which fell straight beneath his jaunty felt-hat. Lucy had succeeded in annoying and discomposing him. He was really attracted toward her, and honest in his admiration. The legends of his regiment, as well as its experiences in passing over a large extent of country, went to prove there was such a truth as "love at first sight." Lucy turned squarely from him in the middle of her seat, and devoted a close attention to her window. She wished that the brim of her hat was wider, for she had an irritating perception that Mr. Torch was intently examining the shape of her ears, her waterfall, and the contour of her head. There was silence for a few miles, and then an avalanche of magazines and papers came sliding over beside her.

"Do look at them," begged Mr. Torch in a beseeching tone. "I meant no offense. Excuse me."

"Thank you," mumbled Lucy, and took up a Magazine.

"First-rate article there," he said, eagerly; "but, by jingo, there isn't a mite of common-sense in it. How are the writers paid your way for writing moonshine?"

"In finding critics like yourself, possibly."

"Very good again. The article is called, 'The Skull of the Negro before and after Freedom.' Now will you be good enough to tell me, Miss, whether the happy and enlightened colored brother, who never is allowed to come into the family with you, is different in the formation of his head from the miserable, ignorant nigger, the associate of the whites at the South? Recollect I am no secesh.[3] No, Sir-ee."

What should she do? Be driven mad by this creature, who had sprung up like a mushroom in the atmosphere of the car! She felt powerless against his familiar, horrible good-humor. She laid the Magazine down, looked at her watch, and queried how much longer she could endure it before attempting "justifiable homicide!"

"My watch run down," he said, "just as we passed Marcus-Aurelius-ville. What time is it?" She felt compelled to inform him; but unwisely held up the watch for him to see the hour.

"Why, what an old-fashioned time-piece!" he exclaimed. "Left you by some relation, I think;" and he attempted to take it in his hand. She drew it away adroitly, and yielded to the temptation of another impertinence.

"It came in with the Torches, and, like them, it never runs down."

He roared and clapped his hands; and Lucy, with a burning face, gave up the contest and concluded to accept the situation of victim till the cars should stop, and there she would run into the prairie if she saw one.

Shortly the train stopped.

"Hillo!" cried Mr. Torch, "what is all this? What are we stopping for at four o'clock to get our suppers? There is a long night before us!" Lucy shuddered. "It really *is* for refreshment. What shall I bring you—apple-pie? ham? cheese? coffee? Do now; I haven't seen you eat a mouthful to-day. Have you taken a bite since we left Chicago? Own up."

"Yes, yes," she replied, crossly, "I purchased rolls and buns this morning; I require nothing more."

"Rolls and buns! poor fodder those; there is no nourishment in them—saw-dust. The train will not stop till we get to Alton. If you would only stop *there* at my mother's and get a cup of her coffee! Why won't you stop and risk yourself? Your parents could not but approve of such an opportunity for you, and I should be the happiest—"

"Mr. Torch," said Lucy, in a stifled voice, "the time is passing, and you will lose your own refreshment."

"If you take nothing, here goes!"

And he darted out. Lucy rose with a forlorn hope of changing her place to be beside some one who might keep Mr. Torch at bay. Mr. Torch, she was confident, would go from bad to worse and make loud, imperative offers of marriage, which she might in her misery be induced to accept to silence and confound him with happiness! She cast a helpless look toward the veiled crinoline statues; they were women, and should aid her to escape from the clutches of an admirer! But their veils were still down, a slight movement behind them betrayed that they were alive, and in the act of eating such fragments as could be concealed beneath them, and she felt repelled. Better find some old gentleman, she thought; but there was no old gentleman present; she had seen none since her dear father left her at Dropville. Why had he not accompanied her? No impudent warrior would have presumed to admire her then. It seemed to her that it was growing dark. Would Mr. Torch talk all night to her! It *was* dark, though the sun had not set; but the sky must be overclouded with a rising storm. Suppose a tempest. She was afraid of thunder and lightning; and what a companion to appeal to was Mr. Torch! It couldn't thunder, for it was October, and too late. Why didn't these troubles shadow forth in her mind while she was having her fine dreams of a journey and making fine plans? A journey, in fact, was tiresome, stupid, dirty. The romancers of the pen must be characters of the most mendacious and venial description. If on her arrival at St. Louis her disappointment should continue, and the city should prove a sham, she hoped she should not find her Uncle John, as her father said he had been, a trouble always; and now he was the cause of her acquaintance with Mr. Torch!

With an air of desperate resignation she resumed her seat, thankful, at least, that no one had witnessed this humiliating acquaintance. As she leaned her head back wearily her eyes rested on the little mirror at the end of the car, a hat was rising in it, followed by a face, followed by shoulders—there was no room in it to reflect further and she sought the reality. The reality, in the shape of a handsome, dignified young man, had already found her, and was looking at her with an expression which gave a relief as profound as it was sudden. Unconsciously she made an imploring gesture, and he moved toward her, feeling an intangible recognition, which he thought he must look into Kant, Fichte, and Spinoza and find a reason for it.[4]

"Will you permit me?" he asked, pointing to the seat Mr. Torch had vacated.

"Certainly," she answered.

"The obtrusive looking-glass yonder would reflect the behavior of your enthusiastic friend," he continued, "and I could not avoid learning that you were annoyed. This sort of man is an unhappy feature of our civilization. I am almost sure I have before this attempted to spare some unprotected traveler from his tongue. If you will allow it, I will go on with my book in your neighborhood." He opened the volume in his hand, and bent his head to the studious perusal of a treatise upon "The Moral Use of Aesthetic Manners."[5] The brim of Lucy's hat was too wide now; but she contrived to get a clear glimpse of his face from under it, and somehow felt as if she had been scolding unreasonably a few minutes since, on the subject of journeys. To him it appeared as if the language of the treatise was more obscure and complicated than the papers which he had read previously; besides, he could not help seeing that Lucy was very pale, that her hands trembled, and thinking there was a tremor in her sweet voice. She was indeed nervous and exhausted for several reasons, and was on the point of having a good crying fit.

"By-the-way," he said, shutting his book, "there is famous tea at this station. I am going to get a cup for you—there is time."

He was gone and back again, with a bowl of tea set in a plate, round which was a wreath of small biscuits.

"I am going back for a second one for myself," he said, disappearing again before she could thank him. She drank the tea and ate the biscuit with gratitude, and her inclination for weeping vanished.

"All aboard!" being cried, he hurried in before the crowd.

"The bowl and the plate, Sir?" said Lucy, interrogatively.

"I was in a dilemma," he answered, with a smile—"if the bowl went out, I feared our friend would come in before me. We must throw them both out of the window if they are too troublesome. The bowl *not* being stronger his song won't be longer."

With the rush back of the passengers came Mr. Torch; he looked puzzled when he saw his place occupied. Lucy felt afraid he would push in beside her, and he was debating within himself whether he would do so when a heavy overcoat deposited itself in the desired spot.

He cast an irate glance at the owner, and said to himself:

"One of those muscular college pups, crammed to the hilt with other men's ideas, which they report as their own. I'll do picket duty; if he gets over the line, I am no longer fit for Company A."

He threw out his chest and folded his arms with a military swagger, which proved the adaptability of the young American to any station, for the swagger was at least equal to that of a Brigadier-General, and said between his teeth:

"There's going to be a tornado, Miss."

"Where?" interposed Lucy's champion.

"Perhaps you have been too much engrossed with your lesson," said Mr. Torch, "to notice that the sky is like brass—isn't that a sign?"

"The appearance of brass sometimes is the sign of failure."

Lucy let the bowl and plate fall with a crash, to divert an impending quarrel, and looked a reproof. Mr. Torch thought she was afraid he was going to do mischief. His crest grew haughty as he spoke again.

"And, perhaps, Sir, you have not observed that we are in the last car."

"What of that?" asked Lucy.

Mr. Torch shrugged his shoulders alarmingly.

"Unless the train stops in time we may be blown into kingdom come."

"Pooh!" said the young man.

"Pooh! yourself!" replied Mr. Torch, "and Boo! if you are so inclined."

The young man rose up to an altitude of six feet and one or two inches, and whispered some mystery in the ear of Mr. Torch, and sat down again, and plunged into the depth of his treatise. Mr. Torch looked doubtfully at Lucy a moment and retreated slowly to the single corner seat behind the one he had formerly occupied. There was no talking to Lucy over the tall head of the reader, and Mr. Torch grew uncomfortable and fidgety, muttering something to the effect that he guessed he could find friends in the smoking-car; got up, and, with an ominous grimace at Lucy, passed out. As soon as he was gone the book was closed and "that day he read no more."

"If the wind blows more than wind should blow under the circumstances, no doubt the rain will stop," he remarked.

"It is an ill wind that blows nobody good," she answered, referring to the absence of Mr. Torch.

"I recollected, at last, that I saw him in St. Louis," he said. "I told him so, and he did not appear to like it."

"I hope he will not be seen there again, for it is to St. Louis I am going."

"So am I. I live there."

A curious hope and longing sprang up in both hearts, which lent them a charmed forgetfulness of every thing outside for some moments. The train whirled on with its rhythmic motion, sounding an agreeable refrain (Staccato)—

> "Begun-begun-to-be-as-one!
> Not-to-part-and-be-undone!
> Apart-apart-and-ever-miss
> This-this-advancing-bliss!
> No-no-no-begun-begun!"

The relentless brakeman, with his ignis-fatuus lantern, came round and lighted some ineffectual lamps.

"Night has come," said Lucy, "but not the tornado."

"Yes; but why is it thought necessary to expose the roof of the cars only with these lamps—is it from some occult astronomical feeling?"

But the semi-darkness was favorable for conversation, they conversed on abstruse, learned subjects, as young foolish persons are apt to converse, and every moment felt drawn nearer and nearer to each other. They continued talking, in a low tone, till every body had taken to nods, and the extraordinary contortions which sleep produces on the helpless frame when unsupported by a bed. It was suggested that one seat should be turned opposite the other, for Lucy to rest upon and sleep; though she protested against it, the matter was accomplished, and the young man retired to the corner seat to meditate, and watch for Mr. Torch. A period of silence ensued, long to him, for Lucy slept: it appeared the normal condition of man to be on an everlasting, straight, swift, banging journey! He pulled up the car-blind and tried to peer into the darkness, something hurtled in the air outside, then he heard a distant roar; it was coming nearer! Lucy heard it, and started to her feet—all heard it; the car was astir!

"A tornado sure!" was cried. "Are we in the woods? Stop her! Back her! Where is the conductor? It's nothing but a gust! Sit down, all hands!"

Lucy saw the door fly open, and Mr. Torch trying to get in; but it flew back, and shut him out. The roar increased, and mixed with it was a strange, sharp shriek close round them; the train staggered, then came a jerk, the car grated, tipped, was off the track, and went smashing against the stone sides of a culvert. Lucy was thrown forward, and caught in the strong arms of her watcher, who braced himself against the upper side of the slanted car.

"Keep still!" was now shrieked; "the danger is over; the car is detached; the train's ahead. The Company ought to be sued for damages. It's well no trees fell on us; we are under a bridge."

Lucy was not as frightened as she should be; her attention was distracted by the beating of a strong heart her cheek was close to—as novel a sound to her as the roar of the tornado.

"Are you afraid?" he asked.

"Not now."

His arms tightened their clasp. It was pitch-dark, for the lights had been knocked out, and he could not see that she lifted her face toward his; but he knew it, and bent his head. As in any darkness and chaos lips will meet, unmindful of all except that which they seek, so theirs sought a meeting—they kissed each other with a kiss of surprised passion, and then they were full of an insane joy.

"I should have been so unhappy if you had not been here," she murmured.

"I never shall be happy if you are away from me again," he whispered.

They felt like indifferent spectators in the midst of the confusion. He was the first to rally from their natural, but, under the circumstances, idiotic happiness.

"My head is badly thumped," he said. "I think I must have made the tour of the roof."

Lucy reached her hand up to touch the wound, but merely succeeded in obtaining kisses on it.

"Oh!" she said, "my arm is hurt; I just feel it."

The tornado passing on, the passengers got out of the tilted car and took another; the locomotive got under way, and the train proceeded. Several persons, it was soon ascertained, were injured. A sprightly young man by the name of Torch had his arm broken—how, it was not known; but Lucy felt, with compunction, that it had been done in his effort to reach her.

"The ass was right after all about the tornado," said her friend. "I'll look him up, set his arm, and apologize."

"Are you a doctor?"

"I am Dr. John Tavish, at your service."

"I am Lucy Tavish," she said, in an agitated voice.

"By Jove! that accounts for it."

"Accounts for what?"

"Explain the Tavish pedigree to me, if you please."

"Seth and John Tavish are brothers."

"Just what I have been saying all along; and you are on your way to our house to make a visit. I am glad you did not meet my brother Seth first; he is a good deal handsomer than I am; he looks like you."

Lucy's mission was accomplished. She never performed a second journey like that, which ended with entering her uncle's house as his son John's cousin, and leaving it as his wife.

A Study for a Heroine

To our little world outside I was a "spirited" child; in my own family a "pest." Somebody must take the ungrateful charge of me; and, having worn out the patience of every one in turn, Mother engaged Sarah Brett, a young girl in our neighborhood, to keep an eye on me, and "manage" me. She was the daughter of "Uncle Siah" and Sally Brett, an impecunious couple, whose individuality was so different and so marked that they were known to everybody, and were a common quotation. Uncle Siah was a church-member, and very pious. Sally's moral nature was so narrow that time and circumstance never made any chink through which a conscience could creep. She had capacities, though, one of which admitted her everywhere; she was excellent in sickness. Piety and nursing thus kicked the beam in the scale of their inferiority. Uncle Siah's persistent prayers were tedious; he wept over them with quavering voice in vestry and conference, and nobody understood a word. He was a nuisance to Mother, pious as she was; but she believed in him, and the *esprit du corps* prevalent in New England Congregationalism, kept her faithful to his needs, and she kindly answered him when he queried if her righteousness was as filthy rags, and if she "wrastled with the sperrit, prevailin' 'g'inst the enemy." His means of livelihood were clam-digging, collecting herbs, garden work. He was also a sort of oral mail for misfortunes; and, if any accident happened, he was the first to know it.

But Mother could not abide Sally. Her hook nose, inquisitive eyes, the way she curried favor, was an offense; and when Sally called, not to beg, but to inquire whether those bottles that had stood so long on the shelf in the pump room were of any use, or if those bits of old carpet in the back entry were going to be thrown away, or to say how she heard that the minister said Mrs. Hilliard was the most benevolent woman in the village, Mother called her, between her teeth, hypocrite and cheat; and gave her the bottles, carpets, and a pail of milk.

The Bretts lived in and owned an old, tumble-down house in the center of the village. It was permeated with a smell of ancient smoke and decayed wood. The dark red beams and doors were worm-eaten, the worms long since gone to decay themselves. When Sarah took me there,

I opened the worm-holes and pretended to make dishes from the powder and Uncle Siah's empty clam shells.

In the Spring Sally earned a little money by making spruce beer. She was also famous for a salve which the suffering came for from far and near. The pair never quarreled; but Sally felt a secret contempt for Uncle Siah, and he bore a nameless dread and doubt of her, mingled with a pity which found its vent in prayer, frequent and ubiquitary. Sally often tartly asked a caller: "Don't you hear him whining in the shed?"

Long after this I learned the development of Sarah's character; her faith in her father; the respect which was never turned aside by the weak and ridiculous part of his nature; her sad suspicion of her mother, and revolt against her greedy meanness and cunning and sharp vulgarity. The shadow of what Sarah was to be rested upon her; from out these sordid surroundings a heroic soul developed for the tablets of hereafter.

Perhaps Sarah was a proof of "heredity"; like neither father nor mother, neither garrulous nor cunning, her talkative power was good, and her insight was clear. It astonished me to be so soon found out. My designs were interpreted before they were fully prepared, and she shamed me from their consummation, yet showed me a laughing sympathy. There was a spice of good-natured malice in her. She liked to invent terrible stories to enjoy my terrors, and improvise upon my "capers" till she scared me out of them. I did not love her; she was too plain, and children love the beautiful. There was something, besides, that stood between us—I could not define it—something far away that I did not reach. I saw looks in her eyes which made me turn round suddenly to see what was behind me.

So Sarah and I passed from stage to stage. First with play; dolls and toys, or out-of-doors on the shore, or in the fields—always together; as her mother said: "Trapseing forever, Sarah follerin' me like a dog from pillar to post, and wearing out shoe leather." Then I was placed in school, merely to learn the three R's, which Sarah fought with, and conquered sooner than I, "capers" ever standing in the way of my advancement—eternally patient with me in her help to force knowledge into my empty head.

Sunday-school was added to our weekly trials; and Sundays were dreadful to me before I could read well. The long sessions of sermons and Bible class aggravated my temper, and finished me off as an accomplished "torment."

Uncle Siah was prayerfully moved by Sarah's proficiency as a Bible scholar; but he warned her that "larnin'" would not save her; she must humble herself, and be "as nothin' and nobody, before she could enter the house of the Lord."

Sally's black eyes snapped, as she added that such business would help her along in the world.

"Just as it has father," Sarah replied.

In family councils a change was proposed; but as our family was a happy-go-lucky one, not doing to-day what could be done to-morrow, nothing was done until a little affair brought about a move in my destiny.

One day in school, at recess, I heard a big girl malign an absent friend; I surprised her by as hard a blow on her cheek as I could give.

Consternation and silence prevailed for a moment. Sarah stood near me, with her hands on her hips, her stony, steadfast glance fixed on my enemy, which so exasperated her that she screamed:

"And you, Sarah Brett, scum as seaweed, with your factory cotton gown. Can't the Hilliards raise a decent one for you? I wouldn't be a waiter this year nor the next on a tom-boy, because her father's rich and your father is a clam-digger."

Not a word from Sarah. I was about to "pitch in" again; but Sarah drew me away.

The teacher handed her a note as we left.

"Yes," she muttered, on the way, "it is only a factory cotton. I am glad I did not knock her down. Is it wicked for me to wear good clothes? Would puff me up, maybe."

"Puffs?" I said, feeling rather ashamed of her poor dress. "My French cambric is puffed. Don't you like it?"

"For you. Your Aunt Dora says the flesh must be mortified. Mortification has taken place often with me."

"O, Sarah! Will you turn black and die, like that woman you told me about?"

She laughed, and looked pleasant again.

We did not return to school.

Another crisis followed soon.

With no word of warning, Sarah appeared in church wearing a pink bonnet, of so new a fashion, so large, and so much trimmed, that the attention of the congregation was given to our pew. Mother was greatly disturbed; but grace restrained her till Monday, when she burst out with St. Paul, and ended with: "Where did it come from?"

"My cousin sent it from Whitestone," Sarah replied, "and she wants me to learn a milliner's trade of her."

Aunt Dora was in her rocking-chair. She shook her head, and remarked that all young folks's heads has turned nowadays.

"How, Aunt?" I asked. "Because Sarah wears a factory frock, does it turn your head to work lace veils to wear on your bonnets?"

They both told me to "shut up."

Sarah's eyes wore that strange look which always set me pondering. I think it affected Mother to asperity. If the pink bonnet was a specimen of her taste, she doubted whether her cousin could teach her much; and there was great pretension about it; very unsuitable.

"Mrs. Hilliard," said Sarah, "aint I as good flesh and blood as any folks who wear pink, red, green, or yellow bonnets, made every which way?"

With each color her voice rose, though in attitude and expression she was very calm.

"I hope so; I hope so, Sarah. But that is not the point," Mother answered, quite subdued.

"It's all points. Laura's father is called Squire Hilliard, my father is called Uncle Siah. What is the reason? Whatever it is, maybe, I guess it is all right. But if the first ladies here wore to meeting any kind of a bonnet, would the folks stare? Oh! no. Next day they'd borrow the pattern of it."

"Well, I never!" said Aunt Dora. "The world is coming to an end when young girls put themselves forward with an idea."

So Sarah and I were parted: and she went to Whitestone.

I took my liberty cheerfully, roaming the place at large, and happy in the vacuity children are blest with. I came across Uncle Siah, one day, and inquired when Sarah was coming home.

He put his basket and hoe on the ground, to keep a wary eye upon me, lest I should startle him with a "caper."

"Little gal, I dunno. What doth your Ma say? Has *she* gin her up? Sary's my darter, though, for all the world, and I pray the Lord not to lay a heavy hand on her. Little gal, you've a good Ma, and a good Pa, but remember where the wicked go. Do your folks want any clams today?"

Tottering on his way, his gray hair fluttering in the wind, I heard him strike up:

> "My flesh shall slumber in the ground
> Till the last trump's joyful sound."[1]

The following Spring Sally Bratt died suddenly; died, as Uncle Siah said, "while her spruce beer was farmenting, and afore she house-cleaned."

Her death aged him greatly. Sarah came home, intending to return; but his condition and wishes altered her plans.

"First and foremost," she said, "I must watch Father, and keep him from wandering. He may pray all over the house, and in the back yard; but he must not go into any other house or place for that purpose. He shall never do a stroke of work; he can play at digging clams, or gathering wintergreen, if he likes, or potter round the kitchen."

We were interested in her plans of starting millinery and dress-making. Mother and Aunt Dora united in praise of her improved appearance; she was the same to me. I thought her bonnets hideous, and her dresses were no fit for me; but I never thought of her plainness now, and was sincerely attracted to her.

The small room on one side of the door was arranged for the shop; the larger one opposite Sarah fitted up and called it "father's arbor." She effaced the ancient odors, papered the smoked walls, placed plants in the windows, cleaned and mended the furniture, and trimmed the wide fireplaces with the feathery asparagus. Under the dim, sloping eaves she found stores which Sally had laid away to sell sometime, or for a "rainy day," braided rugs, intricate patch-work quilts, cushions covered with bright bits of cloth, and yarn for numberless stockings.

"Lord ha' mercy!" cried an old neighbor, stepping in. "If I aint a-treading right on Sally Brett's mat. I give her my baby Billy's yaller petticoat for the sunflower in the middle. She was a master hand for rugs; and now she's where she can't braid any more."

"Nor needs any," said Sarah.

"Oh! I don't begrudge you her savings. It's only my way of speaking. We are all poor creatures. I s'pose you would not like to let me know the price of that bonnet?"

Step by step Sarah advanced. Work came in, and, whether it was tact by nature or acquired, she obtained and kept her custom. Those who knew themselves her superiors perceived she made no attempt to equal them, and her inferiors were sure they were not looked down upon. The window of her little shop-room rivaled the post-office; for almost everybody stopped to tell her the news, or to get what had been told.

"Uncle Siah," relegated to the kitchen, the "arbor" was made the rendezvous for the church choir to practice in; for Sarah, singing "alto," sat in the gallery, from which no weather or interference kept her. When a dancing school was started, her name was early on the subscription list, in spite of opposition.

"I can't argify with her," said Uncle Siah to a "brother." "Somehow, as she takes it, she's doing a good turn to somebody."

At this dancing school we met, as country people generally meet. Class distinctions are kept out of sight, though they exist.

"Why do you look after and dance with all the gawky fellows?" I asked. "And you take it as seriously as if you were distributing tracts."

"When my toes are trod on, and I am bumped against and pulled about, I can't help being serious. And it is too bad the girls refuse to dance with them. They know you are above them; but when they dance with me they are a little proud, because you notice me. Don't you see?"

"Yes, your logic I see."

At this period of Sarah's life, a few were disposed to make invidious remarks. She, it was plainly seen, knew which side her bread was buttered? Why not? Sally's own daughter! Politic where Sally was cunning. This setting of herself before folks to preach the Devil was dead, that everybody had beautiful traits, and meant well—she knew better!

Sarah heard of these opinions, and thought it rather "discouraging"; but she hoped they were not meant. I found her in the "arbor" one day, with a lot of little girls, busy with their needles.

"Experiment," she motioned with her lips. Then aloud: "Come, see how nicely my girls are learning to sew, and help their mothers." "Nuisance"—she motioned again—"sometimes; but they have been brought up so badly."

A table was covered with odds and ends of silk and ribbons, for pincushions, and bags, and so forth. While they were at work she read them stories, and when the afternoon closed they were regaled with tea and ginger-bread.

"How long have you been at this performance?" I asked.

"Oh! three or four months. Some of them walk a long distance. Poor little souls! I wish their mothers would wash them before they come."

"I wonder you don't give them a bath."

"I dare not. It would anger the mothers so, they might not be allowed to come at all."

"You should have a sign out, 'Humanity taken in and done for.'"

She explained that it was the best way to reach the girls, and bring Baptists and Universalists together. She believed in all the religions. She hoped I would not think her "forward."

I note nothing especial for a year or two. Sunrise and sunset, the ebb and flow of the tide, and human life in its ordinary diurnal changes; nothing more.

Passing Sarah's open window, one day, I heard voices, and stopped by it.

She was at work on a delicate silk.

"You may say what you please," quickly remarked a person I knew well. "He has not had the most to do in that bargain. We all are aware that he is well off; owns a piece of the 'Arab,' and the house he lives in. She hasn't a cent to her name. Of course she wants a good home. I wonder if he did not buy that silk."

"Nonsense!" Sarah replied. "No."

"You seem to know. Some folks say you are the go-between."

"Very likely. Just feel the silk; thick as a board."

"What is it, Sarah?" I interposed.

"Mary Green's wedding-gown. She is to be married next week to Abner Hamon. Are you surprised? You know how bashful he is. You remember how you laughed, how he poked his umbrella into me, when he meant to offer his arm?"

"And something else," I was about to say; but, recollecting who was by, desisted.

"Bashful?" the person remarked. "It's all put on. Anybody can purse up their mouth, and turn up their nose, and act as if people were to be taken up with tongs."

"He was good to his mother," said Sarah. "He will be a first-rate provider. I know he hasn't the gift of the gab; but Mary will make up for that."

"If you," began our friend and pitcher—

"Oh! Mrs. Jameson," Sarah broke in, "I have a new receipt for cake, and made it this morning. I know what your cake is. Just take your bonnet off and stay to tea."

"I don't care if I do," answered the mollified lady, "though I have no occasion to."

"Oh! you artful Sarah!" I whispered, as I moved off. Everybody knew that her name had been coupled with that of Abner from the time he joined the church choir to sing "bass." It was also commented upon that Mary Green, a very pretty girl, sought Sarah, and hung upon her, especially when Abner was in the vicinity.

"Serves Sarah Brett right to walk into that trap blind-fold. Fool as Mary Green was, she knew how to set it. Abner ought to be grateful as he stood by for Sarah to pull his chestnuts out of the fire."

Whatever hand Sarah had in the affair, she stood by them; saw them married; and, perhaps, like a faithful robin red-breast, covered them with the leaves of her charity, her hopes, and her regrets.

I was called away from home for several months, and meanwhile "Uncle Siah," grown decrepit, departed this life, deeply mourned by Sarah.

"If he could only have seen his funeral," she said, tearfully, "and heard the choir sing 'Soldier, go home,' he would have cried for joy.[2] The church insisted upon his being buried in this public way. Everybody wanted to do something for me. Abner Hamon left his sick wife—poor Mary, you know—to be one of the pall-bearers. Trouble stalks ahead of him, I am afraid. Mary is in a decline. I wish," she concluded abruptly, "I could go away; but I mustn't. There will always be something for me to do here."

It was true about Abner. With the fall of the leaf that year the pretty, frail, useless creature fluttered like a butterfly over the confines of this world to some other.

Before her headstone was placed at her grave it was surmised that Sarah Brett might have her chance yet, if she played her cards right. But Sarah's play was not in that direction. We were not young girls merely, but matured women. I had money, was educated, as the phrase goes, had traveled, owned to a circle of gay and prosperous friends; and yet Sarah steadily continued to attract me. I was bound to observe her, and compelled to acknowledge a force which I did not quite comprehend; for she was still obscure, poor, her interests confined within the sphere of our small community. She was not "goody" at all, or strict in her views. She liked to sit up till midnight reading a clever novel; she was fond of whist, and it was reported that she had been seen "playing backgammon in the forenoon!" She was as lively as useful in our picnics and sailing parties. It was a source of speculation to the church, because she declined to make a "profession" and become a member. The year following Uncle Siah's death a great revival swept over our region; Sarah went to all the meetings, and sat unmoved by the adjurations to repent. The celebrated revival preacher, Payson Boggs, called on her by request. When he began on total depravity her eyes looked into the invisible world only known to herself. He felt at bay, besides being irritated by the yelping of an ailing dog which she had rescued from the street.

"I see you can take pity on a poor animal," he said, recovering himself. "Can you take pity on your ailing soul?"

"What if I do, sir? The soul must ail, and I must bear it."

"But you can repent."

"I do not; never could feel the least occasion to do so."

"Do you believe in prayer?"

"I don't know. I instinctively yearn for the aid and protection of a Higher Power at times; but I feel it is an impulse there is no accounting for."

She jumped up; for there was a mew at the door. When she opened it to let in a tailless cat, Mr. Boggs took his leave. When asked about his visit, he replied that she was a "singular anomaly."

"Truly," affirmed old Grace Aken, one of the pious, "I feel different about Sarah ever since she helped me when my daughter was sick. Let her jine, or not, she will be 'accepted,' in answer to Uncle Siah's prayers. She don't pray with the tongue, as he did, but with the head and hands."

"I must have liberty," she said to me. "Why should I set myself above all other sects because I am a Congregationalist? I can't do it; and I do enjoy my little specks of wickedness—novels and cards, good things to eat, and so on."

"About liberty, Sarah, I hear things about you and Abner Hamon. Keep your eyes this way, and tell me something mundane?"

"If mundane means matrimony, I can tell you something. I do expect to marry him."

"And the millinery, menagerie, and your goings to and fro at the beck and call of the afflicted?"

"He understands. My affairs will not interfere with his; he is a still man, but in his way a deep one. I wonder if he will ever recall Mary's beauty when he looks at my brown visage? At any rate, I can make him comfortable."

They were married, and went to housekeeping. Sarah let her own house to a couple of old maids, the terror of all landlords, and passed the honeymoon in house-cleaning and voyages of discovery in Abner's premises. As he was a "boss" carpenter, he was from home all day; and many an hour she and I passed together in the sunny, old-fashioned house built by his father.

"I opened a closet, yesterday," she said to me, on one of my morning visits, "for the first time. It gave me a turn to see poor Mary's wedding-gown hanging there. He has never looked at it, because, he said, he never had seen the key, and all her possessions were there."

She gave me a queer look, and was silent for a while.

"It is so large a house," she remarked, presently, "that I can do all sorts of things."

"For others, I suppose?"

"Well. Wouldn't you?"

"No. And are you still meaning to trim bonnets, and go out nursing?"

"Bonnets for somebody in a hurry, now and then, to keep my hand in. I am sure I should be thankful for all these good things; and mustn't I show it?"

For many months life flowed pleasantly and peacefully. Abner was a man of few words. His day's work, his evenings at home, in the large "sleeping-room," where he sat, with his chair tipped against the wall, noting all that passed before him, sufficed for his contentment. Sarah understood his limitations, and never attempted to widen them.

"Sarah keeps public house," he said once. "It beats me how she does it. As long as she allows me a place, it suits me well enough."

"Abner, would you have it different?"

"If you would be satisfied not to attach an outside hospital, I should like it better." Turning to me: "It has got so now that I am not sure whether any one can draw their last breath till she reaches them; and when they do that, she stays on to help the survivors bear the loss. I vow"—and he brought his chair on its four legs—"I'd rather whittle out ship's-knees with a jack knife than do what she does."

"It is strange to me, Sarah," I remarked, with little tact, "how little marriage has changed your habits."

To my surprise, she blushed deeply, and glanced doubtfully at Abner. It was not noticed apparently; his chair was again tilted back, and his face wore its usual expression. I thought then what I think now, that they were alike in an enforced self-control and a natural reticence.

The fates were already spinning a web with as much assiduity as if it were for crowned heads on rulers, instead of a single pair. Abner allowed himself one diversion, that of fishing. He owned a boat, built by himself. When he took a day off, Sarah put up a careful dinner for him. She approved of his excursions, he said, because she could give away the fish he caught.

One June morning, when Sarah's roses were blooming, he decided to go down the bay. Sarah went to the gate with him.

"What a beautiful day you will have," she said. "Not a cloud to be seen."

"The fish will bite, this morning. But the wind is chopping around. If it begins to blow before noon, I shall put back. At any rate, I shall be in by five."

"Old Anice Weaver was in, inquiring when you were going fishing.

She said nothing seemed to relish with her, and she hankered arter [*sic*] some of your catching."

"Doubtless you are glad I go, then?" pulling her ear, as she opened the gate for him.

"Stop a moment!" she called.

He turned, and she twisted a lovely rose in the handle of his dinner pail.

"I hope you think that is a pretty attention, Abner."

He nodded, and she watched him out of sight.

By noon the wind rose, and the sky darkened; fog rolled in from seaward. Sarah went up-stairs to look at the bay; in the lifting of the fog she got a glimpse of the turbulent waters, and the boats scudding under bare poles.

"I must put out some clothes; for he will come in wet through."

The afternoon sped. It was past four when one of Abner's carpenters called for certain directions.

"I knew he had gone, Mrs. Hamon, but thought he might be in," he said. "For Tabor's boat got in two hours ago. It is mighty rough outside. But you are not uneasy, Mrs. Hamon? Abner is a capital boatman; and maybe he'll run into harbor somewhere till after sundown. I hope it won't blow off shore," he added, in a lower voice.

For the sake of occupation, Sarah prepared supper, but could not take a mouthful. It grew dark early, and began to rain. It dashed against the panes, and the wind wailed round the old chimneys.

"Oh!" she cried, passionately, "I hope nobody will come in. I cannot speak to anybody."

She sat alone all night. After midnight the storm died away, and the morning broke clear and glorious. Sarah opened her door, and saw the roses sparkling with rain-drops. "I shall never break a rose off again for him," she whispered. She wrung her hands, and walked the place a few moments, and then waited, in calmness, for what she knew would come.

The boat was found that day among the rocks below Whitestone Point. Abner's hat and the little pail were brought to her. They were caught in the rope of the tiller.

I went to her at once.

"Why am I punished? Why am I punished?" was all she could utter.

That she who had stayed by the bedside of the dying so many times, and performed the last offices for the dead, should be so cut off, deprived of those consolations in regard to her husband, seemed very hard and strange to me.

"It must be borne, dear," she spoke, as if in answer to my thought; "and I must be as calm as he would have me."

From that time she never talked of her sorrow. If necessary, she spoke of Abner as one does of an absent friend. Much more property was left her than was expected. To her surprise, he left a will, and everything to her, because, in his "knowledge of her, no other would make so wise a use of it." She made little difference in her habits. As we knew she never was an ascetic; so she allowed herself a carriage, in which invalids and convalescents rode more than she did. She also enlarged her flower garden, and engaged a gardener who aided her in distributing her flowers. My father, with whom she made some investments, said that she was a sharp business woman, and as she grew old would grow fond of her money. A speech I denied. As time passed, the happiness she deserved, or at least its shadow, came to her; for she never appeared dull nor depressed. The first hearty laugh she gave after Abner's death was when she told me that Deacon Zacheus Bangs had offered himself to her. He thought they might put their means together, and work in the Lord's vineyard. Besides, she had known how handy it was to have a man in the house; and he never would call upon her to draw the water even to wash her own hands!

"I thought of his seven boys and girls, growing up like weeds, and almost wished I could have taken them. I shall never change my name."

"But Abner married twice?"

She gave me a curious look.

"Since we are on that subject, I will tell you something. I wished him to marry Mary. I never should have had a moment's peace if I had then married him; she told me that she should die if she did not have him. I was really afraid she would. She was always delicate. As for him, he was moved by her beauty, as with men generally it took and kept the place of desirable and lacking traits."

"What a woman you are Sarah. I never shall find you out wholly."

"I can't always find myself out. What you look for does not exist; a text does not promise a sermon always. Deacon Bangs says he has found me out; he said he knew I was no Christian by the cut of my jib." This was after the refusal. Sarah spoke the truth. I was baffled in my speculations concerning her; for she was nothing more than what she appeared to be, probably; no mystery to herself, except when perplexed by circumstances outside.

A change in our domestic affairs sent me from home for several years. On my return, I heard that Sarah Brett was in a city hospital for the present; and I gathered this account of her. She adopted a harum-scarum boy, a distant relative of Abner's, who only proved a help to her by pleasing himself. At first it was thought that he, Joe Weed, absorbed her attention. She ceased to go out, except when called to the sick; there her old cheerfulness prevailed. She looked care-worn, too, but made no complaint. The world rarely perceives that one who is an embodiment of unselfish devotion to others may require or wish any service in turn. The observing neighbors noted that her house was turned into the yard; carpets, curtains, and furniture were aired and mended. The blinds of the unused rooms were thrown open, and shut again. The entire premises were set in order.

Some of the curious called to question her. They were answered with her usual cheerfulness; but they left none the wiser. Her aspect was the same in church and the prayer-meetings. When Joe, dressed in his best, went off in the cars one day, and returned the next, with two gentlemen with small bags, who went straight to Sarah's house, the astonishment and anxiety culminated.

She then sent Joe for Mrs. Mason, a trusted nurse; and through her it soon came out. Sarah had been operated upon, for cancer.

"For two years," narrated Mrs. Mason, "has Sarah borne her burden secretly, and in silence. Day by day she watched the growth of the evil, and made ready for death. She dreaded to tell her condition, from the fear that everybody would shrink from the loathsome fact. But she loved life. Somehow, it seemed her work was not quite done. She would live, if possible. It was the curse of man upon her, not the will of God. So she wrote a letter to a celebrated physician she had heard of. When he read it, he said it was so touching that, had she been a poor woman, he would have done the job for nothing."

So he came with his assistant. He told her an operation might save her life. There was always a little doubt; but he trusted it did not exist in her case. She was fully aware of that, Sarah answered; she was prepared, although she could not say she was ready.

"I believe I understand you," he replied, as Sarah said, with an alert air of anticipation, as if he were about to have a "beautiful case."

Her will was made, every article tied up, mended, ticketed for whomsoever she had willed them.

As these tidings spread, human nature for once rose above its level; the community was deeply moved at this spectacle of dignity, patience and fortitude. Her doors were besieged; she was pelted with flowers and loaded with delicacies. And Sarah cried over these attentions as she never had cried over her woeful state. "Why should everybody be so kind?" she asked. "What have I ever done to merit so much?"

But the crowning point of the strength and unselfishness of her character remains to be told.

On the second visit of the great Doctor, he told her the case was a unique one. There were certain complications, which, with her consent, would greatly be to the interests of science if she were removed to his hospital in the city, where his students could make the necessary observations. The benefit these might be to future sufferers was incalculable. She gave him a look of anguish; and then, for the first time her life, fainted.

The next day, Sarah Hamon, my heroine, was taken to the hospital accompanied by the Doctor.

Mrs. Jed and the
Evolution of Our Shanghais

At this time of year, plowing and planting time, sister and I recall the experiences of our life on the farm at Belden's Hole, when we were much younger.

Our farm was two miles beyond the village, which was on the coast. The population there was mostly seafaring. In Grandfather's time, it was said the farm yielded two rocks to one blade of grass; but when Father came into its possession it had been blasted and cultivated into good shape, and at his death some good meadow and woodland were left to us two young girls, and there we lived for many years.

The shore and farm folk alike were poor in regard to money, but that fact kept us on a social level; no one ventured to put on airs, not even the Squire Freemans—meaning him and his wife, who lived in a house so large it was called a "mansion," who kept two horses, and had a Turkey carpet in their best room—behaved as if uplifted. Nor did Mrs. Cragie, who owned the best farm in the country and an eighth of a ship, look down on us. The land was poor, but the sea was a storehouse for food; shoals of herring ran up our weir every spring, and shellfish were plentiful. Even the poorest among us owned the dwelling he lived in.

The fashions of the outside world were of little account with us. Mrs. Cragie had a city cousin who sometimes paid her a visit; with her came a whiff of fashion; from her we got new patterns, and we heard what the best people wore. Still, it was a relief when this elegant cousin went home; her fashionable ways disturbed our self-esteem. Thus, for years, we plodded on without change or improvement; there was nothing new, and everything was growing old. To keep us from the last refuge of poverty, the poor-house, we were obliged to earn our bread in various ways, but it was without enterprise or interest.

The stagnation was dropping into decay, when the California gold fever broke over the country; a pulsation reached us; some of the young men proposed going to the mines, but the old men did not believe in it. Old Jed Buck had been in that country when his ship went into port in the thirties; he said it was a "pizen country, but full of miraclus things, and the skin of the natives was yaller as gold."

This old Jed was a surly, close-fisted man, with a pale, silent wife and one son, also named Jed. They were dependent upon their "salt mash" and a bit of pine woods for their support.

The Buck family were somewhat apart socially; they would have been, from choice likely; they were quite indifferent to public opinion. Jed was eighteen now, and always at work; in spring he went about with a cart and a pair of lean oxen, with brush to stick peas, and poles for beans; in summer he sold berries; in the fall fish and oysters. He was a "solid" boy, with thick hair and a stern face; he never haggled over his wares, it was take or let alone! Sister and I used to pity him, because he had no education. After the California fever died away, he occasioned remark by a quarrel he had with his father. Jed said he was going to school again. Old Jed did not believe "in book larnin'," Jed could read and write, that was enough! But Jed carried his point, and astonished everybody by his application to his books, which he got by selling bark to a tannery. His teacher was an educated man, which rarely happened in our schools, and he was a great help to Jed. Months passed; he was either at his studies or his work, for his father taxed him heavily; from a "solid" boy he grew into a tall, pale, thin man.

"No matter," said Old Jed, "how high whale ile is, his mother trims a lamp every night, and they fool over books together."

In the beginning of the second year, Jed disappeared. When questioned his mother replied that in one week, and no sooner, an explanation would be made. At its end she made it. Jed had started for California, with his books, in a sailing vessel. The past year they had planned, pinched for, and raised money in every way they could think of. Mrs. Buck sold eggs, and the milk from their one cow, all except what Old Jed needed. She was known as the spinner of a mixed yarn, which she walked over the country and sold. She sent her grandmother's solid gold beads, and her maiden silver spoons to a distant jeweler, who bought them; and it may be said here that Jed was grateful; her memory brought him home again. He was energetic and industrious on his part in earning the necessary money. He made turpentine salve, distilled essences from boxberry leaves and peppermint; dried herbs, and made cases for them; in a ramble, he came across the owner of a beehive, and made a bargain to sell the comb and honey on shares; he did all he could without trenching on his father's perquisites. Then he borrowed a horse and wagon, traveled round the country, sold his wares, and returned with money in his pocket.

"I'm darned, and it beats me," growled Old Jed, "how that feller got away; *I* didn't give him a copper."

If his mother heard from Jed she kept the tidings to herself; when he had been gone two years the devoted soul died.

Old Jed's demeanor was in nowise altered or his way of living; he traveled somewhere and returned with an old woman, who kept his house thereafter.

Jed had been gone about five years when a rumor reached the village that he had become prosperous, and known as a mining engineer. In a few months we knew it for a fact that he was coming home with his wife, and that he wished to engage a house to live in.

Jed Buck prosperous, and professional! We all felt interested in his getting a proper abode. No one dreamed of his going to his father's house, or thought of consulting him about one. Nobody exactly could say who suggested Squire Freeman's mansion; he had been dead a year, and his wife had moved elsewhere. The matter was arranged, and we waited for Jed's arrival. Loads of furniture came in advance; and, before we knew it, Jed, his wife, and two persons, supposed to be the help, were in the house. We were led to conclude we were not expected to call.

The following Sunday everybody turned out to meeting, expecting to see the newcomers. The minister entered, followed by Jed and his wife, and they took their seats in his front pew.

Jed Buck was not the Jed who departed from us, it was an Old Jed returning, taciturn, masterful, but well-dressed and refined. He evidently had done it in California, as in the days when he sold turpentine and honey.

But Mrs. Jed! her mark was made at once; we might say that we were *branded* by her. What was she? A tiny, dark woman; her great eyes restless, searching; her firm mouth steady and determined. A strange surprise fell upon us, what did it mean? How she looked at us; eying us more than Tappertit ever did; and how we looked at her![1] At the close of the service we hung back. Jed walked down to where his father was, and put out his hand, very pale. Mrs. Jed watched them, and then spoke to the minister, coming from the pulpit. Mrs. Cragie, naturally, as our foremost woman, stepped forward and asked him for an introduction. We saw Mrs. Jed speaking to her as they moved down the aisle toward Jed, who bowed and spoke to those who passed him, but without shaking hands with anybody. Sister nudged me to look at Old Jed, who was paralyzed before Mrs. Jed's regards; he said, afterward, "that she drawed him like a plaster."

She slipped her hand in her husband's arm, and they went away.

We heard that she said to Mrs. Cragie, that everything here reminded her of the nap of the Sleeping Beauty, without the Beauty.

Mrs. Cragie had a smart reply, but a look from Jed stopped her, which meant, she was sure, "No use."

Well, we were to feel soon that the old order of things must change; we had done little for ourselves, and less for others. We thought of a visit from Mrs. Cragie's cousin to help us meet this new force. Mrs. Jed's taste in dress was undeniable; she was a picture to look at, her dress and ornaments were so beautiful.

> We were like a field of grain,
> Bowed by a tempest of wind and rain.

Her influence was felt first by the petition she got up to have Belden's Hole changed to Braganza; the idea of her letters being mailed for and from a Belden's Hole was insupportable![2] We signed the petition; it went to the Legislature, and Belden's Hole ceased to exist.

We next learned what a pedigree the Bucks brought over in the "Mayflower" and lost in the troublous times and it was a fact!

As a duty, Mrs. Jed called upon the older families, and sister and I were among the favored. How our faces burned! We knew she saw all that was poor and plain with us. As she left she remarked:

"But still your place has capacities. You are so secluded, you might attempt many things."

We never could tell why she roused the spirit in us, which she did. We did not like her, but believed in her. She did not put herself forward; she was no talker; but she made every one else talk as she chose, by a word, a hint, a suggestion.

As I said, before this advent we were worse than at a standstill; property was crumbling away under our eyes, and we allowed it with the excuse, that what one failed to do, another might. Repairs had gone out of fashion, paint had died by stress of age; if our fences fell prone, there they stayed; barns and sheds leaning sidewise from infirmity, were held up by crutches; the ornament of flowers was forgotten, or only remembered by ancient shrubs no neglect could kill, and in our customs, neighborly exchanges of favors had long ceased.

It was not long before reforms set in: an epidemic of paint broke out;

those who could not afford to paint their houses painted their front doors; fences were repaired; the village presented a piebald view, like the woods in spring; individual taste was alone consulted; our houses were of many colors; the garden beds were reset. We imitated Mrs. Jed's windows, and filled ours with plants. The barns and sheds were a job, but here and there newly shingled roofs and "sidings" marked in the landscape; even the one wharf, which had fallen into the water nearly, was mended; vistas and possibilities opened upon us after Mrs. Jed had passed over the ground. We began to improve our ways and ourselves. Mrs. Jed was ubiquitous; she might be anywhere at any moment, walking or driving in her own chaise. She called our place her "terminus," as it was good for a long walk or a short drive. When she came sister and I at her first look were ready to talk, both beginning at the same moment often. Jed had bought the Freeman mansion, and superintended a gang of workmen himself. Mrs. Jed did not interfere with his plans; it was good for him, she said, to have his mind diverted from his intellectual methods.

Old Jed refused any favor from Mrs. Jed; he had enough to carry him through, he said, and new-fangled ways he could not abide. It was pretty well known, however, that Jed visited his father.

It was an unwritten law in Braganza, that meal time was a rite to be performed in secret; hospitality was nearly a lost art. Our doors were closed while we ate our food in silence and seclusion. Open house, good tables, bountiful providers, were legends of the past.

Now we no longer spread a meal on a table against the wall to snatch a hurried morsel! Neither did we attempt to fast for a festival supper. Mrs. Jed called upon the latter occasion, with sister and me, and we heard her murmur:

"A fast with Epicurean motives, is nice."[3]

How we wondered what she meant!

We guessed Mrs. Jed had been a school teacher, she was so learned, perhaps that was the secret of her power, she astonished us perpetually by making us think for ourselves. So far, sister and I had given no tangible evidence of her influence; we were not particularly shabby in any way, our house wore a substantial look still, and the premises were kept in tolerable order by our old man, John Harris, a legacy from Grandfather, a faithful creature, whose interests were ours.

But Fate was marshalling its forces. Jed finished his improvements in house and land, and left for parts unknown. Mrs. Jed remained at home.

A week after his departure on the following Sunday our minister, among the usual notices, read us one which startled the entire congregation:

"Mrs. Jed Buck invites the ladies of the church to her house on the next Tuesday, to confer on the subject of forming a society, for the advantage and pleasure of the community!"

The first outburst was a refusal to go; the second, asking each other if we would go; and the result was that we all went.

It is a long story to tell the result of Mrs. Jed's influence, and the changes wrought since her arrival. They began. Old industries were revived and new ones established; mutual interests brought us together; dullness was voted out of fashion; the young people mixed more with the elders; married people were allowed to be amused outside of domestic pales; a reading club was started because Mrs. Jed was heard to ask Mrs. Goodspeed if she had never heard of one.

Others were started. In all Mrs. Jed put in an appearance, flitting in and out. I think we felt her presence more for her absence, but all she said or did had the effect she intended. Or, had she never any intention concerning us, and was really indifferent? Was the change the natural re-action which time brings round blindly and slowly, beginning with individuals and spreading from mind to mind, till the old yoke is lifted.

When Mrs. Cragie's cousin came on a visit she made a "study" of Mrs. Jed, and informed us she was a remarkable person; that women of her type were never thwarted, and always carried their point. We were astonished at this opinion, and remarked to this cousin that we knew better.

But what were sister and I to do with our rising ambition? We had no money, only income enough to keep us out of debt. We examined our premises and possessions for a promise to start from, in vain. "Oh, if we only had a nest egg!" sister exclaimed, in despair. Prophetic soul! That very day a book fell into our hands upon poultry, the way to keep it, and the assurance of amazing profit. Personally conducted, a little patience and ordinary intelligence, and the result was certain! From time immemorial we had kept hens, as most country people do, but of the old-fashioned kind and few in number. Their breed and keep were little care; their only use a few eggs, and an occasional chicken broth for the sick. We kept them as our cows were, for milk, not to improve the stock.[4] Mrs. Jed did not keep hens; canaries she had, but no hens.

Sister read the book, first, and handed it to me, keeping up such a running commentary, while I read, that I was converted to her view.

"First," she said, "we must prepare for sacrifices, then we must keep all we do a secret from everybody, except John, our hired man; we will never be made ashamed in public. Do you agree?"

Of course I agreed.

"Then, before hens, we must have a hennery."

Inspiration was in the air.

"Come," called sister, at the door, "I have my mind on a spot, let us look at it."

We passed the speckled hen, the black hen, and a miserably, old-fashioned rooster, all comb and tail, and looked into the coop, from mere habit, to see if there were eggs in the nest. "Common hens' eggs," we said, with a superior smile. The inclosure looked on was back of the barn, between it and the orchard; the white-breasted martins were already building in the eaves, and the pink blossoms of the peach were flush in the orchard. One side of the inclosure was bordered by the cow lane, which an old grapevine trellis hid, the corn house and smoke house stood on the other, in military parlance, the inclosure was a hollow square, just the place for secret maneuvers. We called John, who was busy spading, and revealed our plan; he opened his mouth with one of his rare, silent laughs.

"Beats all," he says, "how things is buzzing since that Californy gang settled here; well, marms, I'm up to snuff so far as able, tho I'm a puty old dog for new tricks."

He went back to his spade, and we to the book again; from it we selected the fowl pictured as the largest, the *Shanghai*, and copied out the directions for the hennery, coops, feed, chickens, and everything we thought needful.[5] The book was then returned with thanks, and the opinion "that it seemed very difficult." We knew well that no one would ever dream of our undertaking. If we could but keep it from Mrs. Jed's knowledge!

John suggested, as the inclosure was so sheltered, that a hedge of thick brush round it would be sufficient. This was done; with some old boards he knocked up a shed, with partitions for nests. From the sail loft in the village he got an old sail, which he painted and covered the roof with. When it was done, he was off for the station with an old horse "Bill," a wagon and a slatted box covered with a buffalo robe, with instructions to speak to no one. He was to fetch a Shanghai cock and three hens as we had ordered. He was so late in returning that we began to be alarmed, when we heard him lumbering into the barnyard, and hurried out with a lantern to meet him.

"I guess," he called, "I've brought you an ostrige. I druv home by

Ingin woods, to keep the pesky things out of sight. Arter I left the deepo the crate fell into the road, and a man helped me to get it onto the wagon. He asked me if I had been trading in bullfrogs."

Singular, strangled noises came from the crate, which we suggested should be left where it was till morning. That night was the last quiet one for some time to come. While we were at breakfast John came in, with a sober face, to guess that we had better step out to look arter our new goods—some of 'em was in trouble. We followed him at once.

"You see," he said, on the way, "we had a smart spell of rain afore morning, and I expect it stirred up the critters."

It had. The crate was overturned; happily, the slatted side was uppermost; looking through it we saw an immense mass of feathers and a quantity of coarse, gnarled legs. With great trouble the crate was pushed and hauled into the inclosure, sister and I tugging at it with all our might. What a sight they were when released, with more feathers on their legs than on their bodies, which were variegated with patches of bare, pimply skin. They slowly stepped about sideways, treading upon their own toes with a wise, solemn movement of their foolish heads. We named the rooster *Galahad*, because he evidently had the "strength of ten" other roosters.[6] He was so tall that he began to nibble and pull down the top of our brush hedge; but John thought that when they had filled up with corn, (already they had spoiled a bushel), and when what feathers they had got smoothed down, things would go better; but we went back to the house, still dubious, to be called out in the afternoon again, to find Galahad a picket guard against our old rooster, who was trying to get at him through the brush, both squawking with all their might. The three hens were toeing round in the corners, and uprooting the sod. John said the brush hedge was no go, that the hen families must be separated entirely. We finally concluded to send the old stock to Mrs. Fisher, a poor widow, who lived on a little place near ours. John took the lot to her, and she promised, with tears of gratitude, to keep our secret. If not with honor now, we expected a degree of peace; the Shanghais improved in looks, and grew in size. Galahad grew so tall, that from our chamber window we saw his vivid comb above the hedge; gleaming like a cactus flower. We did not own that we missed the pleasant, gentle old brood, nor that we failed to feel any affectionate solicitude for the new; but it was true. Galahad's next caper was to get entangled in the hedge; he left a good many feathers in it when we pulled him out. John then drove stakes into the ground, and with the clothes line tied down every one of them. At the shore he bought a load of light boards, remarking, to the dealer, "that this time o' year folks felt spunky about mending up things."

"This ere underhanded business makes me feel as if I were going agin the law," he said, when he set about making a fence; "but I s'pose, marms, yer know what you mean to do?"

"We do, indeed, John," sister replied. So he finished the fence, and carted off the brush. Our hopes rose; each hen laid every day, so beautiful, so large a pinkish egg, it was a joy; but they were in a fever to set, and we saved eggs enough for that purpose in a few days. On the seventh day John found the first hen dead under her nest, the eggs chilled; on the tenth, the second he found dead, the eggs still warm, which he put under the third and last hen. How we watched that mother in prospect! Galahad's lonely grandeur moved us to pity; he only half clucked now as he clawed the soil in his loneliness. What joy, and almost with tears, did we look upon eight, long-legged, gaping fledglings; but as the chicks began to skip from under her brooding wings, the mother passed away in her narrow coop.

In the warm air of early June the chicks flourished, and now began other complications. As yet no one had discovered what we were trying to do. It was the month of our first summer club meeting, and the anniversary of the first year. A fine entertainment was expected; it was an opportunity for a display from our best housekeepers. What could we do? We were eggless! We had not bought any eggs at the store or from our neighbors, for fear of exciting comment. Like most country maiden ladies, we ate cake daily; until now we had not known the high value of the egg in cookery; our privations testified to its importance. We inherited a recipe for a "pound cake doughnut," ten eggs to the pound. No one ventured to borrow this recipe, tho the doughnuts were widely known, and purchased at every entertainment. Sister's genius finally triumphed. She sorted the few apples left of a famous tree, "Never fail." She sent John to the creek for the largest scallop shells he could gather. She then made a delicate mess from the apples, filled the shells, covered them with a crust and baked them. They were a success, and the doughnuts were not called for.

We spent a day and night in the village after the festival. On the way home I observed that sister wore a pensive look, and mentioned it.

"What did Mrs. Jed mean, by saying that she knew I was ingenious, yesterday, and murmured, the 'master spirit.'"[7]

"Well, so you are."

"Nonsense; she knows something; said I was happy, and she liked scallop shells, and then she laughed."

"Never mind, sister."

"I have to mind."

John met us with the news of the loss of two chicks, and that he had something to show us. It was Galahad who had taken the chicks under his wings. "I guess now," said John, "we'll raise 'em with this new nurse." An easterly storm set in and we had to take the chicks in the house, and we had a lively time with them; they clawed and nipped at us when we fed them, and were very dirty. One got nearly smothered in the flour pail; another tried to take a sail in a bowl of molasses; another was choked with the cotton wool it tried to swallow in his basket. Besides these troubles we kept watch and ward at door and window, lest somebody should come and get a glimpse of the ungainly bare-skinned creatures. They increased in size and appetite, and kept us boiling Indian meal to stuff them, but they amused us as our fowl pets. The cold rain lasted three days, and then the sun came out; the chickens went back to Galahad, but Galahad had failed, his spirit was broken, and it was all over with him soon. We buried him under the Never Fail apple tree, and were astonished at the size of his mound. It was sad not to feel more regret, for we had learned to respect him, since his conduct with the motherless chickens.

In our simple drama, there were lapses as in all; still our little brood flourished and grew to fowl estate. While feeding them one day, I noticed that sister, spoon in hand, was meditating. Presently, as if to herself, she murmured, "One *white* rooster, two *white* hens. My dear, behold our evolution! and our reward."

"What do you mean?"

"I mean to say you have been very patient through all this business."

The next day we had a roast colored pullet for dinner, and we dined on colored pullets till but three were left, the white ones. The following fall, we had twenty pure white pullets, handsome, well-feathered, but still they stepped on their own toes. It was noised abroad with pride by John, of our superior breed of hens and their remarkable eggs.[8]

"Ah," said Mrs. Jed, "I felt your secluded situation and your faculty were suitable for a large enterprise."

Sister immediately began to relate the whole business from beginning to end, and for the first time I saw a look in Mrs. Jed's face, as she listened, which gratified me. At the County Fair, next year, we got a prize for an "exceptionally pure breed of Shanghais." We then had a hundred pullets as white as the gulls which swooped over our harbor. People came from far and near, in wonder and surprise, to see the fowl and buy the eggs.

Our means increased with their increase. Every spring and fall John sold in the county market the popular poultry known as the "Braganza Chickens."

"How much better Braganza sounds than Belden's Hole," said sister. "We owe that much to Mrs. Jed."

Two

"A Wonderful Promise of Misery"

Stories of Love
and
Other Disappointments

A Summer Story

Agnes Fleming was thirty, Hugh Pennock was twenty. Now and then she found a silvery thread in her smooth bandeaux. His locks were black and silky. Her face was pale, her eyes were weary and wore an inward look. His face was firm and vigorous, his eyes eager and full of humid fire. She was slender, fair, and delicate. He was tall, dark, and robust.

When this pair met, each made a move. She went back, and found something she had never before possessed—youth; while he leaped into the experience of manhood.

Agnes had sent her child, a boy of three years, to his grandmother, who lived by the sea. His absence opened an insidious chasm in the routine of her life, and that alert devil, Opportunity, suggested that the time had come for her to visit some maternal relations, whom she had never known, and who lived at a remote distance in the country. She did not ask her husband to accompany her, neither did he offer to go. They had been married ten years, and could part with composure. Fleming was fond of actresses and claret. With a soubrette he was perfectly at home; as the genius of Agnes did not run in the same direction, she could not make him feel quite comfortable with her. There were periods when they attempted the intimacy which their relation seemed to demand, but these attempts were failures; so the conjugal ship went adrift, and its insubordinate crew suffered, one from irritation, the other from despair. Though claret is the coolest wine in the world, Fleming's hair was thinning. His grey eye looked arid, and his stomach was too spherical. His manner was imperturbable, and he was still handsome in spite of his large jaw. But as we have nothing to do with him, we will leave him in a certain red-paneled room, with a young lady, whose shoulders are exceedingly neat, and whose opaque black eyes wear a flinty sparkle as she sips a glass of Chateau Margaux.

Agnes therefore arrived at Park Farm alone. The grange-like buildings pleased her. The many windowed, angular house of blue stone, was picturesque. Behind it extended a garden, where jonquils, pinks, and damask roses, straggled over the garden paths, and lush grass grew round the knees of venerable pear and plum trees. Before it rose a grove of Norway firs, lindens, pines, and oaks. Hugh Pennock, an Englishman, had planted the trees a hundred years before Agnes was born.

John Pennock, the grandson of old Hugh, his wife Rebecca, and their only child, Hugh Park Pennock, the last blossom which dropped from their tree of life, lived solitary in the dark decaying house. John kept his wheat fields in order, but did nothing else; Rebecca only attended to Hugh and her dairy. Hugh dreamed. So every year the pinks and roses straggled more wildly over the garden paths, and the bed of dead leaves grew thick about the trees in the grove. Old Hugh Pennock was a gentleman. Nature remembered the fact, for when our Hugh was born, she gave him the same impress. Everybody said he resembled the portrait of his great-grandfather, which hung in a small room called the Library, where there were a few leather-bound books, printed in London, for the booksellers 'at the Mitre in Fleet street,' or 'The Golden Lion in Aldersgate street.' This ancestor was Hugh's first idea. He was perpetually asking questions about his history; and he read the old books before he could understand them, but they made an impression nevertheless. When Agnes first saw him, he was grave and self-possessed. His easy silence drew her attention towards him; she wondered at his high-bred face. She thought what strong support there must be in his stalwart arm. He thought, how unreal she looked. There was the tremulous elasticity of a flower in her bearing, and the touch of her cool frail hand, felt like the fall of a dewdrop.

Agnes passed the first days of her visit in a lethargy. Rebecca thought her very ill. Agnes did not know her own ailment. The truth was, that the strain of her old life had given way, and nothing new had come to take its place. She kept her room. It was on the ground floor, with its window in a niche high up in the wall; steps were before it, which Agnes climbed every day, and looked out upon the landscape, stretching away between the park and garden. She saw numberless low hills, undulated ages ago by a wind pent in the earth, which died in a mighty heave along the verge of the horizon. They were crowned with trees, or furrowed with ripening grain. Once inside them, she thought, the clue which led into the world's highway would be lost.

Hugh sent her books and bunches of flowers. Too languid to read, she amused herself by pulling the flowers apart, and throwing them from the window leaf by leaf. Rebecca at last declared that something must be done, or Agnes would die. She must have the morning air. She should ride with Hugh in the wagon. She should not stay in her own room. She had had too much solitude, and not half care enough. Hugh arranged the wagon that day for her, and early the next morning, while the swallows were twittering under the eaves, Rebecca was by her bedside.

"Now, my dear, Hugh is waiting for you."

"A little more sleep," she begged, "I am so tired."

"Not a wink. If you shut your eyes, I'll call Hugh to carry you out to the wagon. Come; I will dress you."

Agnes obeyed her and was soon made ready. Hugh stood outside the door snapping his fingers at his dog Key, who was slobbering and groaning for a caress. Agnes thrust her hand in Key's shaggy coat, who forsook his master at once.

"Help her, Hugh," said Rebecca.

"O no," said Agnes, "Key is helping me." But Hugh quietly lifted her into the wagon, and they started with Key running beside them.

"I shall drive," said Hugh, "where you will have a different view from the one your window gives. I am afraid you are homesick, I have seen you look from it so often, and your gaze was so far away."

"No, I am not homesick; but how could you see me from my perch?"

"From the hammock which swings under that pine," pointing to an old tree, whose top was black with cones but whose lower branches were still green and dense. "It devours all my idle days; I wish you would try it; the carpet under it is dry, you see; the pine does not rustle its leaves above my head; there is no chatter of birds in its boughs; it is always grave and silent."

"It is like you," she thought; then aloud, "I will frequent it from this day."

She drew her shawl about her, and turned her face aside; Hugh saw that she did not wish to prolong the conversation. She enjoyed the scene too much to talk; the cool sweet air was balm to her; the quiet trot of the horses, the noiseless gallop of Key, his scampers into neighboring fields, the long shadows of the trees, and the flying birds, gave her a child-like pleasure. Park Farm was now five miles behind them. The horses were jogging slowly up a long hill, when Hugh suddenly reined them round an abrupt turn in the road. Below, lay a wide magnificent valley full of serrated woods. A crooked river ran through it, the sunrise burnishing its calm surface. Far beyond, the land rose in a series of ridges, extending the prospect till distance was lost in blue haze. Agnes rose to her feet, and gave a cry of delight; Hugh internally thanked her for it.

"I am well," she said, and stretched her hand towards him. He took it, the firmness of his grasp surprised her, and looking into his face she received from his glance an indescribable impression which opened the door of her soul, and encouraged it to step across the dark threshold of her interior life.

"Now for home and breakfast," cried Hugh; "mother will be ready for us." When they arrived at the lane-gate, Rebecca was there to open it. "Agnes, you are better. The great valley is a cure, isn't it? Do you see your breakfast on the porch? I have put my handsome dear old cracked china on it for you."

She had also prepared some dainty dishes, and made the table fanciful with flowers as well as with the old china. Agnes ate a little, and Hugh demolished all his mother set before him. They made her laugh, and then she ate a little more. "The girl's heart is ailing," thought Rebecca; "what can it be, I wonder?" Her tender solicitude smote Agnes with a new feeling. Tears had long since ebbed away from her; but now the tide seemed to be flowing again through some forgotten depth, though none welled from her eyes. A vivid spark gleamed in them, and a tinge of color came to her pale lips.

"How pleasant you are; how sincere," she said. "How positive is the taste of this food; how lovely these flowers are; their odor is delicious. Thank you, Rebecca; I see what you would do. Shall I ride tomorrow?"

"Every day."

"Will you go with me, Hugh?"

"Why, who else can go?" asked his mother.

"Who else?" said Hugh, sipping his coffee; "Where is this woman's husband?" he thought; "I hate him, I believe," and setting his cup down, he sauntered away.

In the afternoon, Agnes went to the hammock. Rebecca sat beside her with her sewing, and gave her a sketch of her mother's girlhood—the mother whom Agnes knew so little of. Rebecca wept gently while she talked. Her emotion moved Agnes, and her words seemed to place her en rapport with her mother; her heart expanded with the feeling, and some of its lonesomeness vanished. An affectionate impulse prompted her to go to Rebecca, and fall on her neck with a kiss. When had she felt such an embrace as Rebecca gave her for that kiss?

The air was full of the golden dust of sunset when they saw John and Hugh returning from the fields. John gave them a kindly nod, asked for supper, and passed into the house. Hugh lingered; looking at Agnes, he commented to himself: "Her countenance has changed again; her features are growing flexible." He leaned against the tree where the hammock was tied in which she was resting. She turned towards him, and thanked him for suggesting the change from her room.

"I shall live out of doors now," she said, "and should even like to pass the night here if Key would be my watcher."

Rebecca told her that the dew fell too heavy at night.

"Dew," mumured Agnes, putting her hand to her forehead, "I wish I could feel it."

Hugh heard her, and folded his arms across his breast with an outward composure, while he felt a slow tug at the heart, as if that organ was for the first time set in motion. A cool wind crept over the earth, and stirred the pine which let its needles fall on Agnes's dress.

"Night is coming," said Rebecca, as she went into the house to prepare supper, telling them to follow her soon. Hugh drew his mother's chair close to Agnes, and dropped his hat in the hammock; she took it with a pretty motion, and twisted in the hatband the leaves which had fallen. He observed all she did with a glance as sharp as that of a young panther.

"Do you like our life?"

"Yes, it is an idyl for me."

"What has mother been talking of?"

"Of my own mother, her early friend."

"Your mother's portrait hangs in my room."

"Let me see it."

"Yes, if you wish. It is a strange, sad face, and makes me dream."

"Come then."

They went up stairs. In the faded picture Agnes saw a resemblance to herself—the same eyes and compressed mouth. Its expression recalled her father to her mind, and she startled Hugh with her question,—

"Was my father a bad man?"

"A worldly man."

"I thought so."

He asked her to look at his books, and they were promising to read together when they heard Rebecca calling them to supper.

As soon as the birds were asleep, Rebecca was by Agnes's bedside again. She put out her candle, drew away the curtain from the window, bade her be ready for the morning's ride, and left her. So ended this happy day, the first of a series.

Agnes wrote Fleming that she was better, described Rebecca and Hugh, said she was happy with them, and asked permission to stay at Park Farm till her child should arrive home, when she wished him to send it to her, and they would, when Autumn came, return together. He gave the desired permission, and promised to send the child. Rebecca soon saw that Agnes required her attention no longer; Hugh must take care of her now, she said; she must look to her dairy, which of late had been neglected. So they were abandoned to the dangerous occupation of learning how to be necessary to each other. Agnes rose in the morning buoyant with the hope which found its fulfilment every hour. The thoughts of Hugh ran towards her, as a river runs towards the sea; his attentions gave her a higher estimation of herself. She decorated her hair with the flowers he gave her, and soon knew which dress he liked the most. The coquetry which exists in refined and sensitive women, so long latent in her, was developed; its inspiration exalted her. She had changed indeed since her arrival at Park Farm. Then, she had the immobility and coldness of a statue. Now, she was a woman with blushes, smiles, and tears—all that belongs to one who has been awakened to the fact that she still has the power to interest and please. John and Rebecca were charmed with her gentle vivacity; they talked about her, and said, how good she was, and how handsome, and wished that they could keep her with them always.

For a time they were contented with this open and innocent friendship; the pleasure of finding a similarity of opinion or a likeness in taste, sufficed them. Their books, their rides and walks, were a great enjoyment. The indolent days of sunshine and shower, the calm, sweet evenings were all delightful; life was beautiful. But this wide circle must needs be narrowed to the vortex of personal sensation. The zest and activity with which they had pursued these simple pleasures died out. Rebecca's unthinking good-nature did not allow her to perceive the change in their pursuits; but changed they were. They kept together still, for the charm of presence was imperative with both, but the book remained unopened in Hugh's hand, the walks were confined to the park, the rides given up. Some spirit presiding over the powers that be, was in the air, and had thrown before them the battle-gage of the souls of Agnes and Hugh.

Hugh was quiet, and looked less at her than he did, but pondered the earth and sky, and examined all things inquiringly. Whatever his mood, she hungered for its meaning. Still she was filled with a vague uneasiness; thoughts came to her of the meaning of all this, but she waved them off, and sought Hugh, mute with a pain she would not analyze.

The wheat harvest was over. Unclouded weather prevailed. The yellow sun rose and set in azure. No dew fell at night. No wind came from the North, none from the South. The moon sailed high over the park, and filled its avenues with misty light. Agnes and Hugh spent the evenings there, under the old pine. John went to bed with the fowls, and Rebecca followed him as soon as the kitchen fire went out. Hugh and Agnes had changed places. She was solicitous for him now, and watched his movements with anxiety. He occupied the hammock, while she sat on the grass beside it. Sometimes she put her hand on his head, and found it bathed in sweat. Sometimes she spoke to him and he did not seem to hear her, for he made no answer; but he sighed, and she sighed back softly. The evenings passed in this way were not counted, but when she thought of them afterward, the period seemed a long one.

When the old hall clock struck ten, Agnes went into the house, undressed with haste, pressed her face to the pillow, and resolutely went to sleep. How long Hugh remained in the park, she knew not. She never heard his step in the hall, and she dared not look from her window, for she had more than once dreamed that he was beneath it. Of late Hugh had absented himself during the day, going away in the morning before she rose, returning at night, and after supper taking his place in the hammock or wandering about the park, where Agnes, and sometimes his mother, joined him. Business kept him away, Rebecca said. She thought Hugh must be growing worldly, or she had a fear that he might put into execution an old plan of going to Europe. Agnes looked down when she expressed this fear, and Hugh made no reply.

One night when the clock struck ten, Agnes did not go in. Hugh counted the strokes expecting her "good-night" with the last, but she was silent. So was he. The moths and beetles flew round them undisturbed. The moon rose; hanging low in the sky, its placid light shone under the dark branches of the pines and revealed their faces to each other, but Hugh's eyes were shut. Bending over him she gazed into his face, till a profound and mysterious melancholy filled her soul. She tried in vain to repress her tears; a sob betrayed them. Hugh opened his eyes and saw that she loved him. It was all clear to them now, they loved each other! He felt as every man feels when a crisis is at hand—resolved and daring. But she felt an inexpressible anguish and humiliation. She wished herself a thousand miles away. "Hugh must feel how wrong she was!" He became conscious of the struggle in her mind, and his better sense strove with his primitive heart, and he remained silent; but his face was so eloquent, she could not endure to meet his glance.

"We will speak of this, but not now," she said; "I must go in."

He walked beside her up the avenue, still without speaking. When they reached the porch, she laid her hand on his arm. He stopped.

"Will you kiss me once?" she asked timidly.

He laughed, but he clenched his teeth. "Good-night, Agnes. Do not try me too far," and stepping back, he waved his hand for her to pass in. The air seemed full of sounds, she was so dizzy. Shutting her door, she listened a moment against it, and then groped for a candle, lit it, and walked about the room. She was crying bitterly. "How criminal I am," she thought; "I have prefigured to Hugh, that which a man should realize but with one—the woman he can ask in marriage. I have wronged some woman besides myself, then! and when the day comes for him to marry, he will think of me and of himself with shame. But what harm has he done?" she asked. She could find no fault with him, and with a woman's pride blamed herself alone. The remembrance of his last words came to her, and she saw that she must not meet him again alone. Then she endured one of those struggles where the mind has a perception that its desires and wishes will be overruled, in spite of all the judgement can calculate, and the specious reasons the heart can invent. She looked about mechanically for a pencil and paper, and wrote a few words with a bitter feeling of revolt, protesting with all her soul against their purport— "Hugh," she wrote, "it is not right for us to be together. It must not be. Let us both be silent. We can guess all that might be said." She crept up stairs, and slipped the note under his door. As she turned back, she stumbled over Key, who had followed her. With a growl he caught her sleeve in his teeth and held her fast. Hugh stirred, as if his attention was arrested. "If he opens his door," she thought, "I will go in." But she clutched Key's collar and dragged him by main strength through the passage. He loosed his hold, and she fled down the stairs, and heard Hugh open his door before she reached her room.

Henceforth Agnes avoided him. She saw that her note had a contrary effect from that which she had intended, for he kept near her as if fearful she would escape him.

To her relief, at last her child and his nurse arrived. As she took him, her heart gave a great throb of pain and love. Hugh's face darkened when he saw him, but he took the child up tenderly and embraced him.

"Now that your boy has come, you can stay," said Rebecca.

"Autumn is at hand," replied Agnes, "and I must back to my busy city life." She determined to return in a few days, and that those days should be spent apart from Hugh. She could not, however, separate herself entirely from him. He had not left home since the night they were last by the hammock under the pine; the business which occupied him before, seemed to be over. He returned to his books, treasures which had long been neglected; perhaps he derived strength and dignity from his counsel with them. He appeared neither to avoid nor to seek Agnes. His behavior was dangerously sweet to her. She spent her evenings by the bedside of her child, or in chat with Rebecca, but sometimes Hugh and she found themselves alone, in spite of her precautions. A struggle was visible in him—a struggle of pride and passion, of right and wrong. He grew moody, and even Rebecca now perceived a change in him, and the two women divined each other without any words; both prayed in thankfulness when the time came for Agnes to go.

The night before her departure was sultry and portended a storm. She was to leave early in the morning; her trunks were packed; she had had her last talk with Rebecca, and had gone to her room. All was still in the house, her child had been long asleep in her bed. The ominous hush outside was occasionally broken by the roll of distant thunder. The air of the room stifled her, its walls seemed narrowing round her, her heart was beating nervously. She unfastened the ribbon on her throat, and took the comb from her hair; but she could not resolve to undress. She avoided the sight of her face in the glass, but employed herself in carefully arranging the books which were on the table under it. She opened them and read over the name on their titlepages—written in ink discolored with age—'Hugh Park Pennock.' Having done this, she walked up and down the room with an irresolute step; she paused by the child and arranged the coverlet over him. At last she looked up at the window, which stared at her blankly. She went up the steps, softly opened it, and saw from it, what she knew she should see, Hugh below with his face upturned.

"Come down," he said in a husky voice, "come down, Agnes."

The desire which had been smouldering in her to be with him once more, for the last time, now broke loose. She yielded to it. As she touched the handle of the door, it turned from the outside, opened, and Hugh and she stood face to face. He was deadly pale, and the expression in his eyes made her quail. He drew her through the hall swiftly, out on the porch, down the avenue. A sharp flash of lightning zigzaged through the gloom, revealing every needle of the pine towards which they were hastening; it daguerreotyped the whole scene in Agnes's memory—the clump of lilies which he trode down—her loosened hair flying over her arms and down her white dress—the tall form of Hugh looming up beside her, his face wild and lurid in the glare—all was impressed there forever. It was utterly dark when they reached the pine. Hugh held her in his arms; she hid her face in his bosom, his head was bowed over hers. The rain-drops began to patter through the leaves. Agnes lifted her face, and Hugh put aside her tangled hair. She withdrew herself from his arms, resting against the tree, for she felt faint, and was about to speak, when her voice was checked by another ghastly flash of lightning. It lighted up the dark end of the house nearest them, where her room was situated, and they caught a sight which froze them. The child, disturbed by the tempest, awoke, and missing her, had crept from his bed, and climbed up the steps into the window, and stood on its narrow ledge, crying for her. She thrust away Hugh, whose impulse was to catch her in his arms and watch with her, for the catastrophe which he saw must take place; but she flew towards the house, deperate with the will to save her child. Something galloped beside her; it was Key. She pointed to the window, now dark again, and tried to speak, to incite him on, for she felt that she only crawled, but in vain; her running was a jest to Key. He impeded her progress by bounding before her in the path, jumping on her shoulders, and loudly barking. The child heard him, and Agnes, by another flash, saw him stretch out his arms, and totter. Key seemed like a black fiend between her and her child. Her heart was breaking, or was it the dull thud of his fall on the wet stones towards the window, she heard? Even then, Hugh's face shot before her vision, as she saw it upturned to her from the very spot where her child lay. When she reached him he was not dead, but she knew as she took him up that he was maimed for life. Hugh shuddered as he heard the wild howl which Key set up, and saw lights moving in the house, from the place where he still stood.

Eros and Anteros

We lived in Third street, my brother and I, in the second story of a house which we hired from the owner, an elderly man, who, with his wife, occupied the lower part of it, except the front basement, which I used as a kitchen. A series of Irish servant girls inhabited this basement, their ostensible business being to prepare our meals, their real one to make it an asylum until they should find something better, meanwhile cooking and cleaning much more to their satisfaction than to mine.

My brother, John Bartlett, was the corresponding clerk of Dimon & Co. When I came to New York to live with him, after the death of our parents, he had been with them three years; he was now twenty-five, and I twenty-two. His salary was fifteen hundred a year—our sole income, for I brought nothing to the new concern in which John and I were to be life-partners, as we promised ourselves, except a good stock of clothes, and a few household relics, which mother had said should be mine, and which my oldest brother, to whom the homestead fell, could not in conscience withhold, although my sister-in-law told him that she considered it perfect nonsense for me to remove them from the spot they looked so well in. Among these relics was a tall, mahogany clock, handsomely carved, with a moon, and the man in the moon, painted on its face; a mahogany bedstead, with high carved posts; and an ancient china tea-set. John thought that my possessions would finally ruin us, they preventing us from boarding in the light and airy manner of those who owned trunks only. We must keep them in some solid resting place, and it would cost something. But I knew all the time that he was tired of boarding, and preferred housekeeping. We wanted little with which to set up our household gods; his savings would more than do it, and when we were settled, could easily live within his salary. After we had hired the rooms and an unbroken Celt, he gave me a hundred dollars and a "Housekeeper's Manual" to begin with; the money was exhausted the first day, but not the "Manual."[1] It went mostly for a lounge bed for the Celt, and a cooking apparatus, including an oilcloth for the kitchen floor, which she declared she must have, putting her foot down, for that was the form of her declaration. I bought a great many pails, (vide Manual), and various ingenious instruments, which none but the inventor thereof could use.

The house machinery adjusted and set in motion, we furnished the upper apartments, three in number—the front room for a parlor, the one back for my bed-room, and a small offset over the hall for John's. The latter, on account of its dimensions, was furnished with a reed-like iron washstand, an iron bedstead, a row of new pegs, and no chairs. The relics, of course, were deposited in my chamber. John bought a dark carpet that harmonized with their sombre aspect, and shrouded the windows, which broke on the walls of a church, in curtains of Turkey red, that produced a gory effect. The naked posts of the bedstead were not picturesque; nor was the loud tick of the old clock melodious. Nevertheless, I soon came to like the room. The parlor was more cheerful. It was adorned with a picture of Lola Montez[2] on horseback in the Kingdom of Bavaria, and one of Jenny Lind,[3] in a wonderful lace berthé, with her hair dressed in rolls and stuck with roses. A good book-case filled one corner, an easy-chair another, and a handsome brocatelle sofa a third. Though the carpet was blue, the table-cover green—for John would buy these odd colors—and the wall yellow, the effect was so agreeable to him that he declared he should *never* live anywhere else. It was November when we began housekeeping, and before I had learned how to make John comfortable, winter was over; but he never complained. Everything would come out right after awhile, he said; besides he had more money now; in January his salary was raised to two thousand dollars. He went out a great deal, but was considerate enough not to bring company home with him. As for me, I went to church, to the grocers and to market. In March I hired a German servant, who proved a treasure. Under her administration comfort crept in, and my brows unbent. I even ventured to be waited upon a little by her. I was not afraid of her, as she spoke but little English. John was so elated by her good coffee, that he bought a new set of china, my ancient tea-set having disappeared, and invited his friends to breakfast. Emboldened by the discovery that she could lard veal in an excellent fashion, and make a fine potato salad, he brought them home to dinner, and we began to live a merrier life; that is, he and his friends were merry—I merely ventured to be useful. Most of his friends were clerks in houses like that of Dimon & Co. Several were the sons of the merchant princes in whose offices they served. Their friendship for John never surprised me, for I thought him their superior. His abilities were cultivated far beyond the needs of his position as a clerk, and he was very handsome. Moreover, there was that in him which we recognize by calling a man *a gentleman*. It was no merit in John to have this gift, but he made the impression of having achieved it. For that reason my oldest brother, who was something of a lout, quarrelled with him, calling him an aristocrat, a puppy, and "My Lord." John left home in consequence of this treatment.

I was politely treated by our visitors though their manner made me feel that I was growing old very fast; but what did it matter? An elderly appendage could fulfill the same duties which fell to me now. One morning when King and Harry Hurlbutt were breakfasting with John, Hurlbutt said something about managing John, as was my duty, I being the elder. John hastily stopped him with:

"You ass, she is three years the youngest."

He looked at me as he spoke, and then at my dress. I turned very red, and my eyes watered with embarrassment; but I contrived to say, setting down my cup with an assumption of ease:

"Nevertheless, I am an old maid, and bound to do as you suggest."

I never saw John look so annoyed.

"Bartlett," said King, "you are under a new conviction; *I* always knew that Miss Bartlett was younger."

"Take some more ham, Mr. King?" I asked.

"No more," he answered, with the deference due an aged person.

When John came home that night, he asked me when I had had a new dress? Not since I came to New York, I informed him.

"For heaven's sake, leave off that frumpish black silk. Here's money, and here's a dressmaker's address. I got it from King."

"From King?"

"Yes; it is the address of his sister's dressmaker. I asked him for it, and he went home to get it."

"Do you expect me to dress *much* better than I do?"

"I have allowed you to do too much for me. I have been thoughtless; how do you get on in household matters?"

"Nicely. Minna manages well; but since we have company so often, I fear she has too much to do. If I could put out the wash, I should like it."

"You must do it at once."

I bought some muslin dresses, for it was warm weather now, and took them to Miss King's dressmaker—a high and mighty personage, in whose hands I was a reed, but who made the dresses well, as she should have done, for her bill exceeded the price of the muslin.

A few days after my conversation with John, I went down to the alley, several doors below our house, which led to a court where there were half a dozen tumble-down cottages occupied by negroes. I could see the cottages, if I put out my head from my window; and it had occurred to me to go there for a washerwoman. I knocked at the door of the first house. It was opened by a stalwart negro, and I entered. A young woman pushed a stool before me without speaking, and went on with her work of folding rough-dry linen. Her appearance astonished me so that I forgot my errand, till reminded of it by the man who said:

"Garcia washes fuss rate. She do up fine gentleman's linen."

"Yes, Madam," she said, composedly, in a musical, broken accent.

"I am looking for some one to wash. Will you come to thirty-six to morrow, three doors above, in Third street?" She looked at her husband, and then consented:

"Yes, Madam."

"Take de candle up de alley, Garcia wait on de lady," giving her a flaring candle, as I rose from the stool. She followed me down the alley, holding the candle above her head. I turned back when I came to the door.

"To-morrow," I said.

"Yes, Madam."

It seemed to me that her expression had changed since she left her house; she looked cowed there, but now an expression of lazy independence was in her face. I could not take my eyes away from her, and she well understood why I could not. She was the handsomest woman I had ever seen—a Cuban quadroon, about twenty years old. She set the candle on her head, which was covered with a Madras handkerchief, put her arms akimbo, and leaned against the wall as if to solicit my inspection.[4]

"You are handsome," I could not help saying.

"Si," she drawled, with an indescribable intonation.

I moved down the street backwards till I reached our steps, and nearly fell over somebody who was going in.

"Did you see her?" I asked.

"Whom?"

"Oh, is it you, Mr. King? Won't the door open? But I hear some one coming."

"Why, Sue," said John, "how came you to arrive with King? What flusters you?"

"An errand up the alley. And I saw such a handsome washerwoman."

"It is for me to be flustered at the sight of a handsome woman, not you."

"She was a quadroon."

"And a devil," said King composedly, lighting a cigar.

"*Per se?*" asked John.

"Si."

"How well you look in the new muslin," continued John. "It's got sprigs all over it—pretty."

"The sprig has no botanical name," I said.

"'Tis the upholsterie," King remarked, throwing his cigar away, and taking a seat beside me, as if to examine my dress further.

"This sash is good, also," holding up one of its long ends, and adroitly pushing his chair round to face me.

"I am tired of these hived-up rooms," John broke out.

"Let us take a walk," said King, "and display this dress in the 'crowded mart.'"[5]

I looked up a little vexed. It was my fate to be astonished a second time that evening. When our eyes met, a belief that I had never seen him before possessed me, and I grew abstracted in my study of his face, for the reason of my belief. It was a wish of his that compelled me to observe him, presenting him in a new light. The wish was, "*I would know you.*" John, doubled in his easy chair, his legs over the arms, and his knees against his nose, paid us no attention. Presently, however, he said:

"Well, we will take a walk, though I know that Sue has no ambition for display."

I put on a new bonnet, at which they chorused, "Oh, oh!" and we went to walk round the willow by the fountain of the park in Fourth street, not far from our house. On the way back we passed, in Broadway, a glittering and crowded saloon.

"Let us go in," King said. "It is the fashion now."

A few feet from the entrance there was a wide flight of steps, where people were going up and down. John's hat came off suddenly to somebody coming down, and a silvery voice acknowledged his salutation.

"Hey, Alice," said King, "how are you? Just going?"

I only caught a glimpse of a slight young girl on the arm of a stout old gentleman. King placed me at a little table before a tall mirror, and ordered a variety of edibles. Every time I looked up he was watching me in the mirror. Strange to say, his air of deliberate inquiry put me at ease, though I avoided meeting his glance again; there was something in his brown eyes—some latent power, which I had not stirred—that affected me deeply.

John roused from a dream to say that he perceived I was talking a great deal; my new dress and bonnet had proved too much for me; but he hoped that it would not be necessary for him to incarcerate me in old black silk again.

"I will go now," I said, "lest Cinderella's fate befall me."

The next day Garcia came. I saw little in her behavior to interest me; she was dirty, vulgar and curious. Minna had brought her to my room, and the old clock amazed her so that I could not make her attend to me at first. When she did, she said, "six shilling a dozen," in imperfect English, and scratched her head with her beautiful slender fingers.

She gave me a slight touch of a dramatic, however, before she went. The organ sounded in the church, and the chant of the priest came in through the open window, for it was a celebration day. She crossed herself, and all her dirt and vulgarity vanished. A gleam of remembrance shone in her colorless face; she clenched her right hand, and with the left slowly rubbed her arm, which was bare to the shoulder.

"You are a Catholic?"

"In Mantanzas," she answered, picking up her basket.[6]

A moment after, I heard her singing in the court.

When the weather was hottest, John proposed that I should go to Glencove for a week; we both needed a change of air. He could leave the city every afternoon, and return in the morning. We would go to a quiet hotel, where I should find no excitement, and I could enjoy the "sad sea waves."[7] Though contented at home I acquiesced, of course. While I made ready, a vague regret stole over me at the loss of the pleasant evenings with King, for he came often now.

On Friday we went to Glencove, and took rooms in a large, noisy hotel—the quiet one John had mentioned, which was full of gay, fashionable people. The voice of the "sad sea waves" was unheard; the band that played every evening was thought a better music. I was troubled with low spirits all day. At dinner, on Saturday, John pointed out the King family, who had just come by the boat with him. Mr., Mrs., and Miss King. King himself was coming down on Sunday morning, team and all.

"Did you know that the Kings were coming here?"

"Oh, yes! I have known the family some months. King introduced me last winter. By the way, he it was who proposed your coming."

I had sprung a trap, and determined to keep very still in it, in spite of Master King. But it is not for mortals to ordain. John conveyed me to a small parlor, and introduced me to his friends. Miss King, a lovely girl, received me with impressment; King, *pere*, with respect; and King, *mere*, with a doubtful air, as was proper, considering that she was the daughter of an ancient dry-salter.

It was not long before I discovered that John and Miss King were in love with each other. Indeed, her beautiful eyes told me so, and asked me "*Are you willing?*" When she said in an under tone, how she had been longing to meet *me*, I gave in and answered in the same fashion, "*I am willing.*" Still I considered that she was Trap number two. Presently John asked her to go to the ball-room to dance, and I was left with Mrs. King solus, for Mr. King had wandered off where there were men and newspapers probably. She entertained me with the platitudes of her class, till I suffered so from internal gapings that my clothes creaked and my muscles ached. Happily the old gentleman returned, and waked me up by a laudation of John. "He was Dimon & Co.'s best man," he said, "and would undoubtedly have an interest in their house." During his conversation Mrs. King accomplished a series of private sniffs and hiccoughs, examined the seams of her dress, pulled out a stray thread, rubbed her teeth with her handkerchief, and as soon as he stopped requested him to look after "Sissy."

Sissy soon came, flushed and warm, hanging on John's arm, who looked pale and cool, with a little ring of curls matted round his forehead.

"If I were not Sue Bartlett," I thought, "I would be 'Sissy' King."

He looked benignly at me, as if he intended that I should have the crumbs which might fall from the feast of his happiness. I adored him for looking so well—adored him for patronizing me. I whispered to him that I was tired, and he said promptly, "Go to bed." Miss King made arrangements for our spending the time together, and bade me "good night" with her eyes on John. It was curious to see his airy, indifferent, unconscious manner, as we went up stairs.

"It is very warm to-night," he said.

"Very."

"It is nearly time for mosquitos, I think?"

"I should think so."

"There is a good breeze?"

"Yes, there is."

"Well, good night; I am going down to have a smoke."

"Good night, John," and I closed my door.

He opened it in a moment.

"Say, are you comfortable, Sue?"

"Yes, indeed! How pretty Miss King is?"

"Isn't she!" and he came in, shutting the door again.

"She is lovely."

The tears came into my eyes. He saw them, and impulsively took out his handkerchief.

"And she is good, too."

"As good as she can be. I guess I won't smoke," taking a chair.

A sudden shyness came over me; there seemed to be nothing more for me to say. The shyness was contagious. He looked around the walls of the room, but not at me; started up with, "I think I will smoke, though," and departed in a sheepish way.

It was a pleasant week that followed. King came down the next morning, and staid through the period of our visit. He could afford to do so, John grumblingly said, for he only made believe that he was a clerk in his father's office. Mrs. King asked every evening, about the time she saw us prepared to be amused:

"Mr. King, do you think a hotel is the place for a young girl?"

"Mrs. King," her husband invariably replied, "you must remember that we were young once."

I learned afterwards that she was only mother-in-law to King, which explained the difference between his age and that of Alice, she being seventeen, and he twenty-eight. The fact also explained to my simple mind the reason of his not living at home. Alice and I became very intimate; but she did not discuss John nor did I discuss King. We examined each other's wardrobes, exchanged presents of ribbons, helped each other to dress, and in short were as childish as young women are generally supposed to be when together. The night before we left Glencove I folded her dresses—(they were legion)—amazing her with my handy qualities, and cleared her room of its rubbish of books, pebbles, and apparel. After that we went in pursuit of John and King. We saw the tops of their hats above the window ledge, outside the parlor, and knew thereby that they were beneath them on the piazza. We crept softly to the window.

"Yes," said King, in his dreamy voice, "two types of women I like, and can't help myself from my likings. Your sister represents one."

I pulled Alice by her dress, to make her come away, but she held me fast, and would not move.

"She is good, clear-minded—her perceptions sharp, ready to be acted upon, yet always so beautifully reticent. The other is represented by an animal—a leopard, say; a creature of pure instincts, and no more answerable for what she is, and what she does, than an animal is. Hey, which woman do I *love*, if I am bound to specimens of each?"

"King," he answered, vehemently "you are damnably sophisticated!"
"I speculate, it is true."
"When you know Alice—"
"She is a child."
"You are a brute, King!" said Alice, knocking off his hat.
"Eavesdropping," he said, "and eavesdroppers never bear any philosophy. But *you* do," he continued, after he had come in by the window, and pushed Alice from her place.
"No."
"Can you understand me?"

My heart beat painfully, not because he questioned me, but because I loved him. I discovered from what he had said to John, *how* I loved him; as he loved my antipodal type—the leopardess! To hold him, I must maintain the bounds he had marked out—for I had no qualification which would entitle me to pass them. My beauty was placid and insignificant; there was nothing striking in my mien and voice, and I had no quickwitted powers of speech. In the inventory which I took of myself, I put down an intuitive trust that a principle higher and stronger than my passion would rule me; but it did not assuage my pain, nor my longing to be able to create in him what existed in me.

"Why don't you speak?" he asked gently.
"Yes, I can understand you."
"Will you?"
"For what reason?"
"I wish to marry you."

I looked round for John and Alice they were beyond hearing. The sense of what I would say oppressed me, but my tongue was tied.

"You heard what I said to John?"
I nodded.
"I *give* myself to you; will you take me?"
"So soon?"
"We have known each other for months."
"I have known you only a week."
"Is it enough?"

He smoothed my hair with a gentle hand, but his eyes were vague and distant. I pulled down his hand and kissed it.

"You are mine!"

He leaned his head on my shoulder with a heavy sigh, and said no more. The notes of a waltz from the distant band, floating into our silence, moved me with a wild longing to rise up and thrust away the man whose hair touched my cheek—to lift him in my arms and cover him with kisses. But I remained a formal, decent statue. No play of the lip, no flash of the eye betrayed me. I repeated under my breath, in the monotone of the waltz:

> "This is the way to be won, won, won,
> This is the way to be wooed."

"It is late," called Alice.

"Let us go then," I said.

King took her hand, when she stood beside me, and placed it in mine.

"Old boy," she said, "are you sentimental?"

When we reached her bedroom, she seized me by the chin. "It can't be possible that Ned is falling in love?"

"Hardly, Alice."

"Something has ailed him all the week."

I whimpered in spite of myself, but she held me fast.

"Are you such a goose as to love him?"

"Something ails me."

"Why, I never thought much of him; he isn't handsome, though he is clever."

"John likes him."

"Is that the reason?"

"I can't help it."

"Pho!"

"Can you help liking John?"

"Oh, *John* is a different person."

"I thought you would be pleased Alice."

"Do you mean to say that there is something between you?"

"Yes."

"Good; I *do* like it. King is a manly sort of fellow, though I can't imagine anybody's falling in love with him."

"Alice!"

"Good-by, my dear." She kissed me and called me sister, which she had never done before; then we both whimpered comfortably, and parted with smiles.

Shortly after our return from Glencove, Alice's engagement was announced. Her mother made some opposition to it, in memory of the ancient dry-salter; but Alice carried her point, for her father and King were on her side.

My engagement to King was not announced, for having no circle of relatives or friends, it was not necessary; besides, it was King's wish. He asked John's consent, in heroic accents, and John consented in a voice broken with emotion: "Take her-r-r and be miserable. Bless you, my sister." He was too happy with Alice to give me much thought, even if he had not resigned me to the care of King, and it never occurred to him that I might not be as happy in my new relation as he was in his. Love was a straight-forward matter in his estimation, with but one beginning and one ending, and he took it for granted that his estimation was the general one. He never noticed that King was a strange wooer, nor that I was in any way changed; he guessed at none of my feelings, which was a relief to me. King's evenings were spent in Third street, except when he went with me to pass them with John and Alice at his father's, or at the theatre and opera. The features of our evenings at home were a succession of cigars, and a handing on my part of matches, varied by his remarks of "How good you are," "Sit beside me," or, "Read to me." I played my role well, for there was a fascination in it which I could not resist. There always remained the privilege of deeper studies in the art I was acquiring—that of living two lives, one for him and one for myself. It had been so soon settled that we were to be married, that we were deprived of the excitement, and the tortures of pursuit, doubt, hope and expectancy; it was natural, perhaps, for him to forget the lover, in the established friend.

But I was happy, with a furtive, fitful, inexplicable happiness. Though passive, the current of his will was set towards me, and his actions ran calmly through it. He exercised a careful watchfulness over me, which was a proof of his purpose in regard to my future. Any approach made me by his or John's friends was intercepted, and conversation with them interrupted. At last those who had been in the habit of visiting us dropped off, and came no more. I never went out except with him. With all this supervision, he never approached me; no caress passed between us; there were no moments of fond, foolish, human weakness. John and Alice, arm in arm, with heads close together, cooing like turtle-doves, appeared to offer him no contrast to our distance and coldness. Once, when we were all at the theatre, in a stage-box, we saw John's arm steal round Alice's waist, under the protection of the curtain, while with his right hand he twisted his mustache for the benefit of the audience. She turned her face to him with so much love in it that it made me sigh—groan almost. King looked at me; for once we met each other's eyes with a questioning gaze. The mask I habitually wore before him dropped off for an instant, but his manner compelled me to resume it.

In January, Dimon & Co. offered John an interest in their house, which he accepted, and his wedding day was immediately appointed. Our Lares and Penates had been nodding their heads for some time, in token of farewell to us.[8] I was more indifferent than formerly to household affairs, leaving them in the hands of Minna, who managed them as she pleased. Garcia came and went every week under her direction. After the cold weather came, I noticed how Garcia coughed; the climate was killing her she said; snapping her fingers, she hoped she should find Cuba when she died. Her temper was irritable; she scarcely ever laughed, except in a vicious way, but in spite of a dark shade under her eyes, her beauty was more splendid than ever, and I felt the same interest in it, as at first, observing all its shades and variations, with jealous, envious eyes. She was still possessed to watch the old clock in my room, and in spite of Minna always went up there, whether I was at home or not.

One night when I was waiting in the parlor for King, I heard the door open which led to my room, from the hall, and a moment after, his step on the stairs; but he did not come in. I went through the little passage between the rooms, pushed back the door, and saw Garcia by the window, her dark beauty in the relief of the deep red curtain. Her eyes flashed, and her mouth was half open, for my entrance had arrested the words she was about to say to King, who stood in the other doorway.

The leopardess was before me.

The clock ticked so loud it attracted my attention, and when I looked from it, King had gone.

Garcia began to take the pieces from her basket, and counted them with loud deliberation as she laid them on the bed, till stopped by a fit of coughing. I went up to the bed and stood behind her. On a corner of the fine handkerchief knotted round her throat, there was a crest worked in red cotton, which I knew, and above it the initial K.

"Forty," she said at last.

"Here is your month's pay."

"They please you, Madam?"

"Certainly."

When I went back to the parlor, King was blowing rings of smoke from his pursed-up lips.

"Where did you pick up that handsome creature?" he asked.

"She lives near us."

"Where's John? At the governor's, I conclude, for Alice is in a world of fuss with the new clothes."

"I know she is."

"Shall we go up?"

"Of course."

As we passed the St. James in Broadway he said: "When shall I quit my bachelor rooms, Sue?"

"Oh, I had forgotten that your rooms were here; where are your windows?"

"They do not face Broadway."

"On this side?" I asked, as we turned out of Broadway.

"Yes, the second story, on the left; but will you answer me?"

"What will our future life be?"

"Serene as the lives of saints, and as blessed. You have so perfect a disposition that I shall always find with you a heaven of repose."

"What shall I find you?"

"Don't you know yet I am what I seem to be—yours. I shall see you and be with you every day of my life; not an action of yours will escape me; not a thought, I hope; I would have you crystallized in me. Can I make you happy?"

He offered me so much, that it was some excuse for my being too great a coward to speak the truth. But a dreary dismay filled my heart at the thought that perhaps there could not exist between husband and wife a relation which should combine the elements of all the relations which bind human beings together, and that men, knowing this, arranged marriage according to their knowledge.

I found Alice in her room with a dress-maker, walking round the room sweepingly, for the dressmaker to decide on the "hang" of a new silk, that was in the process of making.

"After me," said Alice, smiting this side and that, of her skirt, and twisting her neck to see the back of it, "come old Ned and you. Meantime you will live with John, and you shall have a charming room."

A pang respecting my relics smote me; I should be sorry after all to leave our dingy rooms, and an indescribable idea took possession of me, that I should inhabit them for years. I accepted her proposition with cheerfulness, and we were very merry till interrupted by John, who pounded the door and in a surly voice commanded Alice to leave her bosh and nonsense, and come down stairs to entertain him.

When King left me that night, he shook hands with me. The act seemed to seal an unspoken compact.

In a few days Garcia sent a woman to me with the message that she would not be able to come again; her cough was too bad. The woman said that Garcia's husband was a waiter at balls and parties, and at this season made money enough to live upon. I was very glad to hear this, I told her, for it was no longer necessary for me to employ Garcia. Soon after I perceived something in John's manner towards King that troubled me. I saw no difference in King's, and suspected the cause of the cloud which rested on John alone. I must know it fully, for I had promised myself, that no trouble should come to John and Alice through me, and I asked him to tell me the reason of his coolness towards King.

"I have heard something against him, and I doubt him," he answered sharply.

"Is it Garcia, our washerwoman?"

"Good God, Sue, how could you know?"

"Above all, John, Alice must never know it. I beg of you to let your doubt go."

He took me in his arms, and kissed me; I felt his tears on my cheek.

"I am too weak," he said, "to mar the happiness of Alice; to bring misery into the whole family by an exposé. I dreaded lest you should do so, as soon as I told you; but I could not keep it from you. What will you do—how will you act?"

"Leave it to me; don't tell me anything, nor ask me a single question. We will not mention him again."

"Damn him, once for all, then."

On reflection, I found that I had more faith in King than I had suspected; an instinctive rebellion in his behalf, rose against John, in my mind. But my interview with John was a turning point in my determination to know more of King. John's expectation that I would act for myself gave me the impetus to. I purloined his nightkey, had one made by it, and then feigned sickness, declining, of course, to see King; but sending him word, with much love, that I should be up to-morrow. Every evening, as soon as John left the house, on his visit to Alice, I dressed myself in dark clothes, went out quietly, and waited below the alley door. Three nights I waited in vain. On the fourth—a bitter cold evening it was—between eight and nine, Garcia came out with her husband, and I followed them. In Broadway I ventured nearer them, and saw that he carried a white jacket in his hand; he was on his way to some house where there was to be a party. Garcia was well wrapped in a large shawl, and held her head down in its folds. She carried a basket; but from the way it swung about on her arm, I knew there was nothing in it.

They crossed Broadway, opposite the St. James, and Garcia was let in at the side door of the hotel by the porter who sat behind it, while her husband went on with a careless whistle. How should I get in?

The man behind the door whisked about a small broom, yawned, and examined the soles of his boots, with a stolid air, while I stood there watching him. Not daring to remain on the walk any longer, I went down the street and came up on the other side. The man had disappeared. I darted across, and caught a glimpse of him at the end of a long passage, with his broom under his arm. I tried the door; he had forgotten to put down the latch, and I entered, speeding up stairs like a hound; but I walked leisurely through the passage with my shawl on my arm, nonchalantly meeting the eyes of the waiters who passed me.

I went up a second flight of stairs and turned to the left till I came to a narrow passage branching from the main one, with dead walls on both sides of it. At its end there was a window; I looked from it for a moment, and vaguely wondered at the heads I saw passing to and fro in a hall, on the other side of the building. I turned with a shrinking of the heart to my task of finding King's room. It might be that the wall I was now walking against, slipping my hand along its smooth surface, was the wall of his bedroom. It was, I was soon convinced, for I heard Garcia cough. I rushed to his door and raised my clenched hand to strike it, but it fell nerveless by my side. I staggered back to the seclusion of the dark passage. I heard King's gay laugh; it made the blood fly to my head and eyes like splinters of fire. "Will she never come out?" I muttered. At last she passed down the main passage, holding her shawl to her mouth. I knocked at King's door then, and at his "come in," I opened it. He was standing before the mirror, complacently brushing his whiskers with one hand, and holding his hat with the other.

"Did any one see you come in?" he asked.

"Where did you pick up that handsome creature, King?"

"Because, if you were seen," he continued, "you are ruined."

His coolness stunned me.

"Some of your friends saw me, possibly."

"My friends," he echoed, turning as pale as death, and putting his hat down. "Go; you must go alone, too; I cannot leave the house with you."

"Do you know how I divined you, King?"

He would not speak.

"You never ventured to compare my soul with Garcia's body?"

He shrugged his shoulders.

"*Ayudadmi, maestro mio, O morire,*" said a voice at the door.[9]

Garcia had crept back. She showed him the corner of her shawl stained with blood, not heeding me. He looked ghastly now—frozen—but he made no movement. She turned to me. "Water," she said, shaking her finger at me like a child. I went into the bedroom to find some, and saw King menace her with a fearful look, which, however, she did not care for; she suffered too much. She could not drink the water, and grew very faint.

"Give her this wine," he said at last, pouring some from a decanter, and handing it to me.

I held it to her lips, and she slowly sipped it, till she revived. I was about to set the glass down, when she seized it with a hissing laugh, and threw it at him. He did not avoid it, and it struck his arm. The gesture displaced the shawl from her shoulders, which were bare. Even then I saw his eyes drink in her surpassing beauty.

He had chosen the refuge of silence. *I* could say nothing before her. I felt a faintness creeping over me, and pouring out some wine into a little cup, which I took from a table, I drank it. I pulled a chair towards me and sat down. The act made all the receded blood rush back to King's face; his brows were in a flame. Garcia said, in a voice that was entirely hoarse, "Does the clock tick?" I made no reply. As soon as my strength came back, I rose to depart. Some sad and solemn spirit must have touched my face, for, as I reached the door, King uttered a despairing cry, and threw his hands over his head.

John and Alice were married in a few days. King and I were groom and brides-maid.

It is two years since they were married. I see King often. Our engagement was never annulled. I still live alone in Third street.

Lemorne versus *Huell*

The two months I spent at Newport with Aunt Eliza Huell, who had been ordered to the sea-side for the benefit of her health, were the months that created all that is dramatic in my destiny. My aunt was troublesome, for she was not only out of health, but in a lawsuit. She wrote to me, for we lived apart, asking me to accompany her—not because she was fond of me, or wished to give me pleasure, but because I was useful in various ways. Mother insisted upon my accepting her invitation, not because she loved her late husband's sister, but because she thought it wise to cotton to her in every particular, for Aunt Eliza was rich, and we—two lone women—were poor.

I gave my music-pupils a longer and earlier vacation than usual, took a week to arrange my wardrobe—for I made my own dresses—and then started for New York, with the five dollars which Aunt Eliza had sent for my fare thither. I arrived at her house in Bond Street at 7 A.M., and found her man James in conversation with the milkman. He informed me that Miss Huell was very bad, and that the housekeeper was still in bed. I supposed that Aunt Eliza was in bed also, but I had hardly entered the house when I heard her bell ring as she only could ring it—with an impatient jerk.

"She wants hot milk," said James, "and the man has just come."

I laid my bonnet down, and went to the kitchen. Saluting the cook, who was an old acquaintance, and who told me that the "divil" had been in the range that morning, I took a pan, into which I poured some milk, and held it over the gaslight till it was hot; then I carried it up to Aunt Eliza.

"Here is your milk, Aunt Eliza. You have sent for me to help you, and I begin with the earliest opportunity."

"I looked for you an hour ago. Ring the bell."

I rang it.

"Your mother is well, I suppose. She would have sent you, though, had she been sick in bed."

"She has done so. She thinks better of my coming than I do."

The housekeeper, Mrs. Roll, came in, and Aunt Eliza politely requested her to have breakfast for her niece as soon as possible.

"I do not go down of mornings yet," said Aunt Eliza, "but Mrs. Roll presides. See that the coffee is good, Roll."

"It is good generally, Miss Huell."

"You see that Margaret brought me my milk."

"Ahem!" said Mrs. Roll, marching out.

At the beginning of each visit to Aunt Eliza I was in the habit of dwelling on the contrast between her way of living and ours. We lived from "hand to mouth." Every thing about her wore a hereditary air; for she lived in my grandfather's house, and it was the same as in his day. If I was at home when these contrasts occurred to me I should have felt angry; as it was, I felt them as in a dream—the china, the silver, the old furniture, and the excellent fare soothed me.

In the middle of the day Aunt Eliza came down stairs, and after she had received a visit from her doctor, decided to go to Newport on Saturday. It was Wednesday; and I could, if I chose, make any addition to my wardrobe. I had none to make, I informed her. What were my dresses?—had I a black silk? she asked. I had no black silk, and thought one would be unnecessary for hot weather.

"Who ever heard of a girl of twenty-four having no black silk! You have slimsy muslins, I dare say?"

"Yes."

"And you like them?"

"For present wear."

That afternoon she sent Mrs. Roll out, who returned with a splendid heavy silk for me, which Aunt Eliza said should be made before Saturday, and it was. I went to a fashionable dress-maker of her recommending, and on Friday it came home, beautifully made and trimmed with real lace.

"Even the Pushers could find no fault with this," said Aunt Eliza turning over the sleeves and smoothing the lace. Somehow she smuggled into the house a white straw-bonnet, with white roses; also a handsome mantilla. She held the bonnet before me with a nod, and deposited it again in the box, which made a part of the luggage for Newport.

On Sunday morning we arrived in Newport, and went to a quiet hotel in the town. James was with us, but Mrs. Roll was left in Bond Street, in charge of the household. Monday was spent in an endeavor to make an arrangement regarding the hire of a coach and coachman. Several livery-stable keepers were in attendance, but nothing was settled, till

I suggested that Aunt Eliza should send for her own carriage. James was sent back the next day, and returned on Thursday with coach, horses, and William her coachman. That matter being finished, and the trunks being unpacked, she decided to take her first bath in the sea, expecting me to support her through the trying ordeal of the surf. As we were returning from the beach we met a carriage containing a number of persons with a family resemblance.

When Aunt Eliza saw them she angrily exclaimed, "Am I to see those Uxbridges every day?"

Of the Uxbridges this much I knew—that the two brothers Uxbridge were the lawyers of her opponents in the lawsuit which had existed three or four years. I had never felt any interest in it, though I knew that it was concerning a tract of ground in the city which had belonged to my grandfather, and which had, since his day, become very valuable. Litigation was a habit of the Huell family. So the sight of the Uxbridge family did not agitate me as it did Aunt Eliza.

"The sly, methodical dogs! but I shall beat Lemorne yet!"

"How will you amuse yourself then, aunt?"

"I'll adopt some boys to inherit what I shall save from his clutches."

The bath fatigued her so she remained in her room for the rest of the day; but she kept me busy with a hundred trifles. I wrote for her, computed interest, studied out bills of fare, till four o'clock came, and with it a fog. Nevertheless I must ride on the Avenue, and the carriage was ordered.

"Wear your silk, Margaret; it will just about last your visit through—the fog will use it up."

"I am glad of it," I answered.

"You will ride every day. Wear the bonnet I bought for you also."

"Certainly; but won't that go quicker in the fog than the dress?"

"Maybe; but wear it."

I rode every day afterward, from four to six, in the black silk, the mantilla, and the white straw. When Aunt Eliza went she was so on the alert for the Uxbridge family carriage that she could have had little enjoyment of the ride. Rocks never were a passion with her, she said, nor promontories, chasms, or sand. She came to Newport to be washed with salt-water; when she had washed up to the doctor's prescription she should leave, as ignorant of the peculiar pleasures of Newport as when she arrived. She had no fancy for its conglomerate societies, its literary cottages, its parvenue suits of rooms, its saloon habits, and its bathing herds.

I considered the rides a part of the contract of what was expected in my two months' performance. I did not dream that I was enjoying them, any more than I supposed myself to be enjoying a sea-bath while pulling Aunt Eliza to and fro in the surf. Nothing in the life around me stirred me, nothing in nature attracted me. I liked the fog; somehow it seemed to emanate from me instead of rolling up from the ocean, and to represent me. Whether I went alone or not, the coachman was ordered to drive a certain round; after that I could extend the ride in whatever direction I pleased, but I always said, "Any where, William." One afternoon, which happened to be a bright one, I was riding on the road which led to the glen, when I heard the screaming of a flock of geese which were waddling across the path in front of the horses. I started, for I was asleep probably, and, looking forward, saw the Uxbridge carriage, filled with ladies and children, coming toward me; and by it rode a gentleman on horseback. His horse was rearing among the hissing geese, but neither horse nor geese appeared to engage him; his eyes were fixed upon me. The horse swerved so near that its long mane almost brushed against me. By an irresistible impulse I laid my ungloved hand upon it, but did not look at the rider. Carriage and horseman passed on, and William resumed his pace. A vague idea took possession of me that I had seen the horseman before on my various drives. I had a vision of a man galloping on a black horse out of the fog, and into it again. I was very sure, however, that I had never seen him on so pleasant a day as this! William did not bring his horses to time; it was after six when I went into Aunt Eliza's parlor, and found her impatient for her tea and toast. She was crosser than the occasion warranted; but I understood it when she gave me the outlines of a letter she desired me to write to her lawyer in New York. Something had turned up, he had written her; the Uxbridges believed that they had ferreted out what would go against her. I told her that I had met the Uxbridge carriage.

"One of them is in New York; how else could they be giving me trouble just now?"

"There was a gentleman on horseback beside the carriage."

"Did he look mean and cunning?"

"He did not wear his legal beaver up, I think; but he rode a fine horse and sat it well."

"A lawyer on horseback should, like the beggar of the adage, ride to the devil."

"Your business now is the 'Lemorne?'"

"You know it is."

"I did not know but that you had found something besides to litigate."

"It must have been Edward Uxbridge that you saw. He is the brain of the firm."

"You expect Mr. Van Horn?"

"Oh, he must come; I can not be writing letters."

We had been in Newport two weeks when Mr. Van Horn, Aunt Eliza's lawyer, came. He said that he would see Mr. Edward Uxbridge. Between them they might delay a term, which he thought would be best. "Would Miss Huell ever be ready for a compromise?" he jestingly asked.

"Are you suspicious?" she inquired.

"No; but the Uxbridge chaps are clever."

He dined with us; and at four o'clock Aunt Eliza graciously asked him to take a seat in the carriage with me, making some excuse for not going herself.

"Hullo!" said Mr. Van Horn when we had reached the country road, "there's Uxbridge now." And he waved his hand to him.

It was indeed the black horse and the same rider that I had met. He reined up beside us, and shook hands with Mr. Van Horn.

"We are required to answer this new complaint?" said Mr. Van Horn.

Mr. Uxbridge nodded.

"And after that the judgment?"

Mr. Uxbridge laughed.

"I wish that certain gore of land had been sunk instead of being mapped in 1835."

"The surveyor did his business well enough, I am sure."

They talked together in a low voice for a few minutes, and then Mr. Van Horn leaned back in his seat again. "Allow me," he said, "to introduce you, Uxbridge, to Miss Margaret Huell, Miss Huell's niece. Huell vs. Brown, you know," he added, in an explanatory tone; for I was Huell vs. Brown's daughter.

"Oh!" said Mr. Uxbridge, bowing, and looking at me gravely. I looked at him also; he was a pale, stern-looking man, and forty years old certainly. I derived the impression at once that he had a domineering disposition, perhaps from the way in which he controlled his horse.

"Nice beast that," said Mr. Van Horn.

"Yes," he answered, laying his hand on its mane, so that the action brought immediately to my mind the recollection that I had done so too. I would not meet his eye again, however.

"How long shall you remain, Uxbridge?"

"I don't know. You are not interested in the lawsuit, Miss Huell?" he said, putting on his hat.

"Not in the least; nothing of mine is involved."

"We'll gain it for your portion yet, Miss Margaret," said Mr. Van Horn, nodding to Mr. Uxbridge, and bidding William drive on. He returned the next day, and we settled into the routine of hotel life. A few mornings after, she sent me to a matinée, which was given by some of the Opera people, who were in Newport strengthening the larynx with applications of brine. When the concert was half over, and the audience were making the usual hum and stir, I saw Mr. Uxbridge against a pillar, with his hands incased in pearl-colored gloves, and holding a shiny hat. He turned half away when he caught my eye, and then darted toward me.

"You have not been much more interested in the music than you are in the lawsuit," he said, seating himself beside me.

"The *tutoyer* of the Italian voice is agreeable, however."[1]

"It makes one dreamy."

"A child."

"Yes, a child; not a man nor a woman."

"I teach music. I can not dream over 'one, two, three.' "

"*You*—a music teacher!"

"For six years."

I was aware that he looked at me from head to foot, and I picked at the lace of my invariable black silk; but what did it matter whether I owned that I was a genteel pauper, representing my aunt's position for two months, or not?

"Where?"

"In Waterbury."

"Waterbury differs from Newport."

"I suppose so."

"You suppose!"

A young gentleman sauntered by us, and Mr. Uxbridge called to him to look up the Misses Uxbridge, his nieces, on the other side of the hall.

"Paterfamilias Uxbridge has left his brood in my charge," he said.[2] "I try to do my duty," and he held out a twisted pearl-colored glove, which he had pulled off while talking. What white nervous fingers he had! I thought they might pinch like steel.

"You suppose," he repeated.

"I do not look at Newport."

"Have you observed Waterbury?"

"I observe what is in my sphere."

"Oh!"

He was silent then. The second part of the concert began; but I could not compose myself to appreciation. Either the music or I grew chaotic. So many tumultuous sounds I heard—of hope, doubt, inquiry, melancholy, and desire; or did I feel the emotions which these words express? Or was there magnetism stealing into me from the quiet man beside me? He left me with a bow before the concert was over, and I saw him making his way out of the hall when it was finished.

I had been sent in the carriage, of course; but several carriages were in advance of it before the walk, and I waited there for William to drive up. When he did so, I saw by the oscillatory motion of his head, though his arms and whip-hand were perfectly correct, that he was inebriated. It was his first occasion of meeting fellow-coachmen in full dress, and the occasion had proved too much for him. My hand, however, was on the coach door, when I heard Mr. Uxbridge say, at my elbow,

"It is not safe for you."

"Oh, Sir, it is in the programme that I ride home from the concert." And I prepared to step in.

"I shall sit on the box, then."

"But your nieces?"

"They are walking home, squired by a younger knight."

Aunt Eliza would say, I thought, "Needs must when a lawyer drives;" and I concluded to allow him to have his way, telling him that he was taking a great deal of trouble. He thought it would be less if he were allowed to sit inside; both ways were unsafe.

Nothing happened. William drove well from habit; but James was obliged to assist him to dismount. Mr. Uxbridge waited a moment at the door, and so there was quite a little sensation, which spread its ripples till Aunt Eliza was reached. She sent for William, whose only excuse was "dampness."

"Uxbridge knew my carriage, of course," she said, with a complacent voice.

"He knew me," I replied.

"You do not look like the Huells."

"I look precisely like the young woman to whom he was introduced by Mr. Van Horn."

"Oh ho!"

"He thought it unsafe for me to come alone under William's charge."

"Ah ha!"

No more was said on the subject of his coming home with me. Aunt Eliza had several fits of musing in the course of the evening while I read aloud to her, which had no connection with the subject of the book. As I put it down she said that it would be well for me to go to church the next day. I acquiesced, but remarked that my piety would not require the carriage, and that I preferred to walk. Besides, it would be well for William and James to attend divine service. She could not spare James, and thought William had better clean the harness, by way of penance.

The morning proved to be warm and sunny. I donned a muslin dress of home manufacture and my own bonnet, and started for church. I had walked but a few paces when the consciousness of being *free* and *alone* struck me. I halted, looked about me, and concluded that I would not go to church, but walk into the fields. I had no knowledge of the whereabouts of the fields; but I walked straight forward, and after a while came upon some barren fields, cropping with coarse rocks, along which ran a narrow road. I turned into it, and soon saw beyond the rough coast the blue ring of the ocean—vast, silent, and splendid in the sunshine. I found a seat on the ruins of an old stone-wall, among some tangled bushes and briers. There being no Aunt Eliza to pull through the surf, and no animated bathers near, I discovered the beauty of the sea, and that I loved it.

Presently I heard the steps of a horse, and, to my astonishment, Mr. Uxbridge rode past. I was glad he did not know me. I watched him as he rode slowly down the road, deep in thought. He let drop the bridle, and the horse stopped, as if accustomed to the circumstance, and pawed the ground gently, or yawed his neck for pastime. Mr. Uxbridge folded his arms and raised his head to look seaward. It seemed to me as if he were about to address the jury. I had dropped so entirely from my observance of the landscape that I jumped when he resumed the bridle and turned his horse to come back. I slipped from my seat to look among the bushes, determined that he should not recognize me; but my attempt was a failure—he did not ride by the second time.

"Miss Huell!" And he jumped from his saddle, slipping his arm through the bridle.

"I am a runaway. What do you think of the Fugitive Slave Bill?"

"I approve of returning property to its owners."

"The sea must have been God's temple first, instead of the groves."[3]

"I believe the Saurians were an Orthodox tribe."

"Did you stop yonder to ponder the sea?"

"I was pondering 'Lemorne *vs.* Huell.'"

He looked at me earnestly, and then gave a tug at the bridle, for his steed was inclined to make a crude repast from the bushes.

"How was it that I did not detect you at once?" he continued.

"My apparel is Waterbury apparel."

"Ah!"

We walked up the road slowly till we came to the end of it; then I stopped for him to understand that I thought it time for him to leave me. He sprang into the saddle.

"Give us good-by!" he said, bringing his horse close to me.

"We are not on equal terms; I feel too humble afoot to salute you."

"Put your foot on the stirrup then."

A leaf stuck in the horse's forelock, and I pulled it off and waved it in token of farewell. A powerful light shot into his eyes when he saw my hand close on the leaf.

"May I come and see you?" he asked, abruptly. "I will."

"I shall say neither 'No' nor 'Yes.'"

He rode on at a quick pace, and I walked homeward forgetting the sense of liberty I had started with, and proceeded straightway to Aunt Eliza.

"I have not been to church, aunt, but to walk beyond the town; it was not so nominated in the bond, but I went. The taste of freedom was so pleasant that I warn you there is danger of my 'striking.' When will you have done with Newport?"

"I am pleased with Newport now," she answered, with a curious intonation. "I like it."

"I do also."

Her keen eyes sparkled.

"Did you ever like any thing when you were with me before?"

"Never. I will tell you why I like it: because I have met, and shall probably meet, Mr. Uxbridge. I saw him to-day. He asked permission to visit me."

"Let him come."

"He will come."

But we did not see him either at the hotel or when we went abroad. Aunt Eliza rode with me each afternoon, and each morning we went to the beach. She engaged me every moment when at home, and I faithfully performed all my tasks. I clapped to the door on self-investigation—locked it against any analysis or reasoning upon any circumstance connected with Mr. Uxbridge. The only piece of treachery to my code that

I was guilty of was the putting of the leaf which I brought home on Sunday between the leaves of that poem whose motto is,

"Mariana in the moated grange."[4]

On Saturday morning, nearly a week after I saw him on my walk, Aunt Eliza proposed that we should go to Turo Street on a shopping excursion; she wanted a cap, and various articles besides. As we went into a large shop I saw Mr. Uxbridge at a counter buying gloves; her quick eye caught sight of him, and she edged away, saying she would look at some goods on the other side; I might wait where I was. As he turned to go out he saw me and stopped.

"I have been in New York since I saw you," he said. "Mr. Lemorne sent for me."

"There is my aunt," I said.

He shrugged his shoulders.

"I shall not go away soon again," he remarked. "I missed Newport greatly."

I made some foolish reply, and kept my eyes on Aunt Eliza, who dawdled unaccountably. He appeared amused, and after a little talk went away.

Aunt Eliza's purchase was a rose-colored moire antique, which she said was to be made for me; for Mrs. Bliss, one of our hotel acquaintances, had offered to chaperon me to the great ball which would come off in a few days, and she had accepted the offer for me.

"There will be no chance for you to take a walk instead," she finished with.

"I can not dance, you know."

"But you will be *there*."

I was sent to a dress-maker of Mrs. Bliss's recommending; but I ordered the dress to be made after my own design, long plain sleeves, and high plain corsage, and requested that it should not be sent home till the evening of the ball. Before it came off Mr. Uxbridge called, and was graciously received by Aunt Eliza, who could be gracious to all except her relatives. I could not but perceive, however, that they watched each other in spite of their lively conversation. To me he was deferential, but went over the ground of our acquaintance as if it had been the most natural thing in the world. But for my life-long habit of never calling in question the behavior of those I came in contact with, and of never expecting any thing different from that I received, I might have wondered over his visit. Every person's individuality was sacred to me, from the fact, perhaps, that my own individuality had never been respected by any person with whom I had any relation—not even by my own mother.

After Mr. Uxbridge went, I asked Aunt Eliza if she thought he looked mean and cunning? She laughed, and replied that she was bound to think that Mr. Lemorne's lawyer could not look otherwise.

When, on the night of the ball, I presented myself in the rose-colored moire antique for her inspection, she raised her eyebrows, but said nothing about it.

"I need not be careful of it, I suppose, aunt?"

"Spill as much wine and ice-cream on it as you like."

In the dressing-room Mrs. Bliss surveyed me.

"I think I like this mass of rose-color," she said. "Your hair comes out in contrast so brilliantly. Why, you have not a single ornament on!"

"It is so easy to dress without."

This was all the conversation we had together during the evening, except when she introduced some acquaintance to fulfill her matronizing duties. As I was no dancer I was left alone most of the time, and amused myself by gliding from window to window along the wall, that it might not be observed that I was a fixed flower. Still I suffered the annoyance of being stared at by wandering squads of young gentlemen, the "curled darlings" of the ball-room. I borrowed Mrs. Bliss's fan in one of her visits for a protection. With that, and the embrasure of a remote window where I finally stationed myself, I hoped to escape further notice. The music of the celebrated band which played between the dances recalled the chorus of spirits which charmed Faust:

> "And the fluttering
> Ribbons of drapery
> Cover the plains,
> Cover the bowers,
> Where lovers,
> Deep in thought,
> Give themselves for life."[5]

The voice of Mrs. Bliss broke its spell.

"I bring an old friend, Miss Huell, and he tells me an acquaintance of yours."

It was Mr. Uxbridge.

"I had no thought of meeting you, Miss Huell."

And he coolly took the seat beside me in the window, leaving to Mrs. Bliss the alternative of standing or of going away; she chose the latter.

"I saw you as soon as I came in," he said, "gliding from window to window, like a vessel hugging the shore in a storm."

"With colors at half-mast; I have no dancing partner."

"How many have observed you?"

"Several young gentlemen."

"Moths."

"Oh no, butterflies."

"They must keep away now."

"Are you Rhadamanthus?"[6]

"And Charon, too. I would have you row in the same boat with me."[7]

"Now you are fishing."

"Won't you compliment me. Did I ever look better?"

His evening costume *was* becoming, but he looked pale, and weary, and disturbed. But if we were engaged for a tournament, as his behavior indicated, I must do my best at telling. So I told him that he never looked better, and asked him how I looked. He would look at me presently, he said, and decide. Mrs. Bliss skimmed by us with nods and smiles; as she vanished our eyes followed her, and we talked vaguely on various matters, sounding ourselves and each other. When a furious redowa set in which cut our conversation into rhythm he pushed up the window and said, "Look out."

I turned my face to him to do so, and saw the moon at the full, riding through the strip of sky which our vision commanded. From the moon our eyes fell on each other. After a moment's silence, during which I returned his steadfast gaze, for I could not help it, he said:

"If we understand the impression we make upon each other, what must be said?"

I made no reply, but fanned myself, neither looking at the moon, nor upon the redowa, nor upon any thing.

He took the fan from me.

"Speak of yourself," he said.

"Speak you."

"I am what I seem, a man within your sphere. By all the accidents of position and circumstance suited to it. Have you not learned it?"

"I am not what I seem. I never wore so splendid a dress as this till to-night, and shall not again."

He gave the fan such a twirl that its slender sticks snapped, and it drooped like the broken wing of a bird.

"Mr. Uxbridge, that fan belongs to Mrs. Bliss."

He threw it out of the window.

"You have courage, fidelity, and patience—this character with a passionate soul. I am sure that you have such a soul?"

"I do not know."

"I have fallen in love with you. It happened on the very day when I passed you on the way to the Glen. I never got away from the remembrance of seeing your hand on the mane of my horse."

He waited for me to speak, but I could not; the balance of my mind was gone. Why should this have happened to me—a slave? As it had happened, why did I not feel exultant in the sense of power which the chance for freedom with him should give?

"What is it, Margaret? your face is as sad as death."

"How do you call me 'Margaret?'"

"As I would call my wife—Margaret."

He rose and stood before me to screen my face from observation. I supposed so, and endeavored to stifle my agitation.

"You are better," he said, presently. "Come go with me and get some refreshment." And he beckoned to Mrs. Bliss, who was down the hall with an unwieldly gentleman.

"Will you go to supper now?" she asked.

"We are only waiting for you," Mr. Uxbridge answered, offering me his arm.

When we emerged into the blaze and glitter of the supper-room I sought refuge in the shadow of Mrs. Bliss's companion, for it seemed to me that I had lost my own.

"Drink this Champagne," said Mr. Uxbridge. "Pay no attention to the Colonel on your left; he won't expect it."

"Neither must you."

"Drink."

The Champagne did not prevent me from reflecting on the fact that he had not yet asked whether I loved him.

The spirit chorus again floated through my mind:

> "Where lovers,
> Deep in thought,
> *Give* themselves for life."

I was not allowed to *give* myself—I was *taken*.

"No heel-taps," he whispered, "to the bottom quaff."

"Take me home, will you?"

"Mrs. Bliss is not ready."

"Tell her that I must go."

He went behind her chair and whispered something, and she nodded to me to go without her.

When her carriage came up, I think he gave the coachman an order to drive home in a round-about way, for we were a long time reaching it. I kept my face to the window, and he made no effort to divert my attention. When we came to a street whose thick rows of trees shut out the moonlight my eager soul longed to leap out into the dark and demand of him his heart, soul, life, for *me*.

I struck him lightly on the shoulder; he seized my hand.

"Oh, I know you, Margaret; you are mine!"

"We are at the hotel."

He sent the carriage back, and said that he would leave me at my aunt's door. He wished that he could see her then. Was it magic that made her open the door before I reached it?

"Have you come on legal business?" she asked him.

"You have divined what I come for."

"Step in, step in; it's very late. I should have been in bed but for neuralgia. Did Mr. Uxbridge come home with you, Margaret?"

"Yes, in Mrs. Bliss's carriage; I wished to come before she was ready to leave."

"Well, Mr. Uxbridge is old enough for your protector, certainly."

"I *am* forty, ma'am."

"Do you want Margaret?"

"I do."

"You know exactly how much is involved in your client's suit?"

"Exactly."

"You know also that his claim is an unjust one."

"Do I?"

"I shall not be poor if I lose; if I gain, Margaret will be rich."

"'Margaret will be rich!'" he repeated, absently.

"What! have you changed your mind respecting the orphans, aunt?"

"She has, and is—nothing," she went on, not heeding my remark. "Her father married below his station; when he died his wife fell back to her place—for he spent his fortune—and there she and Margaret must remain, unless Lemorne is defeated."

"Aunt, for your succinct biography of my position many thanks."

"Sixty thousand dollars," she continued. "Van Horn tells me that, as yet, the firm of Uxbridge Brothers have only an income—no capital."

"It is true," he answered, musingly.

The clock on the mantle struck two.

"A thousand dollars for every year of my life," she said. "You and I, Uxbridge, know the value and beauty of money."

"Yes, there is beauty in money, and"—looking at me—"beauty without it."

"The striking of the clock," I soliloquized, "proves that this scene is not a phantasm."

"Margaret is fatigued," he said, rising. "May I come to-morrow?"

"It is my part only," replied Aunt Eliza, "to see that she is, or is not, Cinderella."

"If you have ever thought of me, aunt, as an individual, you must have seen that I am not averse to ashes."

He held my hand a moment, and then kissed me with a kiss of appropriation.

"He is in love with you," she said, after he had gone. "I think I know him. He has found beauty ignorant of itself; he will teach you to develop it."

The next morning Mr. Uxbridge had an interview with Aunt Eliza before he saw me.

When we were alone I asked him how her eccentricities affected him; he could not but consider her violent, prejudiced, warped, and whimsical. I told him that I had been taught to accept all that she did on this basis. Would this explain to him my silence in regard to her?

"Can you endure to live with her in Bond Street for the present, or would you rather return to Waterbury?"

"She desires my company while she is in Newport only. I have never been with her so long before."

"I understand her. Law is a game, in her estimation, in which cheating can as easily be carried on as at cards."

"Her soul is in this case."

"Her soul is not too large for it. Will you ride this afternoon?"

I promised, of course. From that time till he left Newport we saw each other every day, and though I found little opportunity to express my own peculiar feelings, he comprehended many of my wishes, and all my tastes. I grew fond of him hourly. Had I not reason? Never was friend so considerate, never was lover more devoted.

When he had been gone a few days, Aunt Eliza declared that she was ready to depart from Newport. The rose-colored days were ended! In two days we were on the Sound, coach, horses, servants, and ourselves.

It was the 1st of September when we arrived in Bond Street. A week from that date Samuel Uxbridge, the senior partner of Uxbridge Brothers, went to Europe with his family, and I went to Waterbury, accompanied by Mr. Uxbridge. He consulted mother in regard to our marriage, and appointed it in November. In October Aunt Eliza sent for me to come back to Bond Street and spend a week. She had some fine marking to do, she wrote. While there I noticed a restlessness in her which I had never before observed, and conferred with Mrs. Roll on the matter. "She do be awake nights a deal, and that's the reason," Mrs. Roll said. Her manner was the same in other respects. She said she would not give me any thing for my wedding outfit, but she paid my fare from Waterbury and back.

She could not spare me to go out, she told Mr. Uxbridge, and in consequence I saw little of him while there.

In November we were married. Aunt Eliza was not at the wedding, which was a quiet one. Mr. Uxbridge desired me to remain in Waterbury till spring. He would not decide about taking a house in New York till then; by that time his brother might return, and if possible we would go to Europe for a few months. I acquiesced in all his plans. Indeed I was not consulted; but I was happy—happy in him, and happy in every thing.

The winter passed in waiting for him to come to Waterbury every Saturday; and in the enjoyment of the two days he passed with me. In March Aunt Eliza wrote me that Lemorne was beaten! Van Horn had taken up the whole contents of his snuff-box in her house the evening before in amazement at the turn things had taken.

That night I dreamed of the scene in the hotel at Newport. I heard Aunt Eliza saying, "If I gain, Margaret will be rich." And I heard also the clock strike two. As it struck I said, *"My husband is a scoundrel,"* and woke with a start.

"Boots"

For the month of July my family were absent, at a distant watering-place, by way of contrast to their ordinary life on our secluded estate. Having lately returned from a pleasure-trip myself, home appeared so attractive, that I decided to remain in close quarters with Solitude. The charms which sages had seen in her face might be discovered in so fit a place—no vista from it opened into any haunt of man; the stage-road, the railroad, the post-office, and the shire-town, were from one to ten miles away. The neighboring farms and estates were of great extent, and the houses upon them concealed by woods, gradual stretches of slopes, and valleys. Our own two hundred acres were circled by a deep fringe of lofty trees. The country outside was generally as silent as a cemetery; the sounds breaking the stillness were the *crick-crack* of a mowing-machine, a far-off dinner-horn, and the cries of the crows. To see any thing beyond the woods, I must go, like sister Ann, into the tower, from which could be discovered the curling smoke rising from hidden chimneys, specks of cattle grazing invisible grass, and a dim blue ring, at the north, which denoted that somewhere a river rolled and a town stood.

I had been making merry among a fashionable set in the city. Built bouquets, high-flavored dinners, Etruscan jewelry, five-feet high beaux, boned turkey, and an eternal din of music in the street, drawing-room, stage, and hall, attuned me to my present situation. Extremes meet. The transition-point is the effective one. I appreciated the present by remembering the past. The great house was empty; nobody in any room to be "introduced." My bruised panniers, peplums, and paletots, were hung on the closet-wall for monuments. For a day or two, what a possession mere time seemed to be! The weather was idyllic; out-of-doors was as secure as in-doors. The mornings were dewy, sweet-scented, wrapped in tender mist, or red with a dry sun, and fixed in shadows. The evenings were calm and clear; bright with a swelling moon, or soft with fleecy clouds and the high-steering stars. If the hours grew long between them, I looked at the backs of the books along their shelves, and studied my rather vacant face in the several mirrors, or knocked the slugs and bugs from the flowers on the lawn and terrace. A regular piece of industry was impossible; there was no nucleus to hitch it to. Hermits never accomplished any thing; neither have those who contemplate Nature habitually.

Thanks be to youth, I slept soundly, and ate well, though Becky, the housekeeper, constantly predicted a failure of appetite, because I was alone, and bad dreams, because I did not go to bed early. Owing to my hermit-like position, I suppose, I began to stare a great deal at the clouds, trees, and grass, and for this purpose occupied the veranda, the terrace-steps, and the benches under the walnut group and the chestnut group. A pleasant numbness took possession of me. It was all the same whether I was about to melt into a cloud or to become steadfast in a tree, so long as I was somehow ebbing into the great harmony of Nature.

"My goodness," cried Becky, "you are getting the dumps. Moping under the trees so—I wish the folks would come home, or I wish your friend Miss Bell would make the visit she has promised you so long."

"Becky, I am now a dryad;[1] don't disturb me. Pan is not dead."[2]

"Miss Anna, you are crazy. If me and Hannah talked so in the kitchen, what would you say? *Pan*; well, I must go to my milk-pan."

So long as I heard no clatter, I cared not where she went; but the house was still, no one besides myself went into the rooms which opened on the terrace and lawn. The gardener swept the veranda, watered the flowers, and removed the rubbish, before I was down-stairs in the morning. He, with the farmer, occupied tenements, which were situated at the end of the place, beyond a lane in the woods. Jimmy, the ostler, slept in the stable; consequently the only persons in the house were Becky, Hannah, and myself. By sunset, we three were the only creatures astir; the work-people were away, and Jimmy, having somnolent traits, and being at present left to his own devices, was generally asleep. Hannah's evening amusement was darning stockings in the garret, and Becky's that of dozing on the settee in the best kitchen, till nine o'clock, when she went to bed, stupid as an owl, by candle-light.

In the early twilight of one of those long days, after the funeral of the world apparently, so lifeless was the landscape, I was sitting on the top step of the terrace, with my fan, and very little speculation either in my eyes or mind. Below the terrace were gravel-walks, crossing the upper part of the lawn, and winding round flower-beds and clumps of shrubs. At the angles of the straight paths stood cedar-trees, whose thick, feathery foliage, as everybody knows, grows to within a foot of the ground. The lawn beyond was bordered, on each side, by a hedge-row of wild vines, hawthorn-bushes, low sumacs, and tall walnuts, and its immense space dotted with oaks and cedars. The ground gradually sinking, and my being positioned at the widest part of the lawn, I commanded a view which included any sudden appearance of beast, bird, or man, within the area. I should have said so, at any rate, if I had been asked any question concerning stragglers or ghosts. The clouds were beautiful. I watched the slow passage of their silver masses, stained by the sunset, till cramped in the neck; I dropped my eyes, and idly scanned the deep shades along the gravel-walk to the right, but my vision was violently arrested. Under the boughs of the cedar, at the first turn, not more than forty feet from me, I saw a man's heels and the lower part of his legs. He wore boots, and light-gray trousers; one foot was before the other; he was in the act of stepping away! My heart jumped, and stood still. I helplessly turned my head toward the house; it had a merciless air—all the upper shutters were closed, and all the lower open windows, of course, vacant. When I looked at the cedar again, the man had vanished. An invading army could not have pervaded the place as this invisible man did for the next half hour. I remained on the step, but saw nothing; no bush nor bough moved or rustled; the swallows dipped and rose above the lawn, making ready for dim night, and the bits of brown birds hopped over the walks, as if no alien had appeared among them. Whether the mysterious creature had wormed himself beyond our lines, with his curiosity satisfied, or whether he was lying in wait in the hedge-row, I could not decide; that he was a stranger in the country, I knew—the fashion of his boots and trousers was a city fashion. How could a city burglar know that our house was at present defenceless, or that we did not own a safe for the silver? I pondered on the matter, till it grew quite dark, and my mind got confused like the forms before me. Could my eyes have deceived me? For the past two weeks I had been a mild-eyed lotus-eater.[3] "Falling asleep in a half dream,"[4] I had watched the "cloud towers by ghastly masons wrought,"[5] and, descending to the earth, had fancied myself an eremite in the desert. Possibly, as was the way with the latter, I had become the victim of an hallucination. Some of the saints had visions of girls dancing in the most charming style of the ballet; and I had had a vision of a handsome pair of boots!

Going into the house I felt "creepy," and was ready to scream, if any thing should touch me. I concluded not to tell Becky; she would howl at all events, and not only insist upon sitting up all night herself, but would keep Hannah and myself awake. I opened the kitchen-door; the room was pitch-dark, but, hearing a faint snore, I called, "Becky!"

"What's wanted?" she answered; "I ain't here."

I asked her where Rover, our watch-dog was; whether at the stable, with Jimmy, sharing his slumbers, or on the alert outside.

"Oh, it's you, is it? If you will believe me, Rover has not been on the premises for the past three nights. Jimmy says so. He is after game of some sort; he does have such spells. Rover is good for nothing—lazy, worthless rascal."

"What if thieves should visit us, Becky?"

"We only have thieves in water-melon time, or peach-time. The niggers come up from Troy then, and spread themselves. I have always lived in the neighborhood, and I never heard of any thing besides being stolen, unless it was chickens; in the fall of the year it is hard to resist fowl. So you need not be concerned about Rover, nor thieves, and I am going to bed; did you slip the window-bolts?"

With a forced courage I hastened back, and fastened the windows down. I saw Becky and her candle disappear with regret; I would gladly have begged her to pass the night in my room, but I denied myself that pleasure, and retired alone.

Rover's deep bay down in the woods startled me about midnight; he was coursing, for his yelp now sounded near, now far. He was a powerful dog. I had seen him spring upon a strange boy, in our yard, and throw him with ease; but I doubted whether he would attack a man, especially a well-dressed man; he might also be intimidated by a cane, or weapon of any sort, and it was not likely that my friend of the boots was unprepared for defence. If this intruder knew any thing, he must know that all country-seats have watch-dogs, as well as the farms. If he happened, at that moment, to be passing Mr. Welford's, the adjoining property, he would encounter four, so savage, that by day they were chained in their kennels behind the wall. There was a hole in the wall before each kennel, and many a time, when riding by, I had shuddered at the sight of four red-tongued animals tugging at their chains in the vain hope of getting at me.

Rover was now silent, but I could not sleep; *Boots*, if I might so familiarly name that dread segment of a man, had murdered sleep. Not only that, but he had destroyed my loved *Solitude*.

Freedom shrieked when a celebrated Polish hero fell, and, although I did not hear this sister-spirit, I have no doubt but that she, shrieking, fled.[6] Henceforth it would be impossible for me to feel alone, though I might, and must appear so.

My window being open, I heard all the sounds of the night: little owls hooted at each other from the cedars, attracted by my dim night-lamp;

moths struck their downy bodies against the window-panes; the negro-minstrels of the sod, the multitudinous crickets, sent out their monotonous lay; all the creeping, nocturnal rodents were abroad, snapping, rustling, squeaking creatures of the woods. Among all these peaceful noises I soon heard another, stealthy but distinct; it was a step on the zinc roof of the bay-window on my side of the house. I rose from the bed in terror, with the cry at my lips of, "Becky, pistol; Jimmy, club; Rover—" but the cry would not utter itself; I was dumb. A spot of moonlight glimmered through the inside shutter, like an oblong, Chinese sort of eye, and I gazed at it with the mild imbecility which we feel when screwed up in a dentist's chair, and behold the monster dentist selecting, with infernal deliberation, steel instruments of torture. *I* expected the entrance of *Boots* by that light of the silver moon. A minute or two glided by, and he did not come; but Rover arrived. With a suppressed groan, he flung himself against the wall with a thud, which must have bruised him; then he skurried round the window with a mad howl, which ended in his being throttled. The dead silence which followed made me impatient, and diminished my terror; I crept to the window and peeped through the blinds. I saw neither man nor dog anywhere; within the reach of vision were the garden, a wide meadow, and an open summer-house; they were quiet and shadowless; the full moon, directly overhead, revealed every object.

"Well," said Becky, at breakfast, "we heard Rover fast enough last night, making up for lost time by pretending to be on the watch; he is lazy enough this morning; I can't coax nor drive him from the porch. Sakes, didn't you hear him?"

I replied that I had either heard him or dreamed so. I went out to see Rover a few minutes afterward and examined him; his collar was off, but there was no wound upon him. He slavered uncommonly, and beat his tail on the stone floor with violence; but he would not follow me. When hungry, he cried and snarled so, that Jimmy had to take food to him. How tedious and perplexing was the day that followed! At intervals, I thought more catastrophe would be preferable; how dull it would be to make a pause, and not shine in a developed drama! Yet this vague, hidden threatening was terrible—especially after sundown. I might, to be sure, set a watch, rouse all the neighbors, and turn things upside down generally; but I was averse to fuss always. Struck by a happy inspiration, I ordered Jimmy to saddle white Surrey, and ride post-haste to Chellon, fifteen miles distant, where my friend Laura Bell lived, with a note, containing an urgent invitation to come to me. He rode away, returning late in the evening, and brought the welcome news that she would be at the station nearest us the next morning. Becky declared herself thankful at the tidings; I was moping, she perceived, and I need not contradict it. I waited till she had gone up-stairs, and then I called Rover; he understood me, and came into the house quietly, swung himself along like a bear, and dropped on the floor by my door, giving a long, low sigh of relief, as if he had found the spot he had been waiting for all day. But no booted ghost troubled us that night.

When Laura arrived, beaming and gleaming, a green-and-gold bird in her hat, and a large black cross on her breast, I thought she looked as a phantom-banisher should, and greeted her warmly.

"I am here with my Saratoga trunk, you see," she said. "I understood, from the urgency of your invitation, that you were bored to death. You are tired of being alone."

"But I am not alone," I answered, cautiously.

"A cat and a parrot, like Robinson Crusoe—have you?"

"Not those; but there may be a man Friday on the premises."[7]

"What ails you, Anna? Something is on your mind."

"No; it is in the woods, or in the air." She made me explain the matter, and refused to believe it; my imagination had misled me, she insisted. What was Becky's opinion?

"Becky knows nothing of the business, Laura."

"You have gone deranged; that's the long and short of it."

I finally brought her round to my way of thinking, in regard to disturbing Becky and Hannah, but could not convince her of the reality of *Boots*. She declared it was a pleasant excitement, and wished it was a fact. Considering the alarm and anxiety I had experienced, I felt vexed with Laura for laughing at me. I had generally shown the most nerve and self-possession of the two; in fact, she had the character of being flighty, romantic, fitful, easily influenced. Being bright and handsome, these traits did not go for much, however; she was popular in spite of them. We had been intimate all our lives—were forever exchanging visits, going on excursions, during which we disputed and remained devotedly attached. She was rather famous for flirtation, and she believed that she had had one or two heart-rending affairs. I, who was still ignorant of such matters, was sure of my ability to advise and direct her. I did not intend that she should fulfil the prediction of some of her friends, that she would most likely throw herself away on some skilful adventurer. She was, by-the-way, somewhat alone in the world, and possessed a comfortable fortune. I dropped the subject, so interesting to me, and led the conversation into a channel interesting to her—the history of the late past. She had been having a lively time, she said; and, of all the times she had ever, ever had, was the week she had passed at the Garnet House, with her cousin, Mrs. Hall. There she had met with—but no matter about that—and she pursed her mouth up, as it were about to burst with an important secret.

"Flirtation number sixty, Laura?"

"There, miss and friend, I met Fate."

"Light or dark hair?"

"My cousin, attempting your *rôle*, separated us."

"Who was the other half of *us*?"

"John Egbert."

"I do not know the name."

"There may be a gentleman, within the limits of the United States, whose pedigree you do not know."

"Who introduced him? Was he alone? What is his profession?"

"He led the German at the hops we had at the Garnet; he keeps a yacht, and his yachting friends were with him."[8]

"I see, a fast man, and a rich one—patent medicine, or machines."

"He is fast; and, of my own accord, I sent him to the right about. He is off with his yacht, taking a little run, as he calls it, and very likely is at the north pole. Wherever he went, he said, he should never give me up. He is my Fate, whether we meet again or not. You need not exercise your wits upon me."

"You shall have a month to forget him in, Laura."

She shook her pretty head, and gave several patronizing sighs.

"Anna, I think I may regain my composure here. How delightful it is! You seem farther from the world than ever. How thick the hedgerow is! and the ivy on the bay-window!—it has grown enormously."

It was at my tongue's end to say, as I glanced at the tough network of the ivy-stalks, "Yes, *Boots* made a ladder of the ivy-bush, when he ascended the roof of the window;" but I did not speak; I would bide my time. The day went by as usual, and we enjoyed it, as Becky said, in "one continual stream of gab." She was good enough to give us tea under the walnuts; the cup which cheers was more cheery in the open air, with our prospect of lawn, grove, and meadow. Hannah had clattered off with the tea things; I was rolling up my fancy-work, for it was now past seven, when I happened to glance toward Laura; her face was crimson, and her dilated eyes were fixed on the southern corner, at the bottom of the lawn, where the Virginia pines were a thick, dark grove, avoided at this season, on account of a prolific poison-vine there. Trying to hide her dismay, she cried:

"Upon my word, Anna, your nonsense is infecting me; a yellow bird, or white-black bird, has been flying among those pines, and for an instant I fancied somebody was waving a handkerchief at me."

"It was not a bird, but some of the men, of course, digging potatoes, or cutting wheat."

My attempt at irony was received with contempt.

"Let us go back to the veranda," she said; "it grows damp here."

"That was just the effect upon me. I felt a cold perspiration all over me."

"What a dreadful ninny you have grown to be! I am ashamed of you."

In spite of her words, I saw she was frightened, and then my self-possession returned. I concluded to feel as much at home with phantoms as Leonora did, when she answered the "ting-a-ling" of the doorbell, and rode away with her lover's ghost.[9] I did my best to entertain Laura; my mode, hitherto most successful, was drawing her on to relate her own feelings and affairs. Now, she continually interrupted herself to ask questions. Did Jimmy sleep in the house? Was Rover on the watch as usual? Did pack-pedlers ever come into our road, or were we ever troubled with city tramps? I assured and consoled her, mentioned a fabulous pistol, and a mythical Revolutionary sword which Lord Cornwallis did not present my great-grandfather with.[10] I also invented anecdotes concerning the prowess of Rover—the said cowed animal was at that moment waiting to be invited into the shelter of the house. As for calling help, it was an easy thing to do. We had an immense dinner-horn, like that blown at Jericho when the walls fell down; at the sound of ours, the farmer and his laborers would rush to the rescue. But she knew why I had not made any disturbance.

"I should like to 'take a horn' of that sort, Anna," she said, faintly; "I believe I am horridly nervous. I'll go to bed, dear; leave your door open."

With her calling to me repeatedly whether I heard any noise, and Rover's whimpering dreams at the foot of the stairs, I had a night of it. I was fain to anathematize the stupid absence of my family, and the more stupid idea which had led me to stay at home in solitude. The sunlight brought better things. We had a perfect, enticing day; in the afternoon I drove Laura up the country in an open wagon. I chose sequestered, shady roads, crossed by brooks, and bordered with ferns. Laura was loud in admiration; but, in the particularly dark and dense places, I noticed that she looked sharply to the right and left. I made no comments. At last she burst out with:

"Who is he, and what does he want?"

"You believe in *Boots*, then?"

"I do. A handkerchief was waved at us yesterday in the pines."

"What *is* to be done?"

"Run away with me to Chellon."

"Desert a post in danger? Nevare! I might send over to Mr. Welford; but, if nothing should turn up afterward, I should not hear the last of it, either from him or our folks. I cannot bear ridicule; I had rather live in a perpetual terror."

"I never heard so strange a thing. He did not kill Rover; he has not entered the house. He is waiting for something. He may be deranged—gone mad for love of you. *I* know how you treat your admirers, miss. The avenger is on your track."

"He is a foolish, miserable, melodramatic villain. I'll have all the people on the place up and scouring it."

I turned the horse homeward, and drove rapidly, not speaking to Laura on the way; she was too absurd. As we turned into our drive which was long and curving, Laura gave a little shriek which made me jump.

"Do you see something white fastened to the oak-tree just ahead?" she asked.

"It is a tax-notice."

"No. I'll hold the reins, if you will get it."

"You want to make a cat's-paw of me. I am not afraid."

I sprang from the wagon, tore the paper from the tree-trunk, and jumped back. The paper was violet-colored letter-envelope; a man's hand was neatly drawn upon it, the thumb and forefinger of which held up a ring. Was Laura's theory the right one, after all? I looked at her in consternation; her countenance was much changed; she was pale, and in her eyes was a queer light; she held the envelope tightly, as if it were a treasure. I was provoked enough to shake her.

"What is the matter, Laura?"

"'Tis a French paper—that—I know it—I—I do. O Anna! Now it is all clear to me. Drive on—Jimmy's at the porch."

She threw herself upon a seat in the porch, and tossed her hat off.

"Tell me this instant, Laura, the cause of your extraordinary behavior."

"*Boots* is Egbert—that's all," she gasped. "He knew that I intended to visit you about this time. He swore he would carry me off, and I said you would hide me. He expects me to evade my cousin, and marry him."

"Did he expect the ceremony to take place on the roof of our bay-window?" I asked, severely.

"What shall I do? I wish you would not scold."

"On the whole, I approve of the match. But you must go to Chellon to-morrow morning. Perhaps Mr. Egbert's yacht is in the woods, somewhere; *he* may take you."

She laughed hysterically. I went up-stairs in a heat. That I should have been scared out of my wits by a foolish lover of Laura Bell's was too much. I stayed in my room all the evening. Afterward, I knew that Mr. Egbert met Laura on the veranda. Within a month, he wrote me a letter of explanation and apology, and returned Rover's collar to me.

A Dead-Lock, and its Key

"A note for *you*, ma'am. No answer."

I was resting in my own room, after riding—it was six o'clock, too early to dress for dinner, too late to dress twice after taking off my habit—sleeping over a book, and comfortable in my white dressing-gown. I was bored by the interruption. The note was no more than this:

> "*Dear Saleen*,—I must stay where I am, and you must go by yourself to the Lesters'—you won't mind. I saw Jack, and he said there was no party, as it would be troublesome, with the wedding to-morrow, and the dining-room is given up to the breakfast. I've sent back the brougham.[1] Thine,
>
> *Fred.*"

Fred is my brother, and was invited, like myself, to dine quietly with these Lesters, whose pretty daughter was to be married next day to a friend of ours—specially Fred's and mine—Sir John March, commonly called "Jack."

"What keeps Fred?" was my passing thought; then I read a little longer, dressed, and drove to Portman Square.[2] As I turned the corner, I saw visible preparations and signs of the morrow's wedding at the Lesters' door. A cart with flowers was unloading; an awning was being put up over the balcony and hall door; men in white aprons came and went. As the brougham drew up I could see through the open door the bustle and stir within. At home in the house, I opened the dining-room door to see what progress was being made with the tables. Several maid servants and some of the confectioner's men were arranging the ornaments and flowers; the cake, with its conventional erection, stood conspicuous. My friends' maid was putting moss into the flower-baskets, and decorating the high dishes containing the more durable part of the feast. "Well, Barker," I was beginning, when I caught the woman's eyes. She was doing her work with a strange gravity, and her face was full of horror and pain. When she saw me, she let fall the flowers in her hand.

"Oh, ma'am! oh, Miss Sarah! you've come."

"Of course I've come," I answered, "What is the matter?"

"You haven't seen them, ma'am, have you?"

"Seen who?—the ladies? No; I came straight in here to look at the tables. Is there any thing wrong? I suppose we're to dine in the library for to-day? How nice it all looks!"

"Nice! Oh, ma'am, it's a mockery; it's awful! To see it all, and to go on as if—as if—O Lord!" and the woman sat down, and rocked herself to and fro, with the tears running down her face.

I was thoroughly alarmed now. "Barker, *is* there any thing wrong? Is any one ill, or dead? Don't frighten me like this. I'll go and see them if you won't speak out;" and I went to the door. I just saw that Barker had descended to the floor, and that her head was on the chair, which she clutched, sobbing aloud.

I met the butler and another man crossing the hall, both with scared, solemn faces, and went on to the morning-room, on the same floor. There all looked much as usual. The pride of the house and of my friends' rather valuable collection of antiquities stood facing the door—a huge cabinet, with massive clamped doors, and richly cut brass-work—*ciselé* as only genuine brass-work of old time can be; curiously inlaid wood-work; marvelous locks, which no one but its owner understood, and no one else dared meddle with. It was a very old friend, the great *armoire*; playing with the children of the house in my childhood, I knew it, inside and outside, by heart. A mystery and a wonder then—an interest later—always a thing to admire and wonder at even now.

It had three doors. The centre one, about four feet wide, and certainly six inches thick, shut in another, which again inclosed, with a space of about eight inches of waste room, a set of six drawers, of different sizes, and a sort of cupboard above them. We used to stand as little children between the drawers and the inner door, and wonder, supposing we were shut in, whether we could breathe long in that narrow inclosure, or be heard by any one without, supposing—awful thought!—we were forgotten, or the outer door were shut. I remember thinking of it in bed at night, as nervous children will think of such things, till I was cold with horror. Both these two doors shut with a catch which was not a lock; but we children were forbidden ever to open or shut them, except when Mr. Lester was present. It was doubtful if any one else knew how to open them, for no one ever tried. The two side doors opened with curious keys, which stood in the locks, chained to the armoire. They were valuables in themselves. The great key of the centre door, worth a hundred pounds or more, was considered too sacred for common eyes, and lay in a velvet-lined case in Mr. Lester's own keeping—brought out only occasionally to show to those who could appreciate such things.

It stood there in the summer twilight, looming darkly in the quiet room, darker than the rest of the house, as back-rooms in London often are. Chilly, it seemed to me, in my thin white dress, coming from the hall full of sunset light. Turning to leave the room, I saw a man lying prone on his face upon the sofa; so still and so straight and so strange in his attitude that I could only stare for a minute, and wonder whether he was asleep or dead. His hands were over his ears, grasping his hair, as if in pain; and I noticed the soles of his boots turned quite up, as one notices trifles in the midst of alarm or bewilderment. The nails in his boots showed he was not dressed for dinner. His hat was lying on the floor on its side. His face I could not see; but I knew it was Jack March, and I touched his arm in wonder.

"Jack, are you awake? Are you asleep? What is it?" I asked, with growing alarm. Was I to find something strange in every room I entered in this house? "Jack!" I said, again. He turned, and I saw his wild, haggard face, that looked at me with vague eyes that seemed not to see; and then he put his head down with a moan, and covered his ears once more, as if to shut out sight and sound. The room felt darker and chillier for this silent figure; and the gaunt old armoire seemed bigger and more oppressive. I ran out of the room in a sort of panic. Up stairs, the drawing-room door stood open. The glow of the sunset was over the room, bright with flowers and pictures; and the open windows showed the balconies lined with red cloth, and ready for the guests next day. Silence here, and silent figures, two of them—one crouched upon the floor, with arms outstretched upon a sofa; another lying half across an ottoman—the bride's mother and sister. As I came in and spoke, now fairly bewildered and frightened, Mrs. Lester rose up with a despairing wail.

"Saleen, Saleen!" She stood shaking and crying out my name.

"Dear Mrs. Lester," I said, taking the poor woman's cold hands, "come and sit down and tell me what has happened. Kate!" I called to the girl on the floor, "come and give me that cushion." She came mechanically, and helped her mother to the arm chair. "Now tell me, if you can—" But Mrs. Lester's head had fallen back upon the cushion, and she had fainted. The girl roused herself.

"No wonder," she said; "she has eaten nothing all day; and then all this. It's too awful, Saleen. I shall go mad if I think; and papa has never come back!"

"Where is your father?"

"I don't know. We sent down to the club and to the House; they can't find him. And we've searched his room, and it's not there. It's nowhere. And Jack is nearly wild; and we daren't break it open."

"It! What, child? Can't you say what you are talking about? *I* shall go mad next. *What* can't you find? And what ails you all?"

"Saleen, it's Mary. Mary is in there, and the key is gone, and papa is away; and she's dying there—suffocating;" and the girl flung herself on the floor with wild sobs and tears. Mrs. Lester lay forgotten in her swoon; Kate rolled in unavailing misery on the carpet. I fled down stairs. The servants were as busy as ever. I knew it all now.

"Good God!" I said to the butler, who was carrying in a tray of glass, "are you going on with all this useless folly, and that girl dying in the next room? Is no one going to try to save her?"

Davis stood still and looked at me pityingly; he shook his head sadly, and went on.

I rushed into the street: a policeman was standing near the carts. "Come here," I said. "You"—to another man—"go and get a blacksmith. Run for your life! Tell them to bring tools to open locks and unscrew every thing. Run!—And you get a hatchet; get any thing, come and break open the great cabinet." I gasped to the servants, who came out to see what it all meant: "Don't lose a moment. Great Heaven! the time that has been lost already!" They obeyed me, dispersing hither and thither. It seemed hours before the men came back with tools. "Try the hinges first. Are there screws?" There was that chance; and they worked at them, removing several heavy curious nails and screws, but seeming no nearer the object; the door was fast and firm. "Oh, break it down!" I screamed at last; "break it with the hatchet. What does any thing matter, but her life—her life!"

"Her life!" said some strange voice close to me, and there stood Jack March, swaying like a drunken man, with scared eyes and wild hair. Was his reason gone or going?

"Don't!" he shouted to a workman who was lifting the hatchet to break in the door. "Not up there. Her head." And then he stooped his ear to the key-hole, listened intently a minute, raised his hand as if to demand silence, and, the intelligence fading out of his face, he rose with a discordant laugh and walked away. "Bah!" he said: "her life against Lester's cabinet—her life against a key." We did not even look round to see where he went stumbling through the hall, where he fell in a fit upon the floor.

Fearing to injure that imprisoned figure—living or dead, who could tell?—we left the door, and proceeded to break into the middle compartment from the wings. The grand old workmanship resisted: there seemed no weak point, no crevice, no possibility of breaking into the huge thing without fear of harm to *that* which it held locked and fast, within a few inches of our light and air and living life, done to death by a bit of clever machinery, the work of a dead hand. I would not think of beautiful Mary Lester as she might be, must be, if another hour went by. All this time no questions were asked. I never knew till afterward how it had all happened; how her father, only an hour or so earlier, exhibiting his wonderful cabinet to a connoisseur in such matters, had gone up stairs with his friend to show the key he prized so much, leaving the cabinet door open, intending to return; how Mary and the children, a younger brother and sister, had come in; and how the unusual sight of the open door had attracted them; how she looked in, and told the little ones she had not stood inside it "so" since she was as little as they were, and, laughing, tried to stand in the old place. "I am not too big even now, am I?" she said; and the children ran to see, and pushing the doors against her, the spring caught, and shut her in with death and suffocation; while they went shouting to the others that sister Mary was "in there shut up," and they "couldn't let her out."

No, they could not let her out. Mr. Lester and his friend had gone off with the key, to show it to some one who had doubted its date—so it appeared from one of the boys who now came in. He had heard them talking on the stairs as they went out.

"He said: 'Jarvis knows nothing about it: he has never seen it,'" said the boy, sobbing. "I heard him. I know he said Jarvis."

"That will be Colonel Jarvis, in Charles Street, ma'am," said Davis. "Maybe, if we sent there—"

There were voices outside, and Barker looked in with a white face of horror.

"It's master coming in," she said, in a sort of whisper.

We all stood back. Who would tell him? Who was to say, Your girl is behind that immovable door?

But the boy, frightened enough at his father at other times, went up to him, trying to speak quietly. "The key, Sir. Quick, for God's sake!"

"Key! What—what's all this? Good God! Sir"—seizing a servant by the collar, and flinging him to one side, like a cat—"do you know what you're doing, meddling with that cabinet? Why, it's worth thousands! God bless me! what does all this mean?" He was purple with anger.

"Don't stand staring. Sarah Heriot," he thundered, "you are not a fool. Be good enough to explain this—this—"

I went up to him sick with horror. "The key is wanted," I managed to say. "There is some one inside—dying."

"Some one—dying—in there! Who? What! Who is it, girl?" He shook me by the shoulder till I winced with pain.

"Oh, the key, the key! Never mind any thing else, Sir. Only open it quick, and lose no more time."

He looked sharply round. Mrs. Lester and Kate were standing at the door, with their terrified, miserable faces. He took in the rest of us with a glance.

"Where's Mary?," he said, suddenly. No one spoke. "Why the devil don't you answer me? *Who* is shut in there? How could any one be there? Trash!" But his face was growing ashy gray, and his lips whitened as he spoke. "Ah, my God! I never shut the door! It is not *Mary*, not my girl that's—" He pointed with a shaking hand to the heavy door. "And—I haven't the—key!"

He made one rush into the street. The servants standing about were swept right and left, as he tore past them down Orchard Street into Oxford Street. They could see the hatless, fleeing figure disappearing in the distance.

Mrs. Lester came into the hall. The doctor and others were busy about poor Jack March, who lay on the dining-room sofa, with closed eyes, happily unconscious. The timid mistress of the house stood by the staircase, her face, her voice, her whole appearance changed and aged in the last hour.

"He has gone for the key; he can't be back," she said, speaking like a woman in a dream, "not for half an hour." She looked round stupidly and smiled. "He will kill me, you know; but the cabinet *shall* be broken open—broken to pieces! Never mind. Fancy *waiting* for the key!" she laughed. "Break it down, I tell you! *I* give the order. Do you hear me?"

Two workmen came from the side door, where a fresh and useless attempt had been made to remove the panel without injury to the front or to the imprisoned girl.

"We might loosen the wood-work, and strike it out, mum; and go on taking out screws, same time."

"Do it."

Sharp blows upon chisels now, and several screws removed from lock and hinges.

"Strike at the hinges with the hatchet," came Mrs. Lester's altered voice, hard and wiry, usually so low and hesitating. "Cut them through; it *can* be done—it *shall*."

They struck with a will; the hatchet edge was pressed to the weakest part, and heavy blows from a mallet upon that. The hatchet edge was turned, and a dint made; some of the work injured and broken—but no more.

"Cut through the panel," suggested Kate. "Surely wood can be broken."

"It's all lined with iron, mum," said Davis; "it is as good as a safe. But we might try."

Three telling blows. The room suddenly darker, a chill sough of wind from the window, and the door swung to with a bang. Every one looked round. A growl of distant thunder, and a faint flash of lightning accounted for it next moment. More blows, and a long ominous roll, and the lightning playing across the great armoire; then an avalanche of rain and hail—all strange and incongruous on this fine evening. The room was nearly dark. One of the men spoke: "Is there a step-ladder in the house?" It was brought. "I'll try the top, with your leave, ma'am. Ah, if I had a light now!" He was given a taper from the library table. "Bill"—to his companion—"look here; hold the light, and keep a hand on the side." He lifted the hatchet, and gave a swinging blow— another—an awful clap of thunder, and the next flash showed every white face to the other. Quick steps in the hall, and the door flung wide; a wild, wet figure threw the key among us, and fell in a heap on the floor. With a wrench, the man on the ladder tore off the upper moulding, and half the roof of the armoire. Mrs. Lester took up the key, fumbled with the lock, let it fall with a shriek. Barker caught it from her, put it in, and turned it. "Open it," she whispered to one of the men; "*I* can't." She turned away, sick with dread. It was opened, showing nothing but the terrible inner door, whose spring was only known to the master, lying senseless on the floor.

"Take off more here," one of the men shouted; "it will give air till the door's got open."

Good thought. They worked savagely.

Mrs. Lester was on her knees by her husband. "Oh, get brandy! Get him to speak! He could tell us how!" They did what they could. "William! Oh, speak to me! How can I open it, the spring—the inner door?"

The white lips moved, and the head with its dripping hair rolled to one side, but no sound came. The men worked wildly now. All thought of sparing the beautiful front and brass-work was forgotten. They tore and hammered at the inner door, whose smooth polished surface presented no crevice or join where to strike first—where to insert a chisel or direct a blow. As they worked, consciousness returned to Mr. Lester; he half sat up, supporting himself against the door; but no words came, though his lips moved, and his eyes looked with intense eagerness at the destruction of his precious armoire. He lifted his hand and looked mutely at his wife. She put her head down to his lips. "What is it? What shall I tell them to do?" He beat his hand upon the floor.

Kate sprung forward: "I know! I know! Strike on the floor, at the foot of the inner door! Oh, I remember, it was there!"

Davis felt with his hand all along the polished surface of the lowest shelf. "Here, press here; give me a hammer." He felt a slight rise, and struck gradually all about the spot Kate showed him. A deafening clap of thunder, and a flash, blinding us for the moment, and we all crowded close, and then came a creak, drowned in the awful thunder.

"It's open," said one of the men.

Kate slid to the floor, twisting my dress about her head.

Davis turned from the door. "I daren't look," he said. "Do you," to the carpenter's man. "Open it gently."

Barker stretched forward, turned round, tried to say something, and burst out crying.

"I can't see," said the man, with a strange, thick voice. "Bring the light, some one." For ten awful seconds there was silence in the dim room, then a cry and a heavy fall.

"Saleen," said a voice close to me, "do you know it's a quarter past seven, and you are due at the Lesters' at half past; and not even dressed? Here's your book fallen down."

I had been asleep over an hour.

If I felt like a conspirator at the Lesters' pleasant dinner, it is not surprising, but I did not mention my dream.

Out of the Deeps

Horace Hampden brooded by the fire in his dusky parlor, and his cousin George Hampden sat near him. When a jet of flame darted from the grate and lighted up their faces they saw the grief which was busy at their hearts. For a long time they had been silent, intent upon their cigars; now one moved his hand, and the other his foot, and then each supposed the other was about to speak. Horace and George were cousins. Horace was married, a prosperous man of business, and George was a bachelor, and a lawyer; both were men of means, lived in the same circle, enjoyed the same amusements, and many of their attachments were in common. Consequently they were much in each other's society, and Charlotte Hampden, the wife of Horace, looked upon George as one of her family.

A few weeks before this period, Horace, not able to leave his business, permitted Charlotte to take their only son, a boy of fourteen, to France, to be educated in the college at Amiens. She crossed the sea in safety, left her son, and started on the return voyage in the steamer "Andromeda."[1] When her arrival was nearly due, a terrible gale sprung up, and extended along the Atlantic sea-board, which lasted several days. "Prayers for those at sea" went up from all interested souls, and a raging anxiety devoured both Horace and George. The nominal date of the "Andromeda's" arrival went by. Other steamers came in, more or less ravaged by the storm, news of shipwreck were rife, the underwriters were busy, but nothing was heard of the "Andromeda." At first the papers gave plausible reasons, mentioned the seaworthy character of the steamer, and the ability of her commander—and then became oblivious. Afterwards, when a list of her passengers was published, more than one person read the name of Charlotte Hampden with regret. She was popular in her circle, and deserved to be; still in her brightest prime, handsome, and lovable in all respects. Her friends, in their obituary remarks, said that her life might be compared to a party of pleasure sailing over a calm lake on a summer's day. Now her awful fate had been mysterious—annihilated by the dreadful sea in some sudden spasm of relentless fury, and ingulphed in the dark world of a deep which never gives up its dead! Horace and George watched and waited still, with hopes that hourly turned to despair, and refused to own their fatal dread to each other.

One day a ship came into port with tidings which confirmed the wreck of the "Andromeda." Sailing north of Hatteras she had come in contact with a mass of floating gear, and secured it. There was evidence that a useless effort had been made by some drowning wretches to tie spars and boards together; a portion of a bulk-head was with it. With a coarse brush some ship's hand had drawn the outline of a dromedary with a huge hump, and upon that were the half-effaced letters which composed the name "*Andromeda*." The day this news appeared, Horace and George met on the pier where the ship was moored, with the same errand—that of seeing with their own eyes, and hearing with their own ears, the truth. Hand gripping hand they turned away, and brokenly said that all hope was gone.

"Oh!" cried poor Horace, "to have no last service to perform, to know that this loss must be for ever invisible!"

"As if she were merely absent, no last memories to turn to, but one temporary farewell," replied George.

The evening found them together by the deserted fireside. George broke the silence at last.

"Is dinner nearly ready?" he asked.

"Half an hour yet," replied Horace, holding his watch to the firelight. "Will you have the gas lighted?"

"No. Something lies so heavy at my heart, that I have resolved to unburden myself."

"My dear boy," said Horace, surprised that he should choose the present moment for a personal confidence; but thinking that he meant it for his own distraction, he added that he was all attention.

"We are such complicated creatures," began George, "and circumstances so arrange our consciences that all reasoning is baffled. Were Charlotte living, it would be impossible for me to make this confession—though, living or dead, to her I am the same man. I have long loved her, Horace, as no man should love the wife of his friend, or the wife of any man. By the stress of my suffering and my sympathy for you, I tell you, we are one in this loss."

Horace was dumb; another chasm seemed to open in his life. What else should he see

"In the dark backward and abysm of time?"[2]

"Are you amazed?" continued George. "Charlotte has never dreamed of me. To her I have been *your* friend; the reflection of our friendship has chastely fallen on her affectionate heart."

Unconsciously Horace drew a breath of relief, which George, with deep sadness, perceived, and went on.

"I tell you this, partly because if mere abstract love is noble, mine has been, and partly to prove to you that I have entered into your loss as no other being can, and with the hope that my pure and faithful love may prove a bond betweeen us, and an everlasting solace. To all intents and wordly purposes, your son shall be my son, and together, as white-headed old men, we will watch and aid his progress into manhood and the duties of life."

George ended with a hysterical sob. His instincts told him that Horace was less great than himself at this moment, and he was disappointed. Horace, too, was now conscious of a want of magnanimity; but, how was it possible to resist that vital jealousy which invades the soul of a man, when the woman whose sole possession is his own comes in question with another man? He longed to be alone that he might go back over all the past of their mutual lives; but swallowing something, he knew not what, he rose suddenly, offered his hand to George, and in a husky voice said,

"It's all right, my dear boy; such matters scare one at first, you know. But upon my word, I see no occasion to wonder over what you have told me. I have not now to learn how much we are alike."

"Spare me all criticism, Horace; the Judgment Day may be anticipated sometimes. Charlotte was my ideal of all that was noble and beautiful; why should I not pay her this tribute to you now?"

Dinner was announced. Dinner that comes as inexorably as death—dinner that must be prepared, must be eaten; dinner, like the king, "never dies."

Both felt the relief of the announcement. The dinner passed off with a few commonplace remarks, and soon after George withdrew to his own solitary apartments in an adjoining street. When alone, he questioned his course, and condemned himself for sentimentality. Of what use to reveal the inner life, and show the pure flame of the soul burning on a sacred altar, to one whose limitations suggested a dark lantern, the slides of which shut over its own feeble wick at any approach? Calmer than he had been for many nights, however, he fell asleep, and more than once dreamed of the "touch of a vanished hand."[3] The old ways were resumed in Audley Street; George paid his daily visit there, and he and Horace were seen abroad as formerly. People mentioned them as the inseparable mourners—again referring to Charlotte's blighted life, which had been rounded so completely by such a husband, and such a friend.

It was now in the full tide of falling leaves, more than a month since the confirmation of the "Andromeda's" loss. Horace and George, inhabiting the little smoking den up-stairs—the rest of the house being closed, for they could not endure yet to be where Charlotte's belongings were—felt an additional melancholy when rain fell, or high winds roared round the walls. The picture of a ghastly sea rose before them, rent and torn by the wind like clouds; figures with despairing gestures tossed wildly to and fro, and agonized cries ascended from an unfathomable depth and distance of space, reaching them, lost, mingled, and spent by the wind, whose merciless errand it was to bring them. This made Horace and George close their teeth, and inwardly strangle the strange noises which stifled their own hearts.

"Suppose we were to shut the house at once?" asked Horace. "It grows too dismal; this howling weather drives my spirits down into my boots, and no tugging at the straps fetches them up again. What do you say to a Canadian trip? I want to see my agent in Toronto."

"As you please," answered George with a sigh. "It is all one to me. It seems to me the most congenial place here; there is distraction in travel, though, and if you want to be distracted, go we will."

"I hardly feel it a duty to try and test my feelings, George. Will you remain if I go?"

"Oh confound it—no! We must Ruth and Naomize it, having begun so—I'll go.[4] I believe I have lost all spring; my days are like zinc, my nights like lead."

And so they grimly talked and laughed. The trip was decided on, two days from that time.

There was a little more bustle than usual in Audley Street, at the appointed hour of departure. Horace and George were to leave by an evening train; dinner was ordered an hour earlier. Some stir of packing the trunk of Horace by the housekeeper made things wear a familiar aspect. When Horace turned his latchkey and entered the hall, seeing open doors, lighted rooms, and a general movement of life, the old familiar sense of home smote his sick heart. He looked up in the empty air, and his soul cried:

"My lost life, and love, and home! Oh treasures mocking my memory—would that I could die this moment!" He was mechanically wiping his hot face when George came in, with an assumption of cheerfulness, speaking loudly, and stepping about as if he liked it.

"Old boy," said Horace, putting away his handkerchief, "Maggie is getting up a first-rate dinner for us; she says we must start on strengthening diet. I declare she is a trump. I feel bound to the servants—they all are trumps—showed so much feeling, by George—"

"Good," interposed George, "I am awfully hungry."

"Of course you are," muttered Horace, "and you have been—eating as much as Charlotte's goldfinch this past month."

"We have a fair night to leave in," said George, as they commenced their soup.

"Yes, we have had a calm day."

"Our Indian summer sets in now."

Both dropped in a reverie, remembering the past.

"What have you here, Pat?" asked Horace.

"Beef, of course, sir."

Horace took his carver, as Pat raised the cover.

A rumbling noise was heard in the street, which they listened to. Wheels were thundering up the street, and horses were galloping.

"Too soon for us," said George, taking his watch out.

"But it stops here," answered Horace.

"Pshaw!" cried George, his face flushing deeply.

A carriage was at the door, and the bell was pulled. Its wire was then a true electric wire; it gave the knowledge of a coming event like lightning. A curious cry and stir came up the stairs, and Horace and George sprang from their chairs, and flew down. They saw Hannah, the maid, supporting Charlotte Hampden—Charlotte, alive, but speechless from emotion—pale, altered, but still herself! Behind her stood a young man, with a big railway rug in one hand, and several packages in the other.

"Bless me," he said, with an affected accent, but half-crying too, "our heroine gives out at the last moment."

Horace took his wife in his arms; not a word was spoken. George slid down the stair in a dead faint. Pat's picking him up made a diversion, and Horace carried Charlotte to the dining room, followed by all, except George, who was rallying from his faint by himself, with a host of sensations which he believed no man had ever felt before.

"What does this wonderful Providence mean?" asked Horace, kneeling by Charlotte, whom he had placed on the sofa. "I am afraid to look away from you, lest I should find myself a madman."

"It means," replied Charlotte's companion leisurely, ridding himself of his traps, "that we kept the boat tolerably dry, and that your wife has more nerve than any other woman upon earth. But what extraordinary introductions do I have to America! The denizens of the coast where we were stranded have a very limited view of the earth, but a very comprehensive one of the sea, and their rights therefrom. Consequently we found it impossible to convey tidings sooner of ourselves."

"Dear Horace," said Charlotte, "Mr. Egremont Moyston may joke as he will—he has saved my life."

Horace fell to shaking his hand violently, and stared at him with eyes full of feeling which he could not express.

"Nonsense," continued Mr. Moyston, "we undoubtedly aided each other. Mr. Hampden, we had a touch of brain fever which delayed us. We were thrown only six miles above the Batto light-house, but we might as well have landed in Patagonia. The white trash who kept us had no sense of what country they were in. 'Pomanco Court House' was the idea of their outside world. No conveyances, no comfort of any sort could we obtain. We were compelled to remain there till I was able to prowl about, and get down to the Batto light, to learn our whereabouts."

From point to point the wonderful narrative went on. Dinner was renewed. The servants, stricken with astonishment and admiration, lost their sense of decorum, and even the cook came up and occupied the edge of a chair, without remembering, as was her duty, that her plane was so much lower than the company that no number of kitchen stairs could measure it.

George had recovered himself, and returned.

"And so you missed your poor Charlotte, dear George?" she asked.

"Very much," he replied.

"Do I look badly?"

"As if you had suffered."

"Yet, dear Mrs. Hampden," said Mr. Moyston, very seriously, "if you and I should consult the glass, we could not find the traces of suffering that we may behold in the faces of your husband and brother."

At the word *brother* Horace felt a violent throb in all his frame. Heavens! George was no brother; he was his wife's devoted, life-long lover. In spite of the situation and the circumstances, the blood flew like birds through every vein. It appeared an inexorable necessity that he should go away by himself, and reflect upon his own feelings, and speculate upon those of George, and guess at the management of the clouded future.

"Why," exclaimed Charlotte, "George's hair has grown white."

So it had. Horace's was not changed a whit, and this he acknowledged to himself, when he saw her eyes scanning his ebon locks; he wished they were a dead white.

"No, indeed," laughed George, "being a little worried at your absence, I left off my 'Hair Restorer.' Now that you have returned—" For the life of him he could not utter another word, his lips trembled so. Charlotte rose, went to him, kissed him, and said softly:

"I thank God more than ever for having restored me to those who so tenderly love me. Now, Horace, I must shut my eyes and sense for the night. Pat, take the best care of Mr. Moyston; this house is his home."

"By Jove, Mr. Hampden," said Mr. Moyston, as Horace withdrew with Charlotte, "is there anything in antiquity to beat our case? I've gone through the Greek tragedies, and fed on our stalwart British classics, but I do not find its match."

"By the way," said George, absently, "I am not the brother of Mrs. Hampden's husband, but his cousin; we are very much together, however."

"Oh," answered Mr. Moyston. "America is the most extraordinary place. Home isn't a flea bite."

"Pray accept my gratitude, Mr. Moyston. I divine, by Mrs. Hampden's manner, what the nature of your service has been." He looked at him with so profound a thankfulness that Mr. Moyston was affected by this praise, and for the first time indicated emotion.

"It is just what you would have done for my sister," he replied hastily; and then they shook hands. Horace re-entered. Charlotte had retired, he said; he had tried to keep up his composure before her, for he saw how shattered her nerves were, but he could have no rest till he heard the full account of the disaster, and rescue.

It was gray dawn before the men separated. The occasion had made them firm friends; Horace was ready to give half his money to Mr. Moyston, and George half his affection. The journey was given up, of course. As George looked round for his valise, Mr. Moyston expressed some surprise.

"Do you go from here at this hour?"

A mighty longing came over George to remain under the roof with her who had been so miraculously restored. He looked at Horace, and Horace made no response. Human failing came over him again; he could not be magnanimous, and George turned away with a sigh. Mr. Moyston perceived there was some hidden fact or feeling between them.

"My apartment is very near," said George carelessly. "And by the way, Mr. Moyston, I hope you will share it a part of the time—bachelors prefer their solitary quarters, you know."

"I hate bachelordom from this out," replied Mr. Moyston. "I have lately seen all the virtues under the sun in Mrs. Hampden. Can I find another in this country?"

"Is he in love with her, too?"—thought poor Horace. "I suppose so—confound him! He is a hero—and George's hair must needs turn white."

"I'm off. Horace, bolt the door, to keep Charlotte in. What will Herbert say to these tidings of his mother?"

Herbert! his son—Horace had not thought of him yet; George was in advance even here.

"Boys are boys," he replied quickly. "I'll warrant you he has played cricket to-day."

"As he ought to," laughed Mr. Moyston, making a move towards the door, feeling an internal uneasiness.

"All this has given me a shock," said Horace, vaguely. "I am not equal to it. George, I tell you, I am not equal to it, and I can't bear it. You always were the strongest, and now your hair's got white. By George, do you know she showed me her arm, with a great scar on it, where she was knocked down on deck! I don't believe she is here at all. The scar is here, nothing else, you know, George." He staggered, and grew frightfully pale; he shook his head from side to side, and groaned pitifully.

"The shock, added to his great sorrow, has been too much for him," said Mr. Moyston. "Fetch some brandy, we must rub him; he is about to have a stroke. Just my luck in America," he said to himself.

George, stricken to the heart, but collected, made use of all available means; but Horace sunk momently—babbling at intervals about Charlotte—whom George would not at present disturb—and finally became wholly insensible.

Whatever Fate changes, or returns, God still disposes. Charlotte, bearing the greatest exposure, suffering, and vicissitude, survived; and Horace, in the ease and comfort of his orderly life, was struck with paralysis. His head and heart were not strong enough for the burdens placed upon them. He lingered two years, a helpless, but gentle, childish man, sedulously tended by George, whose secret was carefully protected from Charlotte. Mr. Moyston alone discovered it.

"I forswear England for the present," he said one day. "I find more character in America. George, noble as you are, you need me for awhile, and as I was the means of bringing Charlotte safely out of a crisis, I shall stay till I see you landed in the haven which shall be your right and rest. Not a word. I love Charlotte as I love no other woman, and I honor and respect you. Hurrah for the Colonies of King George! Just you propose going to England, to leave her now, for the fun."

"I have never proposed anything," answered George, "and I shall never propose."

"It will not be necessary, my dear boy."

Three

The De/Construction of Happy Endings

A Partie Carrée

I.

"How is it that I am always seeing Ann Le Barron, and am forced to speculate about her? What attracts me? She is neither talented, handsome, nor good. What is it to me how she looks or behaves? She is no example to follow. She is perplexing, for she lives in ambush; but what for?"

Eliza Mayhew shut up her grandfather's sea-glass, through which she had peered seaward in the hope of discovering a sail-boat supposed to be somewhere in the bay. Instead of the boat she had seen Ann Le Barron walking, like a sentinel, back and forth at the end of Brown's Wharf, where, as it happened, no vessels were moored. By the time Eliza had tied the glass in its canvas case and shut the portico door her grandmother called her to dinner, with a shrill voice, which made Eliza answer loudly, "Coming!" But she went slowly, rubbing her aquiline nose with an air of irritation, lost in an effort at guessing the reason of Ann Le Barron's walking on the wharf in the middle of the day. Eliza was mild, sensible, and twenty years old; but her grandmother, with whom she had lived since the death of her parents, treated her as if she were a wayward child; therefore when she commenced her dinner with a preoccupied air Mrs. Mason attacked her.

"Now do tell me, 'Liza, if you are going to eat these fritters in a dream?"

"No, grandma."

"You do torment me about your eating."

"She's a solid girl, Nancy," said old Mr. Mason; "Something keeps her alive."

"You know nothing about it, Mason; hold your tongue. Will you have a piece more of this beef?"

"Grandfather," said Eliza, brightening at some thought, "may I have Dick this afternoon to go to ride?"

"No; you can't have him."

Now Mr. Mason meant "yes;" but his wife opposing him when he said "Yes," and when he said "No," his speech was contrary to his intention from principle.

"For mercy's sake, why can't she have Dick, who is eating his head off in idleness?"

Eliza smiled at her grandfather, who said again that she could not go to ride.

"Do you go," said Mrs. Mason to a shock-headed boy who was peeling potatoes in a corner of the kitchen, "and see if John is at the barn, and tell him to tackle Dick at two o'clock. Where are you going, 'Liza?"

"On the Neck."

"What for? Why don't you ride Ship Bay way? But if you will go the Neck road, stop at Mrs. Jones's, and get me some of her dried camomile flowers; they are the best in the world."

By two o'clock Eliza was jogging briskly along a leafy, narrow road, running through the neck of land which jutted into the sea on the side of the bay opposite the pleasant village of Shelby. The wild rose was in bloom, and the young briers crept over the rough stone walls to bask in the June sun. The paths that led into the woody swamps were green with delicate moss and pale, stalky plants, and Eliza stopping Dick, thrust her head out of the chaise, and looked into them with a vague delight. The fresh wind fluttered the leaves of the scrub oaks, and trembled in the birches, and broke into low sighs when it reached the dark unmoved pines that dotted the landscape. After riding several miles she struck into a steep cross road, gullied by rains which had washed the soil away, leaving a bed of rolling stones over which Dick was urged with a gay chirrup. The road came to an end suddenly, as if it had just convinced itself that there was little need of its going on to nowhere. She plunged boldly into a marshy meadow, guiding Dick by a row of stakes which pointed toward a clump of ancient, storm-beaten fir-trees. Here she left the chaise, climbed a sandy hill, and saw a wide space of sea, stretching westerly till lost in a misty distance. A boat was anchored in the lee of a little island, and on the boat she anchored her eyes.

"There they are, Dick!" she called.

Dick pricked up his ears comprehensively, although, from his position under the hill, he was precluded from a view of the cause of her exclamation.

For the benefit of the ants, perhaps, she made little sand-mounds with her foot, while she indulged in a reverie, sentimental but allowable, for it was a happy and an innocent one. Presently she smiled, and shook her head with an expression of reproof as she said,

"Come, Dick, we will go back."

She was detained so long at Mrs. Jones's by questions concerning life "down to the shore" that it was five o'clock before she got home.

"What upon earth made you stay so?" her grandmother asked. "Dick has been wanted for a funeral."

"Why didn't you let Bill go instead?"

"Bill does not understand funerals. You know how he run back in the procession at old Mrs. Crosby's funeral, and what confusion there was. Dick takes to them naturally."

"But he is buried safe, I suppose, without Dick."

"After tea you must sew; don't waste your time in reading."

After the sewing was finished Eliza read three chapters in "Thaddeus of Warsaw" and one in the Bible.[1] As a corrective to the dissipation of the afternoon she imposed the penance of not looking out of any window, either down the main street, at the head of which the house stood, or over the bay which rolled before it.

II.

"Where can Eliza Mayhew be going?" said Ann Le Barron, as she saw her pass from her chamber-window.

"She rides often, you know," Mrs. Le Barron answered. "Her grandfather has two horses, and she can afford it."

"I am sick of her praises of Dick; it is so childish in her."

"Mr. Mason bought the horse, I remember, about two years after your father was lost. It will be fourteen years this fall since I heard the news. You might have had a horse too, if he had come home."

"No such luck! I wish you would alter that pink dress; I want to wear it this evening."

The widow went in search of the dress. Ann drummed on the pane, her eyes roving vacantly for some object of interest outside; but as the house stood on a back street there were few passers-by. It was empty, and she turned away. Her eyes falling on an old mahogany secretary which stood in the chimney recess, a thought occurred to her. She opened it, and took from one of its pigeon-holes a morocco case, containing the miniature likeness of a man with pale eyes and a paler complexion, in a sky-blue coat and ruffled shirt.

"I look like him," she soliloquized, rubbing the gold frame with her handkerchief. "He was aristocratic. But I remember seeing him only once, and then he wore a tarpaulin hat. He tossed me in his arms, and I cried, because he tumbled my frock."

She put the picture back in its place, and went to the glass to observe her own features, in which attitude her mother discovered her.

"Mother, how near to a Frenchman was father?"

Mrs. Le Barron, glancing at the secretary as if something there could answer the question better than herself, replied,

"His father was French, I believe."

"Am I like him?"

"Very much."

"I wish he had lived."

"He was very proud, and, I am afraid, not very happy; he couldn't bear any thing that wasn't genteel. But, Ann, you should be happy; although we are not rich, you have more than he had."

"How long may it last? The minute grandfather dies Uncle Tom will swoop up every thing, and turn you and me out of the house. You know it. You know that he is a rascal—a mean, dirty villain."

"Try on your dress," her mother said, shortly. "It is nearly tea-time; here comes father now."

Captain Green, a hale, bluff old salt, stormed in with a string of live fish, which he held up close to Ann, and demanded that they should be cooked immediately for his supper.

"Don't bring them up here, grandfather!" snapped Ann; "a chamber is not the place for fish!"

"Hity, tity, Miss! a sailor's daughter mustn't be so squeamish. But your mother has ruined you; she is weaker than dish-water. Where do you think I got 'em? The young lawyer prig—what's-his-name? that comes to play cards with you—gave them to me. I was on the wharf when he came in; he had a spanking breeze to round the pint in!"

"Mr. Allen, do you mean?"

"That's the man."

"What nice fish they are!" said Ann, with a coquettish voice. "I'll help you to fry them, mother."

"It's more than half past five," said Captain Green. "Shelby has had its supper; we are behindhand."

After the tea-things were put away the pink dress was donned, and Ann, lighting the astral lamp in the parlor, took a seat there, with a patient "will-you-come-into-my-parlor" aspect. The rays of the lamp, however, only attracted two young ladies, who came in, possibly with the hope of meeting other visitors, for Ann's was a regular rendezvous. But none came, and the young ladies soon departed. Ann retired, and, while Eliza Mayhew was interested in Mary Beaufort and her "white muslin cloak," twisted her thin silky brown hair in papers. Her gaping mother was in waiting, for it was her duty to put out the light. Ann's fingers clutched a curl-paper in mid-air as she caught the tones of a manly voice, which came nearer and nearer, singing.

"We have been friends together!"[2]

"I have come up to bed too soon," she said.

Mrs. Le Barron stopped gaping, and swung one foot over the other while she listened; but the voice passed on and was soon out of hearing, and the light in Ann's cold blue eyes faded.

III.

The singer in the street, Henry Allen, went on his way to his room in the Montgomery Hotel, which stood at the lower end of Main Street. As he passed Mr. Mason's square white house, whose inhabitants were undoubtedly wrapped in slumber, he said to himself, "Nice girl! but how strict they keep her;" and hummed,

"You may break, you may ruin the vase, if you will."[3]

In the hotel he met his father, Judge Allen, of Belford, a town twenty miles inland. He had sent Henry from his own office to practice law in the marine locality of Shelby, and was now come to visit him as a judge and as a father.

"You smoke too much, Henry," was his greeting.

Henry threw away his cigar. "How is my mother, Sir?"

"She is well. Any case on hand?"

Henry laughed. "Yes, Sir—a sailor's-rights case; but they are such a rascally set it is hard to get at the truth of a trespass at sea."

"Read your *Story*, Sir."[4]

"Come up stairs and see how my books are thumbed." On the way they met Tripp, the landlord, who informed Henry that a solemn gent had come from Boston with lots of Ingy-rubber cloth, on a fishing lay, he expected.

"That's pleasant," said Henry.

"How's pickerel in your parts, Judge?" inquired Tripp, clattering down stairs without waiting for an answer. The Judge entered the chamber, which, besides the ordinary furniture, was adorned with several stuffed birds (Henry was his own taxidermist), and pictures whose frames were his handiwork also. When the Judge saw on a small table some workman's tools and a work-box in the process of construction, he said "Pish!" but Henry, quickly screwing up the lamp, directed his attention to the open books around it, and said, "This is the way the midnight oil goes."

"I hope so," answered the Judge, taking a judicial seat on the sofa.

"Now for a pump," thought Henry.

A long conversation ensued upon family and business matters, in which the Judge discovered that the amount of Henry's legal earnings for his first year in Shelby, now just ended, was forty dollars. He confessed that he had bought a boat with the money. The Judge admitted that boating might be pleasant. Henry thought the admission was a gain, and grew eloquent on the topic, when his father interrupted him and went on with his practical remarks. In time a moderate but steady practice might be obtained in Shelby, and he advised him to stay. Henry hastily affirmed that he would. Both were satisfied with this arrangement; Judge Allen because he had a suspicion that the vocation of Henry was not that of a lawyer, and Henry because he was sure that he could never come up to his father's ideas of sharp practice. The Judge reasoned within himself that it would not matter if he should not rise in the profession; it would at least give his mind a dignified bent, and add to the respectability of his position.

"I think," said Henry to himself, after the Judge had retired, "that father despises ingenuity. Mechanical skill is below a lawyer's skill, of course. But my motto is 'Ne quid nimis.'[5] Tra-la-la, Tra-la-la," he sang, proceeding to brush his young whiskers into curl. He was so tall that the top of his head rose above the top of the small ancient mirror he was contemplating his visage in. "By Jove, this glass must be fixed!" He found a bit of wood, which he whittled into a cleat and fastened the glass to it slantingly, standing before it to observe its effect. It reflected a good-humored, regular-featured face with no particular meaning; and if it had been large enough, would also have reflected an agile, slender, well-shaped figure, with long, narrow white hands, and long, narrow feet.

"I say," said Tripp, opening the door without knocking, "are you going fishing to-morrow?"

"Not if my father is here."

"When you do go, I wish you'd make up to that feller that's just come."

"Introduce us to-morrow and I'll settle it."

"What does the old man say of Shelby?"

"He likes it."

"Good, you'll stay then and court some of our belles. There's Miss Mayhew."

"You mustn't interrupt my studies, Tripp."

"Oh no, by no means; I hope they won't consume you." And Tripp vanished.

IV.

Judge Allen went home the next day, and Henry resumed his mechanical labors, which were interrupted by Tripp's bringing the stranger who had arrived the evening before, and whom he introduced as "Mr. Bassett, come to Shelby for his health." He left the room immediately after the introduction, with the air of having made an unwonted concession to good manners.

Henry laid down his tools to observe his visitor, whose manners were so cool, and whose countenance was so serious. He discerned nothing very noticeable in his appearance, unless his eyes might be called so; they were gray, open, cold, and penetrating. His hair was stiff, his complexion sallow, and his figure insignificant.

"Can he laugh?" he thought.

"This little Shelby is a pretty place," Mr. Bassett said; "what are your amusements? Your business I see—'Councilor,' to say nothing of mechanics."

"*I* fish."

"Good. Let us put out. 'Where lies the port; what vessel puffs her sail: come, my purpose holds to sail beyond the sunset and the baths of all the western stars until I die.'"

"Well," answered Henry, meekly, "I'll get the lines ready."

In an hour the *Andromeda* was plowing down the bay under a good breeze, with Henry at the helm, while the crew, which consisted of Sam Tripp, baited the lines.[6]

Another hour brought them to the fishing-ground, where they anchored the boat, and cast their lines. But Mr. Basset took no pains with his; he pondered the sea in silence, allowing his hook to rest on the bottom, where it was unmolested.

"Do you feel a bite, Sir?" inquired Sam, from the other side of the boat, where he and Henry were taking in plenty of fish.

"I do, indeed," he answered. After a while he began to pull in his line, saying, slowly,

> "O God, O God!
> How weary, stale, flat, and unprofitable
> Seem to me all the uses of this world!
> Fie on't!"[7]

He threw himself by the folds of the lowered sail, where, shielding his face from the sun, he studied the sky as silently as he had pondered the sea. If his companions could have seen his face they would have detected tears upon it—tears that came from some depth of sadness he would allow no mortal to discover—tears that he was already denying, for he was smiling; his lips were drawn apart from his teeth, which were set together with fierce resolve.

"Hey," he called, presently, "are the finnies shoaling in?"

"Fast," answered Henry. "Let me know when you have had enough of this, will you?"

"I should like to stay long enough to get the secret of these splendid emerald tints; the sea is a kind of rotary grass just here."

Henry looked down into the water, and said, "I have never thought of it before."

"See, a little way beyond us the water is a steely blue, and farther off it is a perfect azure."

"Ain't it green all over off soundings?" Sam asked.

"Good boy," replied Mr. Bassett; "hoist sail, we will go and see."

The sail was hoisted, and the helm was delegated to Sam, for Henry to smoke and chat with Mr. Bassett. The chat was mostly composed of long answers to Mr. Bassett's short questions. By the time they arrived home Henry had been gauged. Mr. Bassett had come to Shelby to be amused, and he had found in Henry one willing to oblige him. As for the latter, mere companionship was enough. The young men of Shelby had little leisure, and Mr. Bassett promised to be a godsend in the way of idleness. Besides, as Shelby was a marine locality, for most of the time there was a dearth of masculine society. Three-fourths of its sons went to the great deep in pursuit of whales, and the village was in a chronic condition of sadness over their departure, or gladness at their return. They made plans for the future, but Mr. Bassett made no reference to his own antecedents or belongings. Henry remained in ignorance of his station and circumstances—an ignorance which proved to be the fate of all who made his acquaintance afterward.

V.

For some occult reason Eliza Mayhew kept closely indoors. Several days elapsed before her solitude was invaded; but the time had not been unhappily employed, for her disposition was cheerful, and her mind preeminently feminine. Pleasant occupations filled each day; if she was ever idle, her idleness was devoid of *ennui*. Her grandmother taught her early to fulfill those laws which create the individuality of home, and make clean the faces of its Lares and Penates.[8] In time she improved her grandmother's system; to her well-scoured boards she applied table-cloths and carpets, and hung curtains before the windows, which remained in spite of Mrs. Masons's declaration that they drew flies. The front yard, devoted in past years to grass, dandelions, and two distracted, barren peach-trees, now bloomed with roses and lilies, and was adorned with gravel paths bordered with box. The windows of her own chamber were filled with beautiful plants. The mantle shelf was covered with splendid sea-shells from the shores of the underworld, and instead of vases or pictures she had curiously woven and colored baskets made by the natives thereof. The old mahogany furniture, inlaid with threads of white wood in spider-like patterns, suited the character of the spacious, low, wide rooms.

Saturday afternoon she went to her chamber for rest and amusement. She looked out of the western window over the wooded shore curving round the head of the bay. A border of salt meadow made desolate that end of the village below the house, but now its coarse, plentiful grass glistened cheerfully in the warm sun. A creek ran its crooked length through the meadow, crossed by a half ruined bridge, at the head of which a wind-mill waved its arms with a faint creak. Eliza was not profound enough to feel the poetic monotony of the landscape, but she liked the sunset when it struck its rosy bars across the waters of the bay, and darkened the woods on the shore. She composed herself for sewing, and had finished a scallop in a crimson merino sacque, when, happening to look out again, she saw Ann Le Barron in the street, nodding with a nod which signified that she was coming in.

"Where *have* you been this age, Eliza?" she said, entering with a bustle; "I have not seen you since Tuesday, when you rode by our house."

"I have been busy at home."

"You are always busy. What a perfect bower your chamber is! How lucky you are with plants; mine always die. What's the news?"

"I have no news. Will you take off your bonnet?"

"I did not come to stay; but it is so pleasant here that I am tempted." Without farther invitation she threw it off.

"Grandmother is making your favorite sweet biscuit to-day."

"Oh, I am so fond of them!"

She arranged her hair before the glass, exclaiming against her complexion, and wishing that it was as clear as Eliza's, sat down near her.

"I should like to be as well off as you are, and then I should not be tired of Shelby perhaps."

"What's the matter?"

"Oh, I don't know. What makes you contented?"

"A thousand things."

"All trifles?"

"Yes, many of them; but we can't have great events here, you know."

"No, and I need excitement."

"I love it too;" and Eliza turned a faint rose color.

"You? why you are the quietest girl I ever saw! You never seem to need any company. Have you seen Henry Allen lately?"

"Not for ten days."

"A Mr. Bassett is staying at the Montgomery hotel. Nobody knows any thing about him; but he has struck up an intimacy with Henry Allen. We may see him at church to-morrow, and of course he will be at the picnic next Tuesday. What shall you wear then?"

"This merino sacque for one thing. It is always damp and chilly at picnics, you know."

"What a good idea! I should like to try it on." Eliza took out her needle and gave it to her. "How I like it!" she exclaimed. "How becoming red is to me! You don't look well in it. I wish I could have one; I am so thin that I always suffer with the cold."

"Take this and wear it."

"But what will you do?"

"I have shawls."

"I know you have. You have so many things that it will not rob you if I keep it. I am delighted to have it. Is it nearly done?"

"Not quite."

She took up her needle again, and Ann looked on complacently, very well satisfied with her afternoon's labor.

"I was puzzled what to wear. This crimson will look well with my brown dress, and my complexion won't look dingy."

It was not the first time that transactions of this sort had occurred between the girls, Ann always obtaining the advantage. Mrs. Mason now made her appearance to consult with Eliza about frosting the cake destined for the picnic. She asked Ann how her mother was, and if she didn't perceive that old Capen Green, her grandfather, was losing his faculties? It was a fact that her family grew childish early.

Ann reddened slightly, but made an indifferent reply. She knew that she was no favorite with Mrs. Mason, who was not sparing of sharp words; but Eliza's friendship was valuable, so she never retorted.

"Tea will be ready soon, Eliza," said Mrs. Mason, going; "don't keep me waiting one minute. We have nothing very nice for you, Miss Ann; I believe you are fond of goodies."

She ate six of the tea-biscuit, and Mrs. Mason was pleased enough with the compliment to her cookery to allow her to depart without a sarcasm.

Saturday eve was a season of quiet in the Mason homestead. The work was dispatched early, and it was still twilight when Eliza went to her chamber with an unlighted lamp. She opened the western window; her head was tired, the fresh air might revive her. She suffered the same dissatisfaction which always troubled her after an interview with Ann, whose power of assimilating others to the tone of her mind could not be resisted. She was surprised and angry that she had made no attempt at self-assertion. The sickle moon was sinking in the clear western sky, against which the wind-mill stood in dark relief, its arms winnowing the air. Her eyes followed their motion, and as they dipped toward the bridge she saw a figure crossing it. A strange place, she thought, for an evening promenade, closing the window.

It was long afterward when Bose, the dog, woke her with his howling in the carriage-house. She sprang up to look into the yard, and saw a man walking slowly by. She watched him out of sight, but as Bose continued his howls she threw on a wrapper and ran down to the carriage-house and pulled him out by the ear. He growled in his throat still.

"What do you see, Bose?"

She looked toward the gate and saw the figure she had thought out of sight, and though her heart stood still she went up to it, Bose following.

"Thank you for your courage," said a melancholy voice. "I am an inoffensive pedestrian, and am here in the hope of quelling the beast. Come here, Sir. You are a deuce of a dog."

Bose sniffed at him through the bars of the gate, and snorted faintly.

"People do not walk about Shelby by night, unless they are on a stealing excursion," said Eliza.

"Are you not afraid of thieves?"

"Dear me, no."

"What is the dog's name?"

"Bose."

"Bose! Bose!"

The dog gave a little yelp, which made her laugh.

"This is awkward," said the stranger. "I think I must go: farewell, my canine foe!"

As he disappeared Eliza boxed Bose's ears and called him a fool, but allowed him to go in with her to sleep before her door.

VI.

Shelby was Congregational—that is, all the elite of the town; there were one or two inferior religions for the lower sort. Eliza was at church early the next day, and Ann entered as the congregation rose for the first hymn and walked up the aisle; for Captain Green's pew was in the rear of the congregation, and Mr. Mason's near the pulpit. Eliza made room, offered her a hymn-book, and went on with the singing, unmindful of her furtive looks toward Henry Allen, who was in the hotel pew opposite. He walked home with them, and Ann, after Eliza had gone, obtained a programme of the picnic, and the news that there would be a dance at Shelby Hall in the evening. Moreover, Henry discovered that he was engaging her to dance with him the first quadrille.

Early on Tuesday Henry Allen drove round with a large wagon to collect information and viands. When he stopped at Mr. Mason's, Eliza talked to him with so much coolness that he fell into a brown study unexpectedly, while unpacking hams on the picnic ground, upon her dignity and apparent want of feeling.

" 'I would I were a boy again!' " he sang.[9]

"You work like a man," Tripp commented; "you are the head and front of this business. I see that I can leave you in charge."

"I shall be down to the house by eleven o'clock. Every thing will then be ready. Mind, I am not to be asked a single question afterward about arrangements."

He got home just before noon, fagged and hungry, and found Bassett lolling on his sofa, and the floor strewed with feathers from one of the stuffed birds which he had beaten to pieces with a ratan cane, a weapon he always carried.

"Now," said Henry, vexed, "I think you might have made yourself more useful. You have spoiled my owl."

> "'Mourn not for the owl, nor his gloomy plight;
> The owl hath his share of good.'"[10]

Henry lighted a cigar, ran his fingers through his hair, and contemplated the ruined bird.

"It was a tiresome, dead thing," said Bassett; "no color in it. Why not keep something beautiful about you?"

"Beautiful!" Henry echoed, with contempt. "I was a week catching that owl."

"Wretch!"

"Shall you condescend to go to the picnic, and to our humble dance?"

"Will a dog named 'Bose' be at either affair?"

"Perhaps a puppy will."

"Embrace me."

"I say, there's a couple of girls I shall introduce you to!" said Henry, his good-humor coming back suddenly. "Get on your good clothes; you needn't appear in your Mackintosh."

> "''Tis not alone my inky cloak.'"[11]

"Have you been an actor?"

"Yes, in a tragedy where the hero was left out in the cold: go on with the couple of girls."

"They are entirely different."

"Is it possible!"

"If you laugh I will not introduce you."

"Am I not called the Solemn One?"

Henry blushed, for it was true; Tripp's name for him had been adopted in Shelby.

"Miss Eliza Mayhew, orphan, lives with her grand-parents, very strict people; sees little company herself; has an immense sense of propriety; is handsome and good. Miss Ann Le Barron, fatherless; lives with her mother and grandfather, Captain Green; poor, but of good standing. It is the jolliest house in Shelby; no formality there. I visit them often—every body does."

"Is Miss Ann handsome and good too?"

"Well, I don't know; there's something nice about her; she always puts me in good spirits."

"There goes the dinner-bell. Come to my room when you are ready to take me along."

Henry found him astonishingly dressed in a light-gray coat and trowsers—a match for his complexion in color—and a green velvet vest. He envied him the tie of his cravat and the fit of his boots. Tripp drove them to the grove, which was already filled with people moving under the trees, which were decorated with shawls, bonnets, and hats. Children were running about, singing, jumping rope, or playing games. Henry found Eliza Mayhew tying up bunches of flowers, surrounded by a group of talking girls. Ann Le Barron sat on the stump of a tree near them, in the crimson sacque. Her light hair fell in delicate curls against her face, hiding its sharp contour; the folds of her brown dress clung about her picturesquely. The group of girls fluttered apart as Henry approached with Mr. Bassett, who recognized her at once; but she did not dream of his being Bose's knight-errant. He bowed to her, and, turning away, began a lively chat with the girls.

"He is as contrary as the devil," thought Henry.

Presently Ann, with an air of abstraction, sauntered up, and addressed some inquiry concerning somebody she had not seen to one of the girls. Henry interrupted Bassett to introduce her. She made a sweeping courtesy and flourished her handkerchief, with a few inaudible words.

"She is coming *la Française* now," whispered the girls.

Bassett fixed his eyes upon her. She felt them, and kept her side-face toward him. When he spoke, and she turned it to answer, something in her cold blue eyes baffled him.

"There *is* 'something nice' about her, as Allen says," he thought.

When it was time to arrange the feast Eliza was stationed at a dry-goods box to pour tea, and Ann was placed by another to serve coffee. Several young gentlemen volunteered to carry cups for them, and it fell to Henry to be Ann's cup-bearer. Tripp was inclined to supervise the kettle of hot water on her box, and, while Henry went to and fro, made comments upon whatever fell under his philosophical eye.

"I've always noticed," he said, running a cup over which she held out to him, "that religious people are awful hungry on such occasions. Do you believe they get up these things to improve their appetite?"

She laughed. "Is Mr. Allen so religious?"

"Well, in the main he is. His family are strict; they keep the church going in Belford. They are Unitarians, though. Unitarianism ain't so costly as our kind; they don't keep so many missionaries. The Allens could pay if it did. The Judge is worth a hundred thousand cool; the young one is a first-rate-catch."

He looked cunningly at her; and she said, without meeting his eye, "I thought that he was a poor lawyer."

She lied.

"Isn't she sly?" he thought.

"Mrs. Higgins says your coffee is full of grounds," said Henry, returning with her cup, "though she has had three cups, and will take a fourth."

"I'll shake the pot for her," said Ann.

"He won't live in Shelby," continued Tripp, watching him as he conveyed Mrs. Higgins her coffee; "He'll grow tired. But that Mr. Bassett there is as contented as an old puss, watching the clouds here, and a-staring at the water there."

Ann looked round and saw him standing by Eliza. "Are any of his friends with him?"

"Not a friend."

"I should think he would object to settling here if his friends live at a distance."

"I don't know where they live—and that's the droll of it—nor where he came from. And I do not know how old he is; but I'll bet he is thirty."

"He must find it dull if he has no business nor profession."

"He has nary one that I am aware of."

"You are wanted, Miss Le Barron," called Henry.

"Shall I give you some tea, Sir?" Eliza asked, when she saw Mr. Bassett standing near.

"If you please."

"It is not over-nice, I am afraid."

"How is Bose?" sipping tea from his spoon.

"Are you the one?" she asked, with an undisturbed smile.

"You did not recognize me, then? I knew you at once."

"How could I? you were black from head to foot."

"How should I have known *you*?" he persisted.

She transparently answered, "I suppose Mr. Allen told you." There was an implication in her words which she perceived when too late, and she turned a vivid rose-color which flashed her face into animated beauty.

"I should like," he thought, "to see that look often from this undeveloped soul. There is enough here to make a man—" A wicked light passed into his eyes and faded, for Eliza cried "Oh!" suddenly. From the swing just behind them a little girl had been tossed high in the air; she caught at a branch which delayed her fall an instant. He sprang forward like lightning, and she fell on his extended arms with so much force that he was brought to the ground. But he held her up unhurt. His face was scratched, and he was so giddy with the shock that he was not conscious of Eliza's wiping his cheek with her handkerchief, which operation she continued till somebody laughed. Then he looked at her and grew still paler. Confusion of tongues arose. Every body left the tables, and told him how lucky he had been in breaking the fall of the child. The mother, when she found her unhurt, shook her, and every body went back again.

"I wish my face was scratched," said Henry.

"Why?" she asked.

"If you can't guess I don't care about being scratched."

> " 'I was a child, and she was a child,
> In a kingdom by the sea,' "[12]

said Mr. Bassett.

"I have a mind to leave on the strength of my accident. Don't you come, Allen; I had rather walk by myself. I shall see you this evening, Miss Mayhew. If you dance—"

Henry made a rapid attempt to interrupt him, but recollecting himself stopped.

"Will you do me the honor of dancing with me?"

"With pleasure, Sir."

Ann Le Barron saw him coming down the field and quietly moved in his way; her arms were folded, and her curls slightly agitated.

"I hope you are not hurt," she said, with an air of anxiety.

"Not in the least."

"You are quite a hero."

"Yes, *now* I am," with a meaning look.

"Shall we meet you to-night?"
"Are you to be at the dance?"
"I think of going."
"I shall be there. How gracefully your curls float!"
"Do you think so?" shaking her head. "Why do you go away now?"
"I have not been able to see you at all."
Before she could answer he had bowed himself away.

Ann went straightway to Eliza and asked her what she thought of Mr. Bassett.

"Oh, that plain man! I haven't thought of him. I liked the way he caught Sophy Smith, though."

"You never notice men."

"Yes I do;" and Eliza blushed again.

"What *are* you blushing for? I wanted to know if you thought that Mr. Bassett's manners were peculiar?"

"No, I did not think so."

At all events he had succeeded in awakening a feeling in Ann, which was so new and delightful that she was disposed to dream over it. There was pleasure, tumult, expectation in it. She had fallen a victim to so slight a matter as a genial voice, a pair of penetrating eyes, and a few trifling words. Or was it something more? Had she received in this way an admonishment that it would be better for her to avoid the experiment of making her life empty-hearted and selfish? It had been her design for months to marry Henry Allen—and since she had learned that he was independent of his profession, and that his social position was higher than her own. There was wisdom in the plan. He was good-looking, amiable, and a gentleman; but neither his approach toward her, nor his retreat from her, had ever tightened her heart or quickened her cat-like breath. Cold, methodical, vain, longing for luxury, should she not have been an intellectual beauty since she must be the heroine of a few written-down facts? The poor qualities of patience and persistence were hers, and the faculty of understanding what she wanted, and of placing her aims within the scope of her powers.

Her advantage was an insidiously compulsive individuality, which few understood. It was, of course, the secret of her attraction.

"Ann!" Eliza called, who was packing plates in a basket, "you look serious."

"I am tired."

"Ride home with me; I shall soon be ready."

Mr. Bassett wended his way out into the road, receiving and returning kindly salutations with many new acquaintances. He struck into a by-path soon, and was out of sight.

"*Mea culpa!*" he cried aloud, tapping his breast. "I can not outlive myself. Where I find lambs there I also find, in myself, a wolf. Have I come to the shores of the sounding sea to suffer from puerile sensations and be visited by debasing thoughts? Will my grief take beside it my besetting sin?" His thoughts went back to the past. He remembered sin, loss, desolation; but, in spite of them and his self-accusations, he entered the hotel in almost good spirits. Why he felt so he would not inquire. He would not be self-troublesome just then.

"How's the scratch?" asked Henry, putting his head in at his door an hour afterward.

"Come in, and blow a cloud and rest."

Henry threw himself on the bed, vowing that he had been up since daybreak. He began to talk drowsily, and Mr. Bassett relapsing into silence he fell into a sound sleep, from which he started to ask the time. It was eight o'clock.

"Time to dress, Bassett; where are your lights? Did you have a good time to-day? You didn't talk to Miss Mayhew."

"She is a fine-looking woman."

"Fine-looking woman, indeed! Don't you wish she had feathers?"

"She is lucent, fair, placid, good."

"Not so lucent."

"You like her, my boy!"

"Your boy does."

"You do not understand her."

"Ah! that is a good idea."

"I beg your pardon."

"Oh, bother! get ready, will you? I am stung to-day with a million mental mosquitoes."

" 'It is a nipping and an eager air.' "[13]

"I say," said Henry, returning for a moment to the room, "have you yourself any feelings in particular?"

" 'I have not loved the world, nor the world me—
But let us part fair foes.' "[14]

"Confound your poetry!"

A second time that day Henry was destined to be astonished, for Mr.

Bassett appeared before him in a full dress-suit of black and patent-leather pumps.

"Lemon-colored gloves!" said Henry, looking at his own wrinkled, dingy-white pair.

"You know I am not a handsome man, and the tailor tries to help me out. Now *you*—"

Henry looked down his length of limb, straightened his shoulders, put his thumbs in the button-holes of his blue coat, and made a small pirouette.

"Donkey!" said Mr. Bassett to himself.

"Bassett is *rather* unfortunate!" thought Henry, starting for the hall, for he was Master of Ceremonies.

He received the young ladies as they arrived in squads, unprotected, as was the custom—invitations having been issued by a committee. Eliza came early, looking as fresh as a flower, in the calyx of a pale-green silk. The bands of her hair shone like jet, and clung so smoothly to her face that its pure paleness seemed framed in black.

Ann Le Barron was the last to arrive. She swept up the hall as cool as Sabrina, in a cloud of tarlatan—cheap, but becoming; skirt rose upon skirt to the slender waist. Her arms and bosom were covered with illusion. At the back of her head was fastened a bunch of delicate flowers and leaves, which trailed down her shoulders, and gave her an air of peculiar grace. From the foot of the hall she looked like a beauty. Bassett thought so as he entered, and thought so more seriously when he saw her dancing with Henry, for she danced beautifully.

"You dance like a fairy," said Henry, half-enveloped in the whirl of her skirts. "Give my this flower," he begged, touching one.

"What will you do with it?" she asked, with cunning eyes.

"I shall keep it forever."

She broke it from its stem, and, after twirling it across her lips, gave it to him.

Eliza was watching them without surprise, but she turned the bracelet on her arm as if she wished it were a flower.

"Are you engaged the next set?" Ann inquired of him while he was pinning the flower to his coat.

"No; will you dance again?"

"Oh no, not the very next; what will they say?"

"Do you suppose that I care what is said?"

"I see the Gurneys and the Haskells are here; I hope they won't insist upon dancing with me."

"Say you are engaged to me when you are bored."

"Thank you. I like to dance with you, your arm is such a support."

"Is it?" he answered, with a look as if he would like to offer her its support again. "By-the-way, while I think of it, shall I come to your house to-morrow evening and teach you to play chess, as I promised?"

"Do; don't fail to come; I am so anxious to learn!"

"How well she looks, don't she?" said Henry, joining Mr. Bassett after the dance.

"Who?"

"Eliza Mayhew."

"Where is she?"

He had just been observing her.

"Over there; where are your eyes?"

"I have been looking at you and Miss Le Barron."

"Easy soul; and how well she dances!"

"She is gossamer."

"I am going to play the second violin for the next dance. It will be your chance for display."

"Now, Music, wake from out thy charmed sleep!"[15]

"Why can't you talk sense?"

At the first scrape of the violin Mr. Bassett was bowing before Eliza. She rose, and, without speaking, they took places in the quadrille that was forming. He felt a dreamy repose stealing over him, and wished neither to break the silence nor to move. When the time came for them to advance she offered him her ungloved white hand, and he felt its warmth striking through his glove. At the first opportunity he pulled it off and thrust it into his pocket. Again their hands met, but the change was unnoticed by her. He still waited for her to speak, and at last she said,

"I dance badly."

"You do."

She looked up and met his grave eyes looking kindly into hers.

"How beautifully Miss Le Barron dances! You observed her."

"She likes dancing; I believe you do *not*."

"Oh yes. Do you like it?"

"No; but then I am thirty."

Eliza pitied Mr. Bassett, because she thought he lacked, in her estimation, all that she thought Henry possessed. Mr. Bassett would have pitied her if he had been certain that she felt a preference for Henry. But she was undemonstrative; even Ann was ignorant of her feeling.

Mr. Bassett continued to chat with her till Henry joined her; and for the remainder of the evening he hovered round her, except when drawn away by Ann, or when he danced with some pretty girl. He was in high spirits, especially when he perceived that Eliza was unmoved by his flirtations. Mr. Bassett sought Ann, more for the purpose of observing her than of dancing; but when a waltz began he placed his arm round her, and they whirled away.

"Does it make you dizzy to waltz?" she asked, fixing her eyes on his as deliberately as if she were sauntering across the floor instead of waltzing with all her might.

"I am not to the manner born as you are."

"I am French, you know."

They stopped and rested against the wall. She opened her gloved fingers.

"You must be warm," she said, glancing at his white hand.

He made no reply; but his expression gave her a desire to temper with him. He watched her while she played with her fan.

"He is not a man to wind round one's fingers," she thought.

"It is your turn to forward," he said.

Returning from her *vis-à-vis*, she showed him a candid, artless face, and asked, "Do you mean to live here?"

"No; what do you think of me?"

"I have no opinion."

"Let me tell you what you would be with me soon."

"What?"

"*Natural.*"

She threw a glance in the direction of Henry and half closed her eyes. He comprehended that he was being compared with him—to whose disadvantage? His swarthy cheek flushed; she saw it, and for an instant her own face changed. "Natural!" she exclaimed, with a laugh. "You think me affected, then?"

"Not that exactly; but—"

He hesitated to say any more, she appeared so disturbed, and looked at him with such a tell-tale expression that he felt a sudden intuition of her intentions.

She complained of being tired, refused to dance again, and took a seat, where she remained silent and thoughtful.

The ball came to an end, as all balls do. A coach conveyed most of the ladies home, Ann among the number; but Eliza walked, accompanied by Henry, who lingered at the door.

"Good-night!" she said, giving a quick sigh.

"Good-night!" he replied, without going.

They stood silent for a moment; then he bent down and kissed her beautiful lips, opened the door for her, waited till he heard her fasten it, and then walked down the street dazed, till he came in contact with several young men—unsated revelers—with whom he adjourned till morning at the Montgomery. None of them were so gay, so rattle-pated as Henry.

Eliza, in her quiet chamber—

> "Where the faded moon
> Made a dim, silver twilight"—[16]

was half-undressed, in happy perturbation, before she thought of the unread chapter. She struck a light, and opening the Bible read, without heeding their import, the dread words: "Whatsoever thy hand findeth to do, do it with thy might; for there is no work, nor device, nor knowledge, nor wisdom, in the grave, whither thou goest."[17]

VII.

Henry was called away on business the next day to Ship Bay, a sea-port near Shelby. Mr. Bassett, with Sam Tripp, took the *Andromeda* and sailed down the bay in the morning and staid out till night. Sam described the voyage to his father as being rather tedious, but added that he thought Mr. Bassett, alone by himself, was a nicer man than when he was with somebody. "He laughed twice to-day, once when I told him a story, and the other time when he dropped a great heap of letters overboard, tearing them into bits first. 'Sam,' says he, 'there's a flock of young gulls for you!'"

Henry drove into the yard of the Montgomery the following afternoon with a sober face. Seeing Mr. Bassett's boot soles on his window-seat he went up to his room.

"I have brought," he said, "awful news from Ship Bay. A vessel arrived there this morning with the tidings of the wreck of the bark *Minerva* and, with the exception of two men taken off by this vessel, the total loss of her crew.[18] Twenty families had relatives on board. She was struck by a heavy sea which swept her fore and aft. Those who were below were drowned in their berths. Those who were on deck clung to the rigging, and after the main-mast was cut away, they crawled into the forward rigging and froze to death."

" 'With heavy thump, a lifeless lump,
They dropped down one by one,' "¹⁹

said Mr. Bassett, with a shudder. "What a picture to bring here in such a bright, warm summer day!"

"I saw one of the men; his account was horrible. Ann Le Barron's only brother was the last that died—'game to the end;' when he fell on the deck his head cracked open as if it had been a dry pumpkin that had fallen! One cry rose above the gurgling water as it poured down the hatchway: after that, nothing was heard. The mate died singing 'Caroline of Edinboro Town.' Ned Mayhew, Eliza's cousin, broke off his fingers and dropped them overboard before he breathed his last. There wasn't much cursing, the man said, nor much praying. They had little hope of rescue, for the weather was thick, and it blew great guns; but they cheered each other, and promised to hold on and not fall on purpose. They didn't mind each other's dying a bit, and when one tumbled all that was said was, 'There goes Jo,' 'Bill is down,' or, 'Tom is off.' 'I tell ye,' he concluded, 'when death comes that way 'tain't much to face it; 'tis as easy to die as it is for me to take this chaw of tobakker.' "

"Who will spread the news?"

"One of the men is on his way here."

They were excited and restless, and agreed shortly to go over to Mr. Mason's and tell Eliza. Henry was more disposed to cry than she when he made the attempt to speak of her cousin's death, who was his friend. She thought of his trouble before she felt her own grief, and would have spoken some words of sympathy if Mr. Bassett's presence had not restrained her. Mr. Bassett noted it, and accused himself of indelicacy in venturing to come with Henry. Mrs. Mason cried bitterly; and Mr. Bassett endeavored, with so much success, to say something to calm her that she begged him to come again when he rose to leave.

That evening the disaster was known in Shelby, and the next day every door stood open for neighbors and friends to come and go with their burden of sorrow. It was not the first time that such an occasion had drawn them together.

Mrs. Le Barron grieved savagely for her son; she loved him better than she loved Ann, and in her bitterness revealed it. The loss of his only grandson made old Captain Green peevish and complaining. Altogether

Ann had a miserable time at home. Her own feelings were shaken. In the last few days since the calamity she met Mr. Bassett daily, in his capacity of a consoler of the afflicted. His gentle goodness had touched her heart. As soon as he became conscious of the impression he had made she ceased to inspire him with any interest. It was her fate to be bereft of power when she rose above her selfish instincts, or lost the equipose of her will.

The day that a funeral sermon was preached in remembrance of the crew of the *Minerva* there were to be funeral baked meats at Mr. Mason's, and among the guests invited to partake of them were Mrs. Le Barron, Ann, Mr. Bassett, and Henry. The parlors were opened each side of the antique porch, and supper was laid in the long middle room. Ann sat apart so pale and sad that Henry, compassionating her, took a seat beside her, and they conversed in a low tone. He too was troubled. Eliza was so reticent; why she should be he could not understand. Everyone, besides, in this time of trouble, carried an open heart! When tea was announced he took pains to be seated next to Ann. Mr. Bassett sat opposite in a reflective mood, sensible of the current which was drawing them together. It was well that it proved easy for him to be a spectator merely; for he had discovered Eliza's heart.

After supper Ann and Mr. Bassett found themselves in one of the deep parlor window seats. The room was in shadow; but outside the rays of sunset still illuminated the air.

"Who would suspect the sea as it looks now?" he said. "It's surface is so calm that white ribbons are woven across its blue. The sermon to-day makes it a fearful illusion."

"Illusion!" echoed Ann, looking out over the bay.

"Do you court illusions?"

"I never had any."

"Must you have mathematical certainty in your mind to be satisfied?"

"Of what?"

"That the wind will rise and render those white ribbons into green wreathing serpents."

She made no reply but kept her eye fixed on the sea, and he was silent too. Darkness crept down the street, turned the bay into a level shield of cold steel, and stole into the room. As Mrs. Mason called Eliza to light the lamps an overmastering impulse seized Ann and made her speak with gasping breath.

"Would to God that what I think now were not illusion, or that what I feel *is*!"

He continued silent and motionless. Had he turned his face toward her, or spoken a word, her soul would have broken loose in some way—in defiance, expostulation, or entreaty. He watched the gradual growing of the light round the lamp-wicks, and when it widened the room into a clear view, he spoke to Mrs. Mason across it on some trivial matter, and then turning to Ann, said,

"Speaking of illusions reminds me that I have had an idea of astonishing Shelby with private theatricals; of course it must be given up."

"It would be nice to have them in the winter," she answered, pleasantly, though she was in a desperate mood.

Her cheeks, usually so pale, were crimson, and her eyes glittered; dark images filled her mind. She thought of her young brother dying on the wreck in the wild, icy sea; of her mother widowed, bereaved; of herself unlovely and unloved; and hot tears battered against her eye-lids, but she would not allow them to fall.

She was glad to get home and be alone. By morning her self-possession was restored, and she was ready to face life with all energy.

VIII.

Mrs. Mason was pleased with Mr. Bassett. He was neither light-headed nor light-hearted, she said, as some folks were, though she would call no names. Eliza knew that she meant Henry Allen; but as Mrs. Mason found fault with nearly every body, she laid little stress on her words. Since the night of the dance she believed that there was a happy understanding between her and Henry. With an egoism which belongs to girls like her, she thought it natural that they should meet, love, and marry. That she had disposed of her affections to the very first presentable young fellow she thought suitable did not occur to her. So much being established on her part, there could be no exaction, suspicion, nor jealousy; nor the foolishness of lovers' quarrels, nor the silliness of love-making. The tranquil acceptance of his attentions had at first given Henry satisfaction and a sense of security which made him dally with opportunity, and put off from day to day the fulfillment of his intention to ask her to marry him. Now he continually felt a vague irritation against her: that it was instigated by Ann Le Barron he did not dream. His own feelings were "all right," he professed. It was hard that he should be left so in doubt, but he could not make a fool of himself by thrusting his love before her unless he knew her feelings. Meantime he devoted most of his evenings to Ann. Several weeks passed and nothing happened—nothing frequently happens in real life. Time, at the best, is filled up with rubbish not worth recording, except by the angel who writes in our Book of Life.

The tide of human affairs in Shelby flowed over the disaster which had thrown it into an agony of grief and remembrance. One evening Henry and Mr. Bassett joined the sewing circle by invitation. Eliza Mayhew was not there, but Ann Le Barron was; and she, Henry, and Mr. Bassett were the last to leave when it broke up. Henry offered his arm to her, and asked Mr. Bassett to walk with them, but he declined, and hastening to the Montgomery entered his room and locked the door.

Some time afterward he heard Henry come up stairs and try the door. "Bassett!" he called, "let me in; I must talk with you."

He heard no answer.

"I'll break the door in!" he called again.

"You haven't the courage," Mr. Bassett answered from within. "I won't let you in. Go to bed."

Early the next morning Henry was off by stage to Belford. Mr. Bassett avoided society for the space of a week, and occupied himself with sailing and horseback excursions. He was not surprised when a rumor reached him before the end of it that Allen had offered himself to Ann Le Barron. Nobody believed it; every body vehemently denied it; still the rumor spread.

When Henry came back he was busy with his papers for several days, and kept his room closely. One evening, however, he called on Mr. Bassett. A desultory conversation set in, which was kept up on both sides with spirit for a few minutes, and then they fell into a dead silence.

"Let's take a walk," said Henry; "it is a splendid night; harvest moon, big and red, lights up every thing!"

Mr. Bassett agreeing, they sauntered through the village and went up the east road, which crossed a hill, on the top of which they stopped to look out seaward.

Though Mr. Bassett quoted

> "The silver margin which aye runneth round
> The moon-enchanted sea hath here no sound,"[20]

Henry did not look up; he was obstinately bent on whipping the hem of his trowsers with a switch. They descended into the village again and walked to the other end of it. When they came to Mr. Mason's house they saw Eliza sitting in the porch watching the moon, which shone in her face. Henry came to an abrupt halt; Mr. Bassett, saying to himself, "Deuce take it!" passed on, with a sweep of his hat in her direction, without turning his head.

She rose impulsively, and resumed her seat with slow dignity, without speaking to Henry. He sat down on the step before her, and imploringly put his hand on her arm. She kept her regards on the moon. He knew no more than the moon what she felt, but he knew better than ever that he loved her, and that he was a fool. He dashed his hat on the ground and began to cry, as men can cry sometimes; torrents of tears fell from his eyes, which he made no attempt to wipe away. Neither did she.

"I *loved* you so," he said at last, with a sob in his throat.

"It is true, then, what I have heard?"

"Would you have it untrue?"

He bowed his head on her knees, and she pulled him up by his hair, full of wrath at his betrayal of her and his weakness. Pride came to her aid, and suggested that, as there was no bond between them, there was no necessity for any revelation on her part. Would it not answer for her to dismiss the subject with a few lies?

"You will give me up?"

"Yes," she answered, her soul turning to the truth. "I place no value on you now; but I thought we loved each other?"

"Let me tell you—"

"No."

"I am not engaged."

She stepped inside the door.

"They have lied about us."

"*Us*! A lie on such a point is enough."

She shut the door.

That night, when he knocked, Mr. Bassett did not refuse him entrance, but allowed him to come in, and exhaust himself in curses, self-reproaches, and raving invective.

"'Man is man,'"[21] quoted Mr. Bassett, with an exasperating coolness. "He will fall whenever circumstances will let him," he thought, after Henry had gone. "What would have been the result if that serious-hearted girl had taken him back?"

In less than a month Henry introduced Ann Le Barron to his mother. She was haughty, as Ann expected she would be; but in time she was convinced by Ann's strategy that Henry, being weak enough to choose her, might have been weaker and chosen worse, so she succumbed, and the olive flourished between them.

IX.

Mr. Bassett left Shelby, "bag and baggage," according to Tripp, in the middle of September. He would go, he told Henry, before

> "The autumn leaves were shed, and wintry rains
> Were sown in swelling seas;"[22]

and gave no other reason. He was regretted, and spoken of, after he had gone, as he would have been had he died. "He was a better man than he looked to be at first," was said, and with that he was laid on the shelf of the past. He was a better man than when he came, for his moral atmosphere was clear. He had discovered the reason of his errors, and had learned to separate his will from his instincts. Tears rose to his eyes as he whirled along the road over which he might never travel again. In Shelby he had found a complete intellectual solitude, and there were born aspirations which he promised himself should guide him.

Out into the world, wherever he has gone, there must he be left with his new-found strength. He is not the first man who has thought himself good and lofty when alone. He will learn whether his old demons lie in wait to leap into his heart, crying, *"We have been faithful!"* and again penetrate him with the lusts which betray the souls of men.

X.

For many nights after her last interview with Henry Eliza read her Bible with a mechanical sense of duty which pervaded all her actions, and then gave up to the trouble she had kept at bay during the day. She pondered over the success of selfishness and duplicity, and the failure of generosity and honesty. She saw that she might have retained Henry, and she despised herself for the thought. How she burned with shame that so weak a man could make her suffer so bitterly! How weak she had been to snatch at such a shadow, and rejoice over it so fatuitously!

After the shock was over, in spite of her elastic temperament she remained unhappy. Life had lost its savor. To all appearance she bade fair to settle, where so many women's souls lie perdu, into the commonplace. Her sharp-eyed grandmother knew her trouble, and cast about for some mitigation of the evils which assailed her, but finding none, wisely let her alone. Faithfulness to routine, however, brought its reward; the old pleasure of habit stole back little by little, and she was already happier than she knew. The patient fulfillment of her social and household tasks restored her her former moral beauty; what she lacked besides would come in time.

One Sabbath evening, early in May, she sat in her chamber, dull and sad. She had seen in church Henry Allen and Ann Le Barron, as man and wife, for the first time. She was thinking of them when it came into her consciousness that they were not the cause of her unhappiness.

She herself must be the cause! Love for Henry Allen was a myth, and hatred against Ann Le Barron also. A sense of the narrowness of her mind, the smallness of her aims and pursuits, smote her. She had whirled on the pivot of selfhood till she could distinguish nothing beyond it. Throwing a shawl over her head, she went through the garden into the level fields lying under the star-lit sky.

"'The firmament showeth his handiwork,' she chanted. 'Night unto night showeth knowledge.'[23] How my soul has been darkened! But I see light, as I see the stars."

How she wept before she left the fields! The rain of tears made her spirit clear. As she walked homeward her self-communings elevated her beyond mundane affairs. It would be nothing to bear the ills of life, since she believed that she could keep a steadfast eye on the life to come.

For a time this exaltation lasted, then her wings cracked in its rarefied air, and she dropped to the earth unsphered again. There was nothing to develop her in the circumstances by which she was surrounded. But Nature came to her aid, and her eyes were opened to her beauty. It was a slow process, however. A year—two years passed, before she came to mental maturity. In that time a change took place in the household. Old Mr. Mason was gathered to his fathers. Mrs. Mason sank into a quiet state from the day of his death, resigning all authority to Eliza. There was not much property left, but enough for her to retain the old house and the old ways. But she changed the old ways somewhat. The material superfluity was cut off, and an intellectual one added. The house looked poetical now, with its books and pictures and harmonious details.

XI.

Ann Allen lived in Belford, but her visits to her mother in Shelby were so frequent and so long that it was supposed she found a freedom and repose there that was lacking at home. It was one of Eliza's crosses that Ann visited her with an assumption of the intimacy of former days. She made no selfish appeals as she did then, but she was the same fritterer away of time. When Henry was in Shelby, Ann postponed going there. He came and went at her direction; it saved him trouble. After obedience to her, his chief pursuits were the cultivation of grapes and pettifogging. Taking into consideration that there was no capacity in him for further growth, and none in Ann, their match might be called a suitable one. It is certain that neither were unhappy—they passed life as the multitude pass it, with a great deal of self-satisfaction.

She had come to Shelby to pass September, and one windy day in the latter part of the month went out to make calls, when she saw a sight that made her heart stand still. It was Mr. Bassett, "bearded like a pard," sun-burned and robust. She stopped, he stopped, and they shook hands with smiles that extended no farther than the stony back-ground of their teeth.

"Have you come to fish? Henry will be so sorry that he has sold the *Andromeda* now."

"He was sold too," he thought, as he said, aloud, "I have come to sketch this time."

"You have learned to paint?"

"I have been an artist for years."

She had a feeling of thankfulness, in spite of the agitation which his presence had thrown her into, that she was not allied to an *artist*. There was something itinerant in the idea.

"Oh my!" she exclaimed.

They bowed with smiles again and parted.

He was on his way to Mrs. Mason's. Eliza received him with calm cordiality. Mrs. Mason said that she shouldn't have known him, but that she was glad he had come back. Her warm welcome put him on the old footing at once. He felt the change in the atmosphere of the house, and saw one in Eliza that the mere time of his absence could not account for. To avoid allusion to his former visit, he plunged into general accounts of what was doing in the world, and he found that her mind had strayed beyond the bounds of Shelby and could follow him. Taking up an *Art Journal* he remarked that he had lately seen the pictures of an artist whose name he mentioned. She said that she wished the artist would come to Shelby and paint its coast scenery.

"By-the-way," he said, "I am an artist, and my desire to paint under these autumnal skies has led me here."

He wondered at the glow which came to her countenance at his words.

"When I was here before," he continued, "I had grown weary of painting, and kept my art out of sight. It was as well; don't you think so?" he asked, with a smile, "considering that I could not have gained popularity if I had revealed my profession."

She asked permission to be his guide to certain spots she had wished a painter might see; a permission he granted, and then fell into a brown study. Eliza's eyes filled with tears as she looked at him, with the recollection of the time when she was sorrowing for the loss of her cousin Ned; and she was surprised that she had not remembered until now the part he took as a sympathizing listener to all who came to him with their grief. How indifferent and unfeeling she must have appeared to him!

"'Liza," said Mrs. Mason, "Mr. Bassett must stay to tea, and it is time for you to see about it."

Is it strange that the wide old parlor, with its white panels, its new windows with large panes, its crimson carpet, and its crimson and blue clothed tea-table, at which Mrs. Mason sat in the quiet of happy old age, and over which Eliza presided in the beauty of womanhood, fair, serene, intellectual, seemed idyllic to him? They lingered at the table, and he, while drinking cup after cup of tea, told them of his visit to Europe. He had been there nearly two years, and was just returned. After tea he lingered till he saw Mrs. Mason dozing in her chair.

They met often, and his old room at the Montgomery saw little of him. When Henry heard of his frequent visits to Eliza he was tormented by pangs of jealousy and envy, for he had taken it for granted that she would allow no man to seek her. He had disappointed her—what right had she to get over this disappointment? He haunted Shelby an uneasy man. Mr. Bassett saw his uneasiness, so did Ann; but she overlooked it: he was her husband, it was safe to do so.

Mr. Bassett took care that Eliza should not meet him with Henry. To his old acquaintance he offered his painting as an excuse for not joining in parties or making visits. He was readily excused. Eliza suspected that he was poor, influenced, perhaps, by the general opinion in regard to artists, and her suspicion removed the restraint that she would have felt had it appeared otherwise. She proposed that he should ride with her to the places he wished to sketch, and invited him to dine, or to tea, almost daily. Mrs. Mason winked to herself now and then, and kept counsel with her thoughts, but said nothing.

One beautiful hazy morning he strolled over there in his painting jacket and with his cigar.

Eliza was alone, and asked him to read to her while she finished a piece of sewing. Mrs. Mason put her head in at the door in the middle of "The Talking Oak,"[24] and took it out again. Presently she sent in word that Mr. Bassett must stay to dinner, and that Eliza need not come out to help her. After "The Talking Oak" *he* talked and Eliza listened till they were called to dinner. During the meal both were a little abstracted, but very polite to Mrs. Mason.

"What do you say," he asked, "to ciceroning me through the Neck this afternoon? There are good effects abroad to-day."

"I say 'Yes;' and we will go as soon as dinner is over."

"I'll go down to the Montgomery for my pencils and board." And he took up his hat.

"Take a shawl extra," he said, when he came back.

"You spoil her," Mrs. Mason remarked.

He blushed a fiery red, but made no answer.

"You must stop to tea," she said. "I don't believe in Tripp's teas."

"Neither do I," he answered.

They were on the road soon, and passing Ann's window. She was there, looking through the blind, as she had looked once before to see Eliza ride by.

"Oh, it is a match," she decided. "Eliza is getting to be an old maid. She is awfully faded; it is time she married."

For a mile or two they talked gayly, pointing out bits of light and shade, groups of trees, rocks, clouds, or glimpses of sea. But when they reached the depth of the old leafy road they grew silent, and each looked on his or her side of the road with serious interest.

"Behind yonder hill," she said, "is the view of all views, and we must stop by the marsh and walk."

The horse was tied to a tree, and they climbed the hill, from which they saw the sea, where she had once seen Henry fishing in the *Andromeda*. She was thinking of that time when Mr. Bassett startled her by speaking.

"I shall not sketch to-day."

"No?"

"Nor any day here, unless you say you love me, for I love you."

She turned her face to him; it was eloquent with joy and pain.

"I love you," she said; "but do you know that I thought I loved Henry Allen?"

"I know it; but you never did."

"He kissed me"—her face turned scarlet—"and I kissed him, and you can not have the first kiss from me."

"Eliza, I can not give you my first kiss. Forgive me for asking you for your love. I, too—"

She interrupted him.

"So you have suffered?"

"Long and bitterly."

She offered him her hand.

"One thing more before I can kiss it and call it mine. Do you remember my asking you the day I came back about an artist?"

"Yes," she answered quickly.

"I am that artist. Bassett is my middle name. Will you take that, with another added to it?"

"What will grandmother say?" she asked, still holding out her hand.

"Let us go and hear," he answered, taking it.

"Before tea," he said, laughing, when they entered the house.

"Mrs. Mason—" he said.

She looked up through her spectacles at him, and then at Eliza.

"'Liza, you will not leave me?" she cried.

"No," they both said.

"Well, go and eat your suppers in peace."

A mist came over her glasses, and she was obliged to take them off to wipe it away, which she did, slowly.

"Ah," she sighed, "I was young once!"

He bent over her, and kissed her withered cheek.

"You must kiss 'Liza, not me—an old woman."

But she kissed him back, patted his head, and told him that she believed he was almost good enough for Eliza. And Eliza said, "He is quite good enough."

Tuberoses

I.

TIME—*A still, rainy day in September; the hour, 10 A.M. Situation—A small parlor, decorated with pictures and book-cases whose doors are open. An overturned work-basket lies on the floor, and the easy-chairs are occupied with papers and magazines for the room is much frequented. Near the window there is a small table with a watch on it, and a Japanese vase filled with tuberoses; their powerful scent comes and goes in the air like a breath.*[1] *Present—*CLARA BELL, *who is seated near the table, regarding the vase of tuberoses with an abstracted air.*[2] *She soliloquizes:*

"Tuberoses,' he said, 'are placed in the hands of the dead, or wreathed about their faces, when they are put into the coffin.'

" 'But I am not dead,' I answered.

" 'You must be to me.'

"What did he mean? I shall stay here till I am satisfied that I know. Sister Charlotte is at the dressmaker's; Aunt Ann has gone to bed, it being one of her going-to-bed days; grandfather is out at the library; and the housekeeper is making preserves, and holding a day of judgment with the servants below stairs. I shall not be intruded upon; still, I will lock the door. If visitors come they must go to the drawing-room and amuse themselves with the new upholstery therein.

"How do I look this morning? The glass answers, 'Pale and lowering.' It reflects the tuberoses. As I move aside they seem to be lying next my face. Am I dead?

"Seven rows of books in this case. Forty-two volumes in blue and gold. Here is Tennyson, worn more than his fellows.[3] I turn over the leaves:

"'Come not when I am dead
   To drop thy foolish tears upon my grave,
To trample round my fallen head,
   And vex the unhappy dust thou wouldst not save'[4]

"Will he come, or won't he? This picture represents a November eve, I think. A streak of pale amber sky drops over the dark line of the woods under the horizon. On the boughs of a leafless oak in the fore-ground three crows are perched, chattering over the head of a man who is passing through a gate just beyond it.

"'You must be to me,' he said. Why did he not offer to bury me? To be buried, for instance, in our old country grave-yard, where mother sleeps, while this soft, quiet rain falls, would not be so sad as to be left here with these bewildering tuberoses—wax things which can not stir from their fleshy stems, but which baffle me with a secret as subtle as their odor!

"The Venus of Milo in the corner puzzles me.[5] What does she expect? For whom is the calm, stately, mutilated woman looking? A pedestal suits her: men may fall at its base, but rows of petitioners would kneel in vain. Such women must be knocked down. Charlotte is a woman on a pedestal, although she has not a Greek face. I saw her look of surprise at George Garth last night. A Greek woman is never surprised.

"This is the gilt goblet she brought him with water in it. There is a little remaining; I pour a libation on the prospective grave between us.

"What did he say to her when he gave the goblet back? He touched her hand and she stood as if arrested, answering meekly. She yields to him. As for me, I never yield to him—never will; I defy his lordly eye, his willful mouth, his resolute bearing—his whole self! I shall not give him any more trouble thereby, since I am dead to him. 'In that sleep of death what dreams may come?'[6] Suppose I am found here with staring eyes and folded palms upon my breast—this way—and some one comes, will the scent of tuberoses ever be forgotten by the person who finds me?"

[A knock on the door.—A servant enters and informs her that it is lunch-time, but that none of the family are at home. Clara tells her that she has some work to do which she can not leave, and orders tea and a 'plate of something' to be brought her. When the servant returns she brings with the lunch a letter.]

"Have you brought a letter too? Shut the door.

"John Prince, George Garth's cousin, writes me, and seals his letter in pearl-colored wax with his crest! The tea is good. I like poached eggs for lunch. How pleasant the room is for a quiet soul! One could easily pass a day alone, if it were not for the tuberoses. But their odor is faint now; I hardly perceive it. What does John Prince write?

> "'Clara, has George gone? Did he present himself to you in uniform? You know we made an application together for an appointment. He got his—he gets everything—but I didn't get mine; my country does not want me. Therefore I have retired to my uncle's in Yonkers to watch the tide of events. Why can't we correspond? Your letters will enliven my solitude; mine to you will be dull, of course; but I think, from what you said the other night, when George and I were with you and Charlotte at the Maison Dorée,[7] that I could adapt them to your wishes. You were in earnest then.'

"What did I say that night? We were merry, I remember; at least John and I were. Now that I think of it, though, George was serious, especially when I fed John with my stick of Italian bread. Charlotte was serious too, but her seriousness was hunger. Perhaps the letter will inform me further.

> "'After we returned to your house, George asked Charlotte to sing one of his sentimental dirges—
>
>> "I must not say that thou wert true,
>> Yet let me say that thou wert fair;"
>
> and you immediately afterward favored us with an Ethiopian lyric:
>
>> "'Way down on the old Pedee.'"

George, being in a fit of heroics, with battle-fields in prospect, harangued us about knights and troubadours.[8] He wished that times now were more like the times of old, when the lady-loves of those gone to the wars remained in castles, pledged to fidelity and worship toward them. "This was," said George, "as it should be. If a woman loves, her life should testify her love."

"A violet by a mossy stone
   Half hidden from the eye,"⁹

you interrupted him with, but our warrior continued:

"'If I returned to find that a woman I had set my heart upon had visited all the public places possible for a woman to visit, or that she appeared even in the ordinary avocations of her life as if I were not, I would renounce her.'

"'How do you expect a woman to understand all this?' I asked, you know.

"'Every woman in association with a man must know whether she is indifferent to him, or whether she is not. What is the fine perceptions of the sex intended for, if not to learn such things?' You said then, Clara, that such ideas were the ideas of a barbarian—a rough-and-ready boor; that, could you surmise you had so vain a suitor, he should be left in ignorance of your feelings till he should come to your feet with his heart in his hand. No man should ever be entirely at rest concerning the return of his love by you; that you should be disgusted with one who thus insisted upon being made comfortable by continual professions and confessions. Dear Clara, I would save you all that trouble. Won't you begin to fancy me in the light you spoke of?'

"John Prince is an ass. So George has gone to the wars! It was late last night when he gave me the tuberoses; could he have been going then?

"It is tedious here; the rain darkens the panes with its meandering tears. The watch says two o'clock; so far through the long day, and I am no nearer the mark. The clouds are piled round the sky in slate-colored ridges; patches of yellow leaves blur the sidewalk, and look like faded butterflies glued to the stones; their day is over. It is a pity that they could not have found sepulchre in the fields and forests. I wish I had some sewing. There may be something in this basket of Charlotte's. At any rate I can sort over its materials. Why does she have three spools of cotton of the same number, sixty? Here is a collar begun; how neatly she sews! Charlotte is what people call a 'solid girl,' methodical, sensible, cold, but how good she is! How she sniffed at the tuberoses last night, pretending that they made her sick. George overturned her work-basket then.

"'Take it up, Sir,' she said.

"'It is rubbish, and rubbish makes me sick.'

"'It is out of place in this room, certainly,' she said, mildly. He made a movement toward it then, but I put my foot on it and he turned away. We did not speak to each other after that. Here is a roll of paper— paragraphs from newspapers, no poetry. Charlotte does not like poetry. What is this?

"'George Garth, captain in the volunteers, has been assigned to a position on the staff of Major-General Dix.' He can not have had his commission a week. Why should Charlotte see this item, and not I? I'll capture it. What is the next? 'Camphor liniment.' And this? 'The Empress Eugénie rode out a few days ago in a white tulle bonnet without trimming!'[10] I find nothing to do in the basket. What if I should sleep! In a dream, maybe, the solution will come of the riddle, 'You must be to me.'

"With shut eyes my thoughts fly back to the time when I first knew George Garth. Four years since. I was sixteen. He began to tutor me then; but happily he went to India to live with an English relative, and my education was completed without him. Six months ago he came back, for life, he said, India was tedious; he was tired of pale ale and of curry. He renewed his acquaintance at the same point where he left me; why does he not see that I have changed? I remember well the day he paid his first visit to us. I was reading 'Faust.'[11] '*You* read Faust,' he said, and laughed. What would he say if he heard me pray with Faust, 'Give me back again the times when I myself was still forming. I had nothing, and yet enough—the longing after truth and the pleasure in delusion.'[12] He would laugh again, and tell me that the sentimental tendency of my mind must be corrected.

"Mother used to say that his temper and mine were alike; but that mine was manifested, while his 'got into his head,' like drink, and made him dull and blind. After that fire in Nolans Street, when he pulled out of a window old Mary Bell, our carpet woman, she grew fond of him and thought him a noble fellow, although old Mary said, when she told us of the affair, 'he swore awful.'

"The house must have fallen asleep, if I have not. Something is crawling in the sofa-pillow; the thud of my heart chokes me! How dumb these books and pictures are! Where can Charlotte be? Engaged in one of her interminable talks, I have no doubt, but I hear her on the stairs; she tries my door. Charlotte, this is the chamber of mysteries; you can not come in."

"Mysterics? fiddlesticks!" Charlotte answers from without. "I met

Ellen Garth at the dress-maker's, and she gave me a letter. Would you like to see?"

A wild light came into Clara's eyes. "Slip it under the door, 'Lotte."[13]

The letter glides over the threshold, and she hears Charlotte running up stairs.

"Unsealed! Why, who is it directed to? 'Miss CHARLOTTE BELL, Present.'

"I am glad that it is short, for it is quite dark. I do not wish to light the gas. The letter is signed 'George Garth;' he offers marriage. I am released, for I know now what he meant when he said 'You must be to me.'"

II.

When Charlotte Bell ran up stairs she repeated what she had said to herself several times before—"George Garth is a fool."

Although it was the dinner hour, she remained in her room to cogitate whether she had taken the wisest way of informing Clara of his letter. Sisters are sometimes ignorant of each other's feelings; but Charlotte, in one particular, believed that she had divined Clara's. It seemed to her, by the rule of contraries, that Clara loved George; there was no other way by which to account for her goading behavior toward him. Had she been indifferent she would have let him alone, she reasoned. From the fact that George was a constant visitor at the house, and forever following them about, whether in good or ill humor, she had concluded that he was drawn by Clara; of herself as being the attraction she had never thought.

"I'll not answer his letter," she thought. "How ridiculous he is! He is but a year older than I am. John Prince is nearer the mark. I hope I have taken the easiest way for Clara; I did not want her to blush or grow pale before me."

She crept down stairs softly to find the parlor door open, and the room vacant. Across the floor fell the light from the street lantern, in whose bright wake the vase of tuberoses was visible.

"Those tuberoses," she thought, "why did he give them to *her*? But he knows that I can't bear them."

She entered the dining-room. Her grandfather, her Aunt Ann, and Clara were at the table. The waiter was putting the second course on.

Her aunt greeted her with, "You are too bad, Charlotte; we waited five minutes for you."

"I have had so many things to do to-day, and my dress was so damp I was obliged to change it."

Clara ate a crust of bread slowly, as if she relished it greatly, and had no other thought apparently but the thought of her dinner.

"I found a new portrait of Laura to-day," said old Mr. Bell.[14]

"Another old one, you mean," Aunt Ann remarked.

"Yes, I do mean that."

> " 'Think you if Laura had been Petrarch's wife,
> He would have written sonnets all his life,' "[15]

said Clara gayly.

"Do not quote that profligate Byron, my dear Clara," begged Aunt Ann.

"What a girl!" commented Charlotte, with her mouth full.

"How would Charlotte receive a sonnet from George?" Clara thought. The picture of Werther's Charlotte cutting bread for the children would be a suitable present for him to make her instead of writing a sonnet.[16] There was something domestic in it—something that must remind one of the present Charlotte. A variety of images presented themselves to her during the dinner concerning the future of George and Charlotte. She determined to dwell on the subject; she would not thrust it from her thoughts.

After dinner Aunt Ann retired to her room again to resume a novel, Mr. Bell went to his library to look over his collection of portraits, and Charlotte and Clara dodged each other with a feint of unconsciousness that was both laughable and sad. In the drawing-room Clara kept a book before her face, reading up and down the same page till Charlotte began to play, then she stole up behind her and held George Garth's letter over her shoulder. Charlotte wheeled round on the music-stool, seized Clara's hand, and said,

"Did you ever know such a donkey?"

"Yes."

She took from her pocket the letter of John Prince, and gave it to Charlotte with, "Enter Dromio of Ephesus."[17]

Charlotte looked at it a moment with astonishment.

"I know what is in it, I presume," she said, rather frigidly.

"If you are a clairvoyant," Clara answered, leaving the room.

"So many hours of torment are done with," she thought, as she went up stairs to the parlor where she had passed the day. "I can never go back to *that* mood again." She opened the window and put out her head; the rain had ceased, and the moon struggled through the scudding clouds. Down the street came the sound of wheels—the wheels of a noisy hotel hack portending travelers. It stopped in front of the house. Clara drew behind the curtain as she saw George Garth jump out. When she heard the bell ring she took from the vase a tuberose, fastened it in her corsage, and sat down in the dark room with folded arms.

"Well," said Charlotte, shortly, when he entered the drawing-room in his uniform.

"Well," and he stopped in the middle of the floor, twirling his cap.

"How is it that you are here?"

"I was not ordered away to-day as I expected to be; therefore I am able to come to you for an answer to my letter."

His confident tone and manner offended her.

"He whistles me on," she thought, "and I'll whistle him off. Come up stairs, George, I will speak with you there," she said, abruptly.

"Certainly."

"Oh, it is dark here!" she exclaimed, innocently; "wait, George, till I find a match. Faugh! just smell the tuberoses."

George shuddered at the smell.

"Why, Clara is here!" she continued, as the gas betrayed her, but the cunning Charlotte had heard her open the window and knew that she was there. This was the mode in which she intended to punish George; she determined that the interview should be before Clara.

"Good-evening, Clara," said George, his eye catching the tuberose on her dress.

"It is moonlight," asseverated Charlotte, "the gas is meretricious;" and she turned it to a dim flame.

"Good-evening," Clara answered, loudly.

The tone of her voice hit him like a bar of iron. When she pinned the tuberose outside her breast she pinned inside another devil of pride.

"Clara," said Charlotte, in a voice which she could not make quite careless, "where is that letter of George's I gave you just now?"

She made no reply.

For once George, comprehending a woman, comprehended Charlotte.

"You mean to victimize me, Charlotte," he said, calmly. "But I like to see confidence between sisters. Clara, do you approve my offer to Charlotte?"

She would not speak.

"I see that you mean to refuse me, Charlotte; but you know that you would make me a good wife. You dare not say that with you I should not be a happy husband. Why then will you not marry me?"

"You are too young," she answered, hotly.

"You do not believe that I am in love with you. I am not; but you have not expected that of any man—it is not your theory."

"No." she muttered.

"Your character, the habits of your mind, your personal behavior, your ideas of the future, the ties of family influence between us, suit me; I desire to marry you."

Charlotte began to feel embarrassed. Clara went to the table, broke from its stem another tuberose, stuck it in a braid of her hair, and resumed her seat.

George ground his teeth at her action.

"I desire to marry you, Charlotte," he said, with a stamp of his foot.

"George," she answered, faintly, "I think I like somebody better than I do you."

"You are all alike; every woman of you plays the same tricks. What a fool I am! I felt sure of *you*, and never dreamed of what you have told me."

He was in too brutal a mood to spare himself or her.

"Who is it?"

She made a deprecatory motion with her hands which Clara noted. "I fancy," she said, "that it must be a gentleman."

Charlotte smiled faintly, but looked beseechingly at her as if she would say, "Get me out of this, Clara; let me leave you two cross-grained creatures together."

Clara started up. "You are tedious," she said; "I am going."

"I am going too," said George; "I have been here too long. Good-by. So you remember my words to you last night, Clara. I could not have said them once. Does this please your diabolical pride?"

She passed him with an ugly smile and said,

"Dead."

"George," said Charlotte, after she had gone, "I am ashamed of you."

"Why?"

"For offering to marry *me*."

"I repeat the offer if you allow me."

"You are blind and selfish, very selfish to me."

"My selfishness won't hurt you; farewell. God knows when I shall return."

They shook hands heartily as if there was some unspoken sympathy between them. Before he went he threw the tuberoses out of the window. "There is an end of these," he said.

III.

Three weeks passed, and John Prince, receiving no answer to his letter, and devoured with ennui, traveled from Yonkers one morning to invite himself to pass a day or two at Mr. Bell's. The sisters had made no mention of George Garth since his departure; therefore, when John asked them if they had heard from him, they looked at each other and simultaneously answered, "No."

"He has not written me either. I met Jo Lowndes this morning, who told me that George had asked leave of the General to go to the front with his regiment, the Fifth Volunteers. You may be sure that he has gone."

"How foolish!" said Charlotte, looking away from Clara.

"Very, for a fellow with a good income," John replied.

"Only paupers should be in the advance, of course," said Clara.

"But he was doing his duty on the staff, probably; why not be satisfied with that?"

"Because 'man is a pendulum betwixt a smile and tear,' I suppose," she answered.[18]

"Especially George Garth, who, when he gets into a mood, is incapable of seeing or feeling any thing that can not confirm it, and stays in it till a miracle brings him out."

"Let us go to the Winter Garden[19] to-night," Clara proposed, "and forget the war; I wish to see Edwin Booth's 'Hamlet.'[20] And as you know grandfather won't go you can escort us, John."

"Of course, though I don't believe in Tragedy. I'll engage seats at once."

When he returned to dinner he informed the girls that he was too late to get front seats, but that those he had taken were favorable for conversation. He looked meaningly at Clara when he said this, and for reply she tossed her head. At the play she was so attentive to the stage that she appeared oblivious of her companions; but when the curtain fell on the second act, and Charlotte was engaged with her glass, John determinedly turned to her and whispered,

"Why did you refuse to answer my poor letter?"

"I hate to write, you know, John. Your letter was nice; I read it all, I assure you. How poetically handsome Booth is!"

"Hang Booth! You have no heart, Clara. George Garth is right."

"After the theatre we will go to Malliard's; Charlotte will be hungry for jelly."[21]

"Confound Charlotte! You madden me."

"Hush, Polonius is coming."[22]

"What does he say?"

"Hush!"

"'Mad for thy love.'"[23]

"Tell me"—she spoke with so savage an accent that a man in the seat before her turned to look at her—"what is George Garth right about?"

"In believing that you are heartless."

"He gave me tuberoses," she muttered, absently.

"I'll give you a gardenful."

"Don't be reckless, John, and never tell me in plain words what your behavior indicates; for I do not care a pin for you, except in the good old ways of our childhood. Why, we grew up together, you goose."

"We *will* go to Malliard's," he said, and was silent for the rest of the evening. He felt that Clara was in earnest, and had never thought her so before; in his opinion she was a haughty, brilliant, bold girl, and he admired her exceedingly. All the fellows of his acquaintance thought so of her, and he believed that it would be a fine thing to capture her. He had of late consulted George Garth on the matter, innocently giving him reason to think that the capture was possible. George had given him excellent advice—advice which he might have thought was disinterested. He had also spoken so freely of her faults that he was more than ever convinced of them. He did not own that he was taken by surprise when John informed him of his hopes, nor that he had had a dim idea that no one had a right to her except himself. He had calmly and silently waited for those changes in character in her which he thought must take place to make her what she should be for him. When he proposed to marry Charlotte he was in a rage with Clara, with John, and with himself; but he was persuaded that he was collected, prudent, and wise. Perception was not one of his predominating characteristics; and when a recognition of this fact was forced upon him, he felt as some animal of the forest—the elephant, for instance—must feel when he unexpectedly finds himself in an inclosure, or with a placid female elephant who has been the means of decoying a rope round his clumsy leg. Before women he was dictatorial and obtuse; but he was a strong, honest man, and Clara loved him. The more she loved him, however, the less he knew it, for she was perverse. A theory that he must be something to Clara, a far-off Providence in the shape of a brother-in-law, possessed him. His programme, starting from this point, for the future, was definite in its details, one of which was the farewell he conveyed by means of the tuberoses he brought her the night before he expected to leave. The matter-of-fact Charlotte had set his matter-of-fact programme at defiance; and there was something so terrible in Clara's demeanor that evening that his lethargic soul was stirred to its very depths, and when lethargic people rouse they also are terrible. He departed for the wars in fighting mood.

The jelly and chocolate failed to animate any of the party at Malliard's; the three appeared to be in a brown study, which lasted all the way home.

"Clara," said Charlotte, as they went up stairs together, "you have refused John."

"Only snubbed him."

"Did he require it?"

"All men do."

"Oh, Clara, what trouble you are to me!"

"And to every one."

"No, indeed, I was in fun. The fact is, *I* have been a trouble to you; the idea of George Garth pretending to—"

"There, go to bed, 'Lotte."

Charlotte groaned, and obeyed her.

"Does Charlotte think that I care for George?" soliloquized Clara. "Is it possible that he has imagined me in love with John Prince? The booby may have seen the reflection of his fancy in me, and mentioned it to his cousin George. I will speak to Charlotte."

She flew to her room, and, breathless with her determination, exclaimed,

"For once let me be weak with you. Have you guessed my secret? You have. I have loved George for four years and six months. How could you let him ask you to marry him?"

"I didn't let him. I have known for at least *three* years and six months that you loved, but not wisely."

"No, you haven't," she said, testily, and then began to cry. The floodgates once open, she poured a life's confidence into the ear of Charlotte, whose sympathy kept her from gaping a long time. When her sleepiness was evident, Clara crept into bed beside her and went to sleep, with the tears still dropping down her face.

IV.

George is reading a letter from John Prince:

> "'Old boy, she never cared a pin's worth for me. I believe now what you said over and over again, that she would not make a good wife.'"

Here George turned the color of his sash, and called himself a slanderous brute:

> "'What a fascinating girl she is, though; and how she can make a chap laugh with her wit! She'll never marry—never. If she had some of Charlotte's qualities with her own still, she would be a stunner. Then she would inspire one with faith for the future, that time when a man wants to see his brood about her knee.'"

"Curse his impudence!" ejaculated George; "he's using my very words."

> "'But it is all a muddle, my boy, whether we get what we want, or whether we do not. I am sick on't. You are such a hard-headed wretch though, you don't mind the ups and downs of life: I envy you.'"

"Envy me!" said George, folding the letter. "Somehow I do not perceive myself in an enviable light. I feel like a cur. It was an act of dirty baseness to ask Charlotte Bell to marry me. What sense she had to refuse! I like to be punished. No decent fellow—and I hope I have become one—would ever ask two sisters to marry him, one after the other. I have kicked the door of my paradise to and brought away the key; to carry it shall be my penance. I may be killed, however, in a day or two. Charlotte will cry for me, and Clara will say in revenge, 'I should like to send him a tuberose since he is dead also.' I understood her looks that night. She was angry with me for presuming to shut my life from her; she would have been angry with any man for taking that privilege. If she *were* my wife I would crush that pride of hers. What right has a woman to assert herself so offensively? House-lovers, housekeepers, tenders of children, guardians of their husbands' personality, that is what women should be; but it is what Clara will never be. '*Viva la guerre!*'"[24]

In an engagement the day following George was shot through the right arm, and through the hip. His seal ring finger was shot away also. Taken a prisoner to Richmond, his finger was taken out at the socket, and the surgeon tried to find the ball in his hip, but couldn't. In a short time he was exchanged and came down to Fortress Monroe, with his seal ring in his pocket, his clothes perforated with bullets, stained with blood, and himself dirty. His brother officers dressed him in their clothes, cheered him with praise, but shook their heads over the wound in his hip. He was not mentioned in the newspapers, except by one poor reporter, who wrote to his paper, that during the engagement his attention was called to the serious and persistent bravery of a captain, whose name he was unable to ascertain; who, grimed and bloody, cursing his men for quailing when their colonel went down on the field, forced them on without a cheer, and on again, with a silent fury, till he fell and was dragged behind a rebel battery. He appeared subdued by the awful scenes he had witnessed, and when his pipe was allowed him smoked it in meditation, which no one cared to break till he laid it aside. The ball was found at last, but he was lamed for life.

"I should think," he said, "that I might go through a naval engagement. I shall have the gait for it—a rolling one."

V.

"He is coming home, Ellen says, in a few days," said Charlotte one day. "He does not rally as was expected; his privations tell on his system as well as his wounds. He walked fifty miles after he was taken prisoner. I shall rush to see him when he arrives! Shall you go, Clara?"

"No."

But when he came, and Charlotte had gone to his mother's house, Clara sought the room where she last saw him. She hardly knew whether she went there to revive her anger and disdain against him, to recall the love and sorrow she had felt that day, or to form some resolution for the future. The room wore a more formal aspect than it did then; for neither of the girls had frequented it of late. The closed blinds cast a cold green tinge over the pictures; no books were out of place; and the chairs were formally arranged. The watch by which she had counted the long, lonely hours was not on the table; but the Japanese vase stood there—empty. She took it up, and for the first time wondered what had become of the tuberoses she had left in it. No servant was allowed to arrange or to remove flowers. Charlotte would not have removed them; it must have been George himself. Why did he take away what he had given her— given her with a purpose too? She wished then, with an angry impulse, that she had some fresh ones, so that, in case she saw him, she might wear them. The door opened softly behind her; she turned her head, and saw George coming in with a crutch.

"Charlotte is at our house," he said. "You would not come, so I have crawled here to see you. Help me, won't you?"

She hesitated a second, put the vase back on the table and slowly went toward him. He had taken a seat on the sofa before she reached him, and had grown very pale.

"See my maimed hand!" holding it out to her. She clasped her own hands together, but did not speak. "Clara, I am a cripple for life."[25]

Down on her knees beside him she fell, but she remained silent.

"My mind was lame, halt, and blind before I went away."

Still speechless, she looked into his face with eyes that seem to be enlarging with his every word.

"Tell me," he said, falling back on the sofa, "why you were holding that vase?"

Before she could answer he fainted dead away, and when he opened his eyes again Clara had her arm round his neck, and was sopping his face with Cologne water.

"Oh!" he sighed.

"May I kiss your poor hand, George?" she meekly begged.

"Do you love me?"

"Do you love *me*?"

"Clara!"

She kissed him. "I was proud, dear, because I loved you."

"What a miserable part I attempted! Can you forgive me for being such a dolt?"

"Will you forgive me for being so willful?"

They kissed each other now.

"What does this mean?" cried Charlotte, entering. "It is well that I came in. George, I have reconsidered the offer you made me, and accept it. I wish to do something for the cause besides making lint; what better can I do than to consent to take care of you?"

"Charlotte," he said, starting up with astonishing energy, considering his late fainting fit, "I know that you would make me the best wife that I could have, but I do not deserve you. Besides, I think I like somebody better; I do not deserve her either."

"Is this my lord Garth?" Charlotte asked.

"You will kill me, between you both."

The tableau was completed by the arrival of John Prince, who was in search of George.

"Hillo," they said, and grasped hands.

"I am a hulk, you see, John."

"You always were."

"John, I am going to be married immediately."

"Oh, oh!" chorused the girls.

"What pitiful creature consents?"

"Clara Bell."

To hide a slight agitation John pulled at his glove-string and broke it. Charlotte turned very red, but Clara said, gently, "Yes, John, I think I can manage him now."

"Upon my word it is a good thing for them both, ain't it, Charlotte?—a kind of a Kilkenny cat business.[26] You and I will be bridemaid and groom."

"Shall I wear tuberoses, George?" Clara whispered.

"Never."

"Me and My Son"

Mrs. Calton mused beside the fire. "Mechanical piety might be of value to me, or that which this novel illustrates—a chaotic piety; if one *could* have the patience to feel or speak stuff with the cheerful heroine, who is driven from all material happiness with a sharp stick. *She* says, 'It is enough to be close *to* things—you haven't time to live 'em all. To know all about it is to have it. I think it's easy for the angels to be happy, so; they know. It's easiest of all for God.' Either way to get from myself!"

Mrs. Calton tossed the book from her, being restless as well as reflective, and looked out of the window. It was a gusty November day, more dismal without than within, and she turned away to throw herself upon the sofa—to sleep, perchance to dream, or any thing else which chance might turn up. She was alone in the house, mistress of it, for Mr. Calton had gone the way of the earth more than a year ago. If grief is to be measured by one's toilet, Mrs. Calton's was modified; bits of violet peeped among her sables, rosettes on her little shoes, knots of ribbon in her black hair, and an amethyst ornament here and there. She was handsome, though her eyes were gray to greenishness, her hair so dense that it rose in waves round her forehead, and her mouth so large that "prunes, prisms, and Peru" could not draw it up; so full too of dazzling teeth that an enemy might remember what Elia says—"The fine lady or fine gentleman who show me their teeth, show me bones."[1]

She laughed little now, for she had fallen upon weary days. Not for the first time, poor girl!

"Yes," continuing her reflections, "beads to count, a formula to repeat day after day, would absorb the hours. As it is, 'nothing gives an echo to the throne where hope is seated.'[2] The arches of the cathedral, the pipes of the organ, the joints of the knees are mechanical; but in space, sound, and attitude they suggest and invoke the unknown and desired."

Mrs. Calton was interrupted. Her quest for the light never seen on land or sea was delayed. The interruption appeared nothing more than a morning call; but an earthquake could not have been more effective, so far as the changing of her mood went. This opportunity gives her biographer a chance at narrative.

Laura Calton, at this date, between the vague twenties and thirties, was born of "gentle" parents, owners of a nail factory, members of a Congregational church, and the centre of a circle as like themselves as one pea is like another. If Laura's mother had a tea-party in August, the neighbors, one after the other, gave the same early in September. If Laura's father, from his money a little in advance of the community, had his barn painted a new shade, or his carriage lining changed, Mr. Allen or Mr. Perkins followed suit, in a cheaper fashion. It was a very respectable town; an excellent one to be born in, and perhaps a still better one to be buried in. The infants and the dead alone were safe in the bare individuality of human nature. Nobody disputed nor governed *their* way; they would come into the world and go out of it upon a mysterious principle which no opinion could disturb. Laura being a girl of some force and originality, kicked in the orthodox walking-stool provided for her by her guardians and friends; even her good mother thought her queer, and no example to follow; and her indulgent father was often obliged, using his own expression, "to wink" at her. Ostracized people, whatever their acts or aims, are never quite happy, and Laura's girlhood was not satisfactory. The curious comprehension of children which some parents show, Laura was a victim to. If she said "yes," they said "no," from a sense of duty; if she asked for twenty-five cents for a doll's tea-set, they gave her twenty cents to buy a watering-pot to water the cucumbers in the garden with. The fine moral instinct, said to be innate, was much twisted in Laura's mind. She was never allowed to be a law to herself, and nobody explained why she should follow laws that were originated by somebody else.[3] Consequently, she was a child of "ups and downs," possessed by Satan, or on the point of being blest, to use her mother's vernacular. When she grew up she was still variable, "as the shade by the light quivering aspen made;" her leaves were either turned inside out to wind and sun, or glittered darkly through mists and showers.[4] She was not loved, but sought for more than any young lady in the county. Neither lilies nor roses sprang up in her footsteps, but the ribbon snakes of envy and detraction; and this fact closed her heart to the manifold springs of mercy, charity, and tenderness. No inner life was developed, and her outward life was cold and empty. At an early age she discovered that her dolls were stuffed with bran; later, that the worm was in every bud, and rose-bugs eating into every flower. At twenty what ennui possessed her! Full of latent abilities, not a single one had been called into play. Mr. John

Calton appeared upon the stage in the nick of time—for himself; in midsummer, her dullest period, when Nature promises all to the senses, but gives nothing. The world's tired denizen, or a child of nature, Thoreau or Emerson, would have delighted in the season and the scene; but Laura had no soul for nature, no sentiments which every "common sight apparels in celestial light,"[5] no dream of that relation between the seen and the unseen, which brings us glimpses of "that immortal sea which brought us thither."[6] The brilliant July sky was a tiresome spectacle to her; she watched it from vacancy. The sovereign summer clouds, solid in base and apex a moment, boiling like yeasty waves and vanishing up the burning ether, or spreading snowy tufts and plumes across the zenith, or rising like walled cities of towers and palaces, were not as much in her mind as the baseless fabric of a dream. She knew also that the sea rolled before the town; but its plaintive monotone, its fitful roar, the tides, the changing atmosphere and motion, the eternal waste and distance of old ocean "poured round" the world, so congenial to the melancholy and profound in feeling, stirred no mental echo in Laura's spirit. The woods, the meadows, never drew her to themselves; the sprites and elves of the secret landscape, hid in moss, fern, and shrub, never showed their faces to her. Life was dull then without human contact and contest, which belongs to the crowd. What made ordinary people contented, she wondered—those who read no novels, had few new dresses, and never came across attractive men? Must she see those white clouds eternally rise in the north, and the white horses in the bay forever chase each other? Was it her doom to walk up and down Maine Street for the rest of her life, to see that Cummings had a peck of clams outside his door, or a basket of cocoa-nuts, or, on the bench at Begg's Emporium, Tom Frost and Jem Cole smoking, and disputing whether the wind was hauling round, and what the minister "went on" to say the Sabbath before? Must she look out of the window to see Daddy Cox gee and haw his oxen, Mrs. Mortmain skurrying to Mothers' Prayer-meeting, and Mrs. Bond toddling along with eggs and blue yarn to sell, and various other tinkers?

"Oh, mother," she cried, "what is to become of me these weary days? It is everlasting between sunrise and sunset. Oh, mother, how can you be so satisfied? I hate this whole place, and every identical thing in it."

Laura "harried" her mother with these questions one afternoon, when there was not even an old novel nor magazine in the house; when the mail had arrived, bringing her no letter; when she found no article to fix over in her wardrobe; when she had looked in the glass as long as she possibly could, and had finished a neat toilet—all for nothing and nobody! The mother was in her own bedroom down stairs, engaged in darning stockings. The house was so still from garret to cellar—it being the interval between dinner and supper—that the buzz of every individual fly was quite trumpet-like. The fat weed on Lethe's wharf was in a lively situation in comparison.[7] Now and then a curtain flapped on the south side of her house, for the sea-breeze was stirring.

"Laura," answered her mother, in a phlegmatic way, "it would be better for you if you were the daughter of a poorer man."

"Why don't father fail then," answered Miss, pertly. "You often say that you and father live for my advantage."

Laura tipped herself back in her rocking-chair, and her mother instantly discovered that she had an old pair of stockings on her pretty feet.

"Laura," she said, sharply, "why don't you wear those open-work stockings I bought you in Ledford the other day? What is the use of buying expensive things if you won't wear them, I should like to know?"

Laura laughed.

"How about the poor man's daughter, mother?"

Then the mother laughed too. She was a kindly woman, embedded in her beliefs, and rather overlaid with ideas of duty, but, in the main, spirited enough to excuse many of Laura's extravagant notions. She owned two selves—one was hers; the other belonged to her church, her circle, and to that mystical relation which she called her obligations. Alas! Laura did not discover the nature nearest her own till it was too late.

The door of the sitting-room opened with a bang, and Laura saw her father, Mr. Lewis, coming in with a strange gentleman.

"Mother, where are you?" called Mr. Lewis, pulling up the shades.

Mrs. Lewis hurried in, followed by Laura.

"Wife," said Mr. Lewis, with dignity, "I introduce you to Mr. Calton, from New York. He has come to buy nails of us. I expect he has hit *the* nail on the head. Ha! He likes the looks of our place so much that he calculates he'll stop a day or two in our midst. This is my daughter Laura, Sir; my only child, Sir. Don't apologize, mother, but I hope you can scare up something for supper. Mr. Calton has consented to take pot-luck with us."

"If you will put up with the want of ceremony, Mr. Calton, we shall be pleased to have you stay," said Mrs. Lewis.

Mr. Calton bowed, and said he didn't like ceremony, and was excessively fond of country diet. Laura darted a glance from her gray eyes, which he observed, and which caused him to say to himself, "By Jove!"[8]

"Yes, Sir," said Mr. Lewis, "that is just what we have, and nothing else—plain, wholesome, country food; nothing new-fangled or Frenchified in our dishes."

"Curds and cream," added Laura, "golden honey, new-laid eggs, and the crispiest of fresh rolls."

Mr. Calton looked at her again, and this time said, internally, "Thunder and Mars."[9]

Mrs. Lewis frowned at Laura. If there was any thing celebrated in the region it was her table, which always groaned with the first quality of the flesh-pots of Egypt.[10] People rarely refused an invitation to dine or sup with the Lewises. And what should possess Laura to talk so—contrary creature!

"I am sorry it is between whiles with our fruit, Mr. Calton," said Mr. Lewis, also fearing that Laura was on the verge of "capers," and anxious to divert attention from her. "Our Hoveys are off, and our Lawtons haven't come on.[11] Wouldn't you like to take a turn in the garden, Sir? Our pears promise well."

"Certainly," replied Mr. Calton; "I can not have too much of out-of-doors life in this delightful country. Miss Lewis, why have I never heard of your scenery? It is by no means common to find so fresh a landscape in the neighborhood of the sea."

"Coming for nails," Laura answered, "perhaps you thought to see ore and slag only. To my accustomed eyes this is but a dull spot."

"You like city life best, possibly?"

"Innately, yes. I have never spent any time in the city."

His look of surprise flattered her; and as he followed her father into the garden, she felt a new impulse. The atmosphere changed—how pleasant the afternoon had become! She felt grateful for living in a handsome house.

"He seems to be a genteel man," commented Mrs. Lewis; "but he is no chicken."

"Chicken," murmured Laura, absently; "are you going to have chicken for supper?"

"Now, Laura, be spry. Open the parlor, and take Mr. Calton in. The table must be set now. I'll bet that Mary Brown is abed and asleep, lazy trollop! but they are all alike. Help is help. The supper will be all right, daughter, though we don't have chickens in July."

Laura rushed into the parlor, threw up the windows, and examined the premises anxiously. She opened the piano and surged up and down the keys. The voice of the summer sea mingled with the music; it had a glad sound, and she wondered that it came so near. It was provoking that there were no fresh flowers in the vases; but to-morrow it should be different; the room should be decorated, and set in order early! It was a delightful task, when any body was there. The whole house woke up—the kitchen was a scene of bustling preparation.

> "The palace bang'd and buzzed and clackt,
> And all the long-pent stream of life
> Dash'd downward in a cataract."[12]

Mrs. Lewis and her help ran to and fro so constantly that the effect of a stage procession was produced, now in the keeping-room where supper was laid, now in the kitchen and buttery.

When Mr. Lewis returned with Mr. Calton quiet and order reigned. Mrs. Lewis was already in her high chair before the tea and coffee. Laura stood at her place with an air of indifference, but inwardly tormented with the fear that Mr. Calton might consider the whole affair "green" and countrified. Her fear was needless. Mr. Calton felt himself well entertained. Things might be verdant, but only in the sense of freshness. He thought Laura attractive, piquant, new. He was pretty well aware of the station and property of Mr. Lewis. Mrs. Lewis was by no means a tiresome woman, neither ugly nor vulgar. Nail buying had brought his lines into pleasant places. All this he pondered, while eating his excellent supper with a relish which Laura hardly approved of, but which delighted the housewife heart of Mrs. Lewis.

His first visit was a type of the second, and of all. Mr. Calton remained a week with the Lewis family; that is, he slept at the hotel, and passed his days in Laura's society. Mrs. Lewis served him with her best viands three times a day, and Mr. Lewis smoked a cigar and held short conversations with him at the same time and immediately afterward, but it was tacitly understood that the old people were not to interfere at any other time. The young pair walked on the shore in the moonlight evenings, and Laura tried to respond to Mr. Calton's apostrophic condition. He was truly moved by this novel contact with Nature; she blended with his sudden passion for Laura, and the illusion was perfect. Laura's thoughts were more wandering. She could not avoid seeing the opportunity that approached her. The monotonous life which surrounded her might be changed for a city life, for the theatre, the opera, and those inevitable engagements she supposed one must have in entering society as a married woman. Still she was maidenly chaotic—in a flutter, and a little proud. Mr. Calton was a superior man—easy, jovial, and self-sufficient, different from the country beaux, so anxious, and so tenderly beseeching when seeking her favor; and alas! different from the young coast surveyor, the lieutenant, who swooped down on the bay last year like a fish-hawk, and vanished like the same, with the help of a revenue cutter, and who was as delightful a hero as Conrad ever was—the corsair of hearts![13] The thought of *him* was put aside with firmness and a sigh.

The end of the shortest week either had known arrived. It was Sunday morning, and Mr. Calton accompanied the family to church, arrayed in snow-white costume, which came by express the night before in cool haste from his tailor. The black suits of the congregation "sang small" beside this fellow in full sail in Laura Lewis's tow! The impression he made was an irritable one. Common people are apt to feel scorn for that which is new to them; and scorn here was expressed by delicate sniffs, snuffs, and smiles. Laura discerned it, and looked at him, even during the sermon, to exchange kind glances. As soon as service was over he offered her his arm in the very aisle, and she took it, blushing celestial rosy red. Papa and Mamma Lewis also exchanged meaning glances when this act took place, proud and important and parental, like a pair of old ducks.

"I must go home to-morrow," said Mr. Calton, as he and Laura turned into a side street.

"You must be tired of us by this time, I suppose."

"Of course I am."

"We shall never see you again."

"If you say so."

There was a dead silence between Mr. Allen's orchard and Captain Jones's sail-loft; then Mr. Calton skipped a pebble with his boot, and said:

"Do you say so?"

"I am sure we should be very happy to see you."

"Could you lower that parasol a trifle? I can not see your face at all."

Laura muttered something about the sun's dazzling her eyes, but nevertheless shut the parasol.

"We are near home," continued Mr. Calton, "but there is time enough for you to answer me one question. My dear, what do you think of me?"

Again Laura muttered something—that she esteemed him highly as a friend—had enjoyed his visit—hoped they might continue friends, and—mum, mum, mum.

"Hereafter the best of friends, Laura; but I mean differently now, or mean more. I am unwilling to return to New York without the hope of making you my wife. I know I am a dozen years older—what do you say? I can give you a pleasant home, and my whole heart."

"Not just now, please," urged Laura. "I should like to get home."

"Five steps more, and we are at your door. Yes or no, my dear Laura. My proposal can not appear so strange."

"No—yes."

He understood her, and shook hands heartily, whereat she laughed, and then he laughed. When they reached the room, where Mrs. Lewis was untying her bonnet, and Mr. Lewis dusting his hat, Mr. Calton, with timid formality, kissed Laura, "asked consent," and it was as if the programme of a hundred years was settled. Within two months the wedding came off, and Laura left home for the new one, in which this November day finds her, alone and unoccupied.

Mr. and Mrs. Calton were a model couple. The prayer of Agur was answered in their love—neither poverty nor riches were in it, but that medium which keeps domestic life in its true orbit.[14] After buying a good deal of jewelry, and going to many places of amusement, Mr. Calton went back to his business with fresh zest, and Laura took up life on a new external plan, which did not admit a bothersome analysis. In the third year of marriage they lost their first-born and only child. For a season Laura dropped, soul and body, into a dark abyss; the sun in heaven was put out, the moon did not shine, men were as trees walking, and she was alone in the world. That period passed, the accustomed life was resumed—a veil between it and the past, a shade upon Laura's beauty, an older look in Mr. Calton's face, and a different, deeper affection between them; but *that*, according to the wont of our undeveloped life, was not brought out and commented upon. By what theory is our wonderful world created? Men and women live together, fulfilling the apparent conditions of existence, and so many facets of their nature are never cut! One man dies at thirty, whose character is only revealed in its tender simplicity by the shadow of death. Another in the hour of danger brilliantly flashes forth his soul, as from a dark lantern, and then turns the closed sides to the world forever. And there are those who, in some unimportant moment, behold each other's souls in the prison of their eyes, feel them in the link between hand and hand, in the kiss, or word of flame from the lips. Sparkles all, darting and vanishing over the wide, misty plain of the commonplace!

At the end of five years Mr. Calton died suddenly—a prosperous man in the prime of life, full of schemes gratifying to Laura's worldly ambition. The "top of the ladder" he promised she should be—the leader of her set. The rings on her fingers and bells on her toes might be conspicuous wherever she went if she chose. Laura agreed with him, and with him drifted more and more into that outer world where the fruit grows which must, sooner or later, become ashes to the taste. All this was at an end now. At first Laura was stunned, then surprised that *her* life could be so changed. At last she fell into a dreary melancholy, which she believed was to last till some fatal disease should seize her and carry her off. Mr. Calton's will was a trifle humdrum in her estimation; the house was settled upon her, and an income enough to keep it up in the old fashion, no more. A relative or two was mentioned in the will; a cousin Martha was one—a widow, whom Laura had never heard of. This Martha was to have fifteen hundred a year paid to her at her home in the West, or at his own house in Darcy Street, provided she would consent to live with his wife, share her solitude, and be her faithful companion. Laura ordered the money to be sent to Ohio, where the cousin lived, refused to hear the letters read which she wrote to Mr. Calton's executors, and would not answer the several letters which Cousin Martha wrote to herself. So a full year passed. Nothing in the present moved her, nothing in the future interested. She told her acquaintants that the world seemed to have been made for the wind to blow in, and who could tell where the wind came from? And she was not going to be left out in the cold. Seriously, she was wretched, as any woman aged twenty-eight may well be with the ordinary experiences of life. Her liberty was restricted because she was a woman, because of Mr. Calton's wishes, and because her fortune was small. The great panacea of change was denied her. It was the groove business with her as with most, but without heart to roll along in it.[15] She felt no impulse toward literature and art, was not "called" to be strong-minded, and had no especial faith to sustain her in this world, and take her to the next.

"When all that I *have* loved, that which has kept me vital, has passed into a blind and obdurate silence, how can I learn your faith?" she said to the Rev. Mr. Crucible. And Mr. Crucible wisely answered, "We must wait."

Still Laura's soul must have been groping for light; there must have been a latent sentiment for the spiritual, a yearning for that invisible but universal hope, or she would not have been knocking at the door of Catholicism, or at that still more obscure portal, Mysticism, or whatever name it goes by.

Her servant, Ann, opened the parlor door and her mouth at the same time, but said nothing, having no opportunity, she was followed so closely by a tall woman who sat down in the chair nearest the door, and began, in a clear voice:

"Me and my son agreed to look you up. Your silence, Cousin Calton, amused him and troubled me. Curiosity on his side, gratitude on mine. I am Martha Knox; John Calton's mother and my mother were sisters. I am just in from Ohio, and have been traveling three days steady. Now, am I to have your good word or not?"

Mrs. Knox set down her carpet-bag with energy, and folded her hands; but, notwithstanding her volubility, she was confused, Laura stared so at her with mute amazement.

"Me and my son," she repeated, as if to stay herself with a watchword.

Laura was seized with a sudden acute perception that she had been very comfortable till now, and suffered a pang of remorse for not properly estimating the goods the gods had bestowed upon her. And here was Nemesis in the shape of "Me and my son."[16]

She started up and rang the bell for luncheon.

"You must be fatigued, Mrs. Knox. Please come to the fire."

"I *am* fatigued; but am I to be Cousin Martha to you, or must me and my son give it up?" Mrs. Knox grasped her carpet-bag again.

"Is your son in that?" asked Laura, smiling in spite of herself, and Mrs. Knox smiled with her.

"I verily believe I shall have to like you," she said; "and me and my son's sense of duty will wear away."

The old lady came toward Laura with outstretched hand, which was taken kindly; and then Laura carried her into the dining-room, and fed her.

"How did you know that I lived alone, Mrs.—Cousin Martha?" asked Laura.

"Mr. Eben Bangs wrote us in the beginning so. Afterward he suggested that we should invite you to Ohio. Later, he sent us word that he thought it unwise for you to remain in the scene of your troubles. Me and my son thought differently, and here I am. But, my dear, I have to learn thereby that a remnant of pride still hangs round my old self."

Cousin Martha did not tell all that the executor had written. *He* called Mrs. Calton "weak, obstinate, and mistaken." As it was, Laura's eyes flashed.

"Mr. Bangs is a goose," she cried; "he exceeds his limits. And what has your son to do with any opinion concerning me? If you feel any necessity of expressing to *me* the obligation you feel toward Mr. Calton, pray do so; but we need not drag your son into the obligation."

"My dear, I *must*. I always yield to him. He is a genius, an artist, is my son Lester Knox."

"Old Woman of the Sea," murmured Laura. "I don't wonder he sent you off, this genius." Curiosity prevailing at last, she asked Cousin Martha what her son had done.

"Oh dear, what a thing fame is! Lester is the young artist who did the statue of Whinny Ha-ha, which stands behind the Speaker's chair in the hall of Congress.[17] Lester is twenty-seven, you are twenty-eight."

Laura colored, and said that she had been in Washington.

"The statue looks like you."

"Mercy! Indeed?"

"You see, Mr. Bangs sent us your photograph. Lester thought your brow was regal."

Laura colored again, and felt rather lively; but was still angry.

"How very curious and fussy in Mr. Bangs to send my picture!"

"Not very, considering that Lester asked him for it, from mere curiosity, for he said—"

Cousin Martha broke her speech abruptly. It was evident to Laura that Lester had something against her. Cousin Martha began presently again:

"My dear, did you think I could receive John's bequest without learning all about him and his? A whole year has passed, and more. Knox nature could not stand it any longer. Me and my son are different. I had to come. He won't come himself; he will never see you; but we agreed about my coming."

Provoking Cousin Martha! Laura was thankful when bedtime came. Bedroom solitude loomed up as a desirable thing, though she had forgotten her annoyance more than once in preparing for Cousin Martha's comfort. She was also ashamed of certain little twinges and pulsations of affection for this downright visitor. She was alone, that was a fact; and womanly sympathy was not so bad, even in Cousin Martha. She fell asleep and dreamed of "my son," as a disagreeable, yellow-haired Hoosier, in slipshod shoes.

"Dear me!" thought Cousin Martha, feeling very sleepless. "I have put my foot in it. I am paying a price for poor John's legacy. There is something I like in the girl too. I believe that John spoiled her. Aunt Liza, his mother, was a weak sister, if she was my aunt. Linen sheets in winter! She don't take the least notice of what her Ann does; there was twice too much bread cut. I hate the Irish. Laura is as handsome and peculiar as Lester said she was. There's a clock striking midnight, and there's tramping in the street yet. Oh dear! I have not taken my Bible out of my trunk. I forgot it. I hope I am excused."

Cousin Martha had reason to forget her old ways, for she was out of place. Laura frustrated all her attempts at usefulness. In vain she begged for work. It was better, she declared, to watch Lester make clay noses and clay drapery than to sit looking at nothing, or into the street, where every body dressed and walked alike. At last Laura took pity, and taught her some simple embroidery, which proved an advantage to both. Cousin Martha was docile, Laura was patient. "Though they pricked their fingers every stitch," they left in every bud a better appreciation of each other.[18] Still one was homesick, the other bored. Cousin Martha grew reticent. She saw that Laura was not heart-broken, and needed no sympathy, and she felt that there was some lack in Laura's nature which her ignorance could not define. It might be profound, it might be repressed, undeveloped, or shallow. She thought it of no avail to remain with the independent, self-sufficient young widow, and decided to go home as soon as the claims of what she considered propriety were settled. It was a long and expensive journey; respect was due to John's memory; her friends and neighbors were aware of her visit to John's widow; pride would not permit a sudden return to them. Besides, she must wait for Lester's orders. She ceased to mention him, and Laura was no longer annoyed by reference to "my son." One day, when a letter came, Laura pleasantly asked her what was the news.

"He is making designs for a monument for General Marley, to be erected by his brigade. He mentions some French pictures on exhibition here—geener pictures he calls them—and tells me to observe the story-telling power painters have.[19] Lester loves to teach his mother. Goodness knows I am ignorant enough."

"Well," said Laura, "shall we go to the picture-gallery?"

"If you please. I shall go back to him soon; he leaves the time to me."

Her face brightened so at the prospect that Laura felt a pang.

"You have had a melancholy visit, I am afraid. We must first go sight-seeing, and then I will allow you to go home. Why will not Mr. Knox come for you?"

"Oh," replied Cousin Martha, with haste, "he says it is quite enough for me to have bored you; besides, he never thought of coming. He surmised that possibly you would like me well enough to make me a visit; we live in a pretty place; but you'll never think of doing so."

The eyes filled with tears, and her lips trembled in spite of her great self-control; and Laura felt so sorry and so ashamed that she kissed her vehemently.

"Dear Cousin Martha, you are worth two of me, and your son would find me a nuisance. What do I know of the artist life! I always thought artists were queer, and utterly irresponsible, vapid and fantastic outside of their art, slipshod in morals as well as in their shoes—not the sort of men to be related to, but exactly the sort to be invited to dinners and suppers, for the roaring element. I have myself met a painting lion or two with a good deal of mane."

"You *should* visit me and my son," replied Cousin Martha, with dignity.

That very day they went to the picture-gallery. On the way Laura asked if statues brought much money to artists in ordinary; of course she had heard the prices which the sculptors received who lived abroad.

"Lester will have eight thousand dollars for the monument; that includes the base with bass-relief designs."[20]

"You are quite rich, then."

"All generals do not have monuments. Orders are few and far apart. We have been extremely poor. Lester has cut cameos, headstones, signs in wood even, Turks and Indians. Poor, grand boy! His father died when he was only five. I have made shirts, dresses, baby-clothes, every thing to keep the wolf from the door; and we did. Nobody starves in the West. Corn-dodgers and pork are free to every body that's honest and industrious."

"Hush," said Laura, for Cousin Martha's voice grew loud over her bitter recollections. "Here we are at Goupil's; we must go up stairs."[21]

There must have been some latent artistic power in Cousin Martha, she so suddenly forgot every thing in her delight; first at the harmonious aspect of the salon, and then over the pictures. It must be confessed that here she rose superior to Laura, and Laura humbly felt it. She followed silently in her wake.

"See!" said Cousin Martha, pointing to a Bouguereau—a mother and child—"the ineffable glory of maternity in this beautiful, simple woman's face, as she watches her sleeping babe, as yet only a degree beyond a new-born kitten."[22]

"Yes," answered Laura, softly.

"And here"—stopping before the "Autumn" of Hamon—"do you perceive the silent buoyancy of the floating figure extinguishing the last flowers in the pale, dusky atmosphere?[23] Dear me, Lester ought not to be living in Lanerk, when such pictures come over the water."

"It is beautiful; but what an impossible idea!"

"Lester says nothing is impossible to the spirit of Art. But here is a different picture; what do you think of it?"

"A Spanish coqatee—what handsome muleteers! One must go to Spain for such men."

"Or to Lanerk, Ohio," said Cousin Martha to herself.

Laura was pupil throughout the visit, and she came home with a sense of relief at the non-appearance of "my son." If the mother gained so much in the atmosphere of art, what would he prove to be? and herself so lamentably ignorant, so behind the times, as she perceived she was. What a musty old street Darcy Street looked! what a dingy old house hers! what an empty, foolish frivolous circle she moved in!

Cousin Martha did not appear the next morning at the breakfast-table. Laura waited, and then went up to her bedroom to find her in bed, feverish, and with headache. By noon, she said, she should be well; Lester's letter, or the pictures, or a cold, had made her a little poorly; a cup of tea would set her right! It was not so. At night she was so ill that Laura sent for a doctor, who declared the illness to be a rheumatic fever, which was always painful, sometimes tedious, occasionally dangerous. Cousin Martha contradicted him with asperity; *she* knew her constitution, he didn't. Besides, she must go home; Lester was expecting her, and she would not disappoint her dear boy for all the rheumatic fevers in creation. The dear boy was not talisman enough to protect her from the fever; it increased, and in her sufferings she became dovelike in patience and gentleness. Laura watched her night and day; the long-stifled traits of compassion, benevolence, and self-abandonment came into full play. Tenderness gave birth to tenderness, and, except in the case of her child, Laura was never so absorbed. She received a shock, however, when the doctor said that Mrs. Knox's family must be told of her illness, and perhaps sent for. A struggle took place in her mind, and then she went to Cousin Martha's bedside.

"Dear cousin, it would be a comfort for you to see your son; shall I send for him?"

Such an appealing expression came over the worn face, that Laura had difficulty to hide her tears. "It would be good of you to ask him to come; but it would make so much trouble to have a strange man in the house. I am not so very sick, am I?"

"I want him to come, to cure you."

Cousin Martha folded her hands over the coverlet with such content that Laura hurried down, either to telegraph or write a letter to her son. She took her little, used desk in her lap, and began to write:

"Sir," That was stiff.

"My dear Mr. Knox." That was conventional.

"Cousin Lester." He was not her cousin. The doctor came in.

"Better telegraph," he said. "Time flies; it is a long distance between here and Ohio. Puss, you have done pretty well lately; I'll give you a diploma."

"Common decency," said Laura.

"Fiddle-stick! The old woman comes of a stock, and you like her; she has done you a good deal of good. I know your appetite is better since she came."

"It isn't a mite better," Laura replied, indignantly. The doctor laughed and went up stairs, and Laura dispatched the message. When Lester Knox received it, such was his consternation that he snatched up his hat and coat, hurried to the station, and jumped into the train just starting. He tried to shut out all thought. It was not possible to admit that his mother, the only woman friend and relative he had, was in danger. What a fool he had been to let her travel so far from him! He confounded Calton's bequest. Why should they cotton to his widow for that? To be sure, it had opened a vista to Italy; and that more confounded photograph of hers, which that old dunce Bangs had sent, had opened a foolish dream vista; he wished them all further—at the North Pole!

In this condition he arrived at Darcy Street early in the evening. He rung the door-bell furiously. Ann, who was in the hall lighting the gas, opened the door, and he rushed in. Laura at that instant was coming down stairs with a glass in her hand. He sprang toward her.

"How is she, Laura?" and he seized her hands. The glass fell and shivered as he drew her close to him and looked anxiously into her face.

"She is no worse, Lester, to-night," she soothingly replied. "I am so glad you have come. This way, please."

She led him into the parlor to a seat, and took off his hat. He was on the point of breaking down; that, with a man, means crying like a woman. She stood before him in silence. Raising his head presently, he looked at her searchingly and said:

"I know that you have been most faithful in caring for her; thanks, Mrs. Calton."

"I have done my best; you are welcome, Mr. Knox."

He suddenly felt conscious of being shabby, and gave an embarrassed laugh.

"Where shall I go, Madam? I am tired, dirty, and hungry. Where's the tailor, the butcher, and the candlestick maker?"

"Stay with your mother, of course. I must first tell her that you are here. She is feeble and nervous. It will not do for you to rush at her as you did at me, Sir. Your room is ready."

His eyes blazed like diamonds. The dust of travel was not over them at all events. He was relieved, but still feared to ask questions concerning his mother.

"Cousin Martha has been better for twelve hours," added Laura. "Ann will take you to your room." Laura paused a moment to think of him. First, he was undeniably dirty; but then he was as undeniably handsome. He had no sentimental nor long-haired aspect; on the contrary, an uncommonly fierce and cropped one. His hair was short, his beard long, both reddish in hue; his nose was large, so was he; tall and broad-shouldered; and his eyes were awfully keen. She felt like having a fight with him, and made up her mind to avail herself of the first opportunity. Very softly she crept back to Cousin Martha's bedside, to break the exciting news of his arrival, and—found him there. Cousin Martha had both arms round his neck, and he was kneeling beside her.

"Of course I asked Ann to bring me here. Ann is a good girl; has she waited much upon you, mother? I'll make her bust," he said, in a low voice.

"Only Laura has taken care of me, Lester dear. I have been a world of trouble to her. Oh, I have ached so!"

"It is nearly over now, old lady. Let me go. I'd like a little water to cleanse me of this business."

She whispered that there were some new-fashioned shirts and gay cravats for him in her trunk. Would he have them now?

"Indeed I will; for it is alone my inky cloak, good mother. I came off without a rag of luggage."

He tossed over the contents of the trunk till Cousin Martha begged Laura to assist him; he never could find any thing. It was a picture to the old lady to see the two heads close together over the trunk, and both their hands in it. At a suppressed giggle from Laura, she closed her eyes in pure thankfulness and remained silent. They left the room on tip-toe.

In the course of a few days Cousin Martha discovered that Ann was her nurse instead of Laura; but she was mending, and could easily keep the discovery to herself. Ann was also significantly silent.

No visitors came to the house now, it being generally understood that Laura's visitor was severely ill, and the opportunity for acquaintance was excellent. Laura and Lester were firm in their resolution not to like each other, or allow any influence between them; but each gave way to the singular curiosity of probing the nature of the other. They told lies constantly, and were as constantly detected. It was a sort of guerrilla warfare—unexpected attacks were made on both sides, although they were as watchful as cats in combat. Then they were terribly moody. If one was melancholy, the other was gay; if Laura was conventional, Lester professed reckless Bohemianism; if she talked what he called cant and caste, he mounted his Ideal horse, and talked her out of sight. Every moment they loved more and more, and grew afraid and timid about winning each other. At last he determined to subdue her or die, and his ferocious determination led him to act as follows:

The dinner was served as usual one day. Ann was with Cousin Martha, and there was no regular waiting. The cook came up when the bell was struck. Lester sat opposite Laura. Placing his elbows on the table, he said:

"You know that I am madly in love with you. By my soul I must come over and sit beside you! Will you kiss me if I come? Then I'll eat my dinner; otherwise I will not. I can not, dare not, stay in your presence another day."

Laura made a cool feint of pressing the bell.

"Ring the bell, if you dare," he said. Their eyes met; a steady light glowed in his, a flickering, willful one in hers.

"Mercy!" she said. "Where am I?"

"In your own house; which I wish to take you out of. Come into my house, Laura; be my wife, and live a new life with me—an artist. Let me teach you happiness. Have you ever known any, my poor girl?"

Laura thought of her dead boy.

"Lester," she cried, passionately, "do you remember that I *have* been a wife and mother?"

"A mother—yes. But you are an ignorant creature still. Laura, decide."

He rose to his feet, and her glance followed his uprising. Should she give way? How he trembled at heart! Was he to lose this woman, who had so knit herself in her beauty and sweetness to his every fibre? But he stood in a quiet attitude, and there was no agitation in his face. Her whole life rolled before her like a panorama. Most of it was a crude waste. All the ordinary experiences of womanhood bringing her to this result! Was the right way before her at last?

"Laura!"

She held out her arms, and he came to her.

"Tell me something," he begged, kissing her passionately.

"Take care of me—save me. I have seen nothing. I am so unhappy!"

"More than this, my love, you must give me. I have been harsh with you."

"I love you, Lester, just as you have loved me, from the instant you dashed the glass from my hand."

A moment of that wonderful, virgin silence passed, and then Lester cried that the soup was cold.

"Go to your place," Laura ordered. There was little dinner eaten that day. Lester left his place continually; and at last they went up stairs to Cousin Martha. Before they could utter a word she said:

"Laura, did I not tell you that me and my son were agreed? Oh, I am so happy! I am so glad I had the fever. Dear children, you belong to each other. But you are queer, and you must make allowances."

Waiting at the Station

"What place did you say?" Mary Sage asked the conductor, as he came along with his collected tickets.

"Chelsford station," he replied. "Passengers in the morning train from the Cliffs change cars here."

"Strange, strange!" said Mary Sage to herself, for her traveling companion, Miss Whitlow, would not have understood her. "Years have elapsed since a drama was abruptly closed, the lights extinguished, and again the cur—cars, I mean—roll me back to Chelsford, where it began."

As the conductor repassed, Mary questioned him, and was informed that she would have to wait at the Chelsford station three hours before the Old Province train arrived, by which they were to travel homeward.

"Dear me!" snapped Miss Whitlow, rousing at this announcement, "are we to be detained here to feed the flies? Mary, you need not have so hurried matters. But you would whisk out of bed to see the sun rise. You are too old for sunrises."

"Yes, Cousin Ann," cried Mary, cheerfully; "'tis the sunset of life that should give me all the mystical lore I require. But never mind. There will be one spring in the hair-cloth sofa; you shall have that, with as many cocoa-nut balls as you choose to add to your milk of human kindness. I am sure your netting is in your sachel. I mean to explore the region; and, hey presto! we shall hear the cry, 'All aboard!'"

"Nonsense, Mary. In trying situations you are so absurd! *Chelsford*," she added, reflectively, "has a familiar sound. Did your mother ever go there? I have some such recollection."

"We passed a summer in the town when you were abroad, during my green and salad days."

"You were a mere child then. It is fifteen years since. Mercy! as we get older the passage of time strikes the mind like a comet."

"I found that I had grown to be a woman before I left," remarked Mary, bitterly.

"Yes," replied Miss Whitlow, complacently; "our family are remarkable for maturing early."

"And the same in fading."

"By no means; not at all." And Miss Whitlow's piebald curls, two to each temple, shook with disdain at the idea. Like Festus, she probably counted years by her heart-throbs; and as she had had small occasion for perturbing that organ, she might consider herself youthful still—younger, in truth, than the pale, tall Mary beside her, about whom no vestige of girlhood lingered.[1]

The train blustered up to the platform, and five or six persons emerged therefrom, hot and frowzy in spite of yellow and brown linen dresses, Japanese fans, and leather bags of comestibles. Several trunks were madly tossed out of the baggage car, and then the train rolled down the cut through a scattering wood, and disappeared. The country wagons in waiting took off the expected passengers with their luggage, the staring schoolgirls strolled home again arm in arm, and the loafers commanding the benches turned over their tobacco quids and silently stole away to their perches along the village stores. The ticket seller slapped down his window, the candy vendor drew a barrier across his den, and silence reigned within the station; draughts of air and solid sunbeams were masters of the situation.

"Ah," said Mary, "behold this dipterous insect. Something to share our solitude."

Miss Whitlow stepped to the window.

"Pooh! a daddy-long-legs," she answered, peevishly, continuing to dabble her mouth and nose with Cologne-water.

"Cousin Ann, try this rocking-chair. I brought away the *Bactrian Advertiser* for you; there is a dreadful murder in it."[2]

"Give it to me. Where can my spectacles be?"

Mary waited patiently till Miss Whitlow was adjusted satisfactorily, and then went out. From every point of the compass she vainly tried to discover some familiar landmark. Away beyond the trees she saw the spires and roofs of the village, and took at random one of the roads in its direction. It was a mere lane through which she passed, opening from a broad street lined with houses and deep yards; from either side other streets branched, and at the farther end stretched a green; near her, in an angle of the street, stood a square white building. When she read the sign on it she knew her whereabouts—"Grafton, Pitt, & Co."

The years dropped from her mental eyesight like scales, one by one, as she stopped a moment. A feeling of rage took possession of her. The power and durability of an inanimate thing, a sign surviving to suggest so vital, so dead a past! She moved on toward the green, going by houses she could not yet recognize, and trees, shrubs, garden beds, and walks all dream-like and confused.

"I am going to Chelsford Green," she said, "to the Elm Walk."

She saw the arching elms gently bending and mingling their tall thick tops, and the great boles padded with short grass at their base; and then a curious collision took place in her mind between two persons—both of them herself—with a third person added as judge or commentator. The first was a girl of seventeen, carelessly dressed, her shawl down her shoulders, her bonnet half off her head, and her hair flying. She was coming up the Elm Walk with a roll of music in her hand, and her attention was absorbed in some object or person at the limits of the walk. How pretty and bright she looked! Mary's eyes filled with hot, aching tears at the picture. The other was a woman beyond thirty, sober and composed in appearance; she carried a large parasol, and was dressed in gray. Her observations seemed to be confined to the capers of a pair of sparrows who hopped tamely, and cocked up their little round heads at her, while she stood still by one of the trees. To this person Mary gave a pitiful smile and a wave of polite dismissal, and returned to her present self. After a momentary hesitation she crossed the green and went out by the farther gate. "I'll just go by it," she said, "and then return to Cousin Ann."

Presently she came in sight of a lonely little stream, spanned by a handsome stone bridge, newly dated. It was changed there, she found, but still the view down the river must be the same. Yes, there were the high palings, the hedge, the roof, and chimneys of Edward Grafton's place.

> "Ay me, ay me, with what another heart,
> In days far off, and with what other eyes,
> I used to watch—if I be she that watched—"[3]

Mary murmured, her whole soul stirred with some recollection that changed her face wonderfully. She felt drawn by invisible threads toward that place, and walked steadily by the orchard, garden, and carriage drive. The gates were wide open; she heard the stamp of the horses in the stable, and saw the stable groom going to and fro; but the house was silent, its doors and shutters closed. The lawn was terraced, and a piazza ran across the front of the house. Some temptation led her by the terrace. Looking up through the spaces in the shrubbery, she caught a glimpse of a man lying upon a settee. His arms were under his head, his feet were crossed; she thought him sleeping, he was so motionless.

"If that is Edward Grafton," she thought, "why does he not divine that I stand near him? What about that electric chain, I wonder? Here is a test. What a fool I am! Mary Sage, go back to your cousin Ann, and behave as you are expected to behave. The idea of mooning after dead romantic episodes at noonday, because railroad companies will not accommodate each other, is too preposterous. Yes, I'll return; I'll just walk by, and come back on the other side of the street. Who would have thought of my opportunity of seeing old Chelsford again, where I took music-lessons, and had such a gay summer? And now mother is dead, and I am dead—an old maid, I mean—and life is a tiresome falsehood." She was walking swiftly, unaware of her footsteps. A clock struck; the wind brought its slow strokes to her ear; an hour had passed since she left the station, and her heart had counted every happy day she had ever spent in that time. As she passed along on the other side of the way she looked at the settee again. The sleeper had changed his position; he was sitting up, his hat was pulled over his forehead, and his head was bent in a listening attitude. An uncontrollable wish to see this man's face seized Mary, and almost involuntarily she turned again and crossed over below the terrace.

"Suppose I do want to see him!" she argued, crossly. "I am the one to be hurt. I intend to write a book, and call it the *Dissection and Analysis of all Human Disappointment through Emotion*—and that covers a ground as big as Humboldt's *Cosmos*."[4] Stepping by the terrace as noiselessly as possible, for fear of being heard, she had come close to the lawn gate, and, with a feeling of forlorn hope, raised her eyes and met those she wished to meet. Their faces were not far apart, hers below, his above—earnest, sad faces now; deep, inquiring gray eyes. For a moment they were speechless, he amazed, she breathless.

"Mary Sage, is it you?"

"Yes, Edward Grafton."

"Come up here! come in!" he urged.

"No."

"Why are you here in this strange way?"

"Because the Old Province train won't come in. Are you a railroad director?"

"Where have you been all these years, and why should I never have seen you, Mary?" he asked, with a rising irritation. She did not reply at once, but looked at him. Indeed, they measured each other with profound wonder and curiosity. How well she still looked, he thought. Her complexion was brilliant yet, her eyes beautiful as of old. And she thought how little he had changed. His hair was a trifle gray under his hat, and he was bigger than ever; his eyes were absolutely the same.

"I wonder," she at length said, in a dreamy voice, "if all these years might have taught us a right understanding of each other."

"Was it a wrong understanding always?"

"On my part, yes."

Quietly unlatching the gate, he held it open.

"Mary I wish you would come in, I am glad to see you."

"It is impossible, for I must return to my cousin, who waits for me at the station. You know what freaks the imagination plays. When I found myself at Chelsford, after so many years' absence, I thought I would test my bump of locality."

"Have you passed the terrace more than once?" he asked, abruptly.

She blushed redder than a rose. "I wasn't quite sure," she stammered.

"Oh, I see: another experiment."

"How curiously things do turn up!" she wisely remarked.

"Very, indeed."

"I suppose I must go now."

"Where did you say you were going?"

"To our town, Walton."

"Your cousin is with you?"

"Yes—Miss Whitlow. Have you lived here ever since?"

"Oh yes, except a few years abroad."

"Well, good-morning."

"Good-morning."

Dizzy and confused, she sprang forward, but at the end of the path looked round, like Lot's wife. He was gazing at her with all his might, and, woman-like, she walked straight back to him, and cried, "You looked so always, Edward Grafton. I know now how few were the words you spoke to me, and yet I thought I had a numberless memory."

"You said as few. I judged you as I supposed you judged me. Our eyes were said to be alike. Was there a language in them for me? Was I dishonest to let mine tell my story? What could I say, then? My circumstances were patent. There came a fine day, and your mother swooped down on you and bore you off. I acquiesced, because you did."

For the first time Mary looked at the windows.

"No one there but my mother," he said.

Questions crowded upon Mary's mind, which she dared not ask—could not bring herself to ask.

"Mary, let me see your left hand." She held it toward him, and he pulled off her glove.

"Ah," was all he said, and kept the glove. Mary wished that it was not a mended one. The longer she staid, the more silenced she felt, and that was the old spell; but somehow she believed that she might now learn to master this man. Why could she not have been thirty-five when she was seventeen!

"Things do come round curiously!" he repeated, with a quiet smile that made her color deepen again. "I never felt more lonely than I did an hour ago when I heard the clock strike its dismal knell. It has been striking my life away hour by hour, and I have not rebelled. Am I not a patient country lout, biding the arrival of the hearse, living alone all these years with an invalid mother, to whom I am tied? Might I have chosen differently?"

"Alone!"

"I never married Helen Banks."

"No?"

"She was wiser than you. She learned what you should have known, and she went to another man's house, did my cousin Helen. Will you call over and help me count her children?"

Once more he opened his gate, and signed to Mary to enter. She shook her head. Not at his mere beck would she go into the house she had left with such sorrow, and left by him also so uselessly.

"May I walk back with you, then?" he asked. She assented. It was time; in fact, the train was nearly due. Miss Whitlow had slept in her chair, and woke with a crick in her neck and in her temper.

"Where upon earth have you been, Mary? What have you been picking up? You must be very weary of my company. Who's that?" she concluded, in a loud whisper.

"The old friend mother and I made years ago. Cousin Ann, let me introduce you to Mr. Grafton."

Mr. Grafton shook hands with the old lady, and expressed deep remorse that they should have suffered so long a detention in such a stupid place, though the detention had been the means of his rediscovery of a valued friend. He learned through her all he wished to learn of Mary Sage. When the train arrived, and they were about to take seats, he cooly asked her if she ever expected to see Chelsford again.

"Not to wait there again. If Cousin Ann made her sea-side resort of the Cliffs, she must, of course, pass through the town."

"Remember, then, that my house is open, if you choose to come to it. If I am there, I will open my gate and welcome you with all my heart."

They shook hands as they parted, and Mary looked back to him as he stood on the platform. He smiled with his old expression, waved his hand, and made the motion of a word with his lips. It was too mad a dream, the last two hours, for her to believe in. She might be sunstruck; it was very hot weather; a good many people were having queer fancies. She examined Miss Whitlow so closely to see if there was any thing strange about her that she asked what the matter was, and Mary said she thought it had been an uncommonly hot day, which Miss Whitlow denied.

"There was a very improbable story in that paper you gave me," she said. "The writers of fiction cram their readers with foolish, impossible lies."

"What was the story?"

"The husband of a young woman, having a quarrel with her, went off. In the course of several years she heard that he lost his life at Vera Cruz as a soldier in Scott's army.[5] She married again, and at the end of fourteen years the first husband returns, with several scars and an intemperate face and professes great love, anxiety, and a determination to regain her. Second husband willingly restores her to his arms, and finds another love immediately. The original pair are remarried, and he strikes her within a week. What a preposterous story!"

"What explanation did Number One make of the fourteen years silence?"

"None given."

"Did not the wife require one?"

"The story does not say so."

"I should demand the history of every day," said Mary, with energy. "Has he one to give, though, that would be admissible?"

"*Has?*" said Miss Whitlow. "It ain't a live character, but a figment of somebody's cracked brain."

"Truth is stranger than fiction," said Mary.

"I have never found life any thing but the plainest kind of sailing, and having got on so far, expect to discover no mysteries. You ought to know better too. What ever has happened to you beyond a picnic?"

"Did you particularly notice Mr. Grafton?"

"Why, yes; I thought him a very good-looking middle-aged man, and quite polite. Where did you come across him?"

"Heaven help me, Cousin Ann, I have loved that man fifteen years, and had to wait at Chelsford station to discover it!"

"Not to him, I hope," said Miss Whitlow, gravely.

"He guesses it well enough."

"It is all nonsense. Of course you refused him years ago, and made a mistake. When I refused Deacon Watkins I never allowed myself to suffer a minute, though he had the best house in Walton. You are flighty in your disposition, Mary, and always will be. You are as red in the face as a turkey-cock this minute."

Mary was thankful when the coach stopped in Sackville Street, at their door. She ran up to her room like a *young gell*, as Bridget, the servant, declared. In its familiar solitude Mary hoped to recover composure, and be able to judge rightly of this, the most astonishing day she ever passed. Afterward, when retired for the night, she looked in the glass, determined to take a strict account of every indication and vestige of age, to uproot all vanity from her mind, and renounce every romantic anticipation. She was still fair enough for a man of forty, said the glass: a smooth cheek, abundant hair, shapely hands, an erect, well-formed person. As for romance, every woman was entitled by divine right to carry that Scripture on the tablets of her heart. As for anticipation, what right to that? *None*, her reason told her. Had not that obdurate Edward Grafton shown himself to-day, as he had shown himself years since, determined to be understood in his own way, determined to be sought and won as he pleased? It seemed to her for an instant as if he had been thus long waiting for her to pass his gate, like a spider in his web. But she had refused to go in, that was a comfort; and then she fell to crying bitterly, and longed to have the chance offered her once more. What was the cause of his mysterious conduct? she queried. The summer she had spent beneath his mother's roof together with her own mother had its history. Edward's cousin Helen, adopted by his mother when she became an orphan—a feeble, eccentric girl—by some hocus-pocus had obtained an unaccountable influence over him, and held him as her promised husband. When Mary appeared, Edward straightway fell in love with her, and in an open way gave evidence of an affection which he believed, when he had reason to suppose Mary returned it, would lead to its proper and inevitable result. Helen herself, his mother, Mary's mother, must see that it was the right thing that they should be united. Love was the be all, end all—the Bible of the soul, teaching a religion before whose mandates every thing must bow. The consequence of this fine theory was that Mary's mother took her home immediately; his own mother was broken-hearted at the failure in choosing happiness for him; and Helen, after playing fast and loose with him, suddenly married a young man in the neighborhood who was devoid of every attraction Edward possessed. Edward went abroad, and only returned, after a long absence, because of his mother's prayers. A rumor reached him that Mary Sage was engaged; then it was contradicted. He thought of her constantly at that time, and could not forgive her for forsaking him. As the years went by he counted them, and finally settled in the conviction that Mary had grown too old to be any longer remembered as a young man's ideal; too old, indeed, for him to seek her with any sentimental object, and so, as he thought, his love ghost was forever laid. After all, reasoning from any ordinary point of view, his conduct was not to be accounted for. Mary concluded as his past had been, so would his future be, unless she should interfere. She ended her speculations here, and very sensibly went to bed.

When Edward Grafton returned to his house that day he entered it with a funereal feeling; a new void was there. The flying joy and hope he had seen fluttering in Mary's eyes had vanished, and left him desolate. He was not satisfied with himself. Not that he blamed his part in to-day, but long ago. He was in fault somewhere. When his cousin Helen jilted him to his content, why did he not follow Mary Sage? Why not, man fashion, ride into Walton town, and sue the woman he loved to be his wife? Simply because he had expected too much of her; the makings of a heroine were not bestowed upon her. He saw to-day that she was just the woman she promised to be, and he had tried to coerce her; opened his gate, like a melodramatic fool, and nodded, like Caesar, for her to cross his threshold. He had always propped his pride and spirits with the belief that she loved him very deeply; now he doubted it, and the doubt was torture. The doubt increased, and became the torment of his life. Day after day passed, and still he kept at home. Mary grew dearer and dearer to him. He invented all sorts of excuses for seeking her: he was rich; she was poor, the companion of a peevish old woman; it was his duty to give her a home. Perhaps she had remained single for his sake; his honor, then, demanded that he should ask her hand in marriage. And then he knocked his excuses down like nine-pins. So these persons remained apart. A short interview had undone the work of years; for they were both longing and miserable, where they had been cheerful and contented. At last the same fate interfered in their behalf. The medium this time was not a railroad. Sick and idle, Edward went up to the city one autumn day to hear a famous prima donna in her celebrated *rôle* of Sappho. Miss Whitlow, busy, and interested in every thing under heaven, made a rush to the same city for the same purpose, and carried, as a matter of course, Mary Sage and her best gown with her. Edward and Mary were at the same hotel, the Pelham, without knowing it. No magnetism passed through the murk air of dinner and general fluffiness from one to the other to cause fresh speculation in those gray eyes so like to each other.

The opera-house was crowded. Miss Whitlow had a costly seat in the front row, and was fanning her old self in a gracious style, and entirely happy. Mary sat beside her in a soft white shawl, and a pretty head-dress of trailing flowers in her handsome hair. The glorious voice and the passionate acting of the prima donna, who was neither young nor beautiful, moved her strangely. She bent her face over her for a moment, when she looked up, saw the man she wildly prayed to see—Edward Grafton. He was in the parquet, exactly beneath the seat where she was. It was the counterpart of the situation at Chelsford, and it so occurred to them; they smiled with the same thought. "What do you see, Mary?" asked Miss Whitlow. "Your attention seems to be fixed elsewhere. For my part, that dreadful creature shakes my nerves with her goings on."

"Mr. Grafton is in the parquet," said Mary.

"Oh! he is; he can locomote, then. I thought him a human lichen, and grown to the walls of his house in Chelsford. Does the man want to come up?"

"I dare say," replied Mary, carelessly.

"He looks distinguished, and he may come when the curtain falls."

Mary looked at her gratefully, and again at Mr. Grafton, with invitation in her eyes. He was at their elbow as soon as the act closed, and greeted Miss Whitlow first. A youthful blush mantled in Mary's face as she felt the pressure of his hand. Some one behind them vacated a seat, and he took it; the owner did not return when the curtain rose again, and the moments that followed were the sweetest Mary ever knew. The music, the brilliant company, lent a magic to the dear reality. Edward forgot himself, his pride, his rights, only remembering his present love; and Mary, forgetting nothing, feeling all, was ready to live or die with him, just as he chose. They were young again; the voice of passion from the stage, its song of longing and rejoicing or of grief and despair, sustained by the ever-recurring instruments of the orchestra, intoxicated them. They said very foolish things to each other. If Miss Whitlow had heard them she would have called for two strait-jackets.

"May I go home with you?" he asked, humbly, when the performance was over, and he was so carefully adjusting Mary's shawl that Miss Whitlow, to speak the vernacular, smelled an animal of the rodent kind, Latinized as *musculus*.[6]

"We go to the Pelham Hotel, Sir," she answered.

"That is my hotel also; we go the same way."

Miss Whitlow graciously asked him to take a seat in her carriage, and all the way along, when a street lamp shone in, two pairs of gray eyes were fixed on each other with delight. Edward whispered to Mary to join him a few minutes in the drawing-room after Miss Whitlow was properly disposed of. They met, and sat in the deep embrasure of a window for half an hour. Little was said, but enough; and then Edward left Mary at the door of her room with a kiss which made her recall once more the days of the past. She sighed.

"What is it, my love?" he jealously inquired.

"Nothing, only that my hair is gray."

He groaned.

"Why, Edward, what ails you?"

"My wrinkles are legion."

Miss Whitlow was interviewed the next morning. She expressed no surprise; said, in fact, she had been looking forward to Mary's marriage. She went into a calculation about spoons and sheets, and was in a hurry to return home to get Mary ready. Edward persuaded her to remain in the city a week, and during that week persuaded her to consent to a hotel wedding.

"Whatever you did in the green tree," she said to them, "I never saw any thing but what you do in the dry. You are as silly as geese."

The old lady's eyes filled with tears as she spoke, and Edward and Mary smiled at each other, as only bride and groom can smile who are destined to

> "Live in peace,
> And die in a pot of grease."

Vide the oldest, truest fairy stories in the world, and the newest love stories in the same.

Notes

Our Christmas Party

"Our Christmas Party" appeared in *Harper's New Monthly Magazine* 18 (January 1859): 202–5.

1. *mistle-toe bough, the Yule-log, the wassail-bowl, and boar's head*: winter traditions of different cultural origins that came to be associated with Christmas. All of them are mentioned and explained in Washington Irving's *The Sketch Book of Geoffrey Crayon, Gent.* (1819–1820), see esp. "Christmas Eve," "Christmas Day," and "Christmas Dinner."
2. *"Baxter's Saint's Rest"*: Richard Baxter (1615–1691), a Puritan divine, author of *The Saint's Everlasting Rest* (1650) which played an important part in the Evangelical tradition in England and America.
3. *"Edwards on the Will"*: Jonathan Edwards (1703–1758), philosopher, Calvinist divine, and famous preacher. His greatest work was *A Careful and Strict Enquiry into the Modern Prevailing Notions of . . . Freedom of Will* (1754).
4. *"Milk for Babes"*: John Cotton (1584–1652) became a religious leader in the Bay Colony. His catechism for children, *Milk for Babes, Drawn out of the Breasts of Both Testaments* (1646), remained a standard work of Puritan orthodoxy for several generations.
5. *Kingsley*: Probably Charles Kingsley (1819–1875), English author and clergyman.
6. *Prodigal Son*: New Testament story of the wastrel son who was welcomed back when he returned home in repentance, see Luke 15:11–32.
7. *Joseph and his Brethren*: Biblical figures from the Old Testament. Genesis 30, 37, and 45 tell how Joseph, the son of Rachel, was sold into slavery in Egypt by his jealous brothers.
8. *Hollands*: Gin.
9. *"fields beyond the swelling flood"*: from the hymn "A prospect of heaven makes death easy" by Isaac Watts (1674–1748).

Uncle Zeb

"Uncle Zeb" appeared in the *New York Saturday Press* 3, no. 8 (February 25, 1860): n.p.

1. *heart's ease*: wild pansy, so called because it was believed to cure the pains of love.
2. *Dryad*: a wood nymph, a spirit of nature in Greek mythology.
3. *kickshaws*: delicacies, fancy food or dish.
4. *Esau*: biblical figure from the Old Testament. The firstborn son of Isaac and Rebecca, who was tricked out of his father's blessing by his twin brother Jacob, see Genesis 25:21–34.
5. *Marryatt's novels*: Captain Frederick Marryatt (1792–1848), popular British author and naval captain. His first semi-autobiographical novel, *The Naval Officer: or, Scenes and Adventures in the Life of Frank Mildmay* (1829), was a great success; fifteen others followed.

6. *Rabelais*: François Rabelais (c. 1494–c. 1553), French writer, physician, and humorist, is best known for his satirical epic, *Gargantua and Pantagruel*, a tale of two giants. Rabelais's work is famous for his wit and obscenity, especially in his minute description of the human body and its functions.

7. *senna*: a medical plant with a laxative effect.

8. *Brandreth's pills*: a laxative; also a nineteenth-century synonym for quack medicine.

9. *Lares and Penates*: Roman household deities, who rule over the house. The Lares were regarded as the souls of the ancestors, the Penates were expected to observe the welfare and prosperity of the family. "Lares and Penates" also stands for one's possessions.

The Chimneys

"The Chimneys" appeared in *Harper's New Monthly Magazine* 31 (November 1865): 721–32.

1. *"The mountain's a coming to Mohammed"*: in his essay "Of Boldness" Francis Bacon (1561–1626) mentions the following anecdote: "Mahomet made the people believe that he would call a hill to him, and from the top of it offer up his prayers for the observers of his law. The people assembled; Mahomet called the hill to come to him, again and again; and when the hill stood still, he was never a whit abashed, but said, 'If the hill will not come to Mahomet, Mahomet will go to the hill.'"

2. *bitter as the waters of Marah*: marah is the Hebrew word for bitter, see Exodus 15:23.

Lucy Tavish's Journey

"Lucy Tavish's Journey" appeared in *Harper's New Monthly Magazine* 35 (October 1867): 656–63.

1. *Baal*: originally any of a number of local fertility gods among ancient Semitic peoples; in the Bible used for the chief deity of Canaan, hence: a false god, an idol.

2. *Harper's Weekly*: the *Weekly* was a vehicle for political discussions that *Harper's Monthly* eschewed. It aimed at a wider readership than the *Monthly* and was renowned for its illustrations.

3. *secesh*: secessionist.

4. *Kant, Fichte, and Spinoza*: the Germans Immanuel Kant (1724–1804), and Johann Gottlieb Fichte (1762–1814), as well as the Dutch Baruch Spinoza (1632–1677), were all famous philosophers.

5. *"The Moral Use of Aesthetic Manners"*: philosophical treatise by the German dramatist and poet Friedrich Schiller (1759–1805), "Über den moralischen Nutzen ästhetischer Sitten" (1796).

A Study for a Heroine

"A Study for a Heroine" appeared in the *Independent* 37, no. 1921 (September 24, 1885): 1246–48.

1. *"My flesh shall slumber . . . sound"*: from "The sinner's portion and saint's hope," a hymn based on Psalm 17 by Isaac Watts (1674–1748).

2. *"Soldier, go home"*: the words "Soldier, go home; with thee the fight is won," appear in the third stanza of the funereal hymn "On the Death of a Minister, Cut off in his Vigor" by James Montgomery (1771–1854). This hymn may have also been known by the alternative title of "Soldier, go home."

Mrs. Jed and the Evolution of Our Shanghais

"Mrs. Jed and the Evolution of Our Shanghais" appeared in the *Independent* 43, no. 2231 (September 3, 1891): 1330–31.

1. *Tappertit*: Simon Tappertit, a character in Charles Dickens's novel *Barnaby Rudge* (1841). Tappertit is the aspiring and anarchic apprentice of the locksmith Gabriel Varden.

2. *Braganza*: Royal family who ruled Portugal from 1640 to 1910, and Brazil from 1822 to 1889. In the context of the story, the name Braganza calls up associations of extravagance and bragging.

3. *Epicurean*: fond of sensuous pleasure, having a refined taste in food and drink. From the Greek philosopher Epicurus (341–270 B.C.), who held that the goal of life should be enjoyment.

4. *improve the stock*: to further evolutionary development of a species through selective breeding. This is directly addressed later in the story ("behold our evolution"). Charles Darwin's *On the Origin of Species* (1859) argued that species evolve by "natural selection" from less complex forms of life. Herbert Spencer translated these ideas into his broader concept of evolutionary progress. He is known for creating *Social Darwinism*, suggesting that human society, too, undergoes a process of natural selection, resulting in the "survival of the fittest."

5. *Shanghai*: Chinese Shanghai fowl, today known as Cochins. This breed of chickens was first imported to America in 1845. In England, their arrival at about the same time started a chicken "gold-rush," rumors about their fabulous fertility fueled a "Cochin craze." Shanghai chickens are very big but they don't lay many eggs; neither do they provide much meat since their size is mostly due to a profusion of soft feathering. Several songs about Shanghai chickens were popular in the middle of the nineteenth century, among them Stephen Foster's "Don't bet your money on de Shanghai" (1861).

6. *Galahad*: The purest, most noble, and chivalrous of the knights of the Arthurian Round Table, who succeeds in the quest for the Holy Grail.

7. *the "master spirit"*: Social Darwinism believed that individuals and ethnic groups achieve success or dominance because of inherent genetic superiority and a resultant competitive advantage. Thus, the "master spirit" characterizes the "master race."

8. *our superior breed*: racist theory holds the white race superior to all others. Such crude racism flourished in late-nineteenth-century America, as is evidenced by Rand McNally's *Elementary Geography* (1894), a textbook for the booming public-school market, which states: "Most of the civilized people of the world belong to the white race . . . The savages belong to the red, brown, and black races. Most people of the yellow race are half-civilized."

A Summer Story

"A Summer Story" appeared in the *New York Saturday Press* 3, no.14 (April 7, 1860): n.p.

Eros and Anteros

"Eros and Anteros" appeared in the *New York Leader* (February 22, 1862): 2–3. *Eros and Anteros*: sons of Aphrodite, the Greek goddess of beauty and love, and Ares, god of war. Eros is the god of love, while Anteros is either understood as the deity of requited love or the "avenger of slighted love."

1. *unbroken Celt*: untrained domestic servant of Irish descent. By mid-century two thirds of New York City's domestics were young Irish women.

2. *Lola Montez*: Maria Dolores Eliza Roseanna Gilbert (1820–1861), one of the most famous women of her time. Born in Ireland, raised in England and France, she traveled widely throughout her life. Endowed with an exotic beauty, temperament, and independent character, she had the "happy faculty of capturing the most accomplished men," as the *New York Leader* observed. One of them was the Bavarian King Ludwig I (1786–1868), who became her lover. Due to the revolutionary turbulences in 1848 he was forced to separate from Montez and to deprive her of her title of countess. She barely escaped imprisonment by leaving for England. From 1851 on she gained great popularity as a dancer, actress, and speaker in the United States. Montez was known for her eccentricity and her audacity to break with every convention possible.

3. *Jenny Lind*: the "Swedish Nightingale" (1821–1887), was adored for her soprano voice and praised for her blonde beauty as well as her chaste and pure simplicity of character. When P. T. Barnum organized a concert tour for her in 1850–1852, the American public was infected by a "Jenny Lind crush." She donated large sums of her income to charities which earned her additional fame. With Lola Montez and Jenny Lind, two opposing images of woman are called upon—the sensous but immoral woman versus the saintly, sexless woman.

4. *Madras handkerchief*: brightly colored and mostly patterned cloth of silk or cotton, often used for a turban.

5. *"crowded mart"*: from a poem by Oliver Goldsmith (c. 1730–1774), "The Traveller; Or, a Prospect of Society" (1764), line 295.

6. *Mantanzas*: Capitol of the Mantanzas province in central Cuba, known as a pirates' haven at the time.

7. *"sad sea waves"*: quoted from Bayard Taylor's book *At Home and Abroad: A Sketch-Book of Life, Scenery, and Men* (1860), p. 6. Taylor was a close friend of Richard Henry Stoddard.

8. *Lares and Penates*: See Note 9, "Uncle Zeb."

9. *Ayudadmi, maestro mio, O morire*: incorrect Spanish, mixed with some Italian, for "Help me, my master, I am dying."

Lemorne versus *Huell*

"Lemorne *versus* Huell" appeared in *Harper's New Monthly Magazine* 26 (1863): 537–43.

1. *tutoyer*: French, meaning "to speak familiarly to." Here it is used to describe the singer's tone of voice. This usage is unconventional.

2. *Paterfamilias*: Latin for father, head of the family.

3. *The sea must have been God's temple first, instead of the groves*: adapted from William Cullen Bryant's (1794–1878) "A Forest Hymn," which opens: "The Groves were God's first temples"

4. *"Mariana in the moated grange"*: "Mariana" is a poem by Alfred Lord Tennyson (1809–1892), for which the quoted line serves as an epithet. The quotation is from Shakespeare's *Measure for Measure* III, i.

5. *"And the fluttering . . . life"*: from Johann Wolfgang von Goethe's (1749–1832) play *Faust*, Part I, Scene III, an excerpt from the Chorus of Spirits that sings Faust to sleep.

6. *Rhadamanthus*: in Greek mythology the son of Zeus and Europa. Together with his brother Minos of Crete and Aeacus he is one of the judges of the dead in the Underworld.

7. *Charon*: in Greek mythology the ferryman who takes the dead in his boat across the river Styx.

"Boots"

"'Boots'" appeared in *Appleton's Journal of Popular Literature, Science, and Art* II (October 30, 1869): 324–27.

1. *dryad*: a wood nymph in Greek mythology.

2. *Pan*: in Greek mythology a fertility god, patron of herdsmen and shepherds.

3. *a mild-eyed lotus eater*: in his poem "The Lotos-Eaters" Alfred Lord Tennyson (1809–1892) speaks of "the mild-eyed melancholy Lotos-eaters." In the *Odyssey*, the Lotus-Eaters are a people who live on lotus-fruit which induces forgetfulnes and makes its eater lose any desire to return to his own country.

4. *"Falling asleep in a half dream"*: from "Choric Song," section V, a poem by Alfred Lord Tennyson.

5. *"cloud towers by ghastly masons wrought"*: quoted from the poem "In Memoriam A. H. H." by Alfred Lord Tennyson, section LXX.

6. *Freedom shrieked when a celebrated Polish hero fell*: a reference to the Polish officer and freedom fighter Tadeusz Kosciusko (1746–1817), who is famous both for his role in the American Revolution, where he fought on the side of the colonists, as well as for his leadership of the national insurrection in his homeland. He is one of the characters in the immensely popular, early historical novel *Thaddeus of Warsaw* (1803) by Scottish novelist Jane Porter (1776–1850).

7. *Robinson Crusoe . . . man Friday*: Friday is the faithful follower and helper of Robinson Crusoe in *The Life and Strange and Surprising Adventures of Robinson Crusoe* (1719), a romance by Daniel Defoe (1660–1731).

8. *the German*: a dance for many couples in which partners are changed often.

9. *as Leonora did, . . . her lover's ghost*: the famous ballad "Lenore" (1773) by the German poet Gottfried August Bürger (1747–1794), tells the story of Lenore, whose grief for her dead lover recalls him to her door. When he rings her doorbell she follows him to the world of the dead. It was translated first by William Taylor (1765–1836).

10. *Lord Cornwallis*: Charles Cornwallis, 1st Marquis Cornwallis (1738–1805), English general and statesman probably best known for his defeat at Yorktown, Va., in September/October 1781, in the last important campaign of the United States' War of Independence.

A Dead-Lock, and its Key

"A Dead-Lock, and its Key" appeared in *Harper's Weekly* 14, no. 775 (Supplement, November 4, 1871): 1042–43.

1. *brougham*: a closed, four-wheeled carriage.
2. *Portman Square*: square in London, near Baker Street. It is rare that Stoddard uses a setting outside the United States.

Out of the Deeps

"Out of the Deeps" appeared in the "*Aldine* 5 (May 1872): 94–5.

1. *Andromeda*: in Greek mythology, Andromeda was a princess of Ethiopia, daughter of the Ethiopian King Cepheus and Cassiopeia. According to most legends Cassiopeia angered Poseidon, the god of the sea, by saying that Andromeda was more beautiful than Poseidon's daughters, the Nereids. Poseidon sent a sea monster to prey upon the country and only by the sacrifice of the King's daughter would he be appeased. Andromeda was chained to a rock by the sea; but she was rescued by Perseus, who killed the monster. Cassiopeia, Cepheus, and Andromeda were all set among the stars as constellations.
2. *"In the dark backward and abysm of time"*: quotation from Shakespeare's *The Tempest*, I, ii.
3. *"touch of a vanished hand"*: quoted from "Break, Break, Break," a poem by Alfred Lord Tennyson (1809–1892), wistfully invoking the memory of the loss of a loved one.
4. *Ruth and Naomize*: a reference to the biblical Book of Ruth. Ruth was daughter-in-law to Naomi, and refused to leave her even after the death of her husband. The expression indicates inseparable companionship.

A Partie Carrée

"A Partie Carrée" appeared in *Harper's New Monthly Magazine* (September 25, 1862): 466–79. *Partie Carrée*: French for a party of two men and two women.

1. *"Thaddeus of Warsaw"*: immensely popular historical novel by Scottish novelist Jane Porter (1776–1850), first published in 1803, and written before Sir Walter Scott established the form of the historical novel.
2. *"We have been friends together"*: title of a poem by British writer Caroline Norton (1808–1877).
3. *"You may break, you may ruin the vase, if you will"*: quoted from the final couplet of the poem "Farewell! But Whenever You Welcome the Hour," by Thomas Moore (1779–1852).
4. *Story*: Joseph Story (1779–1845), associate justice of the United States Supreme Court. While teaching law at Harvard, he delivered lectures that he elaborated into a series of nine legal commentaries which became very influential.
5. *"Ne quid nimis"*: "excess in nothing," from the play *Andria* by Terence (186/185 BC–159? BC).
6. *Andromeda*: See note 1, "Out of the Deeps."
7. *"O God, O God! . . . Fie on't"*: quoted from Shakespeare's *Hamlet*, I, ii.

8. *Lares and Penates*: See Note 9, "Uncle Zeb."

9. *"I would I were a boy again"*: from the poem "Oh, Would I Were a Boy Again" by the English editor and humorist Mark Lemon (1809–1870).

10. *"Mourn not for the owl, . . . good"*: from the poem "The Owl" by the popular British poet Barry Cornwall; his real name was Brian Waller Proctor (1787–1874).

11. *"'Tis not alone my inky cloak"*: from Shakespeare's *Hamlet*, I, ii.

12. *"I was a child, . . . in a kingdom by the sea"*: quoted from the poem "Annabel Lee" by Edgar Allen Poe (1809–1849).

13. *"It is a nipping and an eager air"*: Shakespeare, *Hamlet*, I, iv.

14. *"I have not loved the world . . . fair foes"*: "Childe Harold's Pilgrimage," Canto III, CXIV, by George Gordon Lord Byron (1788–1824).

15. *"Now, Music, wake from out thy charmed sleep!"*: from Barry Cornwall's (see note 10) poem "See where, upon the blue and waveless deep."

16. *"Where the faded moon . . . twilight"*: from the poem "The Eve of St. Agnes," by John Keats (1795–1821).

17. *"Whatsoever thy hand findeth to do, . . . goest"*: Ecclesiastes 9:10.

18. *Minerva*: the Roman goddess of wisdom and the arts, identified with the Greek Athena.

19. *"With heavy thump, . . . one by one"*: from "The Rime of the Ancient Mariner," lines 218–19, by Samuel Taylor Coleridge (1772–1834).

20. *"The silver margin. . . . no sound"*: from the poem "The Sea—In Calm" by Barry Cornwall (see note 10).

21. *"Man is man"*: in the poem "The Marriage of Geraint," by Alfred Lord Tennyson (1809–1892), line 355 reads: "For man is man and master of his fate."

22. *"The autumn leaves were shed . . . swelling seas"*: from the poem "The Fisher and Charon" by Richard Henry Stoddard (1825–1903), Elizabeth's husband.

23. *"The firmament showeth his handiwork . . . knowledge"*: from Psalm 19:1–2.

24. *"The Talking Oak"*: love poem by Alfred Lord Tennyson.

Tuberoses

"Tuberoses" appeared in *Harper's New Monthly Magazine* 26 (January 1863): 191–97.

1. *Tuberoses*: a perennial plant of the agave family with white, sweet-scented flowers, famous for its fragrance. It is considered an aphrodisiac. In the language of flowers the tuberose signifies deep voluptuousness. Blooms given by lovers express strong attraction.

2. *Clara Bell*: the naming of the sisters Clara and Charlotte Bell implies multiple literary references: British author Charlotte Brontë's (1816–1855) pseudonym was Currer Bell and her novel, *Jane Eyre* (1848), is evoked at the end of "Tuberoses." Charlotte Brontë's sisters Emily and Anne also used the last name Bell for their pseudonyms. Further literary allusions are to the famous sentimental novel *Die Leiden des jungen Werthers* [*The Sorrows of Young Werther*] (1774), by German author and poet Johann Wolfgang von Goethe (1749–1832). Werther's beloved is named Charlotte, often shortened to Lotte. Stoddard also alludes to another novel by Goethe, *Die Wahlverwandschaften* [*Elective Affinities*] (1809), that has a similar plot of two men and two women who get entangled in changing trajectories of desire.

3. *Tennyson*: Alfred Lord Tennyson (1809–1892), eminent Victorian British poet often quoted by Stoddard in her work.

4. *"Come not when I am dead . . . save"*: Clara reads the beginning of Tennyson's poem "Come not, when I am dead" (1850), a poem of disappointed love.

5. *Venus of Milo*: most famous statue of the Roman goddess of love and beauty, Venus was discovered in 1820 by Admiral Dumont on the Greek island of Melos, or Milo. The statue lacks the left arm completely, the right one is detached a little above the elbow. Stoddard uses the mutilated statue as an image of incomplete love.

6. *"In that sleep of death what dreams may come"*: quoted from Shakespeare's *Hamlet*, III, i.

7. *Maison Dorée*: an expensive restaurant in New York City.

8. *troubadours*: French aristocratic poet-musicians during the 12th and 13th centuries, famous for their conception of courtly love which inspired later poets like Dante and Petrarch.

9. *"A violet by a mossy stone . . . eye"*: from the poem "She dwelt among untrodden ways" by William Wordsworth (1780–1850), published in his *Lyrical Ballads* (1800).

10. *Empress Eugénie*: Eugenia Maria de Montijo de Guzman (1826–1920), born in Spain, wife of Napoleon III, and Empress of France from 1853–1870.

11. *Faust*: most famous play by Johann Wolfgang von Goethe; Part I was published in 1808; Part II in 1832. The scholar Faust seals a contract with Mephistopheles, selling his soul to the devil in order to gain youth, knowledge, and magical powers.

12. *"Give me back again the times . . . delusion"*: from *Faust*, Part I. These lines are actually not spoken by Faust but by the "Poet" in the "Prologue for the Theatre."

13. *'Lotte*: short for Charlotte; see note 2.

14. *Laura*: the woman who inspired the love poetry of Francesco Petrarca (Petrarch, 1304–1374), an Italian poet and humanist, and the most popular poet during the English Renaissance. Her true identity is unknown.

15. *"Think you if Laura had been Petrarch's wife . . . life"*: quoted from *Don Juan* (1820), canto III, lines 63–64, satiric poem by George Gordon Lord Byron (1788–1824), which derides sentimentality as well as social and sexual conventions. Byron's unconventional lifestyle and his incestuous love affair with his half sister Augusta earned him a scandalous reputation.

16. *Werther's Charlotte*: see note 2.

17. *Dromio of Ephesus*: one of the twin slaves in Shakespeare's *Comedy of Errors*.

18. *"man is a pendulum betwixt a smile and a tear"*: in Byron's poem *Childe Harold's Pilgrimage* (1818), Canto IV, stanza 109, man is addressed as "thou pendulum betwixt a smile and a tear."

19. *Winter Garden*: a theater in New York City.

20. *Edwin Booth's 'Hamlet'*: Edwin Booth (1833–1893), foremost American actor, was acclaimed on both sides of the Atlantic as the leading Hamlet of his day. Booth was a good friend of the Stoddards. His brother John Wilkes assassinated President Lincoln.

21. *Malliard's*: a candy store on Broadway.

22. *Polonius*: the father of Ophelia and Laertes in Shakespeare's *Hamlet*.

23. *"Mad for thy love"*: Polonius in *Hamlet*, II, i.

24. *"Viva la guerre!"*: could be translated as "three cheers for war."

25. *I am a cripple for life*: reminiscent of Charlotte Brontë's *Jane Eyre*, where Jane marries Rochester only after he is crippled.

26. *Kilkenny cat business*: two cats fabled to have fought until only their tails remained.

"Me and My Son"

"'Me and My Son'" appeared in *Harper's New Monthly Magazine* 41 (July 1870): 213–21.

1. *"The fine lady or fine gentleman . . . bones"*: *The Essays of Elia* was the title of a

series by British essayist Charles Lamb (1775–1834), which appeared between 1820 and 1823 in the *London Magazine*; published as a separate volume in 1823. Lamb posed as Elia, an old-fashioned person, a "bundle of prejudices" in Lamb's words, with a strong preference for the whimsical and the eccentric. This particular quote is from an essay entitled "The Praise of Chimney-Sweepers."

2. *"nothing gives an echo . . . seated"*: in another essay of Elia, "Valentine's Day," a similar line is quoted in the affirmative: It "gives a very echo to the throne where hope is seated." See also note 1.

3. *a law to herself*: a reference to the comedy *Phormio* by the great Roman dramatist Terence (ca. 195–159 B.C.), who says: "Quod homines tot sententiae: suo quoque mos."—"As many opinions as there are men: each a law to himself."

4. *"as the shade by the light quivering aspen made"*: from "Marmion" (1808), a historic poem by Sir Walter Scott (1771–1832), named after its fictitious protagonist. Canto 6, stanza 30, opens with "O Woman! in our hours of ease,/ Uncertain, coy, and hard to please,/ And variable as the shade/ By the light quivering aspen made;/ When pain and anguish wring the brow,/ A ministering angel thou!"

5. *"common sight apparels in celestial light"*: a reference to "Ode: Intimations of Immortality from Recollections of Early Childhood," by British romantic poet William Wordsworth (1770–1850); the quote is not verbatim, in Wordsworth the passage is as follows: "every common sight,/ To me did seem/ Apparelled in celestial light."

6. *"that immortal sea which brought us thither"*: from the same poem (see note 5 above) by Wordsworth, almost verbatim. Lines 168–69 of the Ode go: "that immortal sea/ Which brought us hither." Laura, despite her poetic name, has no capacity for romantic feeling and does not respond to nature's grand beauty.

7. *The fat weed on Lethe's wharf*: a reference to William Shakespeare's *Hamlet*, I, v.: "And duller should'st thou be than the fat weed/ That roots itself in ease on Lethe wharf." No particular weed, but an image of the absolute in vegetable inactivity. "Lethe," meaning "forgetfulness" in Greek, is the name of one of the six rivers of the Underworld. According to Virgil's *Aeneid*, the souls gather on its shores to drink and forget before they can be born again.

8. *By Jove!*: an exclamation of astonishment. Jove is Jupiter, the Roman father of the gods.

9. *Mars*: the Roman god of war.

10. *the flesh-pots of Egypt*: biblical reference to Exodus 16:3. A place where luxury and abundance of food are provided.

11. *Hoveys . . . and . . . Lawtons*: kinds of fruit; Lawtons are a sort of blackberry.

12. *"The palace bang'd and buzzed . . . cataract"*: quoted from "The Day-Dream" (1842), a poem by Alfred Lord Tennyson (1809–1892) that retells the fairy tale of "The Sleeping Beauty."

13. *Conrad . . . the corsair of hearts*: reference to the pirate chief Conrad, the chivalric hero of Lord Byron's poem *The Corsair* (1814).

14. *The prayer of Agur*: biblical reference to Proverbs 30, where Agur prays: "give me neither poverty nor riches."

15. *the groove business*: settled routine; a habitual way of doing something.

16. *Nemesis*: in Greek mythology, Nemesis is the personification of retribution or vengeance.

17. *the statue of Whinny Ha-Ha*: there is no such statue; Stoddard probably alludes tongue-in-cheek to Henry Wadsworth Longfellow's famous poem *The Song of Hiawatha* (1855), in which Hiawatha marries Minnehaha, lovely daughter of an arrow-maker of the Dakotah tribe.

18. *"Though they pricked their fingers every stitch"*: adapted from "Imogen," a poem by Richard Henry Stoddard (1825–1903), where the line reads: "But pricked her fingers every stitch."

19. *geener*: Americanized pronounciaton of the French term "genre;" Cousin Martha means genre paintings.

20. *bass-relief*: indicating another mispronounciation of the French "bas-relief," a technique of sculpture in which figures are carved in a flat surface so that they project only a little from the background.

21. *Goupil's*: famous nineteenth-century art dealer with branches in London, Paris, and New York City.

22. *Bouguereau*: William-Adolphe Bouguereau (1825–1905), French academic painter, well known for his mythological, religious, and genre subjects, especially his sentimental portraits of mothers and children.

23. *Hamon*: Jean-Louis Hamon (1821–1874), French painter and designer. Here his heavily allegorical paintings of the four seasons are alluded to.

Waiting at the Station

"Waiting at the Station" appeared in *Harper's Bazar* (July 26, 1873): 470–71.

1. *Festus*: a once very popular drama by Philip James Bailey (1816–1902), originally published in 1839. *Festus* is Bailey's version of the legend of Goethe's *Faust*. Scene v, "A Country Town," has the line: "We should count time by heart-throbs."

2. *Bactrian Advertiser*: Bactria was the name of an ancient country in what is today northeastern Afghanistan. The name emphasizes the out-of-the-wayness of the journal, which seems to be one of the sensational story papers popular in the nineteenth century.

3. *"Ay me, ay me, with what another heart . . . if I be she that watched—"*: adapted from "Tithonus," a dramatic monologue by Alfred Lord Tennyson (1809–1892); Stoddard changed the personal pronoun to 'she.'

4. *Humboldt's Cosmos*: Alexander von Humboldt (1769–1859), German explorer and scientist. His greatest work was the *Cosmos*, a physical description of the universe, published in five volumes from 1842–1862.

5. *at Vera Cruz as a soldier in Scott's army*: Winfield Scott (1786–1866) led the march from Vera Cruz to Mexico City in the Mexican War (1846–1848).

6. *musculus*: Latin, meaning "little mouse."